W9-AGH-449

PRESSURE
POINT

DICK COUCH

BERKLEY BOOKS, NEW YORK

PRESSURE POINT

A Berkley Book/published by arrangement with
the author

PRINTING HISTORY
G.P. Putnam's Sons edition/July 1992
Berkley edition/September 1993

ISBN: 0-425-13900-X

A BERKLEY BOOK® TM 757,375
Berkley Books are published by The Berkley Publishing Group,
200 Madison Avenue, New York, New York 10016.
The name "BERKLEY" and the "B" logo
are trademarks belonging to Berkley Publishing Corporation.

PRINTED IN THE UNITED STATES OF AMERICA

10 9 8 7 6 5 4 3 2 1

In memory of Teddy Hontz

ACKNOWLEDGMENTS

My thanks to those friends and associates, both civilian and military, who assisted with the political and technical details of this book. And to the young men and women serving in the operational components of the U.S. Special Operations Command—the Army Special Forces and Rangers, the Navy Special Boat Squadrons, the Air Force Special Operations Squadrons, and all their vital support elements—my very special thanks. The end of the Cold War has not diminished our country's need for your professionalism and dedication.

BRITISH COLUMBIA

Strait of Juan de Fuca

Duncan Rock

Cape Flattery

Sekiu

Clallam Bay

Crescent B

OLYMPIC PENINSULA

Vessel Traffic Service (VTS) Antennas

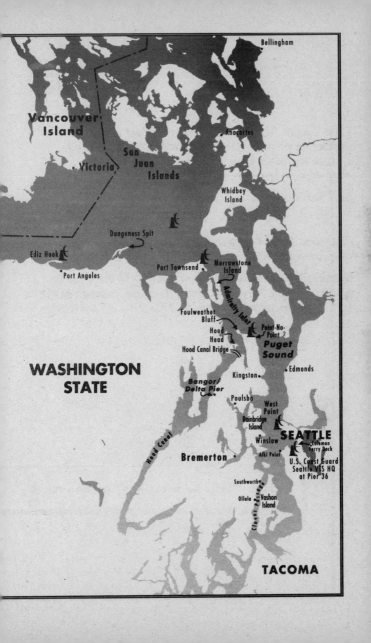

Valor is a gift. Those having it never know for sure whether they have it till the test comes. And those having it in one test never know for sure if they will have it when the next test comes.

Carl Sandburg

Left—port; right—starboard. If you can remember that, your careers are assured!

Guidance provided to the author, and 1,137 other plebe midshipmen, by President John Fitzgerald Kennedy at the U.S. Naval Academy, August 1, 1963

PROLOGUE

Admiral Boris Zaitsev sat with his elbows resting on the huge oak desk, a cigarette protruding from the fingers of one hand while he held the report in the other. It was a red binder with "Top Secret" stamped diagonally across the front. From his high-backed leather chair on the top floor of the headquarters building, he could look across Golden Horn Bay to the city of Vladivostok. Below him were rows of cruisers and destroyers of the Red Banner Pacific Fleet. Farther down the shoreline, Med-moored to the quay, was a long line of rusting, idle state-owned merchantmen. He laid the paper down and concentrated on the cigarette. *Why can't we make cigarettes like this?* The senior officer's commissary at naval base had begun to stock Western cigarettes at his request. Zaitsev absentmindedly brushed an ash from his pants and turned his attention back to the binder on his desk. The report was a detailed analysis of the capabilities of the American Trident submarine, and the ability of the Russian Navy, specifically their attack submarines, to counter this threat.

"Admiral, Captain Molev is here to see you." Zaitsev glanced up at the woman standing half inside the door.

"Thank you, Ludmilla. Wait a few minutes, then send him in."

Zaitsev picked up another file from the corner of the desk. The tab read "Kapitan Pervogo Ranga Viktor Molev." He opened it and scanned the personal history. *Very impressive,* he thought. Working-class family, born and raised in the Russian Republic—*that was very important these days.* Born October

1

16, 1942. *Old for a seagoing officer, but the good ones never tire of operational command.* Graduated with honors from the Nakhimov Secondary School and the Leninsky Komsomol Higher School of Submarine Warfare. Promoted to captain third rank at the age of thirty—*quite a young age to attain that distinction.* A tour as staff intelligence officer with the Red Banner Northern Fleet . . . previous command tours on Oscar and Victor III Class boats . . . taught physics and naval tactics at the M. V. Frunze Naval School—*very impressive indeed. He's an academician as well as a submarine commander.*

There was a sharp knock at the door, and a man in his late forties stepped into the room. His dark-blue dress uniform was adorned only by gold naval piping on the lapels and four gold stripes sewn into the sleeves at the wrists, just below the red star insignia—none of the multicolored rows of ribbons that cluttered the dress of Western naval officers. He held his cap in the crook of his left arm and stood at attention, but there was a casualness about him. Zaitsev recognized the arrogance and self-assurance that was common to those who commanded at sea. He leaned toward the speaker on his desk, but did not take his eyes from Molev.

"Ludmilla, bring tea for me and my guest." Zaitsev pushed himself to his feet and motioned to the two armchairs that bracketed a small coffee table in the corner of the room. "Please, Captain, let us be comfortable." He laid the copy of the report on the table. "I found your work most interesting."

"Thank you, sir." Molev nodded. Ludmilla set the tea service on the table and quickly departed.

"These Trident boats, are they really that hard to find?" Zaitsev asked as he poured.

"As you know, Admiral, the only way to defeat an enemy ballistic-missile submarine is to follow him into his patrol area and shoot him if he attempts a launch. To date, the record for successfully tracking a Trident by one of our attack boats is just under two hours. IR satellite tracking and magnetic anomaly detection by aircraft have been equally disappointing. In the Pacific alone, there are ten of these boats on patrol as we speak, and we have no idea where they are. If the Americans choose, they can launch with impunity. Their warheads are small compared to those used by our rocket forces, somewhere in the two-hundred-kiloton range, but there would be almost three thousand of them.''

''The new missiles,'' prompted Zaitsev, handing a cup and saucer to Molev, ''are they that good?''

''The Trident II system with the D-5 missile is most capable. The warheads can be fitted with standard ballistic reentry vehicles or with maneuverable reentry vehicles should we deploy an effective antimissile defense.'' Zaitsev knew of the costly and marginally effective antiballistic-missile programs the Soviet Union had built in defiance of U.S.–USSR ABM treaties. ''We know the Americans test-fire missiles on a random basis. A submarine coming back from patrol is met with a surprise inspection team that will select one of the missiles for launch. The warhead of the designated missile is replaced by a telemetry nose cone, and the submarine goes back to sea. These tests are made known to us, lest a subsurface launch be misunderstood for a real missile attack, so we are able to observe the launches and track the missiles' flight downrange to their Kwajalein test range. Their success rate is ninety-five percent, and if the launch and initial trajectory are successful, the warheads are deadly accurate. On one test launch, one of our surveillance trawlers was asked to move, as they were in the impact area. The boat moved a few hundred meters, and the nose cone impacted *exactly* where our boat had been.''

''I see,'' the admiral replied. ''Tell me, why can we not track these Tridents with our own submarines?''

Molev leaned forward, warming to the subject. ''American submarine technology is very different from our own. They have had one basic design for their submarines—a single-hull, low-drag configuration. This design has not changed for decades. All their engineering skill and technical expertise has been directed at making their submarines quiet. Their passive-listening capabilities are sophisticated and highly refined.

''In contrast, there have been a dozen or more hull designs in our undersea fleet. Russian submarines are powerful, and their double-hull construction is built to survive an underwater explosion, so our boats are fast and strong, but they are noisy. Our active sonar capability is very good, but the undersea battle favors stealth.'' Molev paused and carefully sipped his tea. ''Their boats are better than ours, Admiral.''

''Better than your Akula, the *S-570*?''

''I'll let you know after this patrol. The boat has a freshly applied, sound-absorbing anechoic coating, and she has been fitted with the new passive sonar suite. We may do better this time.''

''Is it just a matter of technology?''

''That's part of it, but the American missile-submarine crews are very well trained and highly motivated. Their officers receive excellent pay and have schooling similar to our own training at the Komsomol School, although many have advanced degrees from their best civilian universities. But the principal difference between our submarine crews and theirs is in the ratings. American enlisted men are very skilled and competent technicians. Their pay is adequate—quite good compared to Soviet Navy wages—but not nearly what they could earn in industry if they left their navy. Yet they serve well, and they serve with pride. The enlisted men on American submarines have no equivalent in our own navy, and they make it possible for the Americans to keep their submarines at sea for these extended periods of time in a high state of readiness.''

Zaitsev was silent for a moment before he spoke. ''Our leaders talk of more strategic-arms reduction, but the Americans refuse to negotiate on submarine-launched weapons. They give elsewhere, but they will not budge on their Tridents. I am under a great deal of pressure from Moscow to find a way to neutralize these ballistic submarines.''

''I will do my best, Admiral.''

Zaitsev hesitated, then rose and offered his hand. ''Good luck to you, Kapitan Viktor Molev, and good hunting. I want you to report to me in person when you return from your patrol.''

PART ONE

THE *SPOKANE*

Thursday, June 18, 1992, 6:00 P.M.—Vancouver, British Columbia

The man standing near the corner was indistinguishable from the commuters waiting for the 6:05 bus. The Vancouver evening rush hour was nearly over, but the streets were still crowded. Those who waited did so patiently, reading the newspaper or staring vacantly at the passing traffic. There was little conversation. The man held a newspaper, head inclined over the newsprint, but his eyes continually moved over the street in front of him. He wore light cotton trousers, a short-sleeved polo shirt, and woven leather shoes. His skin was a smooth olive color, and he could easily have been taken for a member of British Columbia's large Indian community, but his features were too angular and his dark, close-cropped hair much too coarse.

"Excuse me there, buddy," said a commuter with a briefcase as he stepped past the man toward the curb and an approaching bus. The man's head snapped up from the paper and his eyes flashed. Then, as if by an act of will, he softened.

"Certainly, sir, by all means."

The bus pulled away with fewer than half of those who waited, and the man resumed his vigil. It had rained earlier in the day and the evening promised to be unseasonably cool, but he didn't seem to notice.

Across the street, another man casually worked his way along the block, pausing occasionally to glance into a shop window. He was tall and wore glasses, and carried a paper folded in his right hand. At the corner across from the bus stop, he abruptly turned and walked back to a small café in the middle of the block. The watcher at the bus stop remained in place until the next bus arrived, then moved away from the crowd with those who got off the bus. He crossed the street and followed the second man into the café.

It was a small establishment with checkered tablecloths, and it smelled of garlic. He entered and stepped away from the door, and paused to allow his eyes to adjust to the interior light. A round woman in a dirty apron approached him carrying a plastic-covered menu, but he waved her away. The man wearing glasses who had entered some minutes ahead of him was seated in the corner with his back to the door and his paper on the edge of the table. Satisfied, he glanced around the room and walked over to the table, taking a seat with his back to the wall.

"It is good to see you again, my friend," he said, looking past his companion to survey the room again.

"And you, Jamil. How are you?" The two men worked at a casual conversation, speaking in English. Their accents differed slightly, as one's native tongue was Farsi and the other's Arabic. They had spoken often by telephone, but had not seen each other for about six weeks. After the waitress served them espresso, the one called Jamil leaned forward.

"Now, Ahmed," he commanded in a low voice, "tell me about the preparations."

"The last member of the team will arrive at the safe house tomorrow, and as you know, the weapons arrived last weekend. Salah inspected them and made an inventory of the ammunition. He test-fired them yesterday, and all are in working order. The special weapons and grenades are of the type and quantity you specified. The radios have been tested, and the circuits on the firing devices thoroughly checked. I will pick up the special communications equipment on Friday evening. The system I have assembled will serve our needs. All items have been personally inspected by me, and are staged and ready to go." Jamil nodded his approval. He had worked too long with Ahmed to question him if he said all was in readiness.

Jamil quickly flashed back to when he first met the tall, serious man seated across from him. They were then students at the University of Beirut, back when the fragile Christian–Moslem coalition still governed, and that city was the Paris of the Middle East. In some ways, Ahmed was still the lanky, idealistic intellectual who had followed him when he left the university to join the PLO in the guerilla training camps. *What a waste,* Jamil thought. Ahmed possessed the keenest intelligence he'd ever encountered. *Were it not for the Jihad, Ahmed would have been a great scientist or engineer.*

Ahmed's parents, both physicians in Tehran, had been horrified when their son took up arms with the Palestinians. When they left for Paris after the fall of the Shah, he had disowned them. That was many years ago, and still he followed Jamil. He and Jamil had remained with the Fatah for only a year. Had they stayed longer they would have been killed, or worse, rotting in some Israeli prison.

But Jamil had elected to be an independent—a free agent—working with one organization, then another. For a while they had been aligned with the Popular Front for the Liberation of Palestine–General Command. Then the Hizbollah and the Palestine Liberation Front had bid for his services. His allegiance was to the cause rather than to a specific group. He quickly learned that he was more effective in this capacity, and far safer. Long ago Jamil had learned there were numerous religious factions, sects, and divisions in the Middle East with continually shifting memberships and alliances. He served the Jihad, not the interests of a special group. Their cause was the return of the Palestinian people to their ancestral land in the occupied territories. Or was it? Over the years, this goal had gradually merged with the destruction of the Jewish state. It had become an obsession with Jamil—the destruction of Israel and a hatred for the Americans. The Jews would have been pushed into the Mediterranean long ago had it not been for the support of the United States. He trembled with rage when he thought of America, a decadent land of infidels so far from his homeland who had taken it upon themselves to help the Jewish swine rob his people of their birthright.

God will judge them harshly in the next world for this injustice, he thought, *and I will exact a measure of retribution in this one.* But it had not gone well for the Palestinians. The Gulf War had allowed the Jews to all but crush the Intifada. His people had begun to fight among themselves and seemed unable to organize against the Zionists. Their political capital among the moderate and wealthy Arab nations had been squandered in their disastrous support of that madman Saddam Hussein. What had been seen by many Palestinians as a bold stand against the West was lost in Saddam's brutal conduct in a hopeless conflict. The Palestinians were used, by Syria, Iran, Iraq—all of them—as a cover to legitimize the pursuit of their own national interests. For a while, he had thought the Israelis could be worn down, or at least be forced to yield control of the West Bank and Gaza. But America had destroyed Iraq and continued to arm and rearm Israel, while Russian Jews, spurred by the collapse of the Soviet central government, relentlessly poured into settlements on the West Bank. *Now,* concluded Jamil, *time is on the side of the Jews. A third generation of Palestinians without a country is being born, and our people grow weary. Even Ahmed, my loyal comrade, is growing weary. He tries not to show it, but the years of hiding and clandestine living have made him old—I can see the fatigue in his eyes.*

"The vehicle is ready?" Jamil asked.

"Fueled and recently serviced. We should have no problem posing as a couple on holiday. We move the equipment from Michelle's garage to the motor home tomorrow morning. I plan to leave about five-thirty in the afternoon so we will be in the middle of the weekend traffic headed south."

"Excellent," replied Jamil. Ahmed and Michelle would have little problem in driving the coach across the U.S.–Canadian border. *How ironic,* he thought, *we are going to assault the Great Satan in a motor home.*

"And the rest of the team, they are ready?"

"Yes. They are anxious and a little nervous, but that is to be expected. This group, Jamil, they are a hard lot, more like mercenaries than patriots. I assume you have chosen them with a purpose.'' It was a mild question, but Jamil declined to respond. Ahmed paused to take a drink of the thick black coffee, the demitasse looking small and fragile in the grasp of his long fingers. He had the look of an academician, with his thick glasses and agreeable slouch. He continued, carefully framing his words, ''I don't know how much to make of this, but I have reason to believe that Carlos has been smoking hashish again, possibly even using this cocaine the Americans seem to have everywhere. I cannot verify this, but his actions since he arrived at the safe house have been ... well, suspect.'' Carlos was one of their most experienced fighters. Ahmed did not like bringing this to his leader's attention, but he feared his reaction if it became a problem and he had not mentioned it. A shadow seemed to pass over Jamil's features as he digested this information. Then his face became almost expressionless as he stroked the corner of his mustache with his thumb and index finger.

''Very well. I want you to do or say nothing about this. I will speak to Carlos when I see him on Saturday. Is everything else in order?''

''It is.'' Both men were quiet for a moment before Ahmed continued. ''And now, my leader, may I know why we have come so far from home and made these careful preparations? What is it that we are about to do?''

Jamil lit a cigarette and blew a cloud of smoke between them. His movements were casual, but through the haze Ahmed could see the anger and excitement in his eyes. Jamil again leaned forward.

''The Great Satan thinks we are a beaten people. He orchestrated the Gulf War to prevent a single Arab power from controlling the region's oil. He knew such a power would threaten Israel and ultimately restore our lands. Saddam had his own agenda, but he certainly would have tried to destroy the Jews. And now this fat, rich nation of infidels think they have won— that with their so-called 'new world order' and this sham of a peace conference they force on us, they can dictate our future. They now think we are impotent, and that they are safe!''

Jamil lowered his voice still more and lapsed into Arabic. His eyes glowed and his nostrils flared as the hatred poured out of him. ''What we are about to do to this satan is take from him what he values most—his most prized possession—and hold it up before him while the world watches! If we do this—*when* we do this—the Zionists will see the Americans can be beaten, and our people will take heart. They will rise up as a nation and we will purge our land of the Jewish swine forever!''

Jamil's eyes quickly swept the room, suddenly aware that he had allowed his emotions to surface. He crushed his cigarette and continued in English, speaking in a controlled, measured voice. He described the operation, quickly and methodically, while Ahmed listened to the bold and dangerous plan with increasing apprehension and admiration.

My God, thought Ahmed. *If we are successful in this, the whole Arab world will again rally to our cause.*

Thursday, 6:40 P.M.—Seattle, Washington

Ross Peck stood close behind the helmsman. He was a large man, and his heavy forearms were folded across his chest. His face was dead calm, but his eyes flashed from the officer at the helm to the throttle control to the oncoming dock ahead of them and back to the helmsman. Janey McClure stood near Peck off to one side. Her gaze flickered between Peck and the dock, and she slowly shifted her weight as if trying to impart body English to the ferry as it crabbed toward the dock. She and Peck made an odd couple on the bridge of the *Spokane,* for she was much shorter than he and plump as a partridge.

''Power?'' said the helmsman.

''Not yet.'' Peck wondered about Brad Johnson. He never seemed to quite grasp the relationship of the boat's momentum and the distance to the docking slip. After a while, most officers acquired a feel for the boat and when to apply power to the forward propeller to bring the vessel to a halt. Some never did, and either plowed into the slip's wing walls to make the landing or halted the ferry short of the dock and had to jockey the engines to guide the boat into place. Johnson hadn't yet learned a sense of the boat, so he guessed at when to apply power and was usually wrong. It was the same with the airlines. Some pilots made it hard to know just when you touched down, while others bounced the aircraft along the runway when they landed. Peck had always felt it a matter of pride to bring the ferry to a stop just as the bow on either side of the car ramp touched the dock walls.

"Now," said Peck firmly. He had let Johnson go just a little farther than he should have. Johnson pulled the control lever back, and the free-wheeling forward propeller reversed direction. The fifteen-foot prop bit into the water, causing the whole craft to shudder as green and white water was pushed ahead of the moving ferry. He increased power until the full 8,500 shaft horsepower struggled to bring the vessel to a halt, prompting the bow of the ferry to buck under the strain. The *Spokane* softly kissed one wing wall, then the other as the huge wooden pilings that backed the walls absorbed the spent momentum of the ferry. Johnson then cut the power to the forward propeller and ordered "ahead one-third" to the after screw to hold the ferry into the slip. *Not a totally unacceptable landing,* thought Peck, *but he bounced it in.*

"Well, how'd I do?" Johnson was the second mate, and part of his training was to dock the ferry under instruction. Considering there was no wind and that Seattle's Colman Dock was one of the easier landings, his performance had not been that great. Johnson was a tall, fragile-looking man in his late twenties with crooked teeth and a Beatles-vintage haircut. He was bright, eager, and openly sought Peck's approval.

"You're getting better," said Peck honestly, "but you have to try and feel the movement of the boat, like when you're in your car coasting up to a stop sign." *He probably doesn't do that very well either.*

"Can I do another one this shift?"

"Sure, but first I want you to watch Janey make an approach, and to try to get a better feel for the momentum of the boat. Now you'd better get below and give them a hand on the car deck.'' Johnson disappeared down the stairway as Peck added a little more rudder to hold them more securely against the side wall and keep the *Spokane* from pivoting in the slip while they unloaded.

"I'll stay here if you want to go below, Cap'n."

"Thanks, Janey. How much time till the next run?"

"About twenty minutes. You want me to check on that generator?"

"Thanks, but I think I'll take a walk down there. Can I get you some coffee?"

"You know I don't drink coffee." She smiled. "Why do you always ask?"

"I don't know," Peck replied. "How am I going to make a sailor out of you if you don't drink coffee?"

"You sound like my dad. Like I told him, I don't want to be a sailor—I want to be a seaman." Peck shrugged and headed for the wing of the pilothouse. He wasn't so sure he wanted to be compared to her father. His reference to a sailor, as she well knew, meant a Navy enlisted man, which in Peck's opinion was not all that bad.

"See you on the other end."

"Aye, aye, sir." Janey gave him a mock salute as he headed down the stairs.

You're already a seaman, thought Peck. Janey's father was a tugboat skipper on Puget Sound, and she'd spent a lot of time on the water. She was also the best first mate he'd had in a while. She handled the boat well and would never have made the sloppy landing Brad Johnson just made. More than that, she *knew* the boat. Not just the required learning from the manuals to pass the exams, but she understood the engineering plant, the electrical systems, and the heating and cooling systems. Many of the non–engineering officers on the ferryboats learned only what they had to know to drive the boat. Janey had taken the time to study the workings of the vessels on which she one day hoped to be a master. The last of the passengers were making their way to the boarding ramp as Peck walked through the galley to the large coffee urns.

"What do I owe you for the coffee, Gracie?"

"You know the coffee's free for you, Captain."

"I guess I do. Just don't want to cheat the taxpayer of his cut from the food concession. How's that youngster of yours getting along?"

"Real fine, and she'd do even better if Willard wouldn't keep spoiling her. How're your boys?" Gracie asked.

"They keep growing—must take after their mother."

"You better watch your mouth. I'm gonna tell Sarah what you said next time I see her."

He grinned, placing his index finger to his lips as he left the galley. Peck was a big man, rawboned, with large hands. He was well over six feet and 220 pounds, while his wife was slender and stood under five and a half feet. Their twin sons would be juniors in high school next year, and were as tall and nearly as heavy as their father. He was immensely proud of them.

Peck looked the part of a sea captain in a Spencer Tracy film. He had just turned forty-three, but his hair had been steel gray for several years and now curled from under the confines of his combination cap. He always wore a fresh white shirt, with military creases and four gold stripes neatly sewn to the epaulet tabs that buttoned across the top of his shoulders. The gray hair and the white shirt provided contrast to his tanned, handsome features. He had a broad, even smile and watery blue eyes surrounded by laugh lines when he squinted, which was most of the time. Peck was pigeon-toed, and his powerful shoulders were slightly stooped. Janey kidded him, saying he looked like a cartoon bear when he walked. Nonetheless, there was a certain grace and economy in his movement.

He stepped down two levels to the car deck and opened the heavy metal door marked "Engineering Spaces—Authorized Personnel Only." Another flight of steps and a short walk up the main passageway brought him to the propulsion control panel, the nerve center of the engineering plant. There were two men at the panel, one with a clipboard, making entries, and a younger one sitting on a tall stool, staring into space.

"Afternoon, gentlemen—keeping a tight watch down here?"

"Hi, Ross. What brings you belowdecks on a nice day like this?" Andy Gosnell was the chief engineer on the *Spokane* and like Peck, an ex–Navy man. This was something of a coincidence, since most of the ferry officers came from the merchant marine. Gosnell had retired as a chief machinist's mate with twenty-five years of service, while Peck mustered out as a first-class petty officer after six years in uniform. The two had often worked together since Gosnell had joined the ferry fleet four years earlier.

In contrast to Peck's nautical and softly weathered appearance, Gosnell had the chalky complexion and anemic look typical of belowdecks sailors, or "snipes," as they were called. Peck and his engineer were of the same vintage. When they weren't talking about the boat, the decline of the United States maritime industry, or the "old Navy," they could speak with some authority on the sport or the animal that was in season.

Steve Burns, the *Spokane*'s young oiler, was from a different era. His hair was just a shade off his collar and almost long enough to conceal the miniature earphones connected to the small tape player clipped to his belt.

"Just thought I'd make a social call between trips," replied Peck. "How's that number-two auxiliary generator running?"

"A lot better, but not perfect. Georgie changed out the fuel filters and that helped some, but I don't think it'll be right till the injectors are replaced."

"Where is George, anyway?" asked Peck. He was referring to George Zanner, the first assistant engineer.

"He's back taking manifold temperature readings." Gosnell set the clipboard aside and took out a pack of cigarettes, offering one to Peck.

"Thanks, but I promised Sarah I'd quit. Gawd, I'd like one, though. How's everything else—any problems?"

"Nothin' to speak of," Gosnell replied, lighting up. He had thin arms, with a dragon tattooed on one forearm and a Chinese junk on the other. "I got my suspicions about the lube-oil pump, but the four big Detroits are purrin' like kittens. The rest of the plant is fine, right, Steve?''

''Uh, whatever you say, engineer,'' the young man replied with a smile, dropping the earphones down about his neck. ''You mind if I run upstairs and get a Coke before we leave?''

''How many times I got to tell you it's 'topside,' not 'upstairs,' and we don't 'leave,' we 'sail.' Yeah, go ahead, but take off them damn earphones—people'll think this is a disco instead of an engine room.'' Burns grinned and disappeared while the two older men looked at each other in resignation.

''Y'know,'' continued Gosnell, ''when I was his age I was standing top watch on a twelve-hundred-pound steam plant and overhauling pumps when I wasn't on watch. Kids we get these days don't know shit.''

''Different times, my friend. If the kids knew it all, they wouldn't need old farts like us.''

''You joined up right out of high school, didn't you?''

''Actually, I was still in school,'' replied Peck, rubbing his chin. ''I had a little trouble with the authorities, and the judge said it was the service or the slammer. Good thing there was a war going on, or the Navy probably wouldn't have taken me.''

''No shit,'' said Gosnell, looking at Peck anew. ''You never struck me as the delinquent type.''

''Believe me, I was. The Navy was the best thing that could have happened to me. You should've seen me when I reported in at the Great Lakes Recruit Depot.'' Peck smiled, recalling the day he was inducted into the Navy—tight blue jeans, white T-shirt, a well-oiled ducktail haircut. He made it through boot camp, but not without being singled out as a recruit with an attitude problem.

''Think you're pretty tough, do you, Peck?'' the drill instructor had said at the end of boot camp.

''I can take care of myself, sir.''

''Well, we have a few openings in this man's Navy for tough guys, Peck. I'm going to see that you get one of them.''

Six months later, Seaman Peck was attached to River Patrol Division Five in Vietnam and assigned as a crewman on a PBR patrol boat. Most nights he found himself in the forward gun tub behind a twin .50 mount while they cruised the canals and estuaries of the Mekong Delta waiting to be ambushed. Peck learned two lessons very quickly—that survival meant he had to be a team player, and that a bullet didn't care how big or how tough a man was. By the end of his tour, he was a second-class petty officer and a patrol captain with his own PBR. He had become a leader rather than an intimidator, and the tough guy was gone. He might have been a lifer, but after Vietnam he was assigned to the Naval Torpedo Station on Puget Sound. He married Sarah and they bought a home. When his transfer to Norfolk came through, he put in his papers.

"Peck, you're a good petty officer and you have combat experience," the commander had told him. "The Navy needs men like you."

"Thank you, sir, but I'm all through fighting."

Peck shook his head—that was a long time ago. "Speaking of joining up, Andy," he continued, "don't we have a new man assigned to your gang?"

"Yeah, we do. Name's Gonzales, and he seems to know his way around an engine room. I kind of wonder why he's working here as a wiper since he's got his third mate's ticket." Gonzales was up the passageway crouched on the deck plates near one of the main engines. He wore a soiled pair of overalls and orange Mickey Mouse–type ear protectors. As if sensing they were talking about him, he looked up and smiled.

"Beats shipping out for weeks at a time on a merchantman, and the work's not all that steady. Lots of people take a pay cut or a step down to stay here in the Northwest. I was a craft master and had my own boat over at the Torpedo Station. I quit your Navy and become a deckhand on a ferry so I could stay here."

"My Navy, huh! Hell, Ross," Gosnell said with a twinkle in his eye, "if you'd stayed for twenty, you might even have made chief."

"Might have," replied Peck with a smile, "but would the Navy put an enlisted man in charge of a thirty-three-hundred-ton vessel? Nope, I got the best of it, Andy—I go to work every day, and I go to sea on my own boat. When I'm through working, I park the boat and go home to the family. You can't always do that in the Navy.''

''No . . . no you can't,'' admitted Gosnell. ''But then, you never get a chance to pull a Hong Kong liberty after a two-week transit, either.'' The twinkle had become a sparkle.

The old snipe must have been a real terror on the beach in foreign ports, thought Peck. He glanced at his watch and hurried back up the stairs.

Peck found Janey waiting for him on the port wing of the bridge of the outbound pilothouse, or ''number-two end.'' The *Spokane* had a pilothouse and identical ship-control stations on each end of the ferry. The pilothouses were perched on either end of the promenade deck. Each boxlike structure was thirty feet across on the beam and fourteen feet deep. The doors on both sides of the pilothouse were accommodated by a half-flight of stairs from the promenade deck, and the landings at the top of the stairs served as bridge wings on either side. Second Mate Johnson was now back on the number-one end to monitor the loading of cars and foot passengers.

Peck and Janey watched with a professional eye as the M/V *Issaquah* from Bremerton closed the dock and made her approach on the adjacent slip. She was a smaller boat, about two-thirds the size of the *Spokane*. Peck recognized her captain, Herb Allison, who was at the controls. Colman Dock also housed the headquarters of the Washington State ferry system, and some captains did not want their younger officers bouncing their craft into the home dock. Allison reversed his engines at the precise time, and the *Issaquah* made a perfect landing.

''Pilothouse two, this is pilot one,'' came Johnson's voice over the intercom. ''Captain, the passenger brow is away, and the life rail is in place.'' Peck walked back into the pilothouse and pressed the lever on the speaker box.

''Roger, Brad, standing by.'' A few moments later, Johnson's voice again crackled from the box.

''Car ramp is up and all lines are aboard.''

''Okay, Brad, I have control of the boat.'' Peck moved the lever that shifted control of the *Spokane* to the number-two outbound pilothouse. He brought the number-two rudder amidships and secured power to the number-two propeller, which had been holding them in the slip. Peck scanned the water in front of him. There was a container ship being helped to the loading docks on Shelter Island and several small craft that scurried about the harbor on business. He noted all this as he mentally projected a course for his vessel. Ferries had the right-of-way, but the commercial traffic didn't always honor them as privileged vessels. He then grabbed the wooden handle above his head and allowed the weight of his arm to pull it down. The children and a few of the adults on the forward walkways jumped as the *Spokane* issued a long, throaty bellow. Peck released the handle and ordered ahead one-third to ease the big ferry out of the slip.

The *Spokane* glided out across Elliott Bay, slowly working up to her cruising speed of eighteen knots en route to Eagle Harbor on Bainbridge Island. The Olympic Mountains still carried snow at the higher elevations and formed a jagged, purple-blue and white cut against the western sky. Below this, the haze-shrouded foothills of the Olympic Peninsula and a deep-green band of Douglas fir on Bainbridge Island segregated the mountains from the royal blue of Puget Sound. This splendor always impressed Peck. He was not a particularly religious man, but he felt God had surely blessed him to look at this spectacle from the bridge of his own vessel.

"Janey, she's all yours." He stepped to one side of the pilothouse, allowing her to take the helm. The ferry's control station had not been designed with female pilots in mind, so she had to kick a six-inch wooden platform into place to see out the pilothouse windows and down onto the bow of the ferry. Janey was perhaps in her mid-thirties, but she looked much younger. She had a kind, round face and a smattering of freckles across her rounded nose. Her straight brown hair was pulled back to a ponytail that sprouted defiantly through the hole in the back of her baseball cap just above the adjustable plastic band. She didn't look too nautical perched on top of that box, but she could handle the big ferry.

"Now watch Janey when she maneuvers into the harbor and

makes her approach,'' Peck said to Johnson, who had arrived moments before from the number-one pilothouse. ''I want you to try to *feel* what the boat is doing. It's like waltzing with an old fat lady—you can't change directions too fast, so you have to gently guide her where you want her to go.''

Thursday, 7:35 P.M.—Bellevue, Washington

Fred Lippert stood at the podium and patiently waited to be recognized. Soon there was a symphony of silverware on water glasses, followed by the rumble of moving chairs as many of the seated diners shifted their chairs to face the podium.

''Good evening and welcome to the June meeting of the Puget Sound chapter of the Naval Academy Alumni Association. It's gratifying to see such a large turnout. I'd like to thank the Bellevue Athletic Club for the use of this splendid facility. Normally at this time, I entertain comments from the floor and items of new business from the general membership. This evening, however, in deference to the time constraints of our featured speaker, we'll move directly to the program. The chapter is indeed fortunate to welcome back Rear Admiral MacIntyre, Class of '64 and Chief of the Naval Base, Seattle.'' There was a smattering of applause around the room from other members of '64. ''Most of you know the admiral, so I'll not delve into his background other than to say that he's a naval aviator and that the naval base here is his fifth command tour and his first shore-based command. He and his lovely wife Sally have just begun their second year with us here in Seattle. Without further ado, please join me in a warm welcome for Admiral John MacIntyre.''

Lippert shook the admiral's hand as he surrendered the podium. MacIntyre smiled and surveyed the crowd as the applause died away. He was a squat, intense man who looked more like a middle-aged stockbroker than a fighter pilot. He had spent a career flying jets from aircraft carriers, and his promotion to admiral had only partially compensated him for being taken off flight status. MacIntyre knew carrier aviation was a young man's game and he'd stayed in the cockpit longer than most, but the transition hadn't been particularly easy.

"Thank you, Fred. Distinguished guests, ladies and gentlemen, fellow alumni—it is an honor and a privilege to again be standing before you. As Fred mentioned, Sally and I are beginning our second year in Seattle, and your hospitality and support over the past twelve months have been deeply appreciated. Thank you for making us feel so much at home.

"I've been asked to address you this evening on the proposed military cutbacks and recent reductions in strategic weapons, and to relate those issues to our Navy here in Puget Sound. Briefly, there's good news and bad news. The bad news is that the new home port in Everett and possibly the Sand Point Naval Station are in danger. The good news is that our two major facilities, the Puget Sound Naval Shipyard in Bremerton and the submarine base at Bangor, should continue as before. Bremerton is still the only nuclear-capable yard on the West Coast, and it has scheduled repair contracts and nuclear-ship deactivation work through fiscal year '95.

"The base at Bangor and the Trident program will not only continue, but they will assume a greater responsibility for our nation's nuclear deterrence. All the nuclear warheads have now been removed from our surface combatants. The Strategic Air Command has been off alert for over ten months now, and this summer we will complete the removal of all tactical nuclear weapons from Europe. The START agreements signed last year call for a thirty-percent reduction in warheads, and those cuts may go much deeper. But if you've noticed, all the talk on further nuclear-arms reductions and the elimination of MIRVs, or missiles with multiple warheads, have been directed at land-based weapons. We now have eight Trident-Ohio Class submarines at Bangor, which together with the formidable new D-5 missiles form the cornerstone of our nation's strategic defense. I'm an old airplane driver, but I have to admit that I've really come to admire the professionalism and

dedication of the crews that man our ballistic submarines and to
respect the tremendous capability of the Trident system.''

MacIntyre talked for another twenty minutes about Trident
submarines, the Navy in Puget Sound, and the need for a better
offensive line if Navy was to have a prayer of beating Army in
the fall. The alums gave him a standing ovation as he and Sally
made their way from the room.

''I thought you didn't particularly like submarines,'' she
said as they walked through the lobby.

''I don't, but I'm a dinosaur. The Tridents are the Navy's
most important weapon now, both for national defense and in
the vicious budget battles that will rage in Washington over the
next few years.''

Friday, June 19, 5:25 A.M.—Poulsbo, Washington

Peck turned into the drive and continued past the detached garage to park the car near the back door. He always drove Sarah
to her job on the mornings he worked the late shift. Quietly, he
let himself in and the cat out, and put on a pot of coffee. While
the percolator did its job, he pawed through the mail Sarah had
neatly laid out on the kitchen table. Armed with a mug of fresh
coffee, he stepped through the screen door to the front porch,
which overlooked Liberty Bay. They'd bought the house fifteen years earlier, before the buildup at the Bangor submarine
base on Hood Canal and before Poulsbo had become a fashion-
able cross-Sound commute to Seattle. Waterfront was afford-
able then.

Peck eased himself into the porch swing and wrapped both
hands around his mug to ward off the morning chill. The home
enjoyed a southwestern exposure. The dawn still had a gray
cast, and the bay was a mirror, disturbed only by thin wakes
carved by a pair of mallards that spoke quietly to each other.
The seasoned, rotten-sweet smell of a low tide drifted up the

house. Down the shoreline, two sea gulls argued over a single clam on a beach littered with clams.

Periodically, and it happened most often on those quiet mornings while the family was asleep, Peck reflected on just how lucky he was. He knew of the disappointment and helplessness of some parents whose kids were into drugs or did poorly in school, or wanted nothing to do with their parents. Tom and Jack were both good students, and they were already varsity athletes—this fall they'd both be starters on the North Kitsap football team. Best of all, they liked to spend time with him and Sarah. Not all the time, naturally, but they wanted them at their athletic events, and they brought their friends home a lot.

And Sarah, what a find! Some of the guys he knew had married better-looking women, but they seemed frivolous compared to her. He'd had his chances to fool around and had been tempted a time or two, but that wasn't his way. Sarah's father, a prominent local doctor, had been against her marrying a sailor, but she was the one who insisted they not wait, as her father had wanted. The doctor had come to accept him, even envy him, as overworked professionals will envy a well-paid blue-collar worker who has an interesting job that he likes.

"Mornin'." Sarah slipped through the screen door and joined him on the swing. She huddled next to him in her housecoat, bringing her knees up under her chin. Her waist-length brown hair was piled on top of her head. She wore thick glasses that would be discarded when she was awake enough to put in her contacts. "How's the old man of the sea?"

"Not too bad. Sleep well?" He put his arm around her as she took a sip of his coffee.

"Like a log. You work tonight?"

"Nope. Don't have to go in till Saturday afternoon."

"How about pizza and the movies tonight? *Patriot Games* is playing in Silverdale, and the boys have been after me to take them."

"Sounds fine. You want to go straight from work or come home first?"

"I don't know—let me think about it."

"How're the boys?"

"Still trying to sneak down to the Indian reservation to buy firecrackers. I think you better have a talk with them."

Neither spoke for a while, and soon the sun began to ignite the tops of the Douglas fir across the bay. Sarah didn't always have a need for conversation, which he appreciated. They often shared periods of silence like this together.

The life he and Sarah had built was far different from the one he'd known as a boy. His own father ran off when he was in grade school, and he had to put up with a succession of alcoholic drifters his mother brought home. She was a cocktail waitress with a penchant for good-looking, worthless, and often abusive men. They had lived in a poor neighborhood on the South Side of Chicago, where as a boy he quickly learned that you were either predator or prey—there was no middle ground. He paid his dues until he was big and smart enough to go out and collect them. At seventeen, a run-in with the law had brought him before a municipal judge who had offered him ninety days in jail or an enlistment in the service. His mother's current bum-of-the-month had been in the Army, so Peck joined the Navy.

Sarah stirred and stifled a yawn. "I better get ready for work. You want some breakfast?"

"Let me do it—you get in the shower."

Friday, 5:05 P.M.—Enumclaw, Washington

The old Dodge crew-cab pickup bounded into the gravel parking lot of the Lackland Timber Company and slid to a stop throwing waves of dust over the parked vehicles, mostly other old pickups. There were six rough-cut young men in the cab seats and three more sitting in the bed amid a tangle of ropes, cables, gas cans, and chain saws. The foreman, who was at the wheel, was still wearing a metal safety helmet, and was one of the few who didn't have a can of beer in his hand. Lackland was a jippo-logging outfit that worked small tracts of timber around the large holdings of Weyerhaeuser and the other big companies. Their headquarters—a few equipment buildings and an office created by a plywood partition in one of the sheds—was located just outside Enumclaw near the base of Mount Rainier. Like many small operators, they met their payroll, and whenever they seemed to be getting a few dollars ahead, a log skidder or a cat would break down and wipe out their cash reserves.

"Jesus, Fred, I didn't cheat death out in the woods to have you kill me in the company parking lot," complained one of the loggers.

"You're here, ain't yuh?" growled the man climbing from behind the wheel.

"Fred don't think you've had a full day unless he can put a little blood in your pee from kidney damage."

"It's payday, an' I'm fixin' to put a little beer in my pee."

"Hey, Clancy, where're we goin' drinkin'?"

"I reckon we'll start at the White Horse over in Buckley an' work our way back this way."

The crew clustered around the tailgate of the truck, clutching lunch pails and Thermos bottles as they finished their beers. They were a boisterous crowd except for the foreman, who headed for the office, and another member of the crew who detached himself from the group. He was in his late twenties and dressed in dirty Levi's and a camouflaged military-style jacket. Like the others, he was soiled and sweat-stained from working in the woods, but there was something about him that was a little less clean than the others. His hair was near shoulder length and stringy, and his complexion had a sallow, unhealthy pallor.

"Hey, Billy, you gonna go have a beer?"

"Naw, I got to get home. See you Monday." He climbed into a battered Ford Torino and headed out onto the highway.

"Now, why'd you ask that shit to drink with us?" said one of the remaining crew. "Ain't it enough that we gotta put up with him all day in the woods?"

"Aw, sometimes I feel sorry for him. He's kinda like a stray dog."

"Well, the guy's an asshole. This ain't his kind of work—I wonder why he ever signed on here."

Billy Fenton had been working for Lackland for about three months, setting chokers for five dollars an hour. It was hard and dangerous work, but Ahmed told him it would look better if he were employed, and it was the best he could do. Fenton had never really been one to fit in with the crowd, and the logging crew was not the first group to avoid him.

Fenton had grown up in a well-to-do suburb of Atlanta with two younger sisters who were both pretty and bright. They were his parents' pride, and Billy grew up in the shadow of their accomplishments. He was at best an average student, and the only friends he made were the wrong kind, so he was in and out of trouble—nothing serious, but he was an irritant to his parents and an embarrassment to his sisters. They were all glad when he joined the Army after high school.

Fenton almost made it in the Army. He was promoted to buck sergeant after his first hitch, when he reenlisted for Special Forces training. He earned the coveted Green Beret and was assigned to an A-team training for duty in Central America. Once deployed, the team was billeted in a small village, where they worked with the local militia. Fenton thrived on the attention he received as a member of an elite military training cadre.

One evening while returning to camp after a few beers at the local cantina, he came upon a teenage girl working a small plot of land. At first, she laughed shyly when Fenton made a pass at her. As he became bolder, she pushed him away and finally tried to run from him. He caught her and beat her severely, then raped her. The next day, the girl's father brought his daughter to their camp. Her eyes were nearly swollen shut, but she identified Fenton as the man who assaulted her. When questioned, Fenton claimed she was a tease and that she'd got what was coming to her. After all, she was just a campesina. The platoon first sergeant, a short, muscular Chicano soldier who had never liked Fenton, quickly put him on the ground and hit him five times before the lieutenant and the father could pull him off.

Only the possible implication of the first sergeant for striking a subordinate kept Fenton from a general court-martial.

On their return to the States, Fenton was caught trying to smuggle some marijuana in the bottom of his field pack. He thought he would be busted to corporal and lose a few months' pay at the very worst. But his lieutenant testified against him at the hearing, saying that the Army had made a mistake allowing him to be in uniform. He was given an administrative discharge and a bus ticket home.

A few months later, he was driving a cab in Atlanta and telling anyone who would listen how bad the Army had screwed him. One evening his fare was an Iranian student attending the University of Georgia. He listened, and Billy was surprised to find that he took a genuine interest in his problems.

Fenton hated logging and the other members of the crew, but he had to admit it was the perfect cover. No one thought it odd that a logger would rent an old house twelve miles from town and well away from any neighbors. Enumclaw was a community that tolerated men whose lives centered around hunting and fishing, and who required solitude. The house, a spacious, unkempt four-bedroom rambler with a large detached garage, was located on ten acres of second-growth timber. The property was part of an estate with a lengthy settlement, and Fenton had been able to sign a year's lease. There was state land on two sides, and the nearest neighbor was four miles down the road. He'd stopped for a six-pack of beer on the way home, and when he arrived, he noticed there was another car behind the garage. It was the third to arrive in the last two weeks. The operation had to be going down very soon. *Well, it can't be too soon for me,* he thought. *I'll show them just how much of a soldier I am.*

Off to one side of the house in the shadow of a large cedar tree, a man watched Billy Fenton drive in. He patiently waited to see if anyone had followed him. He disliked Fenton, but then, he disliked all Americans. They were an arrogant, self-righteous people, and they were infidels. The man followed Fenton to the house. He had to admit Fenton had done well in selecting this safe house. It was private and large enough to sleep ten. So far there were six of them, with more to arrive that evening. The garage served as an armory for the weapons and ammunition, and the woods on the property were suitable for test-firing them.

Fenton walked in to find the Palestinian, the Egyptian, and the Latino playing cards at the kitchen table. They played with a fourth man he had not previously met, who looked as if he could be a brother to any of the other three. The room was filled with cigarette smoke.

"Jesus Christ," he said, "you guys got something against fresh air?" Two of them glanced up and returned to their game. The relatively mild summer temperatures in the Pacific Northwest were still cool for them, and they seldom opened a window. Fenton twisted off the cap on a bottle of beer and tossed it in the direction of the wastebasket. He glanced at the dirty dishes and empty bottles around the kitchen. The place was in shambles. He had never been much of a housekeeper, and things had become much worse with the new arrivals. He was about to say something when the man who had watched his arrival stepped into the kitchen. The game stopped and they all looked at him. He was medium height, dark, wiry, and his eyes were very cold. He had a long, prominent nose that gave him the look of a collie dog, but much less affable.

"Hey, Salah, *qué pasa!* When do we go to work and do this great deed you have been planning, eh?" said one of the card-players.

"I have received word that our leader will be here tomorrow. I can only assume that we will strike very soon."

"What is the mission?"

"And just who is 'our leader,' anyway?"

Salah surveyed them. These men had been chosen for their proven capabilities, their strong anti-American feelings, and a passable command of English. They had been given a sum of money up front for "expenses." There was also the unspoken "bonus" that would be paid to them, or their families should they not return, upon the completion of the mission. His instructions in preparation for this operation had come from Ahmed, with whom he had worked in the past. He had met

Jamil only once, and that had been several years ago. He knew nothing of the operation, which was as expected, but he had been quite surprised to learn that the Sayeh himself would lead them.

"Sayeh," which meant "shadow" in Farsi, was Jamil's *nom de guerre*. It had been given to him by the Iranian Revolutionary Guards, who had financed most of his terrorist activities. Jamil was known to be a master planner and had orchestrated numerous acts of terrorism, but to Salah's knowledge, the man had skirted direct involvement and carefully avoided public exposure. It was said that when he did take an active role, he acted alone. Ahmed had called that morning to say that he and Jamil would arrive sometime late that evening. Experience told Salah that in a short while things would start to happen very quickly.

"I know only that we will be told what we need to know tomorrow. The man who will lead us is a man of great reputation and stature, so the work we do is of the highest importance. From now on, no one is to leave the area without my permission, and there will be no more alcohol after the evening meal."

"I'll drink when I want to," said Fenton without thinking. Salah, who never drank, looked at him with disdain. His forced smile was both soft and cruel.

"As a favor to me, please do not." It was not a request. He then turned to the others. "Make all preparations to leave by tomorrow noon. I do not know when we will be called to action, but it will be soon. There will be some new arrivals late this evening, but do not concern yourselves with that. Tomorrow we will be assigned weapons, and perhaps then we will be told of our mission."

Salah walked back outside. *Fenton is weak,* he thought, *and the others seem to want American dollars more than they want to serve God.* He had a contempt for those motivated only by money. But Ahmed had made it clear that they would need capable, professional fighters, and Salah had to admit that those who were the most idealistic did not always perform well in battle.

It was early evening, and the sun would not go down for

another three hours. Salah had spent little time in northern latitudes, and the long summer days were strange to him. He walked a short distance into the woods and knelt down in a small clearing, resting his buttocks on his ankles. Mecca was almost directly opposite him on the globe, but he still faced to the east. Then he placed his palms on the ground in front of him and bent forward to place his forehead on the backs of his hands. On the eve of battle, most men ask their God to keep them safe. Since Salah was a man who didn't really know fear, he prayed for the success of their mission.

Friday, 6:15 P.M.—United States–Canada Border

Ahmed sat in the passenger's seat of the motor home and fretted. Everything was going as planned, he assured himself, but still he was uneasy. The coach had been loaded with those items serious outdoors types would take on a two-week vacation to California—sleeping bags, backpacks, cameras, fishing tackle, a large ice chest. A Honda trail bike had been strapped to the front bumper and two mountain bikes were lashed to the luggage rack on top. There were two complete outfits of scuba gear, including custom-fitted wet suits, fins, buoyancy vests, and tanks. The tanks had proper inspection certifications, and a sticker on the air manifold indicated they had been filled ten days ago at Rick's Dive Shop in Vancouver. Only, these tanks didn't contain air. With great care and at considerable expense, they had been charged with hydrogen cyanide gas. In the storage area under the booth of the kitchenette were six one-gallon paint cans. Externally, they looked like ordinary cans of Glidden Exterior Spread Satin, but inside, a shallow cone had been fitted in the bottom of each can with the apex pointing upward. Semtex, a moldable high-explosive, had been packed on top of the cones, filling the can with the explosive while the space below the cones remained empty. The paint cans were now explosive charges, shaped for a specific purpose. In the storage locker by the toilet, along with the tent poles and fishing rods, were six folded tripods that would hold the cans in place for their designed purpose. These special items had been carefully assembled in a rented Vancouver garage and packed in the motor home that morning.

A litany of memorabilia from vacations past was displayed on the cab and bumper, like enemy kill-tallies on the cockpit of a fighter plane—Rock City, Wall Drug, Sea Lion Caves, Yellowstone, Disneyland—as well as the fraternal orders—Good Neighbor Sam Club and KOA Campgrounds. The twenty-seven-foot Pace Arrow was thirteen years old and a veteran of many border crossings. She looked tired, but the engine, drive train, and transmission were new, as were the tires and brakes.

They were in stop-and-go-traffic on Highway 99, about a quarter-mile from the border. A four-lane river of weekend travelers was headed south, and the dam that held them was the U.S. Customs checkpoint. Their documentation was in order, but crossing the border was never a sure thing. The customs officers had finely tuned instincts for situations that looked the slightest bit out of place. And there was the remote but very real possibility of a random vehicle search. The objective of this border scrutiny was drugs, not terrorists, but it made the threat of discovery no less dangerous. Ahmed had documentation that showed him to be a visiting professor from Saudi Arabia teaching at Simon Fraser University. But their plan to clear U.S. Customs rested largely with Michelle, and Ahmed knew very little about her.

Michelle Frontenac carried an authentic Quebec provincial driver's license and a valid registration for the motor home. Her IDs showed that she was a resident of Montreal and a student at Simon Fraser. She was fluent in German as well as French and English. Ahmed had worked with her for several months as they made preparations for the operation, but she still remained something of a mystery. The others that Jamil had him recruit for the operation had come in service to Islam or for the money. Their hatred for the Americans was their only common bond. With the exception of Fenton, they were a savage lot who had demonstrated their ability to kill without hesitation—they were veterans, and in this case, veteran terrorists. Ahmed sensed that Michelle was different. He knew little about her other than that she was a French national, and that she had connections with the Red Army Faction in Germany and the internationalist wing of Action Direct, a French-based terrorist group. Since the business of terrorism often required that they carry out the most heinous acts, Ahmed suspected people who joined in their work without a motivating cause or, failing that, a healthy appetite for cash. In Michelle's case, he was given contact instructions by Jamil and had met her six months before at a small café in Paris. When Ahmed told her that Jamil would be personally involved, her eyes sparkled, and she had wanted only to know where and when, rather than how or why.

"Relax," she said in English. "Those border pigs have been on their feet for a good six hours. All they want to do is get this traffic backup cleared out and finish their shift." She drove the big coach expertly from a semireclined position, with her left foot on the gas pedal and her right foot on the console between the seats. Her left arm rested on the door window ledge, while her fingers toyed with the steering wheel.

"Let's give the boys in brown a little thrill," she said as she took a Coke from the ice chest behind the seat. She placed the cold can against her stomach under the tight-fitting tank top, causing her nipples to become hard under the fabric.

Customs Officer Roy Collins saw that the motor home was being driven by a good-looking blonde when it was two cars back from his booth. She was sitting at eye level as he looked across the tops of the cars between the Pace Arrow and the tollbooth. It was getting toward the end of his eight-hour shift, and the cars had been backed up for the last half of it. Good-looking ladies helped to pass the time, and this one was gorgeous. The coach rolled to a halt in front of the booth, and he saw at a glance that she had long, well-shaped legs, and that she was wearing absolutely nothing under the tank top.

"Good afternoon. How long will you be staying in the United States?"

"Why, good afternoon, Officer Collins," she replied, reading the name from the tag on his shirt. "About two weeks, unless I can convince the professor here to play hooky for a while longer." Her smile was both intimate and mischievous.

"Uh, are you Canadian residents?"

"I am. Professor Khalid is a visiting scholar at Simon Fraser University from Saudi Arabia. I'm one of his students."

"I see. Could I please see some documentation, Professor?" *A professor,* thought Collins. *I'll bet she gets an A in the class. I hear these Arabs go nuts over Western women.* During the Gulf War and ever since, they had been directed to carefully scrutinize Middle Eastern types. Ahmed handed his passport and working visa to Michelle, who took them with a smile and a wink. The look in her eyes was the same as in Paris when he told her that Jamil would lead them on a dangerous mission. Michelle passed the documents to Collins. He studied them for a moment, trying not to stare at the magnificent breasts that were now pressed against the top of the driver's-side window.

"Do you have any cigarettes in excess of one carton apiece or liquor in excess of one liter per person?" he asked as he placed the visa in the passport and handed it back to Michelle.

"No, Officer, we sure don't," said Michelle. Ahmed just shook his head.

"You folks have a safe and pleasant stay in the United States."

"And you have a real nice day there, Officer Collins." She smoothly pulled away from the booth after giving him one of her most radiant smiles.

"See, that wasn't so hard, was it?" she said as she brought the coach up to the legal speed limit. Her eyes still sparkled, and she wore a triumphant smile.

"No, I suppose it was not," he replied quietly, "but you were pushing it—you took more risk than was necessary. And there was no reason to do so." Ahmed shook his head imperceptibly as he reconsidered the woman behind the wheel. He now knew why she was here—why she had jumped at the opportunity to join the operation—and it was not for the cause or the money. Danger, certainly, and perhaps violence, was like an aphrodisiac to her.

"What's the big deal—he was just a border pig. Christ, did

you see the expression on that asshole's face? I can't wait to tell Jamil about it. Will we be seeing him tonight?''

"Jamil will appear when it is time. You know that."

"Oh, don't be so damned prophetic. God, I can't wait to see him!"

An olive-skinned man, impeccably dressed in a tailored summer suit, sat in a Hertz rental car and watched the motor home several cars ahead of him pass through the customs checkpoint. When his turn came at the customs booth, he stated that he was an engineer with the DeHaviland Aircraft Corporation, and that he was on his way to the Boeing plant near Seattle. His documents were quickly checked, and he cleared customs with no delays.

When questioned just a few days later, Officer Collins would be able to provide only a sketch of the man in the motor home. His description of the woman driving was better, and when he was asked about distinguishing physical characteristics, he was able to report that she had a grand set of knockers.

Friday, 6:30 P.M.—Camp Wesley Harris, near Bangor, Washington

"Ready on the right . . . ready on the left . . . the firing line *is* ready! With one round of ball ammunition, load and lock!"

Gunnery Sergeant McGarther Jennings stood tall at the head of the firing line, feet apart with his hands on his hips. He was dressed in camouflaged utilities and spit-shined jungle boots. He wore a brown broad-brimmed Marine Corps campaign hat tipped low over his eyes, with the black leather strap cinched tightly around the back of his head. Only Marine Corps drill instructors rated wearing that hat—Marine drill instructors and Lee Marvin. Jennings was not as big as he was thick. His chest, waist, and neck were thick; so were his arms and legs. He was a hard-looking man, and his intense dark eyes burned from under the circular hat brim, like star sapphires partially hidden in a fold of black leather.

"Commence fire!" The rich baritone echoed down to the rifle butts.

Crack!

Jennings lifted his binoculars and scanned the target. Six o'clock, again. Jennings stepped forward to the prone rifleman, who was dressed just like Jennings, but with a soft utility cap.

"Now, listen, you're still pushing it—you're anticipating the round going off and you're leaning into it. Remember, deep breath—let part of it out—get your site picture, and it's a steady squeeze-pull straight back. Okay, let's try it again.

"All ready—load and lock . . . commence fire!"

Crack!

Jennings looked again, and a smile split his face. It was a dead-center bull. He dropped to one knee and handed the glasses to the shooter, who now stood beside him.

"Yippee—bull's-eye!" She almost dropped the binoculars as she threw her arms around his neck and kissed him. "Can we shoot some more?"

"That's about it for tonight, pumpkin," he replied, straightening his hat. "We have to clean the weapons, and your mom's waiting dinner."

"Tomorrow, then?"

"I got the duty tomorrow, hon. Maybe on Sunday after I get off. Now, why don't you go give Gunny Carstairs a big hug for keeping the range open for us, and I'll get the rifles."

"Okay, Dad. Meet you in the parking lot." She ran off, pigtails flying, while Jennings retrieved the single-shot, bolt-action .22. It was his first rifle, a gift from his grandfather. He slung it over his shoulder and slid his own match-grade M-16 into its fleece-lined soft case.

He was waiting when she came skipping over the berm to join him. She took his hand as they walked across the gravel lot to the jeep.

Saturday, June 20, 4:14 A.M.—Port Angeles, Washington

''Hey, Mike, you wanna catch that bow line.'' His name was really Muhammad, but sound carried across the water. The hulk on the bow of *Katie B* leaped onto the pier. He slipped the line from the mooring cleat and carried it back aboard. Epps backed the boat away from the slip and well out into the channel. She was a dated wooden forty-six-foot Grand Banks classic cruiser—slow, beamy, and reliable. He twisted the boat midchannel and headed for the harbor entrance at a conservative idle. Epps wiped the heavy dew from the windscreen on the fly bridge with an old towel, and savored the diesel fumes that burbled from the stern, and followed the *Katie B* as she left the Port Angeles marina.

Stanley Epps, much like Billy Fenton, had been in place for a number of months, but unlike Fenton, he loved his ''cover'' job as a charter skipper. At Ahmed's direction, he had bought the boat at a good price and set it up for the summer charter season. A marine survey had indicated she was tired but in good mechanical condition, and the hull was sound. Nonetheless, Epps laid the boat up for a week to change one of the propellers and have the shaft packing glands replaced. He also had the two Gray Marine diesel engines serviced, and installed new injectors and filters. Ahmed had not told him exactly what they would be doing, but he had made it clear that a generous bonus depended on the seaworthiness of the craft. Epps sensed this man and his friends were to be treated with respect, and didn't have to be reminded of the negative consequences if he or the boat failed them.

He was given to believe that any losses in the charter business would be paid by his employers, but so far he'd been able to cover most the operational expenses with charter fees. For the past several months, he had been taking small parties of sportfishermen out into the Strait of Juan de Fuca. Mostly they stayed in the vicinity of Port Angeles and filled the box with

bottom fish, but occasionally they ranged farther west along the
Strait to look for halibut. Still, it had been a fairly slow season
and probably wouldn't pick up until the salmon began to run in
late summer. By then, they would be well clear of Port Angeles
and the Strait.

Working a charter boat and fishing was probably the only
honest work Epps had ever done. He grew up in Crescent City,
California—he knew boats and he knew the sea. Until he quit
high school, he worked summers as a bait boy on the fishing
charters. He then worked full-time on a gill-netter for minimum
wage and a share of the catch. Unfortunately, he had elected to
augment this income as a burglar, and not very successfully. He
had done time on two occasions, and was working as a deckhand on a purse seiner when Ahmed approached him. Now he
felt he was finally in the big time, and he wanted to do a good
job for his new employers. Neither Ahmed nor the others spoke
of it, but he knew they were going to be bringing in a shipment
of narcotics. *What else could it be?* he thought. Epps had always known that the real money was in drugs, and now he had
a chance to get his hands on some of it. Maybe with his share of
this operation he would be able to buy his own boat and be a
legitimate charter-boat skipper. *Captain Epps' Charter Service*—he liked the sound of it. He could tell that these people
were pros. The preparation had been very meticulous, and
these Arabs—"*A*-rabs," as he called them—dealt strictly in
cash.

There were four of them. In addition to the big man he called
Mike, there were two other Arabs. Actually, one was an Iranian
called Haj who preferred to think of himself as a Persian rather
than an Arab. All spoke reasonably good English. Initially,
Epps thought the fourth was Mexican, but had come to learn
that he was a Cuban. Roberto was affable and liked to talk, so
Epps sought him out when he wanted conversation. The others
spoke very little and smiled even less. They had arrived sepa-
rately over the past week. Epps let it be known on the docks that
he had been chartered by a party from Los Angeles for a week
of fishing. For the most part, they had stayed in the cabin and

out of sight. Late last night, all four had gone ashore and returned with two large footlockers.

The leader was a slim, very intense man called Nabil. He was
fine-featured, almost elegant, with a light-chestnut complexion
and skin that stretched tightly over prominent cheekbones. He
wore expensive clothes—V-necked cashmere sweaters and
heavy gold chains. Epps had offered him a pair of deck shoes,
but he preferred hand-tooled patent loafers. He was younger
than the others, but they deferred to him. Nabil had the long,
hard muscles of an athlete and the eyes of a predator. His English was precise and measured, suggesting that he was well
educated. There was a forced cordiality about him. He treated
Epps like a servant, and Roberto little better. These were all
very dangerous men, but Epps was especially wary of Nabil.

They had gone out each day to preserve the appearance of a
working charter boat. He and Roberto fished while the others
slept or sat in the cabin smoking slim, black, foul-smelling cigarettes. Today, Nabil had wanted him to be out of the marina
before daylight. Normally everyone remained in the cabin
drinking tea until the boat was well out into the Strait. This
morning, Nabil came up to the fly bridge just as they were
clearing the breakwater. It was a brisk, clear morning, and
Epps, dressed in a paint-stained foul-weather jacket, steered
the boat with one hand while he blew a warming cloud of steam
through the other. Nabil, who wore only a light sweater and
cotton trousers, moved gracefully from one side of the fly
bridge to the other.

"It's gonna be a great day as soon as the sun gets up," said
Epps, turning to look at the pink light creeping into the eastern
sky. "We can hit some of the bottom fishing holes, or we could
try for a few silvers—the salmon are startin' to come down.
The *Patty Cake* got half a limit yesterday—couple of ten-
pounders."

"How much fuel do you have on board?"

"Like every mornin', we're topped off—four hundred gal-
lons."

"How long will it take you to move us to the Hood Canal?"

"The fishin' ain't that good in the Canal. We'll do a lot better right out here."

"I didn't ask about the fishing—I asked how long it would take to get there." The arrogance in Nabil's voice was lost on Epps, but not the harshness and cruelty.

"It's about a six- or seven-hour run from here at full throttle, nine hours or so at cruising speed."

"Will the boat be missed if we don't return to the marina this evening?"

"I doubt it. Most people would just figure we were on the water late and coming in after dark. I 'spect a few of the other charter skippers will start to ask questions by late tomorrow morning."

"A lot of people will be asking questions by tomorrow morning, Epps. Take us to the Hood Canal at whatever speed you think best. Just make certain that we are at the Hood Canal floating bridge by nightfall."

Saturday, 7:45 A.M.—Enumclaw, Washington

Jamil awoke as the light filtering through the curtains lost its softness and became full daylight. The sun had been up over three hours, but it needed to be well into the sky to reach them through the trees. As he had trained himself, he brought his senses to full alert and eased his right hand around the grip of the Sig Sauer .45 before he opened his eyes. He was momentarily startled by the nearness of the prefabricated wooden cabinet that hung three feet above his head. The sound of birds could be heard through the insulated skin of the motor home, but nothing else. He normally required only five hours of sleep. The seven hours of deep, uninterrupted sleep he'd just had would be invaluable, for there would be little time for rest during the next several days.

He had arrived at the safe house about ten o'clock the night before, just after dusk. Tomorrow would mark the summer solstice, the longest day of the year in the Northern hemisphere. The operation had been planned for this time of year—not for the long evenings, but for the early dawn. The yellow bug light that illuminated the front of the garage indicated that all was well. Still, one always approached a safe house with caution. Jamil swung into the drive and sat with the car idling for a few moments. He switched off the engine, cut the lights, and waited—listening. Even then, he did not hear the man approach the rear panel of the car.

"God be with you, my leader." The voice was respectful but not subservient. Jamil slid from the car and closed the door quietly. The interior lights had been turned off. He clutched the arms of the man who stood waiting in a warrior's embrace.

"And with you, Salah. Thank you for agreeing to come on this mission. It is a long way from our home."

"It is the land of our enemy. Perhaps it is time we brought the fight to his homeland, since he has so recently brought it to ours. I am honored to serve with the Sayeh."

In silent mutual consent, the two men moved a few steps into the trees away from the soft glare of the garage light. Both felt safe but automatically moved into the shadows created by the foliage, where they would be less visible.

"How are the others—are they ready?" Jamil knew the equipment and arms would be ready—Ahmed had said they would be. But Salah was an experienced fighter, known for his coolness and bravery. His opinion of those selected for the operation was a valuable one.

"Since I do not know our mission, it is hard to say. They are here for the money, not for Allah. Even Hassan and Ali, they want to be paid. But I believe they will fight. I cannot say that they will fight to the death, but they will fight."

"And you, my friend, will you fight to the death?" It was a rhetorical question, and not posed as a test of Salah's loyalty.

"Only God knows, but I believe the Sayeh can depend on me."

"I do depend on you, my friend, for soon we climb up on the Great Satan's back and dig our spurs deep into his side."

"Then we should rest while we can. I have cleared a room for you in the house. May I help with your bags?"

"That won't be necessary. A motor home will arrive soon, and I will stay there. Is there a place to park away from the house?"

"The drive swings around behind the garage and another fifty meters into the woods. You will not be bothered there. I will be in the woods and will see that you are not disturbed." Salah was saying that he would stand guard so his leader could sleep. Jamil understood this and squeezed the man's shoulder in gratitude. *If I had a hundred men like this one,* thought Jamil, *I could storm the capitol in Washington, D.C., and seize their government.*

Thirty minutes later, Ahmed and Michelle arrived with the motor home. They had made a brief stop near Seattle for some additional equipment. Jamil directed Salah to show Ahmed to the vacant room in the house. He then took the wheel of the motor home and drove around the garage and into the woods.

Jamil lay very still and mentally brought the day and the tasks ahead into focus. *In a short time we will set events into motion that will capture the attention of the world and focus it on the concerns of our people. If we are successful, our cause and the hopes of the Palestinian people will be dramatically advanced. If we fail, at the very least the Americans will never again feel so secure within their borders.*

He had indeed slept well. Long ago he had mastered the ability to force his body to rest before going into action. This time it had been made easier knowing Salah was standing guard. It had also been made more pleasant by the wild, near-violent lovemaking of Michelle that had driven them both to the point of exhaustion. He knew the prospect of danger aroused her—she became insatiable. He, too, felt it within himself, but he controlled it. If there was one discipline Jamil valued above all others, it was self-control. He slipped from the bed, quickly pulling on a pair of cotton trousers. He slid the automatic into the waistband in the small of his back and donned a dark-blue polo shirt.

"Can't you come back to bed for just a little while?" Michelle pulled the sheet tight across her plump breasts and allowed a slim, tanned leg to part the covers.

"Ah, *chérie,* that would be nice, but I have to see to our work." She started to complain, but thought better of it. "You stay here. I'll be back in a few minutes."

Jamil stepped out of the coach into the crisp morning air. He looked around, carefully searching the trees and clumps of ferns, but saw nothing. He then took a few steps away from the motor home and called to the woods in a conversational voice.

"Salah."

A form materialized from a thicket not twenty meters from where he was standing and walked over to join him. "Good morning, Sayeh. I hope you rested well."

"Knowing you were keeping watch allowed me the luxury of a very sound sleep." He glanced at his watch—7:55.

"Have some food sent over to the coach for me and the woman. I wish to meet with you and Ahmed here at nine o'-clock. I will brief the others at the house when we have finished."

Jamil sent Michelle up to the house shortly before Ahmed and Salah arrived. He set a pot of black coffee on the table and three cup-and-saucer sets, refusing to yield to the American convention of drinking from mugs. The settee in the kitchenette motor home was small but adequate. Ahmed and Salah sat in booths on opposite sides of the table, while Jamil sat on a tall stool at the end of the table, towering over both of them. Spoons and saucers were pushed aside as Jamil spread a chart of Puget Sound across the table.

"Brothers," he began, "our people grow weary from our fight with the Jews, and the debacle of the Gulf War has further weakened them. The peace talks are a joke. They need something to rekindle their spirits. I have long sought a way to combine our limited resources with courage and daring to achieve a stunning victory over the Americans—to hurt them and to humiliate them before the world. Our goal is to hold America at ransom with a prize of great value. Then we will demand that

America and her Zionist allies release control of the occupied territories and clear our land of the Jewish settlers. Ahmed knows of this, but I will now brief both of you on the details.'' He paused to take a sip of coffee and leaned over the map. ''This is my plan.

''The operation has two phases. Phase one will be the seizure of a Washington State ferryboat. We will board the ferry in Seattle with the motor home early tomorrow morning when the boat makes its final scheduled crossing. There will not be many passengers aboard—enough for hostages, but not so many that we will have a control problem. The last ferry out of Seattle leaves at 2:40 in the morning. When the ferry clears the dock in Seattle and sails into Puget Sound, we bring our weapons from the motor home and strike. It should be no more difficult than capturing a bus, and there are none of the security precautions one would find at an airport.''

''I see no problem in doing this,'' said Salah, ''but you did not bring this many people so far, nor assemble such a store of weapons, just to capture a ferryboat. Would it have not been more convenient and safer to capture one of the cross-Channel ferries from a French or English port, or the Hovercraft out of Boulogne or Calais?'' The question was not a challenge—he wanted to better understand the mission.

''You are quite right. We need this particular ferry because of its size and power, and we need to be on Puget Sound with access to the ocean for phase two of the operation. After we gain control of the ferry, we will proceed north from Seattle toward the Strait of Juan de Fuca. But we are not going into the Strait, at least not yet.'' He again directed their attention to the chart. ''We take the ferry north on Puget Sound into Admiralty Inlet. From there we turn south around Foulweather Bluff into the Hood Canal.''

''The Hood Canal?'' said Salah, puzzling over the map. Jamil paused to look at both men before returning to the chart.

''We go south on the Hood Canal to here, the submarine base at Bangor. Phase two, my brothers, is the capture of a U.S. Trident missile submarine.''

Salah looked sharply at Jamil and leaned over to study the

chart more closely, running his finger along their proposed route. Ahmed stared dully at the chart, periodically looking to Salah for an objection to the plan, but the little man was totally absorbed. After a moment, Ahmed nervously cleared his throat.

"The Hood Canal bridge. It is a floating bridge. How will we get past it?" he offered.

"That is being taken care of. The movable section will be opened for our entry into the Canal, and kept open for our return."

"This submarine," said Salah in a steady voice. His eyes danced, but otherwise his face was impassive. "How will we drive it? We are freedom fighters, not sailors."

"That is why we need the ferry—this particular ferry. We will take this Trident submarine—with its nuclear reactor, missiles, and atomic warheads—and lash it to the side of our ferry. Then we will tow it back up the Hood Canal and into the Strait of Juan de Fuca."

Jamil carefully searched the faces of his two comrades. Ahmed, who'd had two days to digest the plan, was still overwhelmed with the idea of actually stealing a nuclear-missile submarine. He tried to keep the doubt from his face, fearing he would be thought disloyal or a coward. Jamil saw this at once and dismissed it. He did not for a minute question Ahmed's loyalty or bravery, knowing that his friend, for all his training and experience, was not a good fighter. He was an adequate soldier, but he lacked the cold and ruthless instinct of a terrorist. Ahmed's value was as a logistician and a planner. His contribution in buying weapons, hiring personnel, and staging equipment was essential to the success of the operation, as was his considerable talent with electronics and communications equipment. When the time came, he knew Ahmed would fight well enough—he would have no choice.

Jamil wanted Salah's reaction. He had been at Munich and had helped with the hijacking of TWA flight 847, among others, and his tactical judgment was to be respected. The smaller man studied the chart and twice referred to the scale. Then he asked a series of pointed questions, mostly about security. He again studied the chart for several minutes and looked up.

"If it is as you say, and the man who drives the ferry is a skilled seaman, then with God's help, we will do it." Jamil met his eyes and saw what he was looking for. Salah did not fear death, but he was not a man to throw his life away uselessly. He believed the plan would work.

"Very well. Now let us discuss the schedule and the individual assignments." For the next hour and a half, they went over the details of the operation. The taking of the ferry was a simple matter, but the capture of the submarine would require the skill and precision of a military operation. They would have to rely on surprise and audacity to compensate for their collective lack of military training. Both Ahmed and Salah were impressed with the meticulous planning and ingenuity of the plan.

"I will brief the rest of the team in fifteen minutes. The briefing will cover only phase one. There is no need for them to know anything more until we have taken the ferry. They will be told that our mission is to capture the ferry and make a run for the open sea, which ultimately we will do."

Jamil rolled up the map and led the others outside the coach. "Salah, see that no one leaves the area until we depart on the mission, and that no one uses the telephone. And tell Carlos I want to see him." Salah nodded his head and strode back toward the house.

"Do you wish me to remain?" Ahmed asked.

"That will not be necessary. I will join you and the others at the house when we are finished."

A short while later, a tall Latino dressed in blue jeans, tennis shoes, and a faded open-collared shirt came walking up the path. He had a handsome face and thick, dark hair. The only suggestion of militancy was a red handkerchief tied around his head in Che Guevara fashion. Carlos was a native of Nicaragua, and had left there shortly after the Sandinistas surrendered power. He was a good revolutionary, but he was undisciplined and had been made unwelcome in the new democracy. He had worked on occasion for the DGI, the Cuban intelligence service. Mostly he was a terrorist for hire, but a good one. Jamil stepped down from the coach as he approached.

"Buenos días, jefe. I am Carlos, and I am at your service." He extended his hand, which Jamil took.

"Carlos, I will come to the point—my associate tells me that you have been taking drugs. Is that true?"

"Perhaps I have," he replied, raising his hands in a gesture of surrender, "but now that we go to work, *no más."*

"Did Ahmed not tell you that drugs would not be tolerated?"

"Maybe he did. But it was just a small amount of powder for the itch in my nose." He smiled agreeably. *"Jefe*—this is America!"

"So it is, my friend," replied Jamil, "but are we like the *yanquis* who have to take drugs for life to have meaning?" Carlos did not have time to answer. Jamil reached behind him to the small of his back and pulled the Sig Sauer from his waistband. The weapon fired as it came level. A 210-grain brassjacketed, hollow-point bullet punched a hole through the pack of Camel cigarettes in Carlos's shirt pocket and continued on into his chest cavity, streaming bits of tobacco and fabric in its wake. The bullet then mushroomed to the size of a dime just before it shredded the left ventricle of his heart and came to a stop by wrapping itself around his fourth rib, an inch from his spine. He staggered backward a step as if punched in the chest by some giant fist.

"¿Por qué?" he managed to gasp as he went to his knees.

"Because I cannot trust someone who uses drugs and does not follow my orders." He then sent a round through Carlos's left nostril that exploded the back of his head like a ripe melon dropped on a supermarket floor. Jamil tripped the release that snapped the hammer forward to the safe position. He replaced the automatic and walked quietly up the road toward the house.

Sunday, June 21, 2:15 A.M.—Seattle, Washington

Jamil brought the rental car to a stop, joining the line of autos waiting to get on the ferry. The car-holding area at Seattle's Colman Dock could accommodate some four hundred cars, and served both Bremerton and Bainbridge Island ferry runs. This morning there were only a dozen vehicles waiting— mostly cars, a few pickup trucks, and one motor home. It was the last scheduled crossing before the 5:35 A.M. Seattle–Bainbridge run. This last crossing was unique in that the ferry would leave Seattle and stop at the Winslow Dock on Bainbridge before continuing on to Bremerton, located on the rugged Olympic Peninsula, which forms the west side of Puget Sound. As Jamil set the brake and turned off the engine, he saw the large, brightly lit ferry slowly making its way to the dock. It looked like some luminescent monster, with the running lights forming red and green eyes and the gaping mouth of the car deck packed with several dozen fluorescent-washed car-teeth. The 1:50 A.M. crossing from Bainbridge Island was right on schedule.

Jamil was dressed in blue jeans and a black turtleneck. He was armed only with his .45 and two flash-bangs—small grenades whose bright burst and noise would temporarily stun those in a small room. He didn't anticipate needing them unless they met resistance. He carried one in each pocket of a royal-blue windbreaker that had ''Seattle Seahawks'' embroidered on the front. An extra magazine was strapped to each wrist under the knit cuffs of the jacket. He could drop an empty magazine and have a reload in place in under two seconds.

Sitting next to him was Hassan, a fierce Palestinian in his early thirties. Like so many others, he was a veteran of nearly two decades of bombings, killings, and living in hovels with dirt-packed floors. The years had blunted his idealism but not his talent. He still fought for the cause, but now he liked to be paid for it. He was dressed much like Jamil and also armed with a pistol. Just ahead of them and one lane over was the motor home with Ahmed, Michelle, and another veteran Palestinian fighter named Ali.

Salah, Fenton, and an Egyptian called Yehya were waiting in the terminal and would board with the foot passengers. This allowed Salah to see if any policemen boarded from the terminal. An odd collection of travelers waited for this early-morning ferry. There were well-dressed theatergoers, a small klatch of very punk teenagers, two sailors who were more than a little drunk, and several workers—complete with boots, suspenders, and metal lunch pails—headed for the Puget Sound Naval Shipyard in Bremerton. All told, there were some thirty passengers who waited patiently for their ship to come in. A careful observer would note that three of those who waited were somewhat apprehensive and seemed to look around more than the other foot passengers, but there were no careful observers on the last run from Seattle.

Jamil waited in silence with Hassan. Nothing more needed to be said, and neither required conversation to relieve tension or pass the time.

The briefing at the safe house in Enumclaw, however, had been tense. All had heard the shots and noted that Carlos was absent from the meeting.

"Carlos will not be joining us for this mission," he had told them. "What we are about to do is far too important to be compromised by one among us who doesn't do exactly as he is told. And there will be risk enough for all of us without having to trust our lives to someone who takes drugs."

He had not killed Carlos without some thought. If it came to a fight, Carlos would be missed, for he was known to be a good man with an automatic weapon, and brave. But the drug thing had bothered him, and the value of Carlos's death as an example to the others made him more valuable dead than alive. Jamil had killed him with the same detachment with which a farmer shoots a fox he has cornered in his chicken house—it is not a personal thing between farmer and fox, but foxes are counterproductive in raising chickens.

Jamil had tacked a schematic of the ferry to the living-room wall and had carefully detailed each assignment—where each member of the team would go, what he was to do, and when. Each was assigned a weapon and a Motorola MX-3000 hand-held two-way radio. Except for pistols, the weapons and the radios were stored in the motor home and would be retrieved when they were on the ferry. Jamil told them that they would be taking the ferry out of Puget Sound and into the Pacific Ocean. From there they would be able to negotiate a list of prepared demands—the release of a number of Palestinian and Islamic fundamentalist leaders held by Israel and several moderate Arab states, and safe passage for all of them to Damascus, Tunis, or some other sanctuary. The plan called for the mission to be aborted if there was any sign of trouble or increased security prior to sailing. Once all were safely aboard and the ferry cast off, the operation was a "go."

The M/V *Spokane,* as well as the city in eastern Washington, was named after the Spokane Indian tribe. She and her sister ship, the M/V *Walla Walla,* were the largest "motor vessels" in the Washington State ferry fleet, and the two boats assigned to the Bainbridge Island–Seattle run. The *Spokane* was 440 feet in length with an 87-foot beam, and could carry 206 cars and close to 2,000 passengers. She drew eighteen feet and could move across the water at nearly twenty-three miles per hour. Her diesel engines powered huge electric motors that turned propellers at either end. It was this diesel-electric drive that allowed for an infinite number of power settings, and the big boat was quite nimble in the hands of an experienced pilot. The car deck of the ferry had two levels along either side with a large single bay in the center to accommodate large trucks, buses, and motor homes. The passenger deck was located immediately above the car deck and ran the entire length of the ferry. It was littered with booths, tables, and chairs and punctuated by newspaper racks, vending machines, and a few video games. The center island of the passenger deck held the rest rooms as well as an office and lounge area for the crew. The galley, which consisted of two short cafeteria lines with restaurant-style booth and table seating for 120 people, was not open on the late-night runs. The next deck up was an open passenger or promenade deck that featured covered seating at either end just behind each pilothouse. This deck was crowded with tourists and commuters alike during the warm summer days. Access to the two pilothouses was from this deck up a half flight of stairs.

The *Spokane* made the landing and discharged her load of cars and a few overnight truckers. Those waiting in the terminal clustered at one end by the loading ramp and watched an equally diverse group straggle off the ferry and into Seattle. Jamil started the car and followed the pickup truck in front of him as a ferry crew member directed them aboard. Since there were so few vehicles, they were all loaded into the center section of the car deck in four rows near the bow. Jamil noted this with some satisfaction, since all of those who drove aboard, as well as the foot passengers, would have to be accounted for. About half of those in the vehicles went up to the passenger deck for the crossing, while most who remained reclined their seats to try for some sleep during the trip. Jamil and Hassan waited in silence as a few more cars were loaded behind them. A short time later, Salah and the other two walk-ons appeared around the corner of the motor home and entered through the rear door.

''Hassan, my friend, it is time to go to work.'' Hassan merely nodded and zipped up his jacket. He got out of the car and followed Jamil to the motor home.

Peck paused midway on the open promenade deck to look at the stars. It was a clear night, and the heavens were only partially attenuated by the lights from Seattle. A bright quarter-moon was already halfway down to the western horizon. Since the ferries ran prescribed routes, there was no need for celestial navigation, only piloting and radar navigation. Nonetheless, Peck had an understanding of and a near-religious respect for navigating by the stars. The act of measuring the angle formed by the position of a star, millions of miles away, and the earth's horizon to plot your position on the globe was almost mystical. It was like finding your exact position on a rotating marble by sighting an object the size of a baseball some two hundred miles away. He quickly found the pointer stars on the cup of the Big Dipper and followed them to the North Star. What a discovery that must have been when the early navigators found that there was a single star that remained fixed in the heavens. Working the night runs, especially in the summer, had its compensation. There were fewer cars and passengers to contend with, and a chance for some quiet time between crossings. He found Orion, Leo, and Altair before moving forward to the outbound pilothouse. Brad Johnson would supervise the loading and transfer control from the other end. A young couple walking hand in hand passed him as he mounted the steps to the pilothouse.

The doors were latched open on either side of the pilothouse to let the breeze through. Only a light chain with a spring clasp and an "Authorized Personnel Only" sign guarded the stairs. Once inside, Peck automatically checked the engine-rpm gauges and rudder-angle indicators. Once satisfied that the boat was well positioned in the dock and ready for the next crossing, he stepped out to the open wing of the pilothouse to enjoy the night until sailing time. After making the Bainbridge Island–Bremerton leg of the run, they would bring the *Spokane* back to Winslow Dock on Bainbridge. From there, it was a half-hour drive home. With any luck he'd be in bed shortly after sunup, and on weekends, Sarah slept in with him. Janey was there looking out over the bow with her forearms resting on top of the bridge-wing combing. She'd been in a pensive mood since they'd come on duty late yesterday afternoon.

"Big crowd tonight?" Peck ventured.

"Not really. Same collection of fools we normally haul on a late-night weekend run. The state's gotta lose a lot of money on these near-empty crossings. You'd think they would cut back on some of them."

"You'd think so. Hey, Janey, what's wrong? You've been moping around here since we came on shift."

"Yeah, I know—guess I'm just a little down in the dumps, that's all."

"Want to talk about it? We're shipmates, after all."

"It's my kid, Cap'n. He got into another fight. I've tried talking to him—I've even grounded him—but it's not working. Jason's thirteen and he's growing up awfully fast. I don't like the kids he's hanging around with, and his grades were pretty bad last year."

Peck pushed his cap back a bit and looked at her. He liked Janey. She had good judgment, and she was a capable mariner. He thought she'd probably be the first female master of a Jumbo Class ferry. Janey had been a single parent as long as he'd known her—going on five years now. Mates and masters alike had their share of night-shift and weekend duty. He knew her parents helped with the boy, but that only went so far.

"I think I may have some idea what you and Jason are going through."

"Really," replied Janey, looking at him sharply. "I thought your boys were doing fine."

"They are, and I've got Sarah to thank for that. No, I meant that I gave my mother a pretty rough time when I was Jason's age."

"Somehow that doesn't seem like you."

"Believe me, I'd have made Jason look like a choirboy. Tell you what, why don't you bring him aboard with you to work once a week. You can show him around the boat, even let him take the helm in open water." *He might have a little more respect for his mother,* thought Peck, *if he can see how well she handles the boat.* "If he gets a little feisty, we'll send him down to Gosnell in the engine room. He'll put him to scrubbing the bilges."

"That'd be great, but isn't it against the rules?"

"Yeah, but I don't see a problem. It'll only be once a week, and we'll both keep an eye on him."

"Thanks, Cap'n. Maybe it'll do him some good, and God knows I'll try anything."

"Pilothouse two, this is one. You ready to go?"

Peck walked back inside and pressed the intercom lever.

"Anytime, Brad."

"Passenger ramp and car ramp are up, Cap'n. All lines are in and the life rail is in place. I'm passing control up to you."

"Roger that, Brad, I have control." Peck took the helm while the *Spokane* was held firmly seated in the slip by the forward propeller. A moment later, Johnson joined them in the number-two pilothouse.

"Did I tell you that was a mighty fine landing you made coming in?"

"Yessir, you did."

"You seem to do better at night. Maybe we ought to have you close your eyes in the daytime."

"Y'know, I really think I might just be starting to get the hang of it."

"So do I. Why don't you take us out of here." Peck stepped away from the control console and over to the radarscope on the starboard side of the pilothouse. The visibility was good, and he could see there was nothing moving on the water, but he still checked the radar. He studied the scope for several rotations of the lime-green sweep line.

"Okay, Brad, whenever you're ready."

The *Spokane* issued a short, polite honk to the empty harbor as Johnson eased her away from the dock and out into Elliott Bay. Janey pulled a tall stool up to the forward windows on the port side of the pilothouse. Standard procedure for nighttime steaming called for one person to be on the helm, one on the radar, and the third to act as a lookout. It was different on other ferries, but Peck discouraged idle or unnecessary conversation during nighttime crossings. He glanced at the radarscope periodically, and his eyes were constantly on the move, watching the water around him. The work was repetitious and very routine, but he still felt a certain amount of pride in knowing that *his* craft was on time, on course, and that his bridge crew was alert. There was no wind on the water that night, and the *Spokane* ran at full speed across a flat, calm Puget Sound like a skater coasting on smooth ice.

Alki Point lighthouse was abeam to port when Jamil and Hassan reached the promenade deck. The stiff breeze created by the speed of the *Spokane* had driven everyone else below. They waited a few moments for their eyes to become adjusted to the darkness before moving forward to the port side of the forward pilothouse. Hassan slipped the catch on the chain across the stairs, and Jamil led them up to the pilothouse wing. He carried the .45, now fitted with a Finnish-made Viame silencer, in his right hand, with the cylindrical barrel pressed vertically along his right temple. Hassan followed close behind, crouching warily behind his weapon. The folding stock of his Uzi was fully extended and tucked into his right shoulder as he held the weapon across his body. Jamil stepped into the pilothouse and quickly to the rear, allowing Hassan to fill the door and giving him a clear field of fire across the front of the pilothouse. Janey saw them first.

"Hey, sir. I'm sorry, but this area is off-limits." She started to turn around to confront Jamil, then saw Hassan. There was enough light for her to see he had a gun. "Captain—"

"What's going on here?" Peck stepped away from the radarscope to the middle of the pilothouse just behind Brad Johnson at the control station. He was answered by the metallic clatter of Hassan's Uzi as the bolt of the submachine gun was pulled back. It told Peck exactly what was going on.

"Captain, we are well armed and prepared to kill. Please turn on a light."

Peck believed him but did not move. Jamil's thumb brought the hammer of the double-action .45 back with a distinctive *ka-click*.

"Captain, the light."

Peck reached over and pressed the slide switch on the lamp that hovered over the chart table. The red night-light bathed a chart of Puget Sound in crimson and created a martian-scape of the rest of the pilothouse. The Sig Sauer and the long barrel of the silencer were leveled at Peck. Hassan was still a shadow in the doorway, but the menacing snout of the Uzi was clearly visible. Janey had stepped away from Hassan and was now next to Johnson, who stood rigidly at the helm. Peck broke the silence.

"Who are you and what are you doing on my—"

"Silence! I will speak and you will listen. I am now in command of this vessel. You will do exactly as you are told and nothing else. We will not hesitate to kill anyone who does not do exactly as they are told. Is that clear?'' Jamil raised the barrel of the .45 and rested it on Johnson's shoulder, but his eyes never left Peck. *He's a big one,* thought Jamil, *and there is more anger than fear in him. He looks capable, and that is good, but he must be brought to heel.* Jamil knew that intimidation, fear, and respect were all factors in controlling hostages, especially when you needed their cooperation.

''Is that clear, Captain?''

Peck glanced quickly to the Uzi in the doorway and back to Jamil. He nodded without speaking.

''Good. Now you,'' he said, prodding Johnson with the silencer barrel, ''turn this boat north and take us toward Admiralty Inlet.''

Johnson was frozen at the controls.

''Now!'' prompted Jamil with a nudge of the pistol.

''Captain . . . ?''

Jamil's hand moved like a snake as he brought it across the side of Johnson's face, smashing his cheekbone. The second mate dropped to the pilothouse deck like a wet rag without making a sound. The visored combination cap tumbled from his head and rolled across the deck. Peck moved for him as Jamil shifted the weapon in a twenty-degree arc and brought it to rest behind Janey's ear. Their eyes locked, and Jamil knew he had won. The battle would have to be fought again, for he doubted this captain would give up easily, but for the moment, he would do as he was told.

After a moment, Peck said, ''Janey, take the helm and come right to three five zero. Do exactly as he says.''

''Thank you, Captain. Now stand over by the far wall, and Hassan will look after your crewman.'' Jamil was a professional. He had learned that it was in the interest of the mission to reward compliance with reasonable treatment. Peck reluctantly backed away to the starboard side of the pilothouse as Jamil pulled out his Motorola and keyed the transceiver.

''This is Jamil. Proceed with your assigned tasks.'' After he received acknowledgments, he directed Hassan to attend to

Johnson, who was starting to moan as he regained consciousness.

Salah and Yehya, a quiet, moody man in his late twenties, were lounging against the starboard rail of the auto deck when the call came from Jamil. Yehya was from Cairo, and had been a student in America for several years. His English was quite good, and he had been the last of those recruited to the group. There were no cars near them, and they were only a few steps from the stairs that went down to the engineering spaces. Salah took the Uzi from under his coat and snapped a long magazine into the handgrip.

''Are you ready?''

''Of course,'' he replied. Salah noticed he was sweating, and that his hand shook when he placed the strap of the Uzi over his head and cocked the submachine gun.

''Yehya, put your weapon on safe.'' He fumbled with the Uzi and moved the selector to the safe position. ''Now look at me!'' he commanded. He looked up but couldn't meet Salah's steady, determined gaze. ''This will not be difficult. They do not have weapons and they are not expecting us. We have nothing to fear from them unless we become careless. But also understand that you will answer to me if you do not do exactly as you were instructed during the briefing. Do you understand?''

''Yes, Salah, I understand. I—I apologize—I'm just a little . . .''

''Enough! It is better to be a little too ready than not ready enough, eh?'' Salah smiled and squeezed Yehya's arm, putting warmth in his voice that he did not feel. ''Now let us see if they are not all asleep down in the basement of this scow.'' *If I didn't need this quivering Egyptian dog, I would kill him right here. Experienced terrorist! Where did Ahmed find this child! Conducting a mission in the enemy's own country is a lot different than machine-gunning synagogues or ambushing Israeli schoolchildren. Well, he will do his job or he will die by my hand!*

Salah motioned him to follow, and they disappeared through

a metal door and down a lighted stairway to the bowels of the *Spokane*.

Fenton, Michelle, and the Palestinian called Ali sat in one of the forward booths on the starboard side of the ferry. Ali was a lean man with dark, leathery skin. He had cunning eyes, but a large gap between his front teeth gave him a perpetual, though misleading, moronic expression. They had two guitar cases with them, resting on the floor between the two facing bench seats. Ahmed soon joined them after making a slow circuit around the passenger deck.

"Everything looks in order. There does not seem to be any policemen aboard. The two sailors we saw in the terminal are sleeping off their drink. There is a group of young people at the other end who are boisterous, but they are harmless. Most of the others are sleeping or reading. Now remember, keep them moving toward the seating area at the other end, and no killing unless it is unavoidable. Any questions?"

"Let's do it," said Fenton.

"We will move when it is time, and not before."

"Yeah, well, this waitin' gives me the creeps."

"Relax, my friend," said Michelle. "You'll get your kicks soon enough." She presented a calm exterior, but Ahmed noted that her eyes flashed and that her complexion was radiant. Fenton started to light up, but Ahmed stopped him, pointing to the No Smoking signs.

"When this vessel is ours, you can smoke wherever you like."

"What the fuck's the difference, we're gonna—" Jamil's voice crackled over the radio and focused their attention to the transceiver on Ahmed's belt. He brought the set to his lips and acknowledged.

"All right," he said softly, "we move now!"

Fenton and Ali opened the guitar cases and began passing out weapons. Ahmed and Ali took Uzis, while Michelle and Fenton grabbed AK-47s. Jamil had insisted on the AKs. Most civilians are unfamiliar with firearms and often think the small Uzis are toys. An AK-47, with its polished wood stock, and foregrip, and black curved banana clip, *looks* like a dangerous weapon.

"Ready?" All nodded. "Let us begin."

Simultaneously they all donned knitted ski masks—the kind that have round holes for the mouth and eyes. This was not so much to protect their identity, but for the effect. One might foolishly question or even try to reason with a man with a gun, but Hollywood and the press have conditioned Americans to fear the Halloween-like effect created by an armed group wearing ski masks—it is the face of terrorism. Ali and Fenton walked across the ferry to the port side, while Ahmed and Michelle stood and turned to face aft, holding their weapons up so they were clearly visible. Horror began to register on those seated nearest them, but no one said a word. Then it started.

"Stand up! Hands behind your head. Now move!"

"Move to the rear—quickly!"

"You there, on your feet! Move!"

"Move to the rear—NOW!"

"Hands up! Move or be killed!"

The game was shock and terror. Any sign of resistance— bewilderment really—was met with shoves and kicks. As the passengers in the forward cabin began to form into groups moving aft, Ali and Michelle raced ahead of them. They pushed through the men's and women's toilets, each driving a frightened passenger before them. Michelle ducked into the second mate's office that was amidships on the passenger deck. A uniformed crew member seated at a desk came to his feet.

"What the hell is this? You can't just . . ." She slammed the butt of the Kalashnikov across his mouth, splitting his lips and carrying away several teeth.

"Walk out of here or die!" She gestured to another crew member, a terrified woman in her mid-thirties. "You—bitch! Help him out with the others, or I'll kill you both!"

There were now two groups, separated by the partition created by the rest rooms, crew spaces, and the galley area, moving toward the stern on each side of the passenger deck. Those in the aft seating area of the ferry were aware of a commotion but didn't yet know what was going on. There was no organized resistance, but the passengers were starting to bunch and to talk.

"What do they want?"

"I don't have any money."

"This ain't right!"

Ahmed knew that they must maintain the initiative and the shock value of their assault. He pointed the Uzi toward one of the exterior windows and stitched it with a short burst. He was answered by a similar burst from Ali on the other side. For most of the passengers, it was the first time they had experienced real automatic-weapon fire. It was like nothing they had heard on TV, but it was unmistakable. Talk was replaced by silence punctuated with the soft weeping of an elderly woman and an occasional sob from someone within the group. They were herded into the aft cabin area, prodded by the pushing and yelling of their four masked assailants. Now they bunched in one group just aft of the galley seating area. A man came up the stairs from the car deck and walked into the aft cabin toward the group. He quickly saw what was happening and turned to run.

"You, stop!"

He took one step and froze, but it was too late. Fenton sent a burst from his AK into the man's back. The bark of the high-velocity 7.62 bullets from the AK-47 was much louder and sharper than the 9mm rounds of the Uzis. The man pitched forward and began to squirm quietly on the deck. A collective wail went up from the crowd.

"Greased that motherfucker!" shouted Fenton as he waved the AK at the huddled passengers. "Okay, who's next?!"

"*On the floor!*" screamed Ahmed, moving swiftly to the other side of the ferry to position himself between the passengers and Fenton. Ali moved with him. "Everyone! *On the floor! Quickly!*"

The terrified group melted to the *Spokane*'s linoleum deck. Those few who were slow about it were threatened or kicked. Ahmed moved quickly, knowing that he must seize the initiative and keep the crowd under control.

"Listen to me! Do not move and you will not be hurt—you have my word!" Then he turned to Ali and motioned to the wounded man. ''Get him out of here—now! And Fenton, you help him.''

Ali grabbed the wounded man by the collar and began dragging him to the two swinging metal doors at the stern of the ferry. Fenton reluctantly slung his weapon and moved to assist him. A dark-red slick on the deck followed them out.

Ahmed circled the prone group while Michelle covered the exits. *That was a close one!* he thought. As long as hostages believe that obedience will enhance their chance for survival, they are compliant and manageable. If they become convinced that death is imminent, they will panic and stampede. Then the terrorist loses control and risks a massacre. *Damn Fenton! Better to have let the man go. Even if he had run, where could he go?* The dark, cold waters of Puget Sound made the *Spokane* a moving Alcatraz. For all his years in the Jihad, Ahmed had never killed—at least not up close, in cold blood. He found that he had to grip the Uzi tightly to keep from shaking. He took a deep breath and stepped atop one of the seats.

''Listen to me! Everyone! This vessel is now in the control of the Islamic Brothers of Freedom.'' This was the name Jamil had adopted for tactical expediency. Experience had taught them that hostages usually behaved better if they felt their captors to be politically motivated or in the service of a cause. It added legitimacy to their actions, and those held captive would be more cooperative, waiting for a negotiated settlement.

''If you do exactly as you are told, you will not be harmed. If you do not, or are slow to obey, you will be punished. Soon you will be made comfortable. For now, you are to lie still, and there is to be no talking.'' Ahmed climbed down and began to circle them, looking for signs of resistance. There was sporadic, muffled weeping that was stifled when he approached. For the moment, he had control.

Fenton helped Ali hoist the injured man to the rail and over the side. The splash of his fall was all but lost in the wake of the speeding ferry. When they returned, Ahmed sent them to the car deck to bring up those who remained in their vehicles. They returned in ten minutes with twelve more passengers, one of them an elderly man with an eye nearly swollen shut and bleeding from one ear. They joined the others on the floor of the main cabin. Ali nodded to Ahmed, who took out his Motorola.

"Jamil, this is Ahmed. The passenger deck is secure."

"And the car deck?"

"It has been cleared, and all passengers are with us."

"Excellent. Salah, are you there?"

Five levels below the pilothouse, Salah held the transceiver in one hand and his Uzi in the other. Lined up on their knees by the main control panel were Andy Gosnell, Steve Burns, George Zanner, and Gonzales. Yehya, who was now confident and fearless, viciously kicked Gosnell, who stared up at him in malevolent defiance.

"I am here, Sayeh. The engines and those who tend them are in our control."

"Very good. Phase one is complete. Ahmed, send Ali up to the pilothouse to stand guard. I will be around to brief each member of the group individually on phase two. Maintain control, and keep me advised of any changes. *Allahu Akhbar!*"

"*Allahu Akhbar!*" both acknowledged.

Jamil stepped to the starboard side of the pilothouse, where he could better watch Peck at the controls. Janey was now tending Johnson, who sat on the floor propped up against the bulkhead at the rear of the pilothouse.

"Captain, we are now in complete control of your vessel. Your life and the lives of everyone on board will depend on your ability to maneuver this ferry and do exactly as I command. You are going to assist us with the next phase of our plan. If you do not, you will watch many of those around you die before I kill you. I do not particularly like to play the role of a sadist, but I can easily do so if it serves my purpose. Now, I want you to listen very carefully to my instructions."

PART TWO

THE *MICHIGAN*

Sunday, June 21, 1992, 2:48 A.M.—U.S. Coast Guard Station, Pier 36, Seattle, Washington

"You sure you're okay?"

"I'm fine, thanks, Chief."

"You want some relief?"

"Nope. As long as I'm awake, I might as well be on the scope."

"Peschel, you should try an' get some sleep before you come on duty—you look like shit."

"Can't sit home on a Saturday night, Chief."

"You sure can, or at least you ought to if you got the midwatch." Chief Radioman John Dearing had been in the Coast Guard for twenty-two years. He had a wife and three kids. It had been a long time since he'd been out on the town before pulling an eight-hour midwatch. *Youth,* he mused—*it's wasted on 'em.* He lit a cigarette and turned to go back into the watch supervisor's office. "You start nodding off, you give me a call."

"Gotcha, Chief."

Radarman Third Class Carol Peschel tried to sound chipper, but she didn't feel that way. She wasn't halfway through her watch, and all she wanted to do was to crawl back to the apartment and crash. She'd been on the midwatch—12:00 midnight to 8:00 A.M.—for the last three weeks. She didn't make a practice of going out before she came on watch. But it was a Saturday night, and she had met this cute guy a few weeks ago, and he had tickets to a rock concert at the Seattle Center. It had been a great evening, but now it was payback time. She wearily turned her attention to the large glass face of the CLU-109-2 radarscope, deftly adjusting the gain and focus controls.

RD3 Peschel, like the other two scope operators on her watch team, wore summer whites. She looked good in uniform—smart but feminine. Her trim figure made the white cotton trousers and open-collar short-sleeve shirt look as if they had been tailored for her. Working nights with the days off had allowed her to acquire a healthy-looking tan. She was short, with a broad, easy smile, and thick brown hair had a slight natural curl that suggested a measure of unruliness. The male members of her watch section rated her an eight on a scale of ten and better than average on the scope. The black chevron and "crow" on her left sleeve were new, since she had only recently been advanced to third-class petty officer. Peschel had been in the Coast Guard a little over a year, having come to Seattle right after boot camp and radar operators' school. Her parents had wanted her to go to college, and her boyfriend wanted to get married. She didn't want to do either, so she and her best girlfriend had enlisted for a three-year hitch in the Coast Guard. So far the experience had been new and exciting—except for the midwatches.

The Vessel Traffic Service spaces occupied most of the fourth floor of the Seattle Coast Guard Station at Pier 36. It was the waterborne equivalent of an air-traffic control net. Ships entering the Strait of Juan de Fuca and transiting on down to Puget Sound checked in with the VTS at the beginning and end of their transit. They were also tracked on the way out. The traffic lanes were labeled by shaded strips on nautical charts. Inbound and outbound vessels sailed along these designated routes, which were well marked by midchannel buoys. A series of radar antennas along the shoreline allowed the VTS to continuously monitor vessels transiting these waters. Ships from the Pacific bound for Victoria and Vancouver, British Columbia, as well as tankers bound for the U.S. refinery at Anacortes, traveled the length of the Strait of Juan de Fuca. Those vessels continuing on to Seattle and Tacoma had to exit the Strait through Admiralty Inlet to get down into Puget Sound. Small craft could roam these waters at will, but vessels of three hundred gross tons or larger had to register their movements with the VTS.

Peschel scanned the status board, noting that no traffic was expected until late that morning when a Japanese merchantman was scheduled to enter Admiralty Inlet, and there was nothing outbound. She glanced at her wristwatch—2:54 A.M. *Three hours down and five to go! This is going to be a long one, and I gotta stay awake.* She folded her leg underneath her buttocks in an attempt to make the chair more comfortable and began checking the sectors of her assigned area—Puget Sound and the southern half of Admiralty Inlet.

The northernmost antenna of her assigned sectors was Point-No-Point, which provided most of the coverage for Admiralty Inlet. Peschel brought that signal up and tuned the scope as it painted the Inlet from the southern end of Whidbey Island to the northern tip of Marrowstone Island. After about ten sweeps she shifted to the West Point antenna, and then to the antenna at Pier 36, which was located on the roof of their building and provided coverage of Elliott Bay. At each stop, she retuned the scope, painting an occasional fishing boat but nothing else. The VTS radar system was exceptional. Under the right conditions, a skilled operator could pick up the towing cable between a tug and barge, and Peschel was a good one. The Day-Glo shadows and irregular lines painted by the rotating cursor were familiar pieces of a puzzle called Puget Sound. She methodically inspected each sector like a lifeguard scanning a crowded swimming pool, quickly seeing everything, but really only looking for something out of place. She had made the circuit and shifted back to the West Point station, which had coverage of northern Puget Sound and the entrance to Elliott Bay. At once, she knew something was out of place, but it took several sweeps of the cursor before she realized what it was.

"Well, hello there," she said aloud.

The ferry bound for Bainbridge Island was well north of its

normal track. She marked the position on the glass face of the scope with a grease pencil—a dot with a circle on it—and noted the time beside the mark—3:02. She quickly checked the sectors to the south and north, and shifted her scope back to the West Point antenna. The phosphorescent blip did not seem to be tracking on a westerly course as it should be. Peschel looked at her watch and entered another dot with a circle on the scope—3:05. Without taking her eyes from the face of the scope, her hands found the control knobs of the floating directional cursor and spun them to move the base of that cursor up to the first dot. She then slewed the directional cursor around until it passed through the second dot and glanced down at the digital directional readout. The ferry was on a course of 355—almost due north. *Now, that's really strange,* she thought. Her left hand reached for another control and moved the blip, or "bug," from the base of the cursor out from the first dot to the second, then checked the distance readout—1,750 yards. Peschel mentally estimated the speed, then checked it on the nautical slide rule. That ferry was making close to eighteen knots, and going the wrong way.

"Hey, Chief!"

"Gettin' a little drowsy there, huh, Peschel?"

"No, I'm not sleepy—come here and take a look at this."

Dearing strolled out of his office and leaned over the scope, resting one hand on the console and another on the back of her chair. His breath smelled like train smoke. "That ferry should be halfway to Eagle Harbor, but after it cleared Elliott Bay it turned north and is running up the Sound."

"So it is. I didn't see anything on the message board about a schedule change, but sometimes they forget. Or the message center didn't post it on our boards. Give 'em a call."

Peschel figured someone had just slipped up, but it was something to do to pass the time on a dull watch. She grabbed the handset from its cradle on the side of the radar console. It was always tuned to channel 14.

"Winslow Ferry, Winslow Ferry, this is the Coast Guard VTS calling. Come in, please, over."

Nothing.

"This is Coast Guard Vessel Traffic Control calling the Washington State ferry that just cleared the Colman Dock and is now steaming north on Elliott Bay. Please respond, over." Peschel was about to repeat the call when the overhead speaker crackled.

"This is the Washington State ferry *Spokane,* over."

"*Spokane,* this is Coast Guard VTS control. I hold you well north of your route and heading north. Are you taking the scenic route to Winslow, over?" Chief Dearing grimaced at Peschel's deviation from prescribed radio procedure, but said nothing. Again there was a silence.

"This is the *Spokane.* There's been a schedule change, and this boat is being moved up to Anacortes for the San Juan Island runs, over."

"Understood, *Spokane,* but we have had no notification of your transit through Admiralty Inlet to Anacortes."

"Roger, Coast Guard, but I just go where I'm told. You better check with scheduler at Colman Dock, over." Peschel looked up at Dearing, who frowned as he absentmindedly scratched his private parts.

"You buy that crap, Chief?"

"Not really, but those ferry captains think they own the Sound, even if they are just a bunch of bus drivers. Probably a screwup in their scheduling. They're shut down now, so I'll give 'em a call in the morning. Tell 'em to proceed." Peschel stared at him for a moment, then shrugged and picked up the microphone.

"*Spokane,* this is Coast Guard VTS Control. You are cleared to proceed on up to Anacortes via Admiralty Inlet—no inbound traffic. Next time, check in with the system per standard VTS user procedure. Please acknowledge, over."

"Roger, understood. Proceeding to Anacortes, and thanks, Coasty. *Spokane* out."

"Did you hear that, Chief? He called me a Coasty! Why, I've a good mind to call that SOB back and tell him—"

"At ease there, Carol. They wear uniforms, but they're still civilians."

The term "Coasty" was an uncomplimentary term, normally used by someone in the Navy. *The whole thing is weird,* thought Peschel. *That captain knows all vessels in transit, including ferries crossing the Sound, are supposed to check in by radio when they get under way. And then he has the nerve to call me a Coasty on the radio—it doesn't make sense.*

"Chief, you think something's wrong with that ferry?" Dearing was back in his office with his feet on the desk.

"Naw, just some ex–merchant seaman turned ferryboat captain thinking the rules don't apply to him."

Peschel turned back to the scope and noted the northbound progress of the ferry before she moved on to another sector. *I'll just keep an eye on that jerk and see if he screws up again.*

In the pilothouse of the *Spokane,* Jamil took the automatic away from Janey's head as Peck returned the hand mike to the clip on the side of the radio. Then Peck placed the two three-by-five cards on the console near the helm. The cards contained a neatly typed script that he had just read over the radio.

"Idiot! I told you not to deviate from the prepared response."

"We always call them 'Coasty'—it's just short for Coast Guard," Peck said, acting surprised.

"From now on, Captain, you will do exactly as I say with no deviation. Now continue on course, just as your Coast Guard has directed us to do."

"You seem to know a lot about our Vessel Traffic Service."

"Your Coast Guard publishes a very helpful user's manual. I'm sure you have one among your nautical charts. They mail them out free of charge." Jamil stepped behind Peck to look at the chart of Puget Sound spread out on the table. Peck exchanged a glance with Janey.

"Hey look, mister, this isn't going to work. There's a floating bridge across the Hood Canal, and the submarine base is very well guarded. You'll never get near a Trident submarine." Jamil turned to Peck and rested the barrel of the silencer on his shoulder. He was as tall as the American, but not nearly so heavy.

"My name is Jamil," he said amiably. "Perhaps you are

right, Captain, but for the sake of your life and the lives of those
aboard, you had better hope that we get that submarine.''

Sunday, 3:22 A.M.—Aboard the *Spokane*

Ross Peck could clearly see the lights from the town of King-
ston off his port beam. He gave the *Spokane* ten degrees left
rudder and brought her heading to 345 degrees. His mind was
reeling, both from the capture of his ferry and by the plan this
Jamil had set before him.

*There's no way I can help them to do this. Even if we get past
the Hood Canal bridge, you simply can't drive up and tow
away a Trident submarine. Security's just too tight. Somehow
we'll be stopped. Hell, the Marine guard force will probably
blow us out of the water!*

Peck had almost refused to follow Jamil's orders, even
though he was supposed to cooperate. State Ferry Service directives clearly stated that in case of armed piracy, he was to
cooperate fully until the authorities arrived to deal with the
situation. *Christ,* fumed Peck, *this isn't a robbery, and I'm not
a friggin' bank clerk!*

When the challenge came from the Coast Guard he had
thought the alarm would surely be sounded. But Jamil had
reached into his shirt pocket and handed Peck a prepared script.
Then he handed him the microphone and placed a cocked pistol
to Janey's head. Someone who planned his moves that carefully was not to be underestimated. There were too many lives
aboard—lives for which he was responsible—for him to do
something hasty or foolish. There was a lot of water and a
bridge between them and the submarine base at Bangor. Peck
knew that his only option was to play along and wait for an
opening. *Time is the enemy of those who take hostages, isn't it?
Maybe the gibe at that VTS controller will make them track us
a little closer.* He thought of the families of those aboard and
the agonies ahead of them. And Sarah—she would awake and

not find him there. Then she'd wake the boys and start calling—and she'd start to worry. A quiet rage began to push aside the fear that had stalked him since the two intruders had stepped into the pilothouse. *Patience,* he thought, *your time will come.*

"How's he doing, Janey?"

"Better. I think he may have a concussion."

"I'll be okay, Captain," said Johnson thickly. "What the hell's goin' on, anyway?"

"*Ekhrass*—not to talk!" The man called Hassan stood on the starboard side of the pilothouse next to the radar. An Uzi, with the handle extended, hung from the strap around his neck. *It will take him a fraction of a second to bring the weapon to a firing position. I might be able to get one hand on the barrel before he can react, and choke him out with the other.* But it was only wishful thinking. Jamil had handcuffed Peck's left wrist to one of the spokes of the *Spokane*'s wheel before he left the pilothouse, and Hassan was well beyond his reach. *Patience,* he told himself—*patience.*

"How many do we have?" Jamil was seated at a table in the restaurant while Ahmed stood nearby.

"Forty-seven. There were forty-eight, but Fenton shot one of them and we threw him from the boat. Fenton is a liability. Do we need him now that we've abandoned the safe house?"

"We'll need everyone until we have the submarine. When the hostages are secure, begin unloading the weapons and explosives. I want those machine guns mounted before we get to the bridge. I will brief the others individually right here. Send Fenton to me first."

The hostages had been forced to empty their pockets and purses, and to remove their shoes. They were scattered around the large cabin in groups of nine or ten. Each group was seated in chairs around one of the steel support stanchions that ran from the floor to the ceiling of the passenger deck. They were then forced to place nylon zip-tie straps around their necks. Michelle and Ali moved from group to group passing a three-sixteenth-inch stainless-steel cable through the zip-ties, connecting the members of the group in a daisy chain around the pole. The loops at the ends of the cable were padlocked together, and the zip-tie collars snugly cinched up around the hostages' necks. The nylon straps, like those used to bundle electrical wiring, were tough and almost impossible to cut, even with a knife. The terrorists carried side-cutter pliers so they could quickly snip the strap of a single hostage to allow them to use the toilet, then reattach them with a new zip-tie. One person with a pistol and a pair of pliers could safely guard the entire group.

"You wanted to see me, boss?"

"Yes, please sit down." Fenton slouched into the chair, holding the AK-47 upright with the butt resting on his thigh.

"Sorry I had to dust that one dude, but the fucker was goin' to make a run for it." He was smoking a cigarette and wearing leather gloves with the fingers cut out. There was an earring in his right ear, a bead dangling from it on a short tether. He also wore a dirty green beret with a faded solid red flash of the 7th Special Forces Group holding up one side over his left eyebrow.

"Tell me, Fenton, are you proficient with an M-60 machine gun?"

"A sixty? Are you shittin' me? I can make sweet music on one of those babies."

"Very well. In a short time you are going to have the opportunity to demonstrate that. Now listen carefully. We are going to make a slight detour before we take this vessel out to sea." Jamil outlined the details of the plan to capture the submarine, then explained Fenton's assignment. Fenton's eyes were wide with excitement and anticipation.

"Hot damn! We're gonna cop a fuckin' Navy submarine. Well, I'll be go t'hell. What's her name?"

"Her name?"

"The sub—what's it called?"

"It is the USS *Michigan.*"

"Boss, you can count on me. Anyone shows their face on that pier an' I'll grease their ass." Jamil regarded Fenton for a moment. His Army file indicated that he had qualified as an expert with a rifle and that he had been trained as a machine gunner. *He can fire the weapon well enough, but will he do as he is told?* Jamil rose from the table.

"Sergeant Fenton, come to attention!" Fenton scrambled to his feet and faced Jamil, holding the assault rifle along the side of his left leg in the order-arms position.

"Sergeant, this is now a military operation, and as your superior, I expect you to do your duty. The success of this operation and our lives depend on your skill and courage. You will carry out my orders without exception, is that clear?"

"Yes, SIR!" Fenton snapped a parade-ground salute. Jamil hesitated, appraising him with his best drill-instructor stare, then returned the salute.

"Now, return to your post and carry on."

"Sir!" Fenton did a clumsy about-face and drew the rifle across his chest on the way out of the cafeteria.

What scum, thought Jamil as he departed. He hated Americans, but he reserved a special dark corner in his heart for feelings about turncoats—traitors on either side. *He's a dead man as soon as I no longer need him. If he's brave and does his job well, he will die quickly. I wonder what his comrades in his Green Beret unit would do if they could get their hands on him? He has soiled their honor, and they would want retribution. It would be a soldier's justice—a bullet to the head or perhaps a bayonet in the groin.* The thought was a comfort to him.

Ali and Michelle each came in, and he briefed them. Then he summoned Ahmed for a final consultation before he inspected the hostages and left the passenger deck for the engineering spaces.

"Is everything in order down here?"

"As you can see, Sayeh," shouted Salah over the machinery noise, "they are being most cooperative." Gosnell and the first assistant engineer were now handcuffed together with one of their hands, while the other hand was cuffed to the long metal bar that ran the length of the propulsion control panel. They had access to the switches and dials on the panel, but they had to work in tandem for either man to reach one of the controls. Jamil approached them and motioned for Salah to bring over

Burns and Gonzales, who were seated on the floor with their hands strapped together behind their backs.

"You will listen to what I have to say, and consider your future actions accordingly. This vessel is now in the control of the Islamic Brothers of Freedom. We will be sailing for several more hours, making a stop to take on some additional cargo before heading out to sea. Your cooperation will be required to keep the engines and the auxiliary machinery operating. If you do not cooperate, then you place our mission in jeopardy. And if our mission is hindered in any way by one of you, then I swear to Allah that not one of you will again ever see the light of day. We will scuttle this vessel, and it will be your tomb." Jamil waited for his words to register. Then he took a block of C-4 explosive from the gym bag he carried and held it up for them to see. It looked like a small block of Velveeta cheese, only it was wrapped in a sheath of brown cellophane. What looked like a flat doorbell button was inset on one side, and a small radio transmitter was attached to the other. A maze of wires surrounded the block, connecting two penlight batteries to a pair of electric blasting caps. He rotated it for their inspection.

"This device will be taped securely to the main seawater cooling intake. Once activated, it can be command-detonated by remote control. If someone tries to remove it, the button will be released, and it will explode. If any of you are bomb experts, you may be able to cut the right wires to disarm it, but it was designed to explode if tampered with. You will remain handcuffed to your stations and attend to your duties. If you do not do exactly as you are told, or if you try to sabotage this vessel, I will not hesitate to set off this charge. You will be able to watch your grave fill with cold water as the sea rushes in. Do you understand?" Neither Gosnell nor his assistant, a former merchant mariner, was immune to the universal terror belowdecks sailors have of being trapped in a sinking ship, although Gosnell hid it well. Steve Burns sat crying silently while the other crewman, Gonzales, stared dumbly at the floor grating.

"Yeah, we understan', yuh asshole."

Jamil ripped Gosnell's face with the back of his hand, and was about to hit him again when he regained control.

"Good, then we understand each other."

Gosnell leaned over to wipe the blood from his mouth on the sleeve of his shackled arm. They all watched as Jamil walked to the end of the compartment and securely taped the block of explosive around a six-inch pipe that went through the deck plating to the skin of the ship below. He rejoined the others at the console and took a small transmitter from his pocket. He switched the device on, and it emitted a short high-frequency chirp.

"The passengers are also fastened to this vessel. If I am forced to use this, then you will share your tomb with them." He fastened the transmitter to his belt and called Salah over to one side. "How is Yehya behaving?"

"He will do to stand guard, but do not count on him if we must fight on equal terms with a determined enemy."

"Very well, we will leave him here. Secure the other two to their stations, and come up to the car deck. I will leave it to you and Ahmed to position the weapons and stage the rest of the equipment for the assault on our prize. I will be in the pilot-house if you need me."

Sunday, 3:45 A.M.—Hood Canal

The floating bridge was draped across the Hood Canal like a long, graceful snake. Each end sloped up to the high ground on either side of the Canal, assisted by trestles that provided ample clearance for small and medium-sized craft entering and leaving the Canal. The mile-long center portion of the highway was supported by huge concrete pontoons or caissons held in place by anchored cables. The moon had almost set, and the symmetrical structure was bathed in starlight, punctuated along its length by cones of light from the evenly spaced gooseneck street lamps. An occasional pair of headlights would sweep down from one side to float across the flat center section and climb the slope at the other side. At the center of the bridge, two forty-foot towers, each offset to one side of the highway and some six hundred feet apart, marked the section of the bridge that could be opened for ship traffic. This was designed specifically to allow supply vessels and submarines access to the base at Bangor from the Strait of Juan de Fuca and the Pacific Ocean.

The Hood Canal was not really a canal but a long, narrow bay that ran some forty-five miles southwest from the bridge before making a dogleg turn to the east for an additional fifteen miles. Only two miles of land separated the tip of the Hood Canal from Case Inlet and lower Puget Sound. If those two bodies of water were joined, the Kitsap Peninsula would become an island almost the size of Long Island. The Olympic Mountains lined the west bank of the Canal like a whitecapped emerald wall, making it one of the most spectacular waterways in the world.

Eight miles from the bridge on the eastern side of the Canal was the U.S. Navy submarine base at Bangor, built specifically to service the Pacific Trident fleet. The base had been carefully constructed so as not to damage the environment, for the submarines shared the clear, deep waters of the Hood Canal with salmon, seals, and roaming pods of killer whales. At the mouth of the Canal, a few hundred meters from the bridge, the *Katie B* idled along, gradually working its way south toward the tower at the eastern end of the detachable spans.

"I want you to dock the boat at the side of the bridge, one hundred meters to the left of the tower on the left."

"You're not supposed to do that unless it's an emergency."

"Just do it, Epps—and don't question my commands." It was there again—that cold threatening tone.

"Okay, the bridge it is. Hey, Roberto! You wanna put the fenders over on the side—yeah, the right side."

The *Katie B* idled toward the easternmost of the two towers. The two-lane highway was some thirty feet above the water, supported by the massive caissons and an iron latticework. Epps put the engines in neutral and let the incoming tide carry them the rest of the way. As Epps twisted the boat parallel to the

concrete float to bring the boat alongside, Roberto and one of
the Arabs scrambled up onto the caisson carrying mooring
lines. Epps noticed that they had automatic weapons slung over
their shoulders. Once they had made the boat secure, they
moved back into the shadows under the highway.

"Epps, we have business on the bridge. You are to stay here.
Turn off the engines and lift the hatches like you are having
engine troubles. Remain here until you are instructed to do
otherwise. No matter what happens, you are to wait for our
return—do you understand?"

"You're the boss," Epps replied as he cut one ignition
switch, then the other. Epps made his way down from the fly
bridge and opened the engine hatches on the stern. The silence
was deafening except for the occasional high-pitched buzz of a
car speeding over the bridge grating above.

Nabil climbed up on the caisson, and Muhammad tossed him
a rifle with a long, curved magazine. He followed Nabil onto
the concrete and to a ladder that led up through the steel girders
to the highway above. Epps turned on a flashlight and set it on
the valve cover of one of the engines. He then seated himself on
the deck, with his legs hanging over into the engine compartment. He was sure that a bridge tender would come to investi-
gate, but none did.

Ben Marcum sat in an old swivel chair with his feet up on the
windowsill. Marcum worked for the state highway department
and had been a bridge tender for over thirty years. This year
would be his last, as he was at the mandatory retirement age.
From his seat in the tower, he had a commanding view of the
automobile traffic in both directions as well as the Hood Canal.
The room was large and comfortable, and served as a control
station and observation platform. The section of the floating
bridge under Marcum was expanded to accommodate the gate
tower located on the north side of the highway. It also marked
the end of a three-hundred-foot "bulge" where the two lanes
of traffic were separated to form a wet well. The space between
the divided highway allowed the eastern three-hundred-foot

section of the bridge to be retracted back into this well when the bridge was opened for ship traffic.

Marcum's attention was divided between the last chapter of a Louis L'Amour novel and the boat that was slowly making its way up to the side of the bridge. It was probably a herring boat looking to see if the fish were schooling up along the bridge, as they often did. Just before the craft was screened from his view by the bulge in the highway, he could see from its shape that it wasn't a herring boat. Probably some sport-fisherman wanting to get out to Point-No-Point to salmon fish at first light, and having some engine trouble. They weren't supposed to tie up along the bridge unless there was a problem aboard, but sometimes they did it anyway. He'd give them a few minutes to sort it out. If they weren't under way soon, he'd go have a look-see. Marcum hadn't turned but a few pages—the Sackett boys were about to catch up with the rustlers—when the door that led to the stair access was suddenly thrown open. A man dressed in Levi's, a dark sweater, and a watch cap stepped inside. Marcum came to his feet and froze when he saw the automatic rifle pointed at him.

"Sit down, old man! One wrong move and you are a dead man." Marcum slowly sat down, his eyes shifting between the man's face and the ugly snout of the rifle.

"What do you want?"

"Right now nothing, but in a few moments you are going to open your bridge."

They waited in silence while Nabil watched two dark forms carrying a box between them move quickly across the steel highway grating to the other tower. After a short while one of them came jogging back. A moment later, Muhammad stepped into the tower and paused to catch his breath.

"The other tower is empty, but we were able to force the door to the stairs," he gasped. "Haj is there setting up the weapons station."

"Weapons. What the hell's goin' on here?"

Nabil brought the barrel of the AK sharply along the side of Marcum's head, knocking him to the floor of tower.

"You will not speak, and you will do exactly as you are told or I will kill you right now. Do you understand?'' Marcum held his hand to the side of his head where his ear had been ripped by the front sight of the rifle. The blood running down his neck was collected by the collar of his flannel shirt. "Do you understand?!'' Marcum nodded as Nabil dragged him to his feet and shoved him back into his chair.

"Return to your station and signal when you are in place. They should be along within the hour.'' Nabil embraced the larger man. "God be with you and with Haj. I will see you back on the boat, or at that place the prophet has reserved for martyrs.'' Muhammad left as Roberto appeared, carrying an M-60 machine gun and a steel olive-drab box of ammunition. Roberto returned a second time with a 40mm grenade launcher and a crate of grenades. A light flashed twice from the far tower, and Nabil answered with his own light.

"It is time, old man. Open the bridge.''

Marcum reluctantly unlocked the panel to the controls that initiated the bridge-opening sequence. He hesitated, and Nabil jammed the muzzle of the AK into his ribs. Marcum threw the master switch, and for a moment nothing happened. Then lights began flashing and barricades dropped to block the roadway just before the highway parted to form the bulge. There was a whirring of electric motors as the concrete-and-steel structure came to life. Hydraulic rams slid the locking bars free and the highway grating of the movable span began to moan as the three-hundred-foot section was drawn back into the well. On the other side, near the western tower, there was no bulge in the highway. A winter storm in 1979 had destroyed the western half of the bridge, so to eliminate the bulge, the new western span had been designed to permit the entire length of highway grating to be elevated some fifteen feet on hydraulic jacks. The caissons supporting this section were built wide enough to fit on either side of those supporting the main road, so the movable section could straddle the adjoining section of highway as it was retracted. The opening sequence was fully automated, and operating commands were sent to the western section by microwave transmitter. Ten minutes after Marcum closed the switch, there was a six-hundred-foot opening to the Hood

Canal. Nabil pulled a silenced pistol from his belt and waved it at Marcum. It was the same make and model as the one carried by Jamil.

"Excellent, old man. Now step away from the panel." Marcum complied, holding one hand to his ear, the other out to the side in a gesture of appeal.

"Please, mister, don't kill me."

"Why not? Is the bridge not open?" The pistol coughed twice and Ben Marcum, aged sixty-four, slumped to the floor. Nabil grabbed him by the lapel of his jacket and dragged him to the door, then kicked him down the stairs. The body tumbled down to the landing and through the railing before dropping to the concrete at the foot of the tower. Then Nabil turned and emptied the rest of the magazine into the control panel. The box emitted a shower of sparks and a single blue flash. The pungent smell of ozone filled the tower room. Nabil took out his Motorola and attached the extended-range antenna.

"Station one, this is station two, over."

"This is station one, go ahead, over."

"This is station two. The door is open, over." The text was designed not to attract attention if overheard, but it did not mask the triumph in the voice transmission.

"Well done, station two. Our boat should arrive there in about thirty minutes. Station one, out."

Sunday, 4:05 A.M.—U.S. Coast Guard Station, Pier 36, Seattle, Washington

Carol Peschel marked the scope and waited another few minutes just to be sure, but there could be no doubt about it.

"Washington State ferry *Spokane,* this is Coast Guard Vessel Traffic Control, over." Chief Dearing came over to the scope and stood behind Peschel with his hands on his hips.

"Try 'em again."

"This is Coast Guard Vessel Traffic Control calling the M/V

Spokane, please respond, over.'' Again there was no reply. They were both looking at the display on the scope from the Point-No-Point antenna, which clearly painted the large blip of the *Spokane* as it turned west across the inbound shipping lane and made its way around Foulweather Bluff. The ferry was about four and a half miles from the antenna and could be seen to move a small increment with each sweep.

''Chief, this has been screwy from the start. There's no reason a Jumbo Class ferry would be going to Anacortes in the first place. Now he's clearly out of the traffic lanes. Either he's headed into Port Ludlow, or he's going south into the Hood Canal.''

''Not enough water for that boat at Port Ludlow.''

''Why would he be going into the Canal?''

''Hell if I know. There won't be anyone at Colman Dock for another few hours. Maybe he has a steering casualty.''

''C'mon, Chief, he's still doing eighteen knots.''

They both watched as the blip moved into the shadow behind Foulweather Bluff and faded from the screen. The other two scope operators, who had responsibility for traffic in the Strait of Juan de Fuca, also had their scopes switched to the Point-No-Point antenna signal. Both looked up at Dearing as the blip that had been the *Spokane* faded.

''We better call the state police, Chief,'' said Peschel. ''Maybe they have someone in the area who could drive over to the Hood Canal bridge and have a look.''

Dearing pondered this and grunted. The chief asked for very few things in life, but a quiet, uneventful watch—normal routine with no flaps—was one of them. Well, this was anything but normal. Small craft did all kinds of stupid things and occasionally a merchantman would stray off course. But the ferry captains knew the Puget Sound waters better than anyone. He had an uneasy feeling about this one.

''Okay, people, back to work. There's a big piece of water out there, and we're supposed to be watching all of it.'' *Why,* he asked himself as he picked up the telephone, *why on my watch?*

Sunday, 4:25 A.M.—Marine Corps Barracks, Naval Submarine Base, Bangor, Washington

Gunnery Sergeant Jennings sat on his bunk in the NCO quarters with his bare feet on the cold tile floor and his forearms resting on his knees. No alarm clock had rung and the blinds were drawn. Still, Jennings knew it was dawn. During the winter months, when the sun didn't rise in Puget Sound until 8:30, he allowed himself to sleep in until 5:30, but in the summer he was always up before 4:30. Jennings draped a towel around his neck and grabbed his shaving kit from the top shelf of the metal locker by his bunk. He slowly made his way into the head, a hand thrust into the back of his olive-drab briefs scratching his butt. His knees cracked audibly as he walked.

Jennings was the senior noncommissioned officer in his watch section. The Marines were stationed at Bangor to provide base security and to guard the munitions stored at the Strategic Weapons Facility, Pacific, or SWFPAC, as it was called. One hundred and twenty Marines were assigned to the base. They stood three-section duty, and there were always twenty-five to thirty Marines in the guard section, twenty-four hours a day. Two second lieutenants and a first louie on their initial assignment out of Quantico were detailed to each of the duty-section platoons. Bangor was considered one of the better duty stations in the Corps. The country was beautiful, and the base housing excellent. Base security duty was not a favorite of the Marines, but Jennings had just finished a three-year tour with an amphibious-ready group. Nearly half of his time had been at sea, mostly in the Persian Gulf. It was nice to be ashore for a while, even if he did pull an occasional weekend duty. He quickly showered and put on a freshly starched set of fatigues, and made his way into the orderly room.

"Morning, Gunny."

"Good morning, Corporal Halasey. You runnin' a tight watch here?" A tall, thin redhead with china-blue eyes and massive freckles sat at the orderly's desk. He had a face that belonged on a box of cornflakes.

"Uh, you bet, Gunny. The El-Tee said he'd be here around zero five hundred for rounds."

It was customary for the duty-section officer and the duty staff NCO to make an inspection of the Marine guard posts and the roving patrols. Many of the NCOs resented the younger Marines, especially the new officers just out of basic school, and joked about their inexperience. But Jennings welcomed a chance to spend time with them. He took every opportunity to teach them the business of being a Marine—they were the future of the Corps. Aside from the Gulf War, Jennings had also spent two tours in Vietnam. He had seen eighteen-year-old privates fight with the best of them, and young second lieutenants die leading their men in combat.

Most of the routine base security was provided by a contract security service. The Marines guarded SWFPAC, and provided a ready response element in case of an intruder.

"Coffee done?"

"You bet, Gunny—just put a pot on." It was also customary for the duty orderly to keep a strong, fresh pot of coffee made when Gunnery Sergeant Jennings had the duty. Jennings carefully filled his mug, a heavy porcelain flagon with "Semper Fi" inscribed under the three chevrons and two rocker arms of a Marine gunnery sergeant's emblem. He gathered the aroma and sipped the coffee cautiously, as if he were tasting a vintage wine.

"Not bad, Corporal, not bad at all. Y'know, it just about takes a full hitch to learn how to make Marine Corps coffee. You be shipping over, Halasey?"

"Not a chance, Gunny. Forty-five days and a wakeup, and I'm a free man."

"You're not running down my Marine Corps, are you, Corporal?"

"Oh gosh, no way, Gunny. I just think it'll be better for me and the Corps if I become a civilian."

"I see," grumbled Jennings. "Well, we'll talk more about

that. I'll be in my office—let me know when the lieutenant is in the area.''

Sunday, 4:30 A.M.—Aboard the *Spokane* near Hood Head on the Hood Canal

Jamil stood in the pilothouse by the radar. The long barrier of lights across the water in front of them was broken by a dark gap in the middle. The break could clearly be seen on the *Spokane*'s radar. Nabil had done his work well, although the hard part would be to hold the bridge open for their return trip. He felt a surge of exhilaration at the success of the operation thus far. Eighteen months of planning and paying informants and recruiting assets and staging equipment. Finding fighting men who could speak English well enough to be brought to America on student visas or work permits. It all came down to the next two hours. He had known taking the ferry would not be difficult, and he assumed that Nabil had little difficulty in capturing the bridge. *But when will the alarm be sounded?*

They had to arrive at the submarine base and next to the *Michigan* before the base security forces were alerted and had time to react. Another call from the Coast Guard came from the speaker overhead. They had known for almost a half hour that the *Spokane* had left the shipping channel and was not bound for Anacortes. Jamil knew they were no longer being tracked on radar, but the Coast Guard would have to know they were near the mouth of the Hood Canal, though they would probably not suspect the bridge was open. *Will they connect the behavior of the ferry with a possible attack on the submarine base at Bangor? The Americans can be so complacent, but they are also very unpredictable.* Then he felt the ferry slowing just a bit.

''Why are we slowing down?'' he demanded.

''Maximum safe speed for going through a bridge opening is about five knots, especially with the tide running behind us.''

"Captain, your safety and the lives of all aboard depend on your getting us to Bangor as quickly as possible. Proceed at full speed."

"Look, I'm responsible for—"

"Enough! That opening is large enough for you to navigate at full speed, and we both know it. And believe me, Captain, it is much more dangerous for your crew and passengers if you do not do exactly as I have ordered."

Peck reached over and moved the throttle indicator to "All Ahead Full." The ferry shuddered imperceptibly as power was added and she began to increase speed. He steered the *Spokane* toward the middle of the Canal to position her for a perpendicular run at the bridge opening. Peck had been mildly surprised to find the bridge open. Then he had hoped to cause a delay by slowing the ferry for the passage through the bridge opening. It would be more tricky than dangerous to go through at full speed. The aircraft warning lights on top of the two towers clearly marked the opening, and the dawn was just beginning to define the length of the bridge.

"This is an unnecessary risk," he said. "It would only take a few minutes to slow to a safe speed." Jamil was standing behind him. He placed the muzzle of the pistol at the base of Peck's skull and hissed in his ear.

"Every second now is vital. Scrape either side of that bridge, and I'll blow your head off."

Nabil heard the *Spokane* before he saw her. It was a quiet morning with no wind, and the rumbling of the speeding ferry carried well across the water. It appeared from behind Hood Head as a dark, moving lump on the water. All the lights, including the navigation and running lights, had been extinguished. The ferry moved from left to right as it approached from the north. When it was a mile away, it turned and headed directly for the opening.

"Station two, this is station one, over."

"This is station two, over."

"We are almost there. Is everything in order, over?"

"Everything is ready for your arrival—good luck, out."

Nabil and Roberto watched as Peck put the *Spokane* into the opening, dead center. The big ferry rumbled through the gap with the noise and speed of a freight train. Nabil's position in the tower was at the same level as the pilothouse on the speeding ferry. There was just enough light for him to make out a figure on the port wing of the pilothouse, and to see that the man had his fist raised in a salute. The *Spokane* charged into the gray mist that had just begun to form over the Hood Canal south of the bridge. Nabil stared at her until he was brought out of his reverie by the honking of an impatient motorist waiting for the bridge to be closed.

"What do we do now, *señor*?" asked Roberto. Nabil turned to him, donning a baseball cap with a Washington State Highway Department logo on it. Then he put on an official-looking green windbreaker that had been hanging on a hook by the door of the tower.

"I will go down and politely inform them that we are having some difficulty with the motors that move the bridge back into position, and that we anticipate it will take another forty minutes to make repairs."

"*Bueno,* but what do we do after that?"

"Continue to declare mechanical problems with the bridge equipment. If they become too restless, then we will have to begin killing them."

Sunday, 4:35 A.M.—Aboard the USS *Michigan* (SSBN 727)

Master Chief Electrician's Mate Vernon Anderson was the Blue Crew COB aboard the USS *Michigan.* The title Chief of the Boat, or "COB," as he was addressed, went with being the senior enlisted man in his crew. The Trident missile submarines were served by two separate crews. The Gold Crew had brought the *Michigan* in two weeks ago, and now Anderson's crew, the Blue Crew, was busy preparing the boat for another patrol. The Tridents were the newest class of ballistic-missile submarines, designed to replace the aging Polaris fleet. The boat was designed to spend more than three-quarters of her life at sea, which meant that the submarine had more endurance underway than the men who served in her. This is not to say that Master Chief Anderson had not endured. He had spent twenty-eight years in the Navy, all in submarines, and by his own conservative estimate, he had spent nine years—nearly one-fifth of his life—submerged.

"Maxwell, why don't you lay below and get us both a cup of coffee."

"Sure thing, COB. You take sugar?"

"Maxwell, do I look like some candy-ass skimmer-sailor? You bring me some strong black coffee."

"Uh, right, COB. Be right back."

Anderson was standing duty as CDO, or command duty officer, responsible for the *Michigan* while most of the crew were ashore. He played the role of a salty old Navy chief, despite his master's degree in electrical engineering. He had just come up on deck to allow Maxwell, the third-class quartermaster who was standing the quarterdeck watch, time to make a head call and get a cup of coffee. It also allowed him an opportunity to check the weather deck and the topside watch standers. Anderson was dressed in a worn set of wash khakis and a leather flight jacket. He was not really overweight, but he had a smooth, well-rounded look typical of sailors who spent long periods of time confined in submarines with the best chow facilities in the Navy. He walked aft along the missile deck, inspecting the numerous mooring lines and shore-power cables that bound the *Michigan* to the pier. There was something despondent and solemn about a warship at night when most of her crew were ashore. The men on watch and other members of the duty section moved about quietly and talked in hushed voices, lest they disturb the huge black monster as she rested.

The Delta Pier was the heart of the Trident complex, providing pierside services to boats like the *Michigan* that came alongside to change crews and take on supplies. The pier was built in the shape of a large triangle, the base of which ran parallel to the shore fifty meters away and formed one side of a huge dry dock that was large enough to handle the big submarines. This whole complex was located offshore to allow for the migration of fingerling salmon along the beach. The other two sides of the pier formed an apex pointed west toward the Canal, and provided berthing for two Tridents. Currently, the *Ohio* was in dry dock and the *Florida* was moored at the other berthing site. The other five Tridents were on patrol.

The Delta Pier was a secure area. Nonetheless, the Blue Crew was required to station one sentry at the head of each of the two brows or gangways that served the missile deck, and a roving sentry on the pier. This was in addition to the vehicle patrols on the pier and surrounding area that were conducted by the contract security service. There was a Marine guard shack at the head of the causeway that led out to the Delta triangle. Several additional layers of security lay between the Delta Pier and the perimeter of the base. The Trident submarines were well protected from any intruder who approached from the land.

The *Michigan* and her sister ships of the Trident Class represented the leading edge of submarine technology and strategic deterrence. They were big, quiet, and fast. The payload of a Trident was twenty-four solid-fueled ICBMs. Each of the new Trident II or D-5 missiles carried twelve MIRVs (multiple independent reentry vehicles) and each MIRV carried a 150-kiloton thermonuclear warhead. She was a 19,000-ton monster that could lose herself in vast reaches of the open ocean, and deliver 228 nuclear bombs on command, reliably and accurately. A Trident didn't even have to be at sea to deliver Armageddon. The 6,500-nautical-mile range of the new D-5s allowed the *Michigan* to hit seventy percent of her targets from pierside at Bangor. All this capability for only $1.4 billion a copy. Advocates in the Navy claimed that the creditable response of the Tridents kept the peace, while it had forced the Soviets to destroy their economy trying to build a weapons system that was its equal. As Master Chief Anderson was fond of saying: "It's one helluva piece of gear."

A shroud was built up around the missile tubes aft of the sail and flattened the lines of the rounded hull to form the missile deck. Anderson paced this area behind the sail, stomping his feet on the steel deck. A damp chill had accompanied an early-morning fog that was creeping in from the Canal. He walked around the six-by-six-foot main access trunk that was sunk in the hull twenty feet behind the sail. This large opening allowed bulk loading of provisions and the change-out replacement of large pieces of equipment. Another identical hatch was located near the stern, just aft of the missile compartment. These openings were positioned over other large hatches so pallets of stores could be lowered to any of the *Michigan*'s four decks or to the keel forty-two feet below the weather deck. The lifelines and chain hoists around and over these access trunks violated the smooth lines of the *Michigan*'s hull and her majestic sail. Several electric blowers whirred quietly on deck by the access trunks, pushing fresh air through flexible eight-inch hoses down into the submarine, where it was picked up by the air-conditioning system and moved throughout the boat.

Balancing two steaming mugs of black coffee, Maxwell stepped through a door in the side of the sail and walked back to where Anderson was standing. He would have preferred cream and sugar, but didn't want to run the risk of being compared to a skimmer, or surface-ship sailor.

"Here y'go, COB. Boy, the fog's really moving in."

"Thanks, Maxwell. The sun will chase it away quick enough."

Anderson looked back toward the bow. The sun was not yet up, but the eastern sky backlit the *Michigan*'s dark sail. Anderson had been around when they called it a conning tower. The term "sail" was more appropriate because the large black fin, with its winglike diving planes, rose from the deck like the tail of a Boeing 737. Out on the Canal, the gray dawn was just starting to press against the fog. Two sailors dressed in dungarees and blue denim jackets climbed up the ladder from the forward access trunk carrying fishing poles. One had a tackle box and the other a bucket of bait.

"Request permission to fish off the stern, COB."

"Permission granted, but I want you wearing life jackets back there."

"You bet. Thanks, COB." The two off-duty sailors made their way to the stern and began to bait their hooks. Ling cod and red rockfish lived under the piers, and they came out to feed at dawn and dusk. It was still a little early for salmon in the Canal.

"Y'know, Maxwell, most people have to pay good money on their day off to go fishing, and we get to do it right here at the office."

"Yeah, but most people don't go to sea and bore holes in the ocean for seventy straight days at a crack, either."

Anderson snorted and walked aft on the missile deck past the forward bow. He paused to savor the peacefulness of the morning. The ripe salt-smell from the barnacle-covered pilings competed with the aroma of his coffee. Overhead, he could just see a hint of blue working through the fog. His watch said 4:45 A.M. Another two and a half hours until his relief came aboard, and he could take the rest of the day off. Time for a plate of steak and eggs at the Chiefs' Club with the COB from the *Florida*. The two of them had a 10:00 A.M. tee-off time on the PGA championship course over at Port Ludlow. *This man's Navy,* he reflected, *is not all that bad.* He walked slowly back to the hatch on the side of the sail to go below.

"Maxwell, rotate your brow sentries and the roving patrol periodically so they stay alert. And to be on the safe side, have those guys fishing off the stern put on safety lines. If anything comes up, I'll be in the chief's quarters."

"Aye, aye, COB."

Sunday, 4:40 A.M.—Aboard the *Spokane* on the Hood Canal

Jamil paced from one side of the pilothouse to the other. Ahmed called periodically and updated him on the preparations that were underway on the car deck. It was now light enough so that he could clearly see the two men on the promenade just below the pilothouse. Fenton and Hassan had carried two M-60 machine guns from the motor home and mounted them on the steel life rail that circled the promenade deck. One was mounted just forward of the pilothouse, and the other on the starboard side right below the pilothouse wing. The two weapons were about ten meters apart, and together they enjoyed excellent fields of fire straight ahead and to the right side of the ferry. Both men had several thousand rounds of detachable-link 7.62mm ammunition coiled in waiting olive-drab metal boxes. Jamil watched as each man put a belt into the breach of his weapon and closed the top cover to lock it into place.

"We are positioned and ready to go down here," came Ahmed's voice over the Motorola.

"Very well, I will be right there." Jamil called Hassan into the pilothouse and pointed to Peck. "If he does anything other than what I have instructed him to do, shoot the woman and then call me, is that clear?"

"I understand, Sayeh." Jamil nodded to Hassan and hurried down the steps of the pilothouse.

On the starboard side of the main car deck, Ahmed, Ali, and Salah were standing together amidships by the rail. Four-inch nylon mooring lines were laid out in long figure-eight coils both fore and aft. Salah and Ali, who would comprise the boarding party, had Uzis strapped across their chests and were further armed with double-bladed axes. Each had a scuba cylinder slung on his back. Both wore dark clothing to blend with the black hull of the submarine, including black sneakers for traction on the rounded steel hull.

"Is everything ready?"

"All is prepared according to the plan," replied Ahmed.

Jamil turned from him, placing his hands on Salah's and Ali's shoulders. "Do you understand your duties?"

"We do," said Salah.

"Questions?"

The two looked at each other, then at Jamil, and shook their heads.

"Very well. The success of our mission is in your hands. Move quickly and carefully." He glanced at his watch. "We will be at the submarine base in ten minutes and alongside the submarine shortly after our arrival. Get your work done quickly and get back aboard—and may God be with you." He embraced each of them and climbed the stairs to the passenger deck.

Michelle strolled among the passengers knowing they were all watching her. One hand held a cigarette while the other was wrapped around the pistol grip of her AK-47, which hung from its sling around her neck. When she saw Jamil, she hurried over to him.

"Any complications?" he asked.

"Like all hostages, they are like cattle in the slaughter pen—restless but compliant."

"Not hostages—prisoners," Jamil replied. "We are at war."

"So we are, *chérie*. How much longer until we get—" He cut her short with a gesture.

"We will be there very soon, and that is not your concern. Have you selected three of them?"

"Over here tied around this pole." She led him to one of the stanchions where a group of wide-eyed passengers formed an irregular circle, joined by their nylon collars and the cable. "These three." She pointed to an older man and his wife sitting together. They were quietly erect, holding hands. Next to them was a teenage girl, weeping softly.

The elderly couple were dressed in formal attire—he in white dinner jacket with the bow tie undone and draped around his collar, and she in an expensive dark-blue ball gown. They were a tall, handsome couple in their early sixties, with tanned faces and silver hair. They exuded an understated wealth. Both were wary, but not so intimidated as the others. The girl was a preppy-looking teenager dressed in loafers, cargo shorts, and a Dartmouth sweatshirt. She had been segregated from a group of young people, and she was terrified.

"Excellent—cut them loose." Michelle roughly pulled the nylon straps away from their necks to insert the jaws of the pliers, and set them free. "We require your assistance in the pilothouse," Jamil said politely. "You will please accompany me there." He stepped away from the group and motioned for them to follow him. Michelle herded them along with the muzzle of her rifle.

"Mister, please don't hurt me. Can't I stay here, please!"

"Quiet, child," the woman said. "For now, we have to do what these animals say. The authorities will be here soon enough and straighten this matter out." The man put his hand on her arm, but she shrugged it off and regarded Jamil with a condescending glare. *One of those,* thought Jamil—*wonderful!*

"The lady is quite correct," he said courteously. "Now, if you will just follow me up to the next deck. Thank you very much." Michelle escorted them to the stairs and returned to her charges.

The man and woman, with the girl between them, followed Jamil to the starboard side of the pilothouse, where one of the M-60s was mounted. The sun was not up yet, but the dawn was rapidly giving way to daylight. A band of fog some thirty feet thick that had formed just before dawn now blanketed the water. Visibility was cut to one hundred meters, and gave the impression that the promenade deck, with the stack in the middle and a pilothouse on each end, was skimming over the white carpet. *God must indeed favor us,* mused Jamil. This condition was not totally unexpected, but he had estimated only a twenty-percent chance of a favorable covering fog. They would be visible on radar, but no one would see the *Spokane* until they closed on the submarine. Fenton stepped away from the M-60 mounted at the front of the pilothouse, and covered the new arrivals with his assault rifle.

"Well, we're here, damn you," said the woman. "Now what do you want with us?"

"Stand over by the rail, please," said Jamil.

"I don't understand—what is it you want?"

Jamil looked past the woman and saw a large barnlike structure rising out of the fog, ahead on the left bank of the Canal.

That would be the Missile Handling Facility, where the Trident missiles were loaded into the submarines. The Delta Pier, where the submarines were berthed, was just a few hundred yards south. They were almost there!

"You, stand here by the rail!" Jamil pushed the girl to the rail between the two mounted machine guns.

"Have you no decency, man? Myself and two other men will do for this. Why the women?"

Jamil looked back at the man as he secured the girl's wrists to the rail with nylon ties. He calmly stood by the pilothouse with one hand in his jacket pocket and the other around his wife's shoulders. Jamil quickly passed a rope around the girl's waist and knotted it securely, which had the effect of pressing her stomach to the rail. This forced her to remain in a standing position against the rail. The woman, now understanding their reason for being brought here, clung to her husband and began to weep softly. The wind from the moving ferry played at the thick white hair that capped the old gentleman's handsome, lined face. Jamil both resented and admired his arrogant courage. The woman began to wail as he secured her to the rail to the left of the M-60 in front of the pilothouse.

"Over here," said Jamil, indicating a section of the rail to the right of the other machine gun.

The man stepped over and placed his hands on the rail, allowing Jamil to secure the ties to his wrists and the rope around his waist. When it was almost finished, he turned his head and spit into Jamil's face. The terrorist blanched and seized the man's face, digging his fingernails into the loose flesh of his cheeks. Still holding him with one hand, he snatched the linen handkerchief from the man's dinner jacket with the other and wiped his face.

"You are brave, and I will permit that. But do not push it, old man!" Jamil released him and quickly climbed the stairs to the pilothouse. The large, boxlike Missile Handling Facility was now abeam to port. "Get to your machine gun, Hassan. We are almost there." Hassan slipped past him and hurried out.

Peck was still at the helm, while Janey and Brad stood on the port side of the pilothouse. All of them stared at Jamil and at the long barrel of the silenced automatic.

"Half speed, Captain, and turn left toward that building." Jamil pointed to a large square structure rising out of the mist on the shore. It housed the offices and repair facilities on the Delta Pier where the Trident submarines were moored. The ferry began to slow as Peck turned to port. "Our submarine is tied to the pier at the base of the building. You are to bring us alongside and hold us there until I tell you to do otherwise. And I want this pilothouse toward the bow of the sub."

"Don't do this!" pleaded Peck. "You can't get away with it!"

The pistol coughed, and the side window behind Janey and Brad shattered.

Johnson started to sink to his knees from fright, but Janey caught him and held him upright. "Steady, now," she said quietly to him. "We'll get through this."

"If I don't get away with it, Captain," replied Jamil, "you and your people will die. Do exactly as you are told, or I start the killing now!"

Peck clenched his teeth and turned his attention to guiding the ferry through the mist toward the buildings on the Delta Pier. The two crewmen clung helplessly to each other in the corner of the pilothouse. Jamil took the Motorola from his belt.

"This is Jamil. We are attacking now! *Allahu Ahkbar!*"

Sunday, 5:00 A.M.—Bremerton, Washington

Deputy Sheriff Bill Cavenaugh was drinking coffee at the Denny's just off Highway 3 near Bremerton. There were only two roving patrols in Kitsap County at night. One car worked the county south of Bremerton, while Bill was assigned to the northern part of the county. Marleen, the waitress, had just brought him an order of toast and a refill on his coffee when the radio on his belt issued a burst of static. It was standard procedure for officers riding alone to carry belt transceivers that were slaved to the mobile units in their cars.

"Roger, this is two seven, go ahead." He held the transceiver to his ear to hear better and for some privacy from the night-shift workers and fishermen at the counter.

"Understood. I'll be up there in a half hour, thirty-five minutes."

"Got an emergency?" asked a man to his left.

"I doubt it. The state police got a call about a ferry being loose in the Hood Canal. The nearest trooper is in Tacoma, so they asked us to look into it."

Cavenaugh wrapped the toast in a napkin and gulped down the coffee. He tossed two dollars on the counter as he headed for the door. It was understood that the deputies could eat on the house, but if he had more than coffee, he always paid.

He almost put the lights and siren on, but thought better of it. The call was unusual but didn't sound like any kind of emergency. There were few cars on the highway this early, so he speeded north at a comfortable seventy-five miles per hour.

"Unit two seven to base, over."

"Go ahead, two seven."

"This is two seven, now proceeding north on Highway Three just north of Bremerton. Did anyone think to call the guy who's supposed to be on duty at the bridge, over?"

"That's an affirmative, two seven, but the operator says the phone is out of order, over."

"Roger, two seven clear." Cavenaugh reached over and flicked the toggle that turned on the flashing lights and eased the car up to eighty-five just as his headlights illuminated a road sign that said "Hood Canal Bridge 27 Miles."

Sunday, 5:00 A.M.—Waterfront, Naval Submarine Base, Bangor, Washington

''Patrol one, this is Harbor Control, over.''

''Patrol one, go ahead.''

''We've got a large radar contact moving down the Canal from the north. We now hold it west of the Missile Handling Facility—do you have it?''

''Just on radar. The soup is pretty thick out here. We might get a visual as he goes past, over.''

''Roger, one. Keep an eye on him. Harbor Control, out.''

Roger Steffins had his head glued to the hood of the radar-scope. They had just been fitted out with a new Furuno 2400 radar, and it provided excellent coverage of the Bangor water-front and the surrounding area. The twenty-eight-foot Bertram patrol boat rocked gently as his partner, Bill Hughs, brought the craft about, and they began to idle slowly in a northerly direction. They were about seventy meters west of the Delta Pier. Looking up from the scope for a visual reference, Steffins could just make out the long flat missile deck of the *Michigan* and the base of her sail as the growing dawn wrestled the fog off the eastern bank of the Canal.

''What do you think it is, Rog?''

''Can't say. Helluva big return, though. Probably a herring boat, although she's really moving.'' Steffins and Hughs, like many serving on the civilian base-security force, were retired Navy. They had worked on the base while on active duty, and were now supplementing their retirement as ''rent-a-cops,'' a term they used a great deal more when they were in the Navy than they did now.

''Why don't you open the beach a little. Maybe we can get a look at her.''

''Aye, aye, sir,'' said Hughs with a smile as he brought the Bertram left to a westerly heading to take them farther out into the Canal.

''Patrol one, Harbor Control, over.''

"Patrol one, over."

"That contact looks like it just turned and is heading for the Delta Pier. You better have a look-see, over."

"Roger, Control. Patrol one, out."

Steffins again stuck his face to the hood of the radar. Control was right. The large blip was heading directly for the pier, and should be coming into visual range just ahead of them.

"Holy shit, Rog, look at this!"

Steffins looked up from the scope and at first saw nothing. He was looking into the fog—low on the water searching for a small craft. Then he looked up and saw the tall superstructure of the ferry bearing down on them. It was less than a hundred yards away and closing rapidly. Hughs swung the Bertram south and gunned the engines to move out of the ferry's path.

"Control—patrol one. You won't believe this, but we got a Washington State ferry heading right for the Delta Pier!"

"Say again, patrol one."

"You heard me, a Washington State ferry, and it's a big one!"

"Patrol two, could you proceed north to the Delta Pier and confirm patrol one's ferry sighting."

"Look, goddammit, it's—aw shit . . ." Steffins dropped the microphone and stepped to the stern of the boat, picking up the battery-powered megaphone. The ferry was on their starboard quarter, and would pass about forty meters astern of them. He could now read the name on the placard mounted just under the front windows of the pilothouse.

"Ahoy on the Spokane. *These are restricted waters. Turn away and stand clear!"*

The big ferry, now a wall of white metal, was slowing but not changing course. Steffins noticed three people by the pilothouse leaning on the rail—and what looked like men with mounted machine guns between them. Then his attention was captured by a man on the car deck looking right at him and holding a short pipe on his shoulder. Suddenly, Steffins realized it wasn't a pipe.

"Hughs! Get down, it's a . . . !" *Whoosh!* Steffins managed to drop below the stern railing before the rocket flew into the cabin of the Bertram. It impacted on the forward bulkhead right beside the coxswain's station, blowing off the fiberglass roof and shattering the windscreen. The force of the blast tore through the small forward cabin like a hot knife through a plastic model boat. Hughs's left arm was severed, and his shredded torso lay over the splintered starboard gunwale as if he were seasick.

Steffins was slammed into the stern railing as shards of metal and fiberglass were driven into his back and legs. He looked up and saw the windows of the ferry ticking by as the *Spokane* hurried past. His eardrums had been blown out, but he could feel the vibration of the ferry. The pain was terrible when he moved, and he was very cold. *If it hurts,* he told himself, *then I've got a chance,* although he couldn't move his legs. The gutted bow of the Bertram, now a twisted mass of fiberglass and aluminum, was starting to burn. *I've got to get out of here,* he thought. Then he smelled it, and realized why he was shivering. The fragments from the rocket had punctured a five-gallon can of gasoline they carried lashed to the inside of the stern combing. He was soaked and the boat was settling by the bow, so the liquid was starting to run forward down the sloping deck.

"No!" he cried. "God, don't let me burn!" He tried to pull himself over the railing, but he slipped and fell back. Then he began to scratch furiously at the deck, trying to get to the fire extinguisher fastened to a stanchion on the port side. He was fighting with the clamp ring around the bottle when the fire leaped up a rivulet of gasoline and torched his pants. He beat his legs with his hands, but his sleeves were now on fire. Steffins's cries echoed across the water until they were silenced by a muffled *whump* as the fire found its way to the Bertram's main fuel tanks.

Salah watched the rocket explode in the cabin of the patrol craft. He quickly loaded another RPG-7 missile into the launcher and again stood ready. It was an older, Communist-bloc weapon but very effective, and he favored it over the American-made LAW rocket or the newer AT-4 that were abundantly available in the illegal-arms market. They broke out of the fog and saw the long, low shape of the *Michigan* seventy meters in front of them. Salah handed the launcher to Ahmed and tightened the straps that secured the scuba bottle to his back. He then cocked the Uzi that hung around his neck, and nodded for Ali to do the same. The three of them crouched behind the solid metal railing on the car deck, and watched the black shape draw closer.

Ross Peck saw the patrol boat explode as it passed abeam to starboard. He'd seen small craft blown apart by rockets before, and for an instant he was taken back twenty years to a time when death had stalked him on canals and brown rivers lined with mangrove and bamboo. Violence, and the smell of burning fiberglass, was so out of place in the tranquillity and beauty of the fog-shrouded Hood Canal, it seemed almost like a dream. *What am I doing helping these people? And where are the Marines that guard the base? Jesus, they're probably waiting for us.* A cold fear stabbed at his gut—an icy dread that was curiously familiar yet very out of place. It was the long-dormant fear of dying by friendly fire.

The Delta Pier was before them, with the magnificent black shape of the *Michigan* resting quietly alongside. She was berthed with her bow pointing toward the shore. He could now see another Trident tied on the far side of the Delta triangle. Wisps of fog blotted portions of the pier and the buildings behind the submarines. The contrast between this peaceful setting and the death of the patrol boat a moment before had frozen him for an instant—then he reacted.

The *Spokane* was still moving at twelve knots and eating the water between them and the *Michigan,* which was dead ahead and lying perpendicular to the advance of the ferry. He cut power to the after propeller and ordered full ahead on the forward one. The pilothouse started to rattle and buck as the big ferry surrendered momentum. *Too late,* he thought. *I'm going to have to turn and slide broadside or risk ramming her head-on.* Peck allowed the *Spokane,* now pushing a wall of foam into the calm water ahead of her, to close within thirty meters of the submarine. Then he put the forward rudder hard to port to bring the bow of the ferry left, and the aft rudder also to port, causing the stern to swing in the opposite direction, pivoting the boat. On the starboard side of the pilothouse, an M-60 opened fire, barking at the submarine and pier below.

Again for Peck, it was déjà vu. *I can't do this,* he said to himself as he looked for a way out. *The shore—I'll put her on the beach.* He started to put the helm over when a scuffle to his right commanded his attention. There was Jamil in the door of the pilothouse, twisting Janey's wrist behind her back with one hand and holding the muzzle of his automatic under her chin with the other—and looking right at him.

"You sonofabitch!" Peck screamed in frustration as he clutched the helm and called for emergency power to the forward propeller.

Maxwell heard muted machinery sounds coming from out in the fog-shrouded Canal, but it was cause for curiosity rather than alarm. Probably a fishing boat. Then he heard what sounded like a loudspeaker or a hailer, but it was too muffled for him to make out what was being said. He was walking across the missile deck to try to better see into the fog when he heard an explosion, and an instant later felt the shock wave.

"What the hell . . . ?" he said aloud. Then he saw the pilothouse and upper deck of the *Spokane* floating in on the layer of surface fog. Again, out loud, "Holy shit!" He ran across the forward end of the missile deck to the trailing edge of the sail and snatched the 1-MC microphone hanging from the communications box on the sail.

"CDO to the quarterdeck—CDO to the quarterdeck! On the double—CDO to the—"

The first several rounds skipped off the metal deck and into the back of his legs and buttocks. Maxwell didn't know what it was that was stinging his legs, but he had to hold on to the communications box to hold himself upright. He stared at the microphone in his hand, seeing it with some detail but no longer holding down the transmit button. "COB, I think I need some help, I—" The next burst found the middle of his back and shoved him up against the sail. Multiple rounds tore through his spine, causing his legs to buckle, and continued into his intestines and bowels. He slid down the sail to the deck, still clutching the microphone. The searing pain was so unbearable, he could not move or speak. Fortunately, the machine gun again raked the quarterdeck area, and a bullet glanced off the plating of the sail and into the side of his head, bringing darkness.

Master Chief Anderson sat with his feet propped on a desk in the chief's quarters, thumbing through the latest issue of *Byte* magazine. Like many aboard the *Michigan,* Anderson was a computer junkie. He immediately knew there must be a problem—no junior petty officer would summon the Chief of the Boat "on the double" unless something was wrong. The CPO quarters was three decks below the weather deck and forward of the sail. He raced back through the wardroom and crew's mess to the forward access trunk ladder that led up through the next two levels to the missile deck. Anderson was not in the best condition, but he was very nimble when it came to moving through a submarine. Twenty seconds later, his head and shoulders poked above the missile deck through the trunk opening. He heard the *pop-pop-pop* of the machine guns and saw Maxwell lying in a pool of blood. Anderson quickly looked around, seeing a pier sentry lying facedown and the *Spokane* rapidly bearing down on them. He had only to climb back down the ladder and he would be safe—but his boat was about to be rammed. Anderson jumped up onto the missile deck and scrambled for the communications box on the sail. Fenton's M-60 found him just as he reached the collision alarm. Anderson heard the initial peal of the siren as Fenton guided the tracers into him. He tried to turn and face his attackers, but had no strength.

"Motherfuckers!" he screamed to the steel plating of the sail as he collapsed on the deck next to Maxwell.

Peck brought the *Spokane* almost parallel to the submarine, with the pilothouse abeam of the *Michigan*'s sail. The ferry had nearly been brought to a halt when the two vessels met. The concave shape of the *Spokane*'s hull at the waterline virtually matched the cylindrical pressure hull of the submarine, bringing the car deck level and within about four feet of the flat missile deck. The jolt caused by the meeting of the two vessels was quite sharp on the *Spokane,* but aboard the submarine, which was five times as heavy and buttressed by the pier, the collision was scarcely felt. The ferry listed slightly to port as it rode up on the hull of the *Michigan* before settling alongside. The diving planes on the *Michigan*'s sail almost touched the side of the ferry just a few feet below the promenade deck. Peck held the ferry's starboard side against the sub, ordering both engines ahead one-third, pushing against each other with the rudders hard over to port. Jamil shoved Janey away from him and back into the pilothouse, and trained the pistol on Peck while he snatched the Motorola from his belt.

"Now, Ahmed! Get them over the side!"

Ahmed acknowledged and motioned to the two boarders. First Salah, then Ali scrambled over the car-deck rail and leaped to the missile deck of the *Michigan.* It was the first time a commissioned American man-of-war had been boarded since British seamen from the HMS *Leopard* boarded the USS *Chesapeake* in 1807—an incident that helped bring about the War of 1812. Salah dropped to one knee by the forward trunk while Ali sprinted the length of the missile deck to the aft main-access trunk. Two sailors emerged from the small hatch at the after part of the sail and were quickly cut down by Salah's Uzi. A third clambered up the ladder of the after trunk. When his head and shoulders were level with the deck, Ali shot him in the face, knocking him back into the shaft, where he plunged four decks to the keel of the submarine. When no more crewmen appeared, they quickly unslung their scuba bottles and placed them on the deck with the manifolds near the blower intakes. They cracked the valves, and the deadly cyanide gas was ingested by the blowers and drawn into the submarine. Then both ran to the rail of the *Spokane,* where Ahmed handed them mooring lines from the ferry. They began dragging the hawsers aboard the *Michigan* and securing them to the mooring cleats on the bow and the stern of the long black hull.

Above, Fenton and Hassan searched the pier for any sign of

movement. The clanging of the general-quarters alarm on the *Florida* competed with the wail of the *Michigan*'s collision alarm. Two marines, armed only with pistols, had started down the pier, but they were driven back and pinned down behind a dumpster. With no movement in sight, Fenton and Hassan began to pour fire into the glass enclosure that served as a control center atop the main building on the Delta Pier.

"Any station this net! Any station this net! This is Bangor Harbor Control, please come in, over!" Seaman William Cassady was a terrified eighteen-year-old sailor. His world had just exploded—literally. There was two inches of splintered glass on the floor of the control booth. Cassady huddled among the shards, cradling the handset and staring up at Master-at-Arms First Class Winston Collier, who was slumped above him in the watch captain's chair with his chin on his chest. Collier stared back vacantly, his hands hanging limply at his sides. The whole front of his blue dungaree shirt was dark with blood.

"Roger, Harbor Control," came a reassuring voice over the circuit, "this is Marine Rover One. Just take a breath and pass your traffic, over." Gunnery Sergeant Jennings drove with one hand and held the mobile unit's microphone with the other. The pickup was five miles from Delta Pier on the north side of the SWFPAC security area, and accelerating through sixty miles per hour in the direction of Delta Pier. Second Lieutenant Billie Calhoun of Valdosta, Georgia, sat beside him, white knuckles pressed against the dash as the truck careened around a bend in the road. Calhoun was a wide-eyed, skinny young man with angular features and acne. He had unusually large ears, like a taxicab with its back doors open.

This was not the first time Gunny Jennings had spoken on the radio to a scared young man under fire. The caller had said nothing about it, but somehow Jennings *knew* the boy was under fire. "It's okay, son," he said reassuringly. "Just squeeze the handset and tell me what's going on."

"We're under attack! There's a boat just came into the Delta Pier and they're machine-gunning everything. They've killed Collier! We need help bad!"

"Help is on the way, son, just stay calm," replied Jennings, bringing the pickup to seventy-five. "What's your name, son?"

"Seaman Cassady, sir!"

"Okay, Cassady, you're doing just fine. Now, tell me—what kind of a boat you got there, over?"

"A big white boat—I think it's a ferry, sir—uh, over."

"Okay, son, can you take another look to be sure, over?"

"No way, sir! They done killed Collier!" Jennings knew better than to press him.

"All right, good job, Cassady, you did fine. Just tell me, where was this boat when you saw it last?"

"It was comin' in on the north side of the Delta, right next to the *Michigan.*"

"Okay, just stay down, and we'll be there to help you in a minute. Break, Base Control, you copy?"

"Roger, Marine Rover One. What is your ETA at the Delta, over?"

"ETA zero three. Recommend that you call away the React Team to the Delta Pier and that you set Threat Condition Delta, over."

"Roger, Rover One. Report when you get to the scene. Break, all stations this net, all stations this net. Threat Condition Delta has been authorized by the base command duty officer. Repeat, Threat Condition Delta is now in effect."

Condition Delta placed the entire base on maximum alert and sealed it from the outside. All external gates were secured and duty personnel were placed on full alert. This condition also meant nuclear weapons were threatened and that the use of deadly force was authorized—the Marines and the base security personnel would now shoot to kill.

"What do y'all think's goin' on, Gunny?"

"Not sure, El-Tee," Jennings replied as he drew his issue Colt .45 from the holster and chambered a round, "but it sure as hell ain't another Greenpeace protest. You better get the scattergun unlimbered." Calhoun nodded as he took the Mossberg twelve-gauge from the vertical rack between them and pumped a shell into the chamber. Then he took another shell from the bandoleer hanging on the dash and shoved it up into the magazine.

Salah took cover at the base of the sail while the scuba bottle finished venting into the submarine. Ali, back on the stern, was more exposed, but he was able to crouch on the pressure hull of the *Michigan* behind the shrouding built up from the hull to form the missile deck. This was the most dangerous time for them—for all of them. It would take about five minutes for the tanks to empty themselves and another five minutes for the gas to find its way to all the compartments of the submarine. Since the *Michigan*'s reactor and auxiliary generators were shut down, they needed to stay alongside the Delta Pier long enough for the blowers on deck and the air-circulation equipment on board, all driven by shore power, to move the cyanide gas throughout the submarine. Meanwhile, the two M-60s poured a withering fire across the pier and into the buildings. The staccato bursts of fire competed with the plaintive wail of the *Michigan*'s collision alarm. Tracer rounds had started a small fire in one of the buildings, and a dark haze was drifting across the pier. A siren wailed in the distance, but no one had come down the pier to oppose them.

"Salah, Ali—that is enough—move!" Jamil shouted from the pilothouse wing. "Cut the lines and get back aboard!" Fenton and Hassan picked up the pace, shooting into the buildings and at access routes to the pier. Salah crabbed over to the scuba tank at the forward access trunk and, holding his breath, carefully picked it up and tossed it down the hatch. The escaping gas had caused a film of ice to form on the neck of the bottle. Back on the stern, Ali did the same. Then they took out their axes and began chopping away the nylon mooring lines that held the *Michigan* to the pier, Salah working from the bow aft and Ali from the stern forward. After all lines were cut, the two men ran back to the main access trunks. On the pier near each main access trunk, a davit fed a large black rubber-coated umbilical from an electrical distribution box on the pier, across to the submarine and into the trunk. Salah swung first, the blade of the ax biting cleanly into the cable. There was a loud snap, and a blue ball of flame encased the head of the ax. The force of the explosion singed Salah's eyebrows and knocked him back onto the deck. A sharp stench of burnt rubber and ozone hung in the air. He recovered the ax and jumped to his feet, ready to swing again, but the cable had parted. He smiled as he inspected the charred head of the ax, knowing now why Ahmed had insisted that they purchase axes with fiberglass handles. At the after access trunk, Ali chopped into the cable, but it came apart with no arcing. Both of them threw their axes over the side and ran to reboard the *Spokane*.

When the collision alarm sounded, Torpedoman Second Class Jesús DeRosales ran to his general-quarters station, which was the torpedo room, located under the leading edge of the sail, four decks below and just above the keel. He dogged the hatch behind him to seal the compartment and began to check the *Michigan*'s complement of Mark 48 torpedoes to make sure they were properly secured to their storage cradles. He still didn't know whether or not this was a drill, but he quickly donned the sound-powered phone headset and reported his space manned and secure. Normally, if it was a drill, they announced it before the alarm was sounded.

The control-room phone talker had taken his report, but now it seemed that there was nobody on the circuit. Stringing the phone cord behind him, DeRosales walked to the after end of the torpedo room and looked through the glass port into the number-one auxiliary machinery room. Machinist Mate First Kent Arnold, also wearing sound-powered phones, was slumped against one of the generator sets. His face was blue and he clutched his throat with both hands—clearly he was choking. Arnold dropped to the floor and DeRosales started to turn the wheel to open the hatch between them. Then he froze, only for a moment, and hurried back forward through the torpedo room, stripping away the headset as he ran. As he had done during countless drills, he quickly donned an EAB mask and snapped the quick-disconnect fitting of his air-hose pigtail into the torpedo-room manifold. He then spun open the manifold valve, allowing air from the emergency air-breathing system to flow into the mask. He breathed greedily, since he had been holding his breath ever since he saw Arnold collapse in the machinery room. After he was breathing normally, he unsnapped the pigtail from the manifold and again walked aft. He quickly undogged the door and entered the compartment, stepping over Arnold to plug into the EAB manifold in the machinery room. When he bent over the prone sailor, he found that his face was ashen-colored and his lips blue, and that he was quite dead. DeRosales rocked back on his heels and pressed against a metal cabinet for support as he crossed himself. *Mother of God, what is happening! Kent and I play on the softball team together. Just yesterday, we beat the* Ohio *Gold Crew for the base championship. He can't be dead!* He thought he was going to be sick, but choked it back, fearing he would foul his mask and chance the same fate as had befallen Arnold. *Relax,* he told himself, *breathe normally. The EAB system is self-contained and totally isolated from the normal atmosphere of the boat. What got Kent won't get me if I just stay cool.*

It took DeRosales several minutes to regain control—then his training took over. He returned to the torpedo room and recovered his sound-powered phone set. He then began to methodically switch through each circuit that should have been manned during in-port general quarters. He was beginning to think that he was the only one alive. Then the lights went out and the boat fell silent.

Jennings almost put the pickup into a drift as he turned off the road and headed down the causeway that led out onto the Delta Pier. He was on the opposite side of the Delta from the *Michigan,* and screened from the boat by the maintenance buildings in the center of the pier. They squealed around another corner, driving north along the eastern side of the Delta triangle. Jennings slid to a stop just short of two Marines who were pinned down behind the dumpster. He and Calhoun leaped from the cab of the pickup and took up a position behind a nearby CONNEX box.

"Jesus, Gunny, are we glad to see you!"

"Keep down and tell me what's goin' on," he called across

the thirty meters that separated the CONNEX box and the dumpster. Periodically, a burst of machine-gun fire would ring against one or the other of the metal boxes.

"They got at least two automatic weapons up there, Gunny, an' they're shootin' up the whole fuckin' pier!"

"Have they tried to come up the pier?"

"I don't think so, but every time I poke my head out they open fire!"

Jennings spun his fatigue cap around in the manner of a base-ball catcher. Then he put the side of his face level with the wooden pier planking and peered around the left corner of the box. After a long second, he jerked his head back.

"Well?"

"You ain't gonna believe this, El-Tee, but there's a ferry-boat alongside the *Michigan* and two guys running around the deck of the sub with broadaxes."

"Axes?"

"Yessir, like a couple of fuckin' lumberjacks. And here we are—four Marines with pistols an' a scattergun pinned down by two mounted machine guns." Jennings snatched another look around the side of the box. "More bad news, sir. Looks like they got some hostages tied up by the machine guns, and I think they're getting under way."

"Under way? You sure?!"

"There's a lotta diesel smoke comin' from the stack of that ferry."

"Gimme your forty-five, Gunny."

"Sir?"

"Ah said, gimme your forty-five."

"Lieutenant," pleaded Jennings, "please don't do some-thin' stupid!"

He slid the pistol over to Calhoun where the young officer was lying prone on the pier. The submarine and the ferry were at least seventy-five meters from their position. Calhoun checked the weapon and thumbed off the safety, holding it in his right hand as gripped his right wrist with his left hand. Then he half-rolled around the right corner of the CONNEX box and leveled the weapon. He saw one man jump from the submarine to the ferry and tumble over the car-deck rail out of sight. The second was right behind him, but he hesitated and lost his footing, catching himself with his elbows on the top of the rail. As he scrambled to get a purchase with his feet, Calhoun got a good sight picture, corrected high, and fired. The .45 slug tore a shallow arc across the pier and slammed into Ali's left shoulder blade. Calhoun rolled back just as a flurry of bullets dug into the corner of the CONNEX where his head had been.

"*Saeedny ya akhy!*"—Brother, help me!

Salah reached for him, but he missed as Ali lost his grip and dropped from the side of the ferry. He bounced off the pressure hull of the sub and rolled down between the two vessels. There was several feet of open water between them, as the *Spokane* had shifted both her rudders and was now straining against the mooring lines that bound her to the *Michigan* to pull the sub away from the pier. The cold water revived Ali, and he again began to call for help, clawing feebly at the rounded steel of the submarine. Salah started over the rail to help him, but was restrained by Ahmed.

"Don't risk it—Jamil needs you more than Ali!"

Salah gave him a murderous stare, but relented. Ali continued to whimper as he clung to the sub's hull, until Peck ordered all engines back full to drag the *Michigan* back out into the Canal. This caused the number-two end of the ferry, from which Peck conned the vessel, to work up against the side of the sub and grind him between the two hulls. Ahmed covered his ears to block out Ali's final screams. Salah checked the magazine in his weapon and recovered the rocket launcher as he ran for the stairs to the passenger deck.

"Faster, Captain! Add more power!"

"The engines are working at full output. It's just going to take a while to get it moving," replied Peck.

The ferry control station was designed for effective visibility across the bow of the ferry but not low on the water to either side, so all Peck could see was the top of the *Michigan's* sail and the pier beyond. The *Spokane* churned water and she strained against the side of the sub, but nothing happened. After what seemed like an eternity, there was movement. Very

slowly at first—a few feet, then a few meters—the big submarine began to slide down the pier and out into the Hood
Canal. The two brows slipped from the side of the submarine
and now hung vertically from the pier into the water. Fenton
and Hassan were still sporadically raking the pier and the sail of
the *Florida* to discourage any pursuit or return fire. When they
were well away from the Delta Pier, a second patrol boat came
into range from the south and the starboard M-60 began to pour
a stream of tracers into the cabin. Soon the craft began to idle in
circles, absorbing more rounds until it finally went dead in the
water.

"Here comes the Peacekeeper and the React Team, Gunny."
The Peacekeeper was an armored Dodge carryall with a ring
turret on the roof. The Quick Reaction Team, a squad of heavily
armed Marines, was inside. "Y'all think we should move out
an' take a position at the end of the pier?"

"Too late, sir," replied Jennings as he saw the open water
between the pier and the *Michigan*. "We could engage them,
but we'd have to kill those hostages to get to the machine guns.
And it wouldn't stop 'em." Jennings, First Lieutenant Calhoun, and the React Team Marines watched helplessly as the
ferry and her prize steamed slowly in a northerly direction.

"Where do we go from here?"

"Our job is to guard 'em while they're here—not go get 'em
back. We already screwed that up. I got an idea though, sir.
Let's get back to the truck." Calhoun and Jennings raced for
the pickup. They squealed around in a tight circle and tore back
down the causeway.

"Marine barracks, this is Marine Rover One, over."

"This is the Marine barracks. Hey, what's going on,
Gunny?"

"This is Rover One. Now, you listen up, Halasey. I want you
to get two helmets, two flak jackets, and the rifle I keep in my
locker, and be out front of the orderly room when I get there.
And bring all four boxes of ammunition on the top shelf of the
locker. Got that, Halasey?"

"Uh, roger that, but your locker has a padlock on it, over."

"Halasey, you shoot it off, you bite it off—I don't give a shit, but you have the gear and the rifle ready when I get there. You read me? Over."

"Loud an' clear, Gunny—Marine barracks, out."

"What are y'all gonna do, Gunnery Sergeant?"

"With your permission, sir, I'm gonna try to head them off at the pass. While I'm doing that, I think you better call the major and let him know why he's probably never going to make light colonel."

"Good idea, Gunny."

"One more thing, Lieutenant. Where did you learn to shoot like that?"

"I was captain of the pistol team at The Citadel—finished second at the NCAAs—so I ain't all that bad with a side arm." Jennings just shook his head and drove. Young second lieutenants! They never ceased to amaze him.

Sunday, 5:25 A.M.—Hood Canal Bridge

While the *Michigan* was being pirated from the submarine base at Bangor, Deputy Sheriff Cavenaugh was completing his run north up Highway 3 to the Hood Canal bridge. He turned left off the highway and immediately drove out onto the trestle that led down to the floating portion of the bridge. From this vantage point, he could look both directions on the Canal.

"Base, this is unit two seven, over."

"Go ahead, two seven."

"I'm on the Hood Canal bridge, and I can't see anything of a ferry. The bridge is open, and it looks like there's some traffic backed up down there. I'm checking it out now. This is two seven, clear."

Cavenaugh covered the half-mile to the center of the bridge in less than thirty seconds. There were fifteen or more vehicles waiting behind the lowered barrier gate. Red lights winked along the barrier arms and on the Bridge Closed signs. Cavenaugh had wheeled over into the opposing traffic lane to pass the line of waiting cars and pull up to the barricade. There were half a dozen men standing around the hood of the car that was first in line. He got out of the car, pushing the broad-brimmed, campaign-style hat squarely on his head as he stepped around to the front of his patrol car.

"Morning, gentlemen—what's going on here?"

"Got a problem with the bridge, Sheriff."

"We been here, some of us more'n an hour."

"Yeah, ever since that ferry went through."

"What's that about a ferry?" said Cavenaugh, turning his attention away from the "bulge" in front of them that held the retractable section of the bridge in the wet well of the divided highway.

"That's right, Sheriff. I got here about four o'clock an' they was jest openin' the bridge. We sat for musta been a half hour or so, an' then here comes this ferry, jesta haulin' ass. Didn't have no lights on it or nuthin.' Jest come rippin' on through the openin'."

"And after the ferry goes by," said the first man's companion, "this feller come down from the tower an' says that the bridge is stuck an' its gonna be an hour or so 'fore they get it fixed."

"Sheriff, I got a load of Sheetrock in the back in my truck," added another. "I got to be in Port Angeles for delivery by six-thirty."

"Okay, everybody keep calm. I'll go see what the problem is and let you know what's going on."

Cavenaugh ducked under the barricade and walked up to the single right-hand lane of the divided portion of the roadway toward the tower that was some fifty meters up from the barricade.

"It will begin now, Roberto. Are you ready?"

"*Señor,* it is maybe not so good to kill a policeman."

"Is there some other way?"

They had removed several of the window sections from the tower to create firing ports. Nabil snapped off a three-round burst that caught Cavenaugh full in the chest. Then he raked the group standing at the head of the line of cars with the remaining twenty-seven rounds in the magazine of his AK-47. The crashing sound of gunfire rumbled between the steep banks of the Hood Canal. As the echoes died away, they were replaced by the screams of wounded men and frightened calls for help.

"Roberto, I want you to disable as many of those vehicles as possible with the grenade launcher, especially the pickup trucks. Americans carry rifles in their pickups."

Nabil tossed aside the AK and took up the M-60. He rested the bipod on the windowsill and began firing into the vehicles, working them carefully to be sure that each one, for as far back as he could see, had a series of spiderwebs in their windshields. Halfway up the line of cars, a grossly overweight man made a run for it. Nabil smiled grimly as he gunned the man down from behind, tossing him forward on his face. He crumpled on the pavement at an odd angle, coughing blood from his nose and mouth. Between the deafening rapid-fire bursts, he would occasionally hear the *thonk . . . krump* of Roberto's grenades and the plaintive cries of wounded men from below. He could also hear the rattle of automatic-weapons fire from the across the bridge opening behind him. Muhammad and Haj had also gone to work. A pall of smoke from a burning vehicle began to stain the morning sky.

Between the tower and the line of cars, Deputy Sheriff Cavenaugh was fighting the searing pain in his chest and stomach and desperately trying not to pass out. He knew he was seriously wounded, perhaps fatally, but he had to hang on. His mind flashed to the FBI training film he had seen some months before. It was about the will to live after you had been shot— about how anger was his ally, and that he must summon and focus a personal rage against his attackers if he was to rally the will to live and to resist. He had rolled over on his back near the guardrail so he was partially shielded from the tower above. His hand fumbled at his belt, and he managed to unsnap the leather keeper of his portable radio. It took all of Cavenaugh's

mental reserves to suppress the pain and force his right hand to
drag the transceiver across his chest to his left cheek.

"This . . . this is Cavenaugh! Officer down, need help—
officer down, need help!"

"Roger, Bill! You are weak but readable—weak but readable. Understand you need assistance. Can you describe your
situation, over!"

"It's . . . Hood . . . Hood Canal B-bridge taken by gunmen—
heavily armed—automatic weapons! Need backup—ambulance . . . !"

Cavenaugh could not get his breath, and a spasm of pain
caused him to lose his grasp of the radio, which tumbled to his
side but out of reach. With superhuman effort, he fought to
retrieve his revolver from its holster. Raising his head off the
roadbed to see the tower, he grasped the weapon with both
hands and extended his arms in the direction of the machine-
gun fire. The deputy managed to get off three rounds, one of
which hit the side of the tower, before Nabil found him with the
M-60. He died instantly, but Nabil pounded his lifeless form
with several long bursts.

Sunday, 5:27 A.M.—Aboard the *Spokane* on the Hood Canal

The *Spokane* had backed the *Michigan* well away from the
Delta Pier into the Hood Canal. Then Peck applied his seaman-
ship and considerable skill to pivot the two boats, turning the
bow of the Trident boat north to head back up the Canal. The
big submarine was still between the ferry and the pier. Jamil
directed an elated Fenton, who was trying to show Hassan how
to do a "high five," to move the forward M-60 to the port side
of the pilothouse. Then he told Hassan to take the three hostages and Brad Johnson, who was still huddled with Janey in
the pilothouse, below to the passenger deck. The three human
shields were unharmed but showed strains of the ordeal. The

woman and the girl had been terrorized beyond tears, and clung to each other as they moved back across the deck. The gentleman fared better and carried himself erect, though he was visibly shaken.

Peck was in a daze. He was sure the Marines would have fired on them or stormed down the pier, killing himself and the others, if they had to in order to protect the submarine. And what about the crew on the sub? Like all Navy vessels, they had a small-arms locker. This Jamil was having it all his own way—taking the *Spokane,* the bridge standing open, now the submarine. *Christ, who's going to stop this guy!* Then an idea began to germinate. *Maybe it's up to me to stop him.*

"And now, Captain, now that we have done what you and many of your countrymen thought impossible, I want you to move us at maximum speed back through the bridge opening."

"If it's still open," replied Peck, trying to mask the empty, defeated feeling in his stomach.

"It will be open, Captain, or some good men will have died trying to hold it open."

As before, it seemed as if the big submarine would not move—then gradually it began to gather momentum. Jamil stood behind him, watching every move. After a while, Peck found that with full power behind the stern propeller and carrying ten degrees left rudder, he could move the *Michigan* along at a brisk six knots. Moments later, Ahmed joined them in the pilothouse.

"We lost Ali."

"What?"

"He was almost aboard when someone on the pier shot him. He fell and was crushed between the ferry and the submarine. He performed bravely and has earned a place of honor with God." *So will we all,* thought Ahmed as he watched his leader digest this new information. Jamil appeared pensive for a moment, looking down and tugging at his lower lip with his nonshooting hand. Then he took Ahmed by the arm and escorted him out to the pilothouse wing.

"Anyone else hurt?" asked Jamil. Already, he had mentally discarded Ali.

"Everyone is safe, and the hostages are all secure on the passenger deck."

"Excellent. Take Salah and Hassan to help you prepare the charges for the submarine. Will you have any problems getting back aboard while we are moving?"

"Salah doesn't think so."

"Then do it. And keep me constantly advised of your progress." Ahmed nodded and turned to leave, but Jamil held his arm. "We are going to do it, old friend. The whole world will know of this, and future generations of Palestinians will speak our names with reverence."

"I know, Jamil, but the Americans will do everything in their power to recover their submarine."

"That is why it is imperative that you get those charges in place. They will be much less bold when we are able to explode the missiles on our submarine. You will see."

Jamil embraced him roughly and sent him down the stairs. From his vantage on the wing of the pilothouse, he looked back at the fading structures on the submarine base. The sun had nearly banished the fog, and it promised to be a gorgeous day.

Sunday, 5:36 A.M.—Naval Submarine Base, Bangor, Washington

Jennings traded his lieutenant for Corporal Halasey at the Marine barracks, and headed for the main gate.

"Gunny, you sure this isn't some kind of a drill?"

"We got a bunch of dead sailors down at the Delta Pier. That sound like a drill to you, Corporal?"

"What do you think we're gonna find when we get there?"

"I'm not sure, but if they're going to take that submarine out of the Canal, they've got to get it through the bridge. If we can close the bridge or keep it closed, they can't leave."

"Can't the React Team be sent up, or at least a full squad?"

"We're not authorized to take action off base unless requested by proper civilian authority, and that takes time. Our job is base defense. The El-Tee stuck his neck out by letting the two of us go without the major's permission. Did you bring a weapon?'' Jennings waved as the sentry opened the gate to let them through. The base was now on maximum alert, and the Marines on the gates were in full battle dress.

"I got my M-16 and six magazines. Who are these guys, anyway?"

"Who knows? Maybe the same assholes who hit the Marine barracks in Beirut, or some of Saddam Hussein's thugs left over from the Gulf War. For terrorists, they're sure as hell organized, I'll give 'em that. I didn't think it was possible to take a sub like they did."

"Hey, Gunny, you're not going to get me shot, are you? I got less than two months left in the Corps."

"I always take care of my men, Corporal, but we're Marines and we'll both do our jobs like Marines."

Halasey swallowed and cinched down on the chin strap of his helmet while Jennings squealed onto the northbound on-ramp to Highway 3.

Sunday, 5:40 A.M.—Sand Point Naval Station, Seattle, Washington

Rear Admiral John MacIntyre hung up the phone and sat on the edge of the bed winding his wristwatch. He had just spoken with Captain Bonelli, the base commanding officer at Bangor. As commander of the naval base in Seattle, he was the senior naval officer in the region. There were various operational, administrative, and logistical components among the shore-based and afloat commands stationed in the Puget Sound area, but when something went wrong—really wrong—it was always placed at his feet.

MacIntyre's first flight instructor back in Pensacola had told him that the first thing you do when the fire warning light goes on in the cockpit of your aircraft is to wind your watch. Good advice for a young pilot, because taking a moment to wind your watch forces you to think before you act. Many years ago, he had been ready to punch out of his crippled F-4 over Haiphong. He didn't actually wind his watch, but he did stop and think. He was then able to nurse the crippled Phantom out over the Gulf of Tonkin, where he and his crewman parachuted into the water and were rescued.

"John, is something wrong?"

"Got a flap over at Bangor. Looks like it might be serious."

"But we've invited the Larsons over for dinner this evening."

"Yeah, I know—you'd better cancel it."

"Now John, I just can't *do* that. We've already put them off once—what'll they think?"

"I don't give a shit what they think, cancel it!"

The admiral walked into the bathroom, carrying the Extend-A-Phone. His thinning gray hair was tousled on top of his head like a newborn's. He punched in a number and held the phone cradled against his ear with one hand while he relieved himself with the other. The duty officer, who had just relayed the call from Bangor, answered after one ring.

"Okay, Lieutenant, listen up. First thing, I want you to send a flash message under my signature to all military installations in the region and order them to go to terrorist Threat Condition Charlie. Then I want an emergency recall of the entire staff. Next, alert the communications center and the watch supervisor there to stand by for a high volume of priority encrypted-message traffic—things are going to get real busy. Then, notify the duty officers at CINCPACFLT, COMSUBPAC, COMTHIRDFLT and the Thirteenth Coast Guard District, in that order, and tell them that I will want to speak with the commander or the senior available command representative by secure phone in ten minutes. Do you have that . . . okay, read it back to me." MacIntyre listened carefully and flushed the toilet. "Okay, Lieutenant, you have it correctly—now get to work and I'll see you in about eight minutes." MacIntyre quickly dressed and, as an afterthought, grabbed his shaving kit from the dresser on his way out.

"Sal, I'm sorry I was short with you, but this may be damned serious."

"I know—phone me from the office, okay?" she called after him, but he was gone.

So far, he had made no decisions, only reacted. By the time he slid behind the wheel of the car, he was beginning to reflect on what was happening. *How in the hell can someone steal a Trident submarine? There was absolute panic in Steve Bonelli's voice.* MacIntyre had met with Bonelli only twice since he'd taken over the CO's job at Bangor last month. Poor bastard—thirty days on the job and this happens. And *Michigan* had just been fitted with the new D-5 missiles. A burning fear began to churn in his stomach—the same fear he had felt when shrapnel from that North Vietnamese triple-A site had struck his aircraft over twenty years ago. MacIntyre pulled up to the flag entrance of his headquarters as a sailor rushed up to open his car door.

Sunday, 5:55 A.M.—Aboard the USS *Michigan* on the Hood Canal

"Do we have everything?"

Salah took a notebook from the pocket of his trousers. "It is all here—the tripods, the charges, detonators, elastic cords, electrical harness, and firing reel."

"Okay," replied Ahmed. "Let us get to work."

Salah and Ahmed assembled the first charge, erecting the tripod and lashing it to the center of the large circular steel watertight hatch that capped a six-foot-diameter missile tube. The attachment of the charge had been well planned, and the bungee cords stretched perfectly from the legs of the tripod to the pad-eyes on the hatch. Next, they secured the gallon paint can, which contained the shaped charge, to the locking ring at the top of the tripod. With the first charge securely in place on the forward-port missile tube, they moved to the second tube on the starboard side. The *Michigan* carried twenty-four tubes in two rows of twelve. Alternating sides, they placed charges on the first six pairs—three on the port side and three starboard. After placing the charges, Ahmed unrolled the electrical firing harness and tested the circuit with a galvanometer. He then carefully placed an electric blasting cap into each charge. This task was facilitated by the plastic filler caps mounted into the lids of the cans for injecting color when mixing paints. The blasting caps were connected to the harness in series, and the harness wire spliced to the leads from the firing reel. Ahmed again tested the circuit and shunted the posts on the side of the reel. He turned to Jamil, who was supervising the preparations from the wing of the pilothouse, and waved, taking the Motorola from his belt.

"The blasting caps are in place, and the circuit checks out."

"Very well, get the wire over here to me." Hassan waited on the starboard side of the promenade deck of the ferry, just above Ahmed and Salah on the missile deck of the submarine. He tossed them a coil of rope and carefully retrieved the firing reel as it paid out cord between the two vessels. Hassan loosely secured the cord on the life rail and moved forward, unreeling cord along the deck and up to the pilothouse. Jamil produced a small radio transmitter with "arm" and "fire" switches on the side. He removed the shunt from the side of the firing reel and connected the wires to the firing device. As a backup to the radio initiator, he wired a friction firing device, or "hell box," to the posts on the firing reel. Then he toggled the "arm" switch on the radio transmitter.

"It is done," he said aloud to no one. "One flick of my finger and the submarine is finished." He took out his transceiver and called to Ahmed. "Check again that the charges are secure, and come back to the ferry."

"Sayeh," said Hassan, who stood on the wing of the pilothouse, "those charges do not look big enough to severely damage such a large vessel. And they are positioned in the air above the deck. Will they truly sink the submarine?"

"Oh yes, my friend," he replied. "They are very special charges, and they will most certainly sink the vaunted Trident submarine."

The six shaped charges were the work of an artist—Marwan Kreeshat, a master Palestinian bomb-maker. He had carefully designed these charges to punch a three-inch hole through the four-inch steel missile hatches and send a three-thousand-degree jet of molten plasma into the center of the missile warhead. If this white-hot jet failed to detonate the high explosives in the warhead, whose function it was to implode the plutonium spheres of each MIRV warhead to initiate a nuclear blast, then this fiery lance was sure to ignite the rocket motor fuel. The *Michigan*'s missile silos would become Roman candles.

Sunday, 6:00 A.M.—Torpedo Room, USS *Michigan*

The darkness, strangely enough, wasn't so bad, but the silence was terrifying. Those aboard ship get used to the hum of machinery and the constant whirring of air-conditioning equipment. Plus, there are the muted sounds of humanity, like the music over the boat's entertainment system or an occasional whoosh of someone flushing a urinal. Now there was nothing, and the boat, ninety percent immersed in fifty-four-degree water, was becoming cold. The torpedo room was never too warm, since it was at the end of the heating and air-conditioning distribution loop.

DeRosales sat in this sensory vacuum and began to sweat, which made him even colder. He felt suspended in space, exposed and surrounded at the same time. He clutched at one of the torpedo racks to keep from falling, but he wasn't falling. *It's a drill,* he told himself, *relax and breathe normally*—although he knew it wasn't a drill. When he felt the boat moving, ever so slightly with an occasional gentle bump, it seemed to help. That in itself was cause for alarm, but it was some relief from the black silence. *Why are we under way?* he thought. *The collision alarm means just that—collision imminent. Maybe there is a fire on the Delta Pier, and a tug has come alongside and moved them away from it. That would account for the movement and the sudden loss of shore power, but what about Kent Arnold? What killed him? Has there been a fire on the* Michigan *that has generated the deadly gas?* DeRosales began to hyperventilate, and he felt his moist breath begin to collect on his skin while it fogged the faceplate of the EAB mask. *Calm down,* he told himself, *one step at a time. You can handle it—you're a submariner!*

He found a battle lantern on the bulkhead and flashed it around the compartment. The visual reference helped. He began to draw long, deep breaths, and the fog on his faceplate cleared. If they had been at sea and the boat's power failed, the emergency lighting would automatically have come on, but it wasn't activated in port. Every five minutes, DeRosales rotated the barrel switch on his sound-powered phone set to check the various circuits that should be manned during general quarters, but he could raise no one. His post was the torpedo room, but he had to find out what was happening. Battle lantern in hand, he prepared to leave his compartment.

He disconnected his air hose, quickly moved aft through the watertight door, and again entered the auxiliary machinery room. He went straight to the air manifold and quickly plugged himself in. During casualty drills when they were at sea, the crew had relay races around the boat wearing EAB masks with blackened faceplates, and DeRosales could find every manifold on the boat, even without a light. Arnold's body looked all the more ghostlike in the lantern's spotlight. DeRosales moved quickly past him and climbed the ladder that led up to the crew's mess. He had to undog the watertight hatch overhead, so he was out of breath by the time he got to the air manifold in the compartment. He panned the light around and found two of his shipmates. One slumped over the table, and another, who apparently died trying to escape, lay at the base of the stairs to the next level. Both were blue. Once more, he was almost overcome by nausea, and the acrid stench of vomit filled his nose. Again, he closed his eyes and concentrated on breathing slowly until it passed. As he gently pulled the sailor aside, he recognized Pearcy, a third-class petty officer who had been aboard for only a week. DeRosales quickly climbed to the next level, where he found two more dead in the missile control center. Another ladder took him up to the *Michigan*'s control room and four more dead shipmates. There was a scuttle in the ceiling of the control room that went through the pressure hull into the sail. The sail was not pressurized, and it free-flooded when the boat was submerged. The hatch was open, and he could see a glow of daylight coming from the door on the side of the sail. He took several deep breaths before he unplugged his EAB mask hose and scrambled up the ladder.

He poked his head through the door and felt the breeze on his face before he dared to take a breath. He saw the bodies of Maxwell and the COB, lying on the deck at the base of the sail. A cold fear stabbed him—*the air out here must be bad too!* Then he realized that something different killed them. They were both bloody, and they didn't have the blue look like the others. The door was on the starboard side of the sail, away from the *Spokane*. DeRosales could clearly see that they were under way as he recognized the eastern bank of the Hood Canal. He leaned out far enough to see the stern of the ferry against the port side of the *Michigan*.

"Somebody's killed my crew and is trying steal my boat!" he said in a soft voice. "But what the hell can I do about it?" Then he saw the ship-to-shore portable radio that the quarterdeck kept as a backup, resting just inside the door combing.

Sunday, 6:05 A.M.—Hood Canal Bridge

"Well, thank God, the Marines are here!"

"You there," said Jennings to one of the men gathered

around the cars and pickups lined up at the entrance trestle of the bridge. "What's going on?"

"Only two of you? Gonna take more than that to handle those guys."

"Just tell me what's happening," he replied sternly. A ricochet whined overhead, and they all crouched lower behind the vehicles.

"I got halfway down on the bridge before I saw what was happening. I been in 'Nam, and I seen it before. Somebody down there in that tower has got a machine gun and a mortar, and they're shooting up that line of traffic. Charlie used to do it on Highway One near Da Nang all the time. They'd shoot up the first vehicle and the last one, an' then they'd plink away at the ones in the middle. Only them poor bastards down there ain't soldiers, an' they can't fight back. I was lucky to be able to back up the road and get out of there." The speaker pointed to a big Chrysler that had two bullet holes in the windshield.

Jennings grabbed his binocular case and carefully made his way from girder to girder to the western end of the trestle where he could get a better view. He surveyed the scene through the Zeiss field glasses and found that the man with the wounded Chrysler was right. It was like an ambushed convoy in Vietnam—or Afghanistan or southern Iraq, for that matter. A county sheriff's car was parked at the head of the column near the barricade. Several vehicles were smoldering, and one that he could see was burning. The line of cars looked like a junkyard. And like Vietnam, there were frightened figures huddled under the vehicles, seeking cover. Whoever occupied those bridge towers meant to fight to keep the waterway open. The Zeiss glasses had mil posts for range estimations, and Jennings placed himself eight hundred yards from the nearest tower. The wind was out of the south, gently carrying the smoke away from the bridge, so it wouldn't be of much help—or a hindrance. One of the two red dome lights on the sheriff's car was still flashing. *It's going to be hard to cross that open stretch of bridge to the cover of cars down there,* thought Jennings, *and then it won't be easy to move along the line of cars to get close to the tower—unless I can cut the odds a little.* He worked his way back across the trestle to the others. They had been joined by another sheriff's car and two deputies.

"Sergeant, we got a call that one of our men is in trouble on the bridge. Is there any way we can get down there to assist him?"

"Not unless that cruiser of yours is armor plated."

"Do they really have a mortar?"

"Maybe a rocket launcher, but probably grenades. Deputy, you carrying anything besides side arms?"

"Nothing but a shotgun."

"Gas?" No response.

"Tear gas?"

"I forgot all about that! We carry a tear-gas pistol and a half-dozen cartridges.

"Great, I want you to put them in the back of my pickup."

"Whoa, hold on there, Sarge, this is a civilian matter."

Jennings firmly took the deputy by the elbow and eased him away from the crowd. "See that down there, sonny—that's a war zone. You ever been to war? Your police academy train you for this?"

"Well, no, but . . ."

"I don't got time for this shit. You got a man hurt down there, an' a state ferry towing one of my Trident submarines is headed for that bridge opening. What we gotta do ain't in your training manuals—it's in mine. Now, you gonna fuck around, or are you gonna give me an' the corporal a hand?" The deputy studied the Marine for a moment, then motioned to his companion.

"Fred, get the tear-gas pistol from the trunk of the car."

"And turn off those dome lights," added Jennings. "I don't want to attract any more attention for a while. Halasey, get my rifle case and ammunition!"

"What do you think they are doing up there?"

"Roberto, it is as I said when you asked that question five minutes ago. They are trying to figure a way to get across the open stretch of bridge so they can rescue the dead policeman and the others, but until they can get regular troops here with an

armored vehicle, I doubt they will try. We are safe for the time
being.''

"*Sí,* but I just hope that ferry shows up soon. We can't hold
out here forever.''

"You won't have to. I believe that is our ship coming now.''

Roberto followed Nabil's gaze to the south and saw the
hump of the ferry in the middle of the Canal. Alongside was
what appeared to be a black cross, formed by the submarine's
sail and diving planes. Bow-on, it looked very small, but Jamil
had said it was many times bigger than the ferry.

"*Bueno,* it won't be long now!''

"Perhaps fifteen or twenty minutes. Keep your attention on
the bridge. We must not falter now that victory is so near at
hand.''

"On the bridge, this is the *Katie B.* Hey, man, we gotta get
outta here! This place is gonna be crawling with cops!'' Nabil
took out his Motorola.

"Remain there, Epps—you will be amply rewarded for your
patience.''

"I'm tellin' you we can't stay here, and don't use my name
on the radio!''

"The others will be here soon. Stand at your station and
remain calm. Nabil out.''

Epps had called every ten minutes since they had opened
fire. He had taken refuge in the cabin of the *Katie B,* occasionally peaking through the curtains. He couldn't see much from
his position below the roadbed except black smoke, but he
could smell the burning rubber. He was becoming increasingly
desperate, but the chance for big money and his fear of Nabil
had kept him there. *If worse comes to worst and the cops do
come,* Epps told himself, *I'll say that they forced me to bring
them here.*

Nabil lit a cigarette before offering one to Roberto. *They
might try it,* he thought as he looked eastward to where the
highway dropped down from the trestle to the floating portion
of the bridge. *But that's well over six hundred meters of open
concrete they will have to negotiate before they can even get
near the cover of the cars.* He held the smoke in his lungs for a

long time before exhaling. Then he placed several short bursts into the line of cars to discourage any organized resistance from the survivors of their previous slaughter.

Gunny Jennings gave instructions to Corporal Halasey and the two deputies before again moving along the girders to the western end of the trestle. There was a wooden walkway on the side of the road, but Jennings moved from I beam to I beam, hoping the men in the tower didn't have binoculars. When he reached the final girder, he dropped to one knee behind it. *I'd like to get closer,* he thought, *but this looks like the best I can do.* With the glasses, he carefully studied the long ribbon of concrete that led down from the trestle and ran above the water to the line of cars and the tower. Smoke from the smoldering vehicles allowed him to gauge the wind but didn't obstruct his vision. It was too early for the effects of heat from the bridge to cause movement in the air over it. Jennings went to a prone position and shoved the stock of the Remington 700 tightly into his shoulder. He shot southpaw, so he tightened the sling around his right biceps. His right hand began to tingle from loss of blood, so he knew it was tight enough. The gunny pulled the bill of his fatigue cap low on his forehead and settled in behind the optic, a thick cigar-shaped 10X Leupold Utimax scope. As a member of the elite Marine scout-snipers in Vietnam, Jennings had killed NVA soldiers and VC at greater distances. Since then he'd stayed active in Marine Corps shooting contests, but he wasn't the marksman he'd once been. And it had been a long time since he'd put a reticle on a man.

He felt the wind lightly brush his cheek and estimated it at five mph. "Looks like four minutes of left windage ought to do it," Jennings said softly to himself as he turned the knob on the scope and counted the clicks. The scope was set for standard high-power rifle competition at one thousand yards so he dropped thirteen minutes with the elevation knob for an eight-hundred-yard shot. Through the scope he saw two men in the tower. One was armed with a machine gun and the other with a grenade launcher. He would rather have taken the gunner, but the grenadier, who was more exposed, was his best shot. Jennings settled the cross hairs on the man's chest and went into his breathing cycle. *Relax,* he told himself. *Watch the smoke— make sure it's moving smoothly and steadily—now breathe deeply, exhale, target center, squeeeeeeze . . . wait for the recoil.* As it should, it came as a surprise when the butt of the rifle dug into his left shoulder.

It took the 180-grain boat-tailed Sierra bullet 1.3 seconds to reach the tower. The round was high and just off center, but it tore into Roberto's left eye and ripped off the side of his head. Nabil was splattered with blood and brains as he quickly ducked below the window ledge. He moved to help Roberto, but drew back in morbid fascination. With a section of his skull gone, Roberto turned and ran straight into the west wall of the tower, smashing into the windows. Twice he bounced off the wall and charged it again as his flailing arms were slashed by the broken glass. The third time, he fell over a chair and thrashed around on the floor for almost ten seconds before he ceased to move. Nabil recoiled into the corner of the tower, wondering if the hideous thing that had been Roberto would jump up and come after him.

The Marine pickup with one of the deputies driving screeched to a halt on the trestle. Jennings vaulted into the back with Halasey as the truck tore down the hill from the trestle to the flat part of the floating bridge. Crouching behind the top of the cab, Jennings began cycling rounds through the bolt-action Remington, jerking the trigger when the windows of the tower danced through his scope. Halasey was firing a round every two or three seconds to make his magazine go the distance. The deputy, looking like a boy playing soldier in Jennings's steel pot, peered over the steering wheel from under the helmet and drove straight down the middle of the road.

A ricochet singing though the tower brought Nabil out of his stupor. There was an occasional slap on the side of the tower from the .223 bullets of Halasey's M-16 and the heavier *thunk* of larger .308 slugs. Then he heard the roar of the approaching truck. Nabil swung the barrel of the M-60 over the ledge and sprayed the bridge, but was forced back down as a round splintered the wooden window casing next to him. By the time Nabil managed to get a steady burst into the pickup, it was almost to the end of the line of cars.

"Everybody okay!" said Jennings. All three men were on the concrete by the side of the truck. The windows were now shot out, and a cloud of steam billowed from under the hood.

"Semper fi, Gunny!"

"How about you, Deputy?"

"Got some glass from the window in my face, but I'm fine. Scared shitless, though!"

"Ain't we all. Deputy, I want you to stay here with the truck. When we begin to move on the tower and start to draw fire, see if you can help some of these folks. There's a first-aid kit under the dash."

"Got it, Sarge," he replied, trying to hide his relief at not having to go forward with the other two. Jennings didn't ask for the helmet back, and the deputy didn't offer.

"Corporal, you remember your fire an' movement drills from basic training?" He spoke as he loaded the long .308 cartridges into the breech of the Remington and ran the bolt forward to chamber a round. He had already removed the scope.

"I think so, Gunny."

"You go when I say, and I go when you say. Stay on semiautomatic fire. Saves ammo and it's more accurate. Be careful of the civilians, and remember, you're a Marine."

Halasey took a deep breath and nodded.

"Ready—go!" Jennings rolled up by the left front fender of the pickup and snapped off a round that dug into one of the window supports of the tower, while Halasey quickly crabbed up to the next car.

Roberto was forgotten as Nabil responded to this new threat. There were only a few of them, but they seemed to be very skillful. He guessed they would try to work their way down the line of cars to get closer. Nabil knew he would have to hold them until the ferry arrived. Possibly, with covering fire from the machine guns mounted on the ferry, he would have a chance to try for the boat and escape. Then, from down on the water, an engine coughed and rumbled as the diesels aboard the *Katie B* roared to life.

"Epps, what are you doing?!" Nabil shouted into the transceiver.

"That's it! The cops are here an' I'm cuttin' out."

"You dung-livered coward! Wait for the others to get here. They will cover our escape!"

"I'm done takin' orders from you fuckin' A-rabs. I'm gettin' the hell outta here!"

Epps cast off and swung the *Katie B* north, heading away from the bridge at full throttle. Nabil ignored the bullets that were snapping through the windows and concentrated on the figure at the wheel of the receding craft. The rounds from the M-60 walked up the teak deck until they found him. Epps pitched forward over the control console as the bullets perforated his heart and lungs. The *Katie B* proceeded up the Canal, faithfully carrying out her skipper's last command.

Nabil swung the machine gun around and raked the line of cars, then dropped to one knee to place a new belt in the feed tray. He guessed there were at least two of them, and they were halfway up the line of cars.

"So be it. I will be honored by God as one who fought to the death and took many infidels with him." His hand was shaking as he closed the top cover of the M-60 and went back to the deadly game of cat and mouse with the two men below.

They were still a half-mile away, and Jamil could clearly hear the firefight on the bridge. An angry smudge hung over a line of cars on the eastern section of the bridge as several continued to smolder. There were only half as many eastbound vehicles on the western section of the bridge, and none was burning.

"Station two, this is station one, over." No response.

"Station two, this is station one. Come in, Nabil."

"This is Nabil. The bridge cannot be closed—the way is open, but the soldiers are close!"

"Get to the boat—escape!" There was a sharp exchange of gunfire, and a moment passed before Nabil spoke again.

"The boat is gone and there is no time."

"Can you jump? We will pull you from the water."

"It is no good. I will fight them from here. *Alwedaa,* Jamil!" Jamil continued to call, but there was no answer.

Peck was herding the *Michigan* up the Canal rather than towing it. Once he had the massive steel tube moving, it was a matter of sustaining that momentum. At first, he found it an unwieldy task, and he overcorrected with the rudder, causing their wake to resemble a long flat S. He carried ten degrees left rudder to account for the *Spokane* being alongside its tow. Soon he found that if he added seven degrees additional left rudder or eased right the same amount and held it, after a minute or two the head of the submarine would start to move. Then it was a delicate matter of judiciously applying rudder in the opposite direction to stop the turn. It was much like what Peck had been told about piloting a supertanker, and he was quite sure it would take a half-mile or more for him to bring the *Michigan* to a stop. For the last ten minutes, he had been carefully aligning the two vessels to pass through the bridge opening. He knew that if he got too far off center, he couldn't turn in time and he couldn't stop.

Maybe that's the answer, thought Peck. *I'll take us into the bridge! The combined mass of the two vessels will probably part the cables holding the floating sections in place, but it also might damage the* Spokane *so they can't continue.* As they got closer, Peck could clearly see the cars on either section of the bridge, so he knew that a collision would certainly cause injuries—perhaps loss of life. *Loss of life! There are those men on the patrol boats and the sailors on the submarine. And how many aboard are still alive, if any? They must all be dead or the terrorists would have stationed a guard on the deck of the sub. How many men in a duty section—thirty . . . forty? My God, what have I done? If I'd held my ground from the beginning and refused to cooperate, those men might still be alive. Was I right to trade the lives of all those sailors for my life and the lives of*

*those aboard my vessel? My orders are to cooperate. Well, I've
cooperated with the bastards, and look where we are!*

Peck's mind raced as he jockeyed the two vessels to pass
through the bridge gap. *Maybe I could just clip the western side
of the opening with the port side of the* Spokane, *and possibly
foul one or both of her propellers in the cables. But then, there
are the charges Jamil set on the* Michigan. He couldn't see
them from his place at the helm, but he didn't doubt they were
there.

There was also another factor in the equation—that subtle
force that compelled all masters and captains to protect their
vessel and those aboard her. Peck recognized this, but he knew
he'd have to try to stop these men. *I have to play the game from
this point forward—no looking back—and wait for an opportunity.* The mounting anger and frustration were almost choking
him as he positioned the *Spokane* and the *Michigan* to shoot the
gap in the floating bridge.

Jennings was pressed against the side of the sheriff's patrol car;
Halasey had taken cover under a pickup truck alongside. There
was fifty meters of open roadway grating between them and the
tower.

"How much ammo you got left, Corporal?"

" 'Bout a magazine and a half, plus fourteen rounds for my
.45."

"On my signal, give me four or five rounds of covering fire,
okay?" Halasey was hanging in there, Jennings thought with a
brief rush of pride.

"Now!" As Halasey fired, Jennings popped over the trunk
of the cruiser with the tear-gas pistol. After the *tonk,* he
watched the canister bounce off the tower just under the windows before he ducked back behind the car to avoid the splatter
of bullets.

"Again, Halasey. Now!"

This time the projectile flew through the window, hitting the
corner of the room and bouncing onto the floor. Nabil first
thought of trying to kick the smoking canister down the stairs,
but already the gas was overpowering, searing his nose and

eyes. He fired a quick burst over the ledge and, grabbing an extra belt of ammunition, scrambled down the stairs. The machinery room at the base of the tower had no windows and a single door that opened out onto the roadway. Ben Marcum stared cloudy-eyed at him from the concrete floor. Nabil burst through the door and ran for the protective western side of the tower building. He almost made it, but Corporal Halasey, sighting on the windows above, was able to adjust his aim and crank off several rounds before Nabil could duck behind the tower. He turned the corner, but both Halasey and Jennings knew he was hit.

"Good shooting, Marine! I think we can take him now!" But before the two Marines could make a move across the grating to the tower, they were taken under fire by the two machine guns on the *Spokane*. There was nothing they could do but crawl under the vehicles and wait.

Peck again hit the opening dead center with the *Spokane*, allowing for a hundred feet of clearance from the starboard side of the *Michigan* to the eastern end of the floating bridge. While Fenton and Hassan poured fire into the line of cars, Jamil's attention was riveted on the lone figure sitting on the concrete with his back to the tower, legs apart and straight out in front on him. He was sitting in a pool of blood. He seemed to recognize Jamil, and struggled to his feet. As the ferry entered the opening, their eyes met and he raised his fist.

"Allahu Ahkbar!"

Jamil weakly raised his arm to return the gesture, but he couldn't speak. Then the man turned and began walking down the grating toward the line of cars, firing the M-60 from the hip.

"No! Nabil, no!!"

Jamil could only watch. The covering fire from the ferry allowed him to get thirty meters up the grating before the small-caliber rounds began picking at his sweater. He managed to shake them off until a larger, well-aimed round punched through his sternum to his heart and crashed on through his spine, knocking him to the pavement.

• • •

Jamil stood at the rail long after they had passed the bridge opening. Fenton was making a show of spraying down his M-60 with WD-40 lubricant and replaying the action with Hassan, who listened and nodded. The deck around the pilothouse was littered with spent brass shell casings and treacherous underfoot.

"Well, we cheated death again," the American said as he swaggered up to Jamil. "Who was that crazy dude down on the bridge—I mean, what kinda dope was he on, walking right out there in the open like that?" Jamil turned and swiftly snatched Fenton by the front of his shirt, grasping both fabric and skin.

"You retched lump of camel shit! That was my brother—my younger brother! And he was 'on' nothing but a crusade for his people and his homeland! He was a patriot—something about which you know nothing. You will not desecrate his memory by ever speaking about this again, do you understand?" Fenton, held in a viselike grip, looked up into the face of death. He couldn't summon the courage to speak, so he bobbed his head. "Now get below and out of my sight!"

Jamil released him, and Fenton fled toward the stairs forward of the pilothouse. In his haste he slipped and fell among the empty shells. He quickly regained his footing and hurried below. Jamil desperately wanted to kill him, but with Ali, Nabil, and the others at the bridge gone, he would need every gun.

"Captain," said Jamil as he climbed the steps to the pilothouse, "make the best course for the Strait of Juan de Fuca. And remember, I still need you—but not as much as I did earlier today." Then, turning to Hassan, "You fought well today. Now guard them closely—I have business on the lower decks."

On the eastern end of the floating bridge, Jennings sat with Halasey's head on his lap, wiping his face with his handkerchief.

"I do okay, Gunny?" he asked weakly.

"You did fine, Marine. You did just fine." Jennings looked up and saw ambulances and police cars streaming down onto the bridge. Several men, some with blood-soaked clothing, began emerging from the line of cars.

"Been thinkin' 'bout what you said, Gunny," he whispered, " 'bout signin' up for another hitch. I dunno . . . I just dunno . . ."

"Stay with me, Halasey! Goddammit, Corporal, that's an order! You stay with me!" But he was gone, and Jennings knew it. His eyes lost focus and started to dilate.

The young Marine had crawled forward for a better shot at the madman from the tower who staggered toward them with a machine gun. As the ferry cleared the bridge opening, one of the mounted M-60s had found the angle on Halasey and shredded his whole right side. Jennings gathered him in his arms and held him while tears flowed down his black cheeks into Halasey's matted red hair. *I'm a soft old woman,* he thought. *I never cried when a Marine died in Vietnam, and plenty of 'em did—why now?* He held him tightly and rocked him back and forth, oblivious to the mounting activity around him.

"Can I help you with him, Sergeant?" said the man who appeared at his elbow.

"No, thanks, Deputy. I brought the corporal down here with me, and I'll take him back."

Jennings gently placed Halasey in the bed of his pickup and covered him with a blanket. Two ambulances loaded with wounded civilians had just left, and a medevac helo was turning on the shore near the trestle. An ambulance had been dispatched from the Navy hospital near Bremerton for his corporal, but it would be a while before it arrived. Jennings sat on the tailgate and waited, with his hand on Halasey's boot. *Next time one of the NCOs at the barracks starts talking about the old days and bad-mouthing the younger Marines,* he swore, *I'm gonna knock his dick in the dirt.*

"Hello . . . hello, is anybody there? This is Petty Officer DeRosales on the USS *Michigan.* Is anyone there . . . hello, come in, over?"

It took only a second for Jennings to understand what he was hearing. He jumped around to the cab of the pickup and snatched the microphone from the dash.

"This is Bangor mobile one! I hear you fine, Petty Officer DeRosales. Can you advise me of your situation, over?"

"Oh, thank God—thank God! I didn't think anyone was going to answer. Something terrible has happened on board, and everyone is dead! I think it's something in the air, but I managed to get to an emergency air mask. There's been a lot of shooting, and I know this sounds crazy, but the boat is being towed up the Hood Canal by a ferry. You got that, over?"

"I got it, and you're not crazy—the men on the ferry are hijacking the *Michigan.* Now listen close—where are you, and do the men on the ferry know you're still alive, over?"

"I don't think so. I'm inside the sail. There's a breeze through the door, and I don't have to wear the mask up here. I've got to get off of here before they find me, over."

"DeRosales, what's your first name, over?"

"It's Jesús. Jesús DeRosales."

"Okay, Jesús, this is Gunnery Sergeant Jennings—just call me Gunny. Are you sure you're the only one alive? The *Michigan*'s a big sub, over."

"I'm pretty sure, at least not in the forward part of the boat. I haven't been back in the engineering spaces or the missile compartment, over."

"This is a tough one, Jesús, but can you find out, over?"

"Well, yes, I can, but if these people find me I'm sure they'll kill me, over!"

"Look, Jesús, I'm going to give it to you straight. Terrorists have taken over the ferry, and now they have your boat. They've probably killed all your shipmates, but we have to be sure. Now, we need you, and we need your radio to keep track of what they're doing. We need you to report back to us, can you do that—it's very important, over?"

"I guess so. Gunny, I'm scared. Those bastards killed my shipmates and I'm afraid they might come for me."

"I know you're scared, Jesús, but you gotta hang in there. I want you to sneak around the sub and see if any of your shipmates are still alive. Be careful and use the emergency air. Then I want you to stay hidden until we contact you. Now, what time do you have, over?"

"Seven o'clock, over."

"Seven o'clock it is," said Jennings, setting his watch. "Here is our communications plan—I'll call you back in exactly one hour, but if I don't call or it isn't safe for you to talk, I'll call the following hour. Do you understand, Jesús?"

"An hour—that long?"

"That's right. I have to do a lot of work on this end if we're going to rescue you, okay?"

"Okay, Gunny, but don't forget me."

"No way, Jesús. Listen up on the hour, and I'll be back to you. Good luck. Jennings out."

Another scared kid on the radio, thought Jennings as he got out of the cab, *and this one's got a real reason to be scared. I hope he can hold on—he's the only thing we got going for us right now.* The ambulance arrived and pulled up behind the pickup.

"What the hell is going on?" said one of the two corpsmen who got out. "First Bangor and now this—are we at war or what?"

"Something like that," Jennings replied. He gathered the blanketed form from the bed of the pickup and carefully placed his corporal in the back of the ambulance. A few minutes later, when the ambulance was speeding south on Highway 3 to Bremerton, Jennings told the corpsman driving to stop at Bangor.

"Can't do that, Sarge. My orders are to get that stiff back to the hospital."

Jennings reached forward and grabbed the sailor by the front of his white jumper and nearly separated him from the steering wheel. "Now you listen to me, you fuckin' squid. That Marine you're driving has a name—it's Corporal John Halasey. Now, you can drive me to the Bangor security office, or I'll drive myself and the two of you can walk. You got that?"

"Uh, whatever you say, Sarge."

"And you don't call me Sarge—I'm Gunnery Sergeant Jennings to you."

Sunday, 7:10 A.M.—Sand Point Naval Station, Seattle, Washington

John MacIntyre laid his half-moon reading glasses on the desk and rubbed his eyes. His life had depended on his eyes for so many years. They had served him well as a pilot, but had deteriorated very quickly during the last few years. It wasn't quite so bad at a distance, but he was now unable to read without the "cheaters," as he called them. *If I wasn't so vain,* he admitted, *I'd get bifocals and be done with it.*

MacIntyre had been on the STU III secure telephone and had briefed the duty officers at the headquarters of Commander, Third Fleet in San Diego, and Commander, Submarine Force Pacific in Pearl Harbor. He knew both commanders were probably en route to their offices right now. He had been able to speak directly to his boss, Admiral Hugh Calloway, Commander in Chief, Pacific Fleet, also in Pearl Harbor. Calloway had stoically received his report, then directed him to send a flash message, "eyes only, special handling," to the Chairman of the Joint Chiefs of Staff. It would be a JCS-directed show from this point—he would coordinate, report, and recommend, but he would make no real decisions. Both MacIntyre and Calloway knew this kind of incident could be a political/military/ bureaucratic nightmare in its resolution, and both knew there would be a lot of finger pointing when it was over. It would probably bring about Calloway's retirement, and certainly his own. *Sally wanted that second star—hell, so did I.*

MacIntyre permitted himself a wry smile. *I flew three years in combat and logged over eight thousand hours in fighter and attack jets—parachuted twice from crippled aircraft. Half of my classmates from the Naval Academy who took jets out of Pensacola are dead. And I get taken out of the saddle by a lunatic on a ferry who steals a submarine.*

"Excuse me, Admiral, I have Captain Bonelli on the secure line," called the yeoman from the doorway of his office.

Bonelli had called every fifteen minutes from Bangor, per

his instructions. MacIntyre sensed that he was starting to come apart. There had been a lot of bloodshed, some of which Bonelli would have to answer for regarding base-security precautions. Not really his fault, since he had only just taken command, but the Navy probably wouldn't see it that way. MacIntyre respected submariners, but he didn't particularly like them as a group. He felt they were technicians and engineers more than warriors. *But it takes a special kind of man—a very brave one,* he admitted, *to go to sea in those ballistic-missile submarines. They spend their whole lives training for one thing—to launch their missiles. They volunteer for this duty knowing full well that if they ever* do *launch those missiles, the world as they know it—family, home, and friends—will have ceased to exist, vaporized in a nuclear firestorm.*

"Thank you, Rita," he replied as he picked up the phone. The yeoman left, and the admiral waited for the series of clicks and a chirp as the secure link made its connection. "MacIntyre here."

"Hello, Admiral. I have the casualty figures and preliminary damage assessment for you." Bonelli spoke for a moment, and MacIntyre made notes on a legal pad. The distortion caused by the encryption did not entirely hide the stress in his voice.

"How about the *Michigan*?"

"She's past the Hood Canal bridge and off Hood Head. I just learned that the entire duty section aboard has been killed by some lethal gas. But we do have one sailor aboard who is alive—he reported in by radio about fifteen minutes ago, and has been able to hide himself from the terrorists."

Christ, thought MacIntyre, *you should have reported that immediately!* He suppressed the urge to reprimand him; it would serve no purpose.

"Are we in contact with this man now?"

"Not now, sir, but he was told to listen for radio contact on the hour."

"The maintenance of that communications link is your number-one priority, understand?! Stay in touch with that sailor! Anything else?"

"Yes, sir. One of the terrorists who was holding the bridge

has surrendered. The Jefferson County sheriff has him in custody, and they're taking him to the jail in Port Angeles. The other three are dead.''

MacIntyre asked several more questions before hanging up. While waiting for his call to go through to Admiral Calloway, he again wound his watch.

PART THREE

STORM WARNINGS

Sunday, June 21, 1992, 8:02 A.M.—Alexandria, Virginia

Frank Sclafani drove the family home from the early service, and he had just eased his large frame onto the recliner. His wife followed him into the family room with two mugs of coffee and handed him one. It was the way he liked it, very strong and well fortified with cream and sugar.

"Thanks, hon," he said as he loosened his tie. When he was home, he and his wife made a ritual of watching *Sunday Morning* with Charles Kuralt. It was a sensible TV program, to Frank and Carla Sclafani's way of thinking. Their daughter understood this and had retired to her room and her own TV.

"Anything special you want to do today?" Carla asked. It was his first weekend home in more than a month.

"Not really. Thought I'd take the dog out for some work, and then I probably ought to get after the grass. You want to drive down to Annapolis for some clams later on—maybe after Ellie gets out of the pool?"

"Perhaps, or we could just stay home and barbecue."

"That sounds even better. You want me to burn beef or a bird?"

"I don't know. Let me think on that one."

Sunday, 7:01 A.M.—Coronado, California

Brian Horner sat on the floor of the apartment with his legs at a forty-five-degree angle, straight out and flat on the carpet. He grasped his left foot with both hands and pulled his muscular frame forward so his chin rested on his left knee. He remained that way for a full minute and changed to the right leg. Horner was close to six three and weighed exactly two hundred and five pounds. He was wearing a ''Bay to Breakers'' running shirt and black spandex biking shorts.

''You going for a ride?'' Pam Horner was tall and tan, with a lean, athletic build and sun-bleached hair. Around the apartment complex they were known as ''Ken and Barbie.''

''Why not? The race doesn't start until three this afternoon.''

''You're not going far, are you?'' They were entered in a Jack & Jill 10K run through Balboa Park. The male-female teams placed according to their combined times.

''Just down to Imperial Beach and back—fifty minutes tops. Relax, I've been to hack-it school.'' He had chiseled features and striking blue eyes, and a perpetual crooked grin that saved him from being pretty.

''Okay, but I need you to go to the store when you get back.''

''No sweat,'' Horner replied as he pulled on leather gloves, the kind with no fingers worn by bums and bikers. He snapped the chin strap of his helmet and wheeled the bike out of the spare bedroom. ''See you later,'' he called as he headed out the door, but she was busy in the kitchen with the espresso machine.

Sunday, 10:15 A.M.—Atlantic Ocean off Martha's Vineyard

''Give us a little room here, boys, we've hooked into a real whopper.'' A handsome man in his mid-sixties braced himself against the roll of the boat. When the call "fish on" rang out, the skipper immediately cut his engines and the forty-five-foot cruiser wallowed aimlessly in the trough. "He may not be a trophy winner, but he does have some spunk." The fisherman tried to sound casual, but there was a measure of excitement in his voice. His fish caught a glimpse of the boat and made another run, bending the rod sharply and causing the reel to shriek as it peeled out line. It was a strong run, but it was his last. *I wonder,* mused the fisherman, *why a fish, once hooked, is always referred to as a "he."* As soon as the fish was netted and brought aboard, the skipper brought the boat into the waves, allowing those clustered on the stern to move about more easily. It was a soft, cloudless New England summer day with a gentle three-foot swell rolling in from the southeast. The tall angler now leaned casually against the transom, holding his rod in one hand and displaying a fourteen-pound bluefish with the other. He'd rather have been back in Missouri fishing for smallmouth bass, but this wasn't all that bad.

"Nicely done, Mr. President."

"Wait'll Tom Foley sees this!"

"He's a real beauty!"

Much had been made in the press about the President's inability to catch fish on his summer holiday, and the Speaker of the House, himself an avid fisherman, had just last week made a particularly biting remark that was quoted in *The Washington Post.* Both the President and the fish endured while the cameras clicked and whirred.

"I guess the White House press corps is going to have to shift their coverage to problems I've been having with my backhand." The cameras stopped, and an aide appeared to collect the fish and hand the President a towel. While President Bennett was wiping his hands, he noticed Buck Williams had just emerged from the cabin wearing a very grim expression. Williams, in a Marine Dress Blue Delta uniform—blue trousers with a red stripe, short-sleeved khaki shirt and white combination cap—was in sharp contrast to the casual dress of the others aboard. Aside from the marksmanship medals, he wore only a single row of ribbons, but they consisted of the Navy

Cross, two Silver Stars, and three Purple Hearts. The silver eagles of a full colonel nested on the points of his collar. He quickly made his way through the entourage to the President's side.

"What's going on, Buck?" Williams had a message in hand, but knew the President liked a short verbal brief when something came up.

"Sir, we have a situation—a serious one."

"Okay." The President turned to the entourage crowded on the stern sheets of the cruiser. Some had sensed that something was not right, but most were still talking about the fish. "Could you all please excuse me for a moment." A measure of gravity swept through the group, and they melted into the cabin or up onto the flying bridge. "Let's have it, Buck."

"There has been a terrorist incident on the West Coast— near Seattle at the Naval Submarine Base at Bangor, Washington. It seems that a group of terrorists has taken control of a Washington State ferry and is holding the passengers hostage on Puget Sound. Furthermore, Mr. President, they've managed to capture a Trident submarine from the base at Bangor and are towing it into the Strait of Juan de Fuca." The President stared at him for a few seconds before he spoke.

"Give me that again, Buck."

Williams repeated himself and placed the slip of paper in Bennett's outstretched hand. The President seated himself on the transom rail and read the message. Thanks to cellular-phone coverage and encrypted-fax technology, it was a clear and concise synopsis of what had taken place. The JCS crisis-management center had passed along the full, unedited text of Admiral John MacIntyre's report.

"I need a map," the President said without looking up. Williams held out a sheet he had torn from a Coast Guard chart table index. It was a crude line drawing of Puget Sound and the Strait of Juan de Fuca, but the only chart available. The President acknowledged it with a "humph" and began to study the chart, periodically glancing at the message.

"No contact from the terrorists or list of demands?"

"No, sir." The President continued to study the chart and reread the fax.

"As I understand it, these people and our submarine are about here." Williams stepped to Bennett's side as the older man pointed to where the Hood Canal joined Admiralty Inlet.

"That is correct, Mr. President."

Bennett handed the chart to Williams but kept the message. He stood abruptly and turned his back to Williams, gazing out across the Atlantic. There was no other craft in sight except for a white Coast Guard patrol boat that always escorted the President when he fished these waters. He remained there for some time while the Marine waited at attention.

"Contact Mr. Keeney and tell him I want increased security at all military bases and federal buildings. Have him make all preparations to give us the broadest range of options for negotiations as well as military action, but tell him to take no action that would endanger the hostages. I want a report on the armament aboard that submarine as soon as possible. Also, direct him to have Secretary of State Noffsinger fully brief Prime Minister Mulroney on the situation and ask the Prime Minister if he would please hold this information closely until we learn more about the situation. Have him assemble a working group from the National Security Council to convene immediately on my return to Washington to discuss damage assessment and to entertain alternative courses of action. I want the meeting expanded to include those agencies and the armed forces reps required to fully explore our options." The President hesitated, as if there were something he had forgotten, then grimly shook his head. "That's all, Colonel," he said, turning back to Williams. "Take charge and get me back to the capital as soon as possible."

"Aye, aye, sir." Williams saluted and strode purposefully back into the cabin. Within seconds, the two Caterpillar diesels exploded to full rpm, and the President had to hold on as the craft swung smartly to an easterly heading. He remained seated on the transom, alone and lost in thought, until Williams returned.

"Your instructions have been sent and receipt acknowledged, Mr. President,'' Williams said. He handed Bennett a copy of the fax transmission. "The helicopter will be turning on the dock and *Air Force One* is standing by and ready at Providence Airport. Your ETA at Andrews is 2:00 P.M., sir."

"Very well, Buck, stand at ease." Williams went to parade rest, but relaxed only slightly. The President remained seated and read the outgoing fax copy while he tugged thoughtfully at the loose skin under his chin, a habit his wife always admonished him about. Then he looked up at Williams. "What do you think happened out there, Buck?" he asked in a quiet, confidential voice. "How in the hell could a bunch of damn ragheads put their hands on one of our Trident missile subs?" The President's tone was familiar and invited a candid response. The last time he had spoken to Williams like this was last year when he told Williams that his son, a Marine lance corporal, had been one of the few Americans killed in the Gulf War. The sincere compassion of the President and Mrs. Bennett had been overwhelming. Williams's loyalty to this president ran far deeper than required by his official role as military aide to the Commander in Chief.

"I honestly don't know, sir. I'm sure some good men died trying to stop them. I think it's safe to say we're dealing with a highly organized and motivated group—and probably well led."

"Any thought as to who might be behind it?" It was not an idle question. Williams had several years' experience in the Middle East and had written a respected thesis on terrorism at the Naval War College. He was not in Beirut when the Marine barracks there was bombed, but all Marines shared the bitterness of that attack. Williams thought carefully before he answered.

"No, sir. Ahmed Jibril is capable of this, but we've been keeping pretty close watch on him. The Abu Abbas faction would certainly try it if they had the backing. Abbas Musawi is probably the most capable terrorist in the Middle East now, but neither he nor Abbas could do this without a state sponsor. State sponsorship, if it exists, is hard to prove, so I doubt we'll be able to track this terrorist through his sponsor."

"Qaddafi?"

"I doubt it, sir. This was a complex operation. He talks a big game, but he's never been good for much more than military posturing or a nightclub bombing. The air strike on Tripoli scared him pretty badly, and this kind of an action invites retaliation. It would seem that Syria has the most to gain, because if Palestinians are involved, it could threaten the peace talks. Tehran hosted that big terrorist conference last October. Maybe the Iranians know something." The President handed the fax back to Williams and began to slowly pace the deck. Dressed in a burgundy cardigan sweater, tan cotton sailing trousers, and Top-Siders with no socks, he still looked presidential. He walked slowly across the small deck a few times and stopped abruptly, facing Williams.

"Dammit, Buck," he said sharply, "what do they want with that Trident sub?"

"Mr. President, I honestly don't know."

Bennett pursed his lips and slowly shook his head. "Why don't you get us both a Coke and some sandwiches," he said quietly. "It's going to be a long day."

After Williams left, the President continued to pace—starboard side, port side, and back to starboard. On one circuit his attention was taken by the bluefish, stretched out on the top of a large plastic cooler, appraising him with a milky eye. He hooked a finger under its gills, hoisted it over the side, and released it—then resumed his pacing.

Sunday, 10:42 A.M.—Washington, D.C.

Morton Keeney sat at his desk and reread the fax from the President. *This,* he told himself, *could be a nasty piece of business.* He was dressed in a dark three-piece suit and Oxford tie, having been called from the middle of mass at St. Matthew's. Across from him sat Navy Captain John Buntz and Army Colonel Robert Starr. Buntz was in a golf shirt and slacks, while

Starr wore an old sweatshirt and grass-stained trousers, neither having been at church when the summons came. Keeney, the President's National Security Advisor, would have handled it a little differently, but he essentially agreed with the President's direction. He set the message aside and took a legal pad from the corner of his well-ordered desk. He wrote in silence for several moments, neatly drafting various columns of names and connecting them with lines to form an elaborate diagram. Buntz and Starr waited patiently. This was familiar ground for the two NSA staffers—the calm before the storm of activity they knew would follow.

"Gentlemen, this is the situation," said Keeney, turning the tablet for the two men to see and holding it at an angle from the desk. "A group of terrorists are holding hostages aboard a ferryboat on Puget Sound near Seattle, and they have captured a nuclear ballistic-missile submarine"—he pronounced it "miss-isle." "Our task is to open negotiations as soon as possible and to position all counterterrorist forces for direct action should those negotiations prove ineffective. The President wants increased security, so we set Threat Condition Charlie nationwide." Using a gold Cross pen as a pointer, he continued. "I'll contact State and the intelligence agencies. Bob, I want you to notify the Joint Chiefs, the Special Operations Command and the FBI. John, you attend to the rest on the list. These are the priority they are to be called. Any questions?"

"Just one, sir," said Starr. "Is this a code-word operation?" The assignment of a code word from the National Security Advisor, who acted for the White House in these matters, meant that any reference to the incident was classified "SECRET NOFORN"—no foreign dissemination. It compartmented all information on a "need to know" basis and restricted all government and military personnel from discussing it with anyone not cleared for the operation, and specifically, from talking with the press. Keeney thought a moment. The National Security Advisor had a reputation for being able to deftly manage the media during crises. Part of this presumed ability was that he was careful not to underestimate the press. He recognized this as a situation that couldn't be kept under wraps for long.

"For now, yes. The press will sniff this one out pretty quickly. There's been too much loss of life. If we keep it closely held, even for a few hours, it may give the response elements a chance to mobilize and get airborne without media attention."

"And the code word?" asked Buntz. The NSA pondered this, pursing his lips over steepled fingers. Standard procedure called for him to go to a computer-generated list and select a code word at random, but this was not his way.

"PRESSURE POINT," replied Keeney. *Not as catchy as JUST CAUSE, the code word for the Panama invasion,* he mused, *or DESERT SHIELD/DESERT STORM, used in the deployment to Saudi Arabia and the Gulf War, but it will have to do.*

Within two minutes, all three men were on the phone, calling other men away from those personal and family activities for which they had reserved their Sunday morning.

Sunday, 11:15 A.M.—Mount Vernon, Virginia

"Rachael, mark!" Rachael stared intently across the field of rye grass.

"Rachael, mark!" A different direction, and again Rachael was locked on and tracking. It was the same thing with the third mark. Rachael was holding, but with some difficulty, quivering about her chest and shoulders. Sclafani then pointed to the second mark and said in a conversational tone, "Rachael . . . back!"

The Labrador exploded away from his side as though she were spring-loaded. She returned on a dead run, circled her master, and sat down beside him. Rachael surrendered the white rubber bumper and sortied twice more on command to make her retrieve. Sclafani tugged at the dog's ears fondly and was about to set up another retrieve when the phone rang. He walked over to the cellular phone resting on the hood of his pickup and took the handset.

"Sclafani here."

"Mr. Sclafani, this is the duty officer. We have a situation, and they need you here at headquarters as soon as possible."

"What's the priority on this?"

"Urgent, sir. The deputy director will be here in fifteen minutes, and he said he wanted you here when he arrived." Sclafani glanced at his watch.

"Tell the deputy director that I'll be about ten minutes behind him unless he wants to send a helicopter." He rang off and dropped the tailgate for Rachael. The dog leaped into the back of the pickup, but gave him a quizzical look.

"Sorry, girl, but we have to quit early. Next time." He again stroked the Lab's soft black ears. The dog was only partially mollified, and said as much with her sad brown eyes. Sclafani dialed as he drove away.

"Hi, hon—I gotta go in. I'll be home in about ten minutes, and I'll have to head right out."

"Oh, Frank, that's a shame. Ellie's not going to be pleased. She was counting on you to take her to swim practice. Don't they know this is the first weekend you've been home in a while?"

"I know, and I'm sorry, but this's a hot one. Could you have my travel bag and briefcase at the door? I'll trade you Rachael for both of them. She's not happy about this either."

"She'll live, but I don't know about Ellie. How about a sandwich for the road?"

"Hon, you're a mind reader. See you in a few minutes." He winced as he hung up the phone, knowing how much Carla hated these calls. She put up a good front, but it only added to his guilt.

Fifteen minutes later, Frank Sclafani was speeding north on the George Washington Parkway. A large leather briefcase rested on the seat beside him, the suitcase in the bed of the truck. He found that he could defuse a measure of the stress his job created if his bags were carefully packed and ready to go. Carla still dreaded the calls, but not as much as when he had been one of the team shooters.

Sclafani was the senior negotiator on the FBI Hostage Rescue Team. As the negotiator, he directed the operation and made most of the decisions. Unlike in the movies, negotiations with terrorists were done over the radio or on the telephone. Only once had he conducted the negotiations face-to-face, and he never told Carla about that one. Sclafani had been the chief negotiator on the HRT for the past three years. The younger guys on the sniper and SWAT elements kidded him about being too old for their job, and in truth he probably was. But he loved what he did now. As a shooter or a part of the SWAT, it was all mechanics and standard procedure. It was the negotiator who had control.

The longer the negotiations took, the more effective Sclafani became. Last summer they were called in by the local authorities to a small North Carolina town. It was a bank robbery that had gone bad. Two men held three tellers, two customers, and the manager for three days. When he persuaded the bandits, both two-time losers, to walk out, they couldn't believe that the voice they had finally come to trust belonged to the man standing before them. His clothes were wrinkled from sleeping in them, and he had not shaved. His shirt was well sweated, tie askew, and his hair was matted and dirty. Sclafani looked much like the bank robbers. He found that if he subjected himself to the same deprivation as those he negotiated with, he quickly began to think like them—and that gave him an advantage.

Sclafani had taken his law degree from CUNY with honors, and had he accepted one of the many offers he received from prestigious New York firms, he would have made an impressive income negotiating oil leases or corporate mergers. Instead he had become a special agent in the FBI, and now he reasoned with and subtly threatened volatile, desperate, and often deranged outlaws. He appealed to their vanity and sold them on the benefits of reason and restraint. Sclafani empathized with them and understood why they had to do what they did, and they often understood why he had to do what he did. Time was usually on his side—not always, but usually. The hardest part came when he sensed that the talking was doing more harm than good, and that time had become his enemy. He was the one who determined when that moment had come, and it was he who picked up the radio and said to the SWAT leader: "I'm all done here—take him." It was like knowing when to spank a child. He knew it was the right thing to do, but he never felt good about it.

Sclafani arrived at the Hoover Building and hurried inside with his bags. One of the staff would put his truck in the FBI garage, where it would be waiting for him when he returned. Sclafani was second-generation Sicilian and had joined the Bureau back in the late seventies. He knew they had hired him for his ethnic background and language skills. Fortunately, the Bureau had learned that good investigative work was more profitable than agent penetrations, and that bribing well-placed informants was cheaper than the cost of replacing agents and settling with widows. Sclafani had been handsome as a young man—tall, with an angular face and sturdy, prominent nose. Too much of Carla's pasta had given him a rounded appearance. His features were strong but kindly, and his thick black hair now laid siege to a large round bald spot, like that of a Franciscan monk. Sclafani puffed up the stairs rather than wait on the elevator. Deputy Director Parker was waiting for him in the second-floor briefing room.

"Frank, glad you're here," Parker said. He looked at his watch and handed Sclafani a sheaf of papers as the negotiator slouched into one of the leather armchairs at the long briefing table. Two other agents sat across from Sclafani. He jammed a cigarette into the corner of his mouth and immersed himself in the documents, mostly classified fax and telex traffic. Sclafani read for moment, then began to pat down his pockets for a match. One of the agents reached across the table with a gold butane lighter. Sclafani accepted the light without comment or taking his eyes from the paper. They waited in silence for him to finish.

"Any communication from them?"

"None."

"How about from the guy on the submarine?"

"Just the initial contact and one radio check. I understand he's pretty shocked about all that's happened."

"No shit. Has the guy they captured been interrogated?"

"The Seattle field office has two agents en route to take him into custody. They've been instructed to conduct a field interrogation on the spot and get a report on the wire as soon as possible."

"HRT and SWAT?"

"They left Quantico about a half hour ago," said Parker. "There's a C-141 waiting at Andrews to take all of you to Seattle. We hope to have a boat or possibly a naval vessel available to serve as a command post." Sclafani rubbed his jaw and again scanned the reports. He looked up at Parker.

"This one's got an ugly feel to it. First of all, I don't see the HRT as a player—we've worked ships, but only tied up alongside a pier. And these guys don't seem like your normal wide-eyed, expendable extremists. They had to be pretty good to have taken that sub and got to where they are. They've planned well, and I bet they've anticipated some of the countermeasures we might take."

"You're probably right," replied Parker, "but it's domestic. They may want to rule out the military, so it's ours until Congress says differently."

The statute of *posse comitatus* forbade the domestic use of federal troops unless specifically authorized by Congress. This placed the FBI, the nation's senior police force, in charge of all terrorist actions within the United States. It was customary and quite common for the Bureau to request military assistance under the statute when required, and Sclafani could see that if force was necessary, it would be well beyond the Bureau's capability. But there was a catch-22. The Bureau didn't want to throw in the towel too early—there was turf to defend. On the other hand, they didn't want to botch the operation and get blamed for it. *Well,* thought Sclafani, *that's why guys like me are in the field and guys like Parker are in headquarters.* Sclafani knew Parker had no love for terrorists, but watching out for the Bureau was a ranking priority with him. Parker looked like a deputy director. Even for an emergency on Sunday morning, he wore a dark suit, white shirt, and conservative striped tie. The two other staff agents were younger, but dressed exactly the same.

"Have we asked for help?" said Sclafani.

"Not yet. The President has asked for a total effort on this, but for the moment, it's still our jurisdiction. I would anticipate that Seattle will be the destination for several military response units. The agent-in-charge of the Seattle office will meet you on that end with transportation, probably an Army helicopter from Fort Lewis. Any questions?"

"Who's the on-scene commander?"

"He hasn't been designated yet. Perhaps it will be you, although I doubt it." *Which means,* thought Sclafani, *that the Bureau is already trying to pass this off to the cavalry.* "By the way," Parker continued, "you did bring a suit along, didn't you?"

"It's in my suitcase. No sense getting it wrinkled on the flight. Don't worry, sir. If I need to, I can look like a real FBI agent."

"I see." Parker pushed himself up from his chair and extended his hand. The two other agents also got up. "Well, good luck and have a pleasant flight."

Sunday, 8:25 A.M.—Coronado, California

Brian Horner waited, resting heavily on his forearms across the handle of the shopping cart so the front wheels were almost off the ground. He was on line at the express checkout register at Von's Market. Except for the half-gallon of Gallo Chablis, nearly everything in the cart was fresh produce. The few packaged items had been carefully screened for salt content and preservatives. He thumbed though one of the scandal tabloids while he waited. While he avoided oral consumption of trash, he enjoyed the printed variety. Dolly Parton admits illicit liaison with Prince Charles—my goodness!

"You don't really think they're having an affair, do you?" Horner fumbled the paper back onto the rack and moved his cart to the counter. The girl at the register might normally have said something a little more caustic, but this guy was a hunk.

"Dolly told me herself that the pompous-Englishman routine is all an act," Horner replied, and added conspiratorially, "She said that when the lights go out, the prince's a real animal—if you know what I mean." The girl laughed and then blushed as Horner met her eyes and smiled. She checked him through at less than her normal speed, and was trying to think of something cute to say when she noticed he was wearing a wedding band. *The good-looking ones all seem to be taken,* she thought. Horner was counting the change when his beeper sounded.

"Oh, are you a doctor?"

"Well, in a way," he replied as he took the beeper from the elastic band of his running shorts and read the number. "Telephone?"

"Right over there—doctor." He smiled again and walked over to the wall phone. The nylon shorts hung loosely on his slim hips, but his broad shoulders stretched the fabric of the faded gray T-shirt. She stared after him for a moment and turned back to a cart full of potato chips, bean dip, and beer. Horner dropped a coin in the slot and dialed.

"Quarterdeck—SEAL Team Three. This is not a secure line and subject to monitoring at all times. Petty Officer Barnes speaking. May I help you, sir or ma'am?" It was the correct response, but normally it got abbreviated on weekends.

"Barnes, this is Lieutenant Horner. What's up?"

"You're recalled, sir."

"Aw, for Christ's sake!"

"Hey, don't blame me, sir, I'm just on the quarterdeck."

"Where'd this come from, Barnes—what's going on?"

"C'mon, Mr. Horner, you know the deal; you're recalled." He thought Barnes might give him a hint over the phone, but he was playing it by the book.

"Okay, Barnes. How about Mr. Santee and the master chief?"

"Both on their way, sir."

"Right—I'll be there in five minutes." Horner hung up and quickly fed another coin into the slot.

"Hi, babe."

"Brian, you forget something?"

"Naw, I just got recalled—I gotta go into the team."

"No, Brian, not today!"

"Sorry, babe, but I have no choice. It's probably some staff weenie running a drill—muster the troops and secure."

"Bri, we've been training for this race for over a month. Call me from the team as soon as you can, okay?"

"You got it. I'll probably be home in less than an hour."

"I hope so. 'Bye."

Horner blew out his flip-flop as he wheeled the cart out of the supermarket and hobbled across the parking lot. He crowded the groceries in the passenger seat of the Porsche and sped away from the store faster than he really needed to.

Forty minutes later, Pam Horner got a call from the executive officer of SEAL Team Three informing her that her husband's platoon was participating in a flyaway mobilization exercise, and that he might not be home for several days. It was a shock and it was upsetting, but it had happened before.

Sunday, 11:30 A.M.—Fort Bragg Army Base, North Carolina

"Down—FORTY-EIGHT!"

"Down—FORTY-NINE!"

"Down—FIFTY!"

"Reeeecover—AIRBORNE!"

"Fall in, column of twos—AIRBORNE!"

"Sergeant Blackwood, take charge!"

"Yes, SIR!"

A wiry man in his mid-thirties with the rakish look of a feral cat trotted up to the front of the double column. He led them out of the barracks area and along a dirt road that threaded its way into a stand of jack pine. The captain who had led PT for the last forty minutes fell in behind his men. The temperature was already over ninety degrees, and the air was very humid. Normally they held their PT and run earlier in the day, but on Sunday it was delayed for church services, even though none of them went to church. Like his men, the captain was sweating profusely but not breathing hard. It would be hard to find a better-conditioned group of men—perhaps a college cross-country team. But then, the strike teams of the Army's Delta Force prided themselves on their physical conditioning, as well as their military and counterterrorist skills. The captain's team was an eighteen-man element and the "on-call" team, which meant that they could be on the tarmac at nearby Pope Air Force Base with their weapons and equipment in thirty minutes.

Four miles into the run—about halfway—a six-by-six chased over the dirt road behind them, blasting its air horn. The captain, a taller and younger version of the sergeant, called the men to a halt as the truck braked to a stop in a cloud of dust.

"Cap'n Sherrard, you got a mission. An' the major said to tell you this was no drill!"

"Load 'em up, Blacky—on the double!" Sherrard jumped up to the cab beside the driver and slammed the door. "The major say anything else, Corporal? Any idea where we're going?" Sherrard's team could do a lot of things, but they were a Mideast response element, which meant they were highly trained in urban and desert warfare, and most of his men could speak Arabic.

"The major didn't say nothin' 'bout where, but he did say I was to tell you to gear up for CQB and maritime operations."

"Close-quarter battle and maritime ops?"

"That's what he said, sir." The ride back was a rough one, less so for Sherrard than for his men, crowded onto the wooden bench seats in the back of the six-by-six.

Sunday, 8:32 A.M.—Aboard the *Spokane*

Some semblance of a routine had descended on the *Spokane*. The passengers either dozed in their chairs or stared dully into space. The terror of their capture and the fight for the *Michigan* had emotionally drained them. For the most part they were listless and manageable, and their fear had largely been overcome by fatigue. Jamil had organized his prize crew into rotating duty stations. Fenton, Hassan, Yehya, and Michelle were to stand regular watches—one in the engine room, one with the passengers, and one walking the promenade deck as a roving lookout while the fourth was free to rest. Ahmed and Salah had busied themselves with hauling the cases of radio equipment up to the pilothouse, setting up antennas, and sorting out cables. Fatigue was beginning to be a factor with the terrorists, too, but the flush of their victories kept it well masked.

Jamil sat on a tall stool by the starboard door of the pilothouse. The .45 automatic, with its long silencer still attached, rested on his lap. He leaned against the wall with his feet propped casually on the radar console. Peck stood at the helm of the ferry, as he had for most of the time since the *Spokane* was captured. They were now well clear of the Hood Canal and into Admiralty Inlet, steaming in a northwesterly direction. They had just passed the tip of Marrowstone Island to port. Jamil had had Janey relieve Peck for a short time just after leaving the Hood Canal. She managed to keep the two vessels moving in the right general direction, but their heading wandered as much as thirty degrees either side of the intended course. Jamil could see that it took considerable skill to hold the two vessels on a steady course.

"So tell me, Captain, do you still think I will not get away with it—that we will not succeed?" Jamil had allowed Janey to go to the galley and get them some coffee. He correctly guessed that she would not make trouble so long as her captain's life was pledged against her behavior.

"You've managed to capture my boat and to steal a submarine," Peck replied, "and you've killed a bunch of American sailors in the process. I'd say you're in a lot of trouble."

"Trouble? Do you seriously think the police or your navy will do anything while I control the lives of the passengers aboard this vessel or while I can destroy the submarine?" Peck did not respond for a moment. He sensed that Jamil wasn't just boasting or talking to amuse himself—the man was too careful for that.

"Okay, you have hostages and you can sink a Trident submarine. You have a position from which to negotiate. What is it you're after—money, recognition—what do you want?"

Jamil dropped his feet to the rungs of the stool and leaned forward, his eyes blazing. "That is typical! That is so typical of you Americans! Most certainly an American would not risk his life unless there was money to be made. When I began this journey, do you not think that I considered death a possibility—perhaps a likelihood? And you think I would do it for money? You are a fool, Peck, or you are not the man I thought you might be." Jamil was now up, pacing the length of the pilothouse. Peck glanced at Jamil and saw the passion in his face. Janey had returned with the coffee. She set it down and stood silently in the corner. Jamil took no notice of her. He stopped behind Peck and continued in a quiet voice.

"Tell me, Peck, have you served in your armed forces?"

"Yeah, I was in the Navy."

"Did you see action—did you ever have to fight?"

"I spent a year in Vietnam."

"Excellent! And you were in combat there?"

"Yes."

"And you were paid well for this? They gave you money and honors and medals to pin on your chest?"

"My country was at war, and I had to do my hitch in the service," Peck replied, trying not to sound defensive.

"I accept that, Peck. But can't you conceive, just for a moment, that I too have been drafted into the service of my country? No, I didn't receive my conscription papers in the mail, but I was drafted as surely as you were. My country, too, is at war—we are occupied by a foreign power and still we fight on.

The Israelis have taken our land, our right to self-determination, and, most importantly, our dignity. They continue to build settlements as Jews from Europe and Russia pour into my country. Soon there will be nothing left for us. We have no choice—we have to fight.''

''But why are you here?'' ventured Peck. ''Your land and your fight are a long way from here.''

''They are. But Israel will continue to have her way with us so long as the United States provides money and weapons. We are here to show America that if you are in league with the Jews, then you, too, are at war and must be willing to suffer the consequences of war.'' Jamil once more rested on the stool, but he was far from relaxed.

''What will make you go home, Jamil?'' asked Peck carefully. ''What will it take for you to give back the submarine and my boat?''

''The Israelis must allow us a land of our own. They must allow the right of the Palestinian people to live in peace as a sovereign nation. They must abandon the West Bank and Gaza, and recognize them as the State of Palestine. They must also remove their settlements from our land.''

''Isn't that what all these peace talks are about?''

''Since they began in Madrid, the Jews use talk as a delay tactic. They must give us our land now.''

''And if they don't?''

''Then I will destroy the submarine. Your life and the lives of the others aboard will be used to bargain for our freedom. And if your country will not bargain, then we will both become martyrs in this war between us.''

Sunday, 8:35 A.M.—Sand Point Naval Station, Seattle, Washington

Admiral John MacIntyre sat at his desk, reflecting on all that had happened. He'd just had two stale doughnuts, and was on his third cup of coffee. No wonder his stomach burned. But it was more than just the coffee. When he received orders to Seattle as the commander of the naval base, he had been mildly disappointed in that it was an administrative command. His duties were that of a caretaker for the old Sand Point Naval Station, with considerable responsibility for relations between the Navy and the local community. His military duties consisted of coordination between the various bases and afloat commands in the Pacific Northwest. The job mandated an active social calendar, and the people in Seattle had been wonderful to them. His wife had liked it well enough, but it wasn't why he joined the Navy or why he had worked to get to senior command level. He knew the situation that had developed was as dangerous as any he had faced in his career, but there was little he could do but stand by and await word from his boss, the Commander in Chief of the Pacific Fleet. MacIntyre also expected to hear from Commander, Third Fleet, who also worked for CINCPACFLT and had operational control of all surface forces in the Eastern Pacific. Commander, Submarine Forces, Pacific, whose property had been stolen, would also have a say in this matter.

Since the incident had been code-worded, none of these fleet commanders could speak to the press. Any statement that came from his headquarters would be well screened by the Chief of Naval Information, or CHINFO. Any military action would be authorized only by national command authority, which meant the White House would be calling the shots. Orders would come directly from the President through the office of the Joint Chiefs of Staff. MacIntyre speculated on just who would get the call. The FBI had primary responsibility for domestic terrorist activity, but this was a whole lot more serious than the hijacking of an airliner or a postal bomb. The U.S. Special Operations Command, or USSOCOM, controlled all military special operations forces—they would certainly be a player if military force was used. Then there was Delta Force, the Army unit trained in assault tactics for terrorist actions and hostage situations. MacIntyre assumed he would be tasked to provide support in the way of logistics and communications for those forces and agencies that he presumed must surely be airborne by now.

But the admiral had done more than just sit by the phone and await a decision from Washington. He had directed Captain Bonelli at Bangor to dispatch a patrol boat to shadow the *Michigan* and the *Spokane* at a discreet distance. Aboard the craft was the Marine sergeant who had made the initial contact with the survivor aboard the *Michigan.* Bonelli reported that they had successfully reestablished radio contact with the man. MacIntyre had sent for a copy of his personnel jacket from Bangor—whoever was placed in charge of the operation would want as much information about that young man as possible. He had also called the commander of the Naval Air Station at Whidbey Island and authorized a photoreconnaissance of the two captured vessels by a P-3 patrol aircraft.

The admiral had also taken steps to bolster his staff in the two areas where they would be hard-pressed—communications and public affairs. His communications team was a good one, but like most nonoperational staffs, they were shorthanded. When this thing got going, there would be a nonstop flurry of message traffic. He had informally mobilized a local reserve communications unit—something which could legally be done only by the President or Congress. Communications officers and radiomen routinely carried top-secret clearances. When he explained the situation to the CO of the reserve unit, a stockbroker at Shearson Lehman Brothers in Seattle, he got the response he hoped for: "Admiral, say no more. My men will be there as soon as I can track them down—we'll worry about the paperwork later." His public affairs officer—PAO—was a young lieutenant and capable, but short on experience. He had directed his chief of staff, a senior captain with several tours of command, to supervise all contact with the public and the media. They had already received a number of inquiries from the local papers to the governor's office. The code-word guidelines allowed MacIntyre to brief the commanding general of the Washington State National Guard, who was now en route to Olympia to brief the governor. This would solve part of the problem and effectively mobilize the local law-enforcement agencies.

The press was another matter. The Gulf War had shown them that the media can make a nonstop TV miniseries out of a foreign war. *What will they do with a domestic crisis like this?* The reporters from the local media had been told that there had been a mechanical problem reported aboard a Washington State ferry and nothing about a Trident submarine. The story would hold up at best for a few hours, but those were the instructions passed to him by CHINFO. The newspeople had been polite but skeptical, and MacIntyre knew this was the lull before the storm. As soon as they had confirmation that the ferry was attached to a submarine and headed north, they would be on the air. Too much had happened, and there had been too many deaths. The national networks would soon cover them like a cheap suit, and they were not polite like the local press. The military had rapid response capabilities, but they were amateurs compared to the national news media.

"Sir, I have Admiral Tate on the STU 3." One of the more pleasant working relationships he had encountered since coming to Seattle was Jim Tate, Commandant of the 13th Coast Guard District.

"Very well, put him through." MacIntyre picked up the handset and waited for the scrambler to click in.

"John, are you there?"

"Yes, Jim, go ahead."

"The *Mellon* got under way fifteen minutes ago from Pier 36. At best speed she can overtake the *Spokane* in about three and a half hours. She has no helo aboard, but I have three H-65s at Port Angeles on standby, and they're at your disposal. Any Navy vessels able to respond?" Tate asked.

"You're it, Jim. There're two frigates in the yard at Bremerton, but they're not ready for sea. The *Florida* can get under way by tomorrow morning, but I don't know what we'd do with another boomer out there. A carrier battle group off northern California has just turned north, but they're three days out. Anyway, I think the white hull of a cutter is a lot less threatening than one of our greyhounds."

"I concur. *Mellon*'s skipper is Don Libby. I think you've met him—real solid guy. He called me from ship-to-shore, reporting that he left without a full crew but he can get the job done." MacIntyre vaguely remembered meeting Libby at a Chamber of Commerce function.

"His comm gear up?"

"One hundred percent—UHF, VHF, and HF on-line crypto. Anything else?"

"One thing, Jim, and it's not easy to talk about. Is the *Mellon*'s gun operational?"

The Coast Guard admiral hesitated a moment. "Well, yes, as far as I know. I'll verify it and get back to you. They've got the new three-inch Mark 76 system, and it's a damn fine gun. I know they've trained it out on a few drug boats, but I can't tell you when they last fired a round."

"I understand your concern, and I'll keep it in mind." Jim Tate was reflecting his own reservations about the possibility of having to fire on a friendly vessel. "Jim, I have no authority but to position assets and await further orders. Have *Mellon* close on them slowly to about two thousand yards on their stern quarter, and we'll wait it out from there. I'll send you a message to that effect." He knew Tate would want it in writing, and MacIntyre didn't want to make him ask—friends didn't do that.

"Understood, John, thanks. I'll keep you posted, and good luck."

MacIntyre sat lost in thought for a few moments until he was interrupted by another call.

"MacIntyre here. . . . Yes, I'll hold." His chief staff officer stuck his head in the office and, seeing his admiral busy, started to leave, but MacIntyre motioned him to a seat.

"Yessir . . . Yessir . . . Yessir, I understand . . . I understand perfectly, Admiral, and I'll do my best. . . . Thank you, sir." MacIntyre put down the phone and looked at his chief of staff.

"That was Admiral Calloway at CINCPACFLT. For the time being, I've been made on-scene commander of PRESSURE POINT."

Sunday, 8:35 A.M.—Coronado, California

Lieutenant Brian Horner pulled up in front of the SEAL Team Three compound and walked across the parking lot. The sailor behind the desk just inside the door stood up and noted the time of his arrival on a clipboard.

"Morning, sir, they're in the briefing room. You're supposed to go on in."

"I saw the skipper's car outside. Barnes, what's going on?"

"I dunno, but I'd say you're gonna stand up for this one."

"Aw, shit."

"Hey, sir, remember, you *are* a volunteer."

"Screw you, Barnes." Barnes laughed as Horner headed for the briefing room. The rest of Echo Platoon was milling around the room, most of them dressed like Horner. They were a handsome, tan, athletic-looking bunch. A short, trim man with a grim expression stepped away from the group to meet him. He was the only one in uniform, dressed in freshly pressed camouflage utilities and polished jungle boots. His fatigue cap, starched board-hard, accented his graying temples.

"Everybody here, Master Chief?"

"Everyone but Peppard and Thomas, and Thomas is home on emergency leave, so we'll be one short of a full platoon." Just then, another man walked through the door. Master Chief Watson noted his arrival and turned to Horner. "Echo Platoon all present and accounted for, sir."

"Anybody know what's going on?" asked a third SEAL who joined Horner and the chief. Ensign Dave Santee, the assistant platoon officer, was as tall as Horner, but younger.

"No word yet, Mr. Santee," replied the chief, "but I'm sure we'll mount out."

"Dammit, Master Chief, we don't need this shit," said Horner. "We leave for a seven-month deployment in two weeks—you'd think they'd cut us some slack."

"Sir, I don't think this is a drill."

"What!"

"Just a guess on my part, sir, but I don't think the skipper'd let them put us through this for a drill—not this close to a deployment. I think something's going down." The three men stood in silence for a moment. Both Horner and his master chief had been through this before—not a drill, but a mount-out for the real thing. It could be a terrorist action or a Third World response like Grenada or Panama. But a mount-out did not mean action—only about one time in ten did an emergency recall and mount-out result in an actual mission. Usually the mission was canceled, negotiations prevailed, another team took the action, or it was a false alarm. Twice during his four years as a SEAL, Horner had gone out for real, and both times they had been aborted.

"You really think this is a live one?" asked Horner.

"We'll know in a minute," said Santee. "Here comes the skipper."

"Okay, gentlemen, take a seat." The fifteen SEALs shuffled into the three lines of folding chairs. Commander Gary Sullivan was the commanding officer of Team Three, and he wasted no time getting to the point. "This is not a drill, and you're all in isolation from this moment on. There's been a terrorist incident in Puget Sound, and Echo Platoon is the SEAL response element. It's Team Three's duty, and you're my best C-1 platoon." Sullivan was a short, stocky man with large hairy forearms and a receding hairline. He stood before the platoon, feet apart, with his hands on his hips. "Men, this one looks like a real no-shitter. A well-armed group of terrorists have taken a ferryboat with hostages and managed to use it to capture a Trident submarine. There's already been an estimated fifty people killed, and if this thing goes the distance, there's a good chance it will be a maritime operation. This is a code-word operation, and isolation discipline will be strictly enforced. Now Commander Walker, the staff intelligence officer from Naval Special Warfare Command, will give you what information we have on this thing."

Sullivan stepped aside and was replaced by the staff N2. The briefing room was dead silent. Walker had little information, reading two messages he had received from their immediate senior command, USSOCOM at MacDill Air Force Base in Tampa. He was armed with a pointer, and periodically tapped a chart of Puget Sound tacked to the wall of the briefing room. The casualty figures indicated that they were dealing with an opponent that was more of a military strike team than a band of terrorist irregulars. He passed on a few comments he had obtained in a phone call with the SOCOM watch officer and surrendered the floor to the Team Three CO.

"Men, this is as real as it gets around here. Mr. Horner, I want you prepared for surface, subsurface, parachute, and fast-rope attack. The master-at-arms is standing by outside and will provide your isolation supervisors. There's a C-130 standing by at North Island to fly you to McChord Air Force Base in Tacoma. You'll receive further orders when you arrive." Sullivan paused and swept the group with his eyes. "Gentlemen, there's nothing more to say. Remember—you're Navy SEALs, and this is what you've trained for. Good luck and good hunting. Mr. Horner, carry on."

While Sullivan and Walker had been talking, Horner's mind raced. They'd trained for it, all right, but he'd never thought they'd really have to do it. Chances were they still wouldn't, but this sounded very real. He knew why Echo Platoon had been tapped for this job. For the last fourteen months they'd been training together for their deployment to the Western Pacific, and they were in a very high state of readiness. Some platoons were specifically trained for submarine operations and underwater attacks in minisubs called SEAL delivery vehicles. Others were specialists in arctic operations or area-designated with heavy emphasis on language skills. Echo was a direct-action platoon. In many respects, they were generalists—flexible with a broad range of mission-profile capabilities. But their specialty was strike operations—small-unit tactics, stealth, and firepower. They had also been well trained in counterterror, or CT, tactics and close-quarter battle. *Relax,* Horner told himself. *This* thing may be big, but chances are it will be solved without committing the platoon. He stood up and nodded to the CO.

"Aye, sir." Then he turned to his men. He put one foot on

the seat of his chair and leaned across his knee on his elbows, like a coach in the locker room. The young faces around him were flushed with excitement and anticipation.

"Okay, guys. For now it's just a mount-out drill—nothing more. But since we may have an action, make sure your equipment is complete and in order. We'll need full rubber and Draegers, chutes and reserves, and I'll want to take our own fast-rope rig. Draw weapons for the full range of CT work and CQB."

It was a lot of equipment, but Echo Platoon was ready. Their weapons, parachutes, and the Draeger LAR-V shallow-water scubas had been staged for the upcoming deployment and carefully packed in crates for air shipment. There would be a last-minute shifting of equipment for this particular contingency, and they would have to draw ammunition and grenades, but they were ready to go.

Horner stood up and turned to Watson. "Master Chief, they're all yours."

Master Chief Watson stood up, flipping through pages of his notebook. Watson had been a Navy SEAL for twenty-five years. He was forty-three years old, but he seemed closer to thirty. He had a light, compact build, and looked more like an accountant than a SEAL, except for the short waxed handles of his neatly trimmed mustache and a scar that cut across one cheek. Most people pictured SEALs as big men, and many of them were. But Chief Watson knew it was a little man's game, especially when you got older. He worked hard and could keep pace with the younger men, but he doubted he could do so if he were a six-foot, two-hundred-pounder, which was the standard in Echo Platoon. Watson was a much-decorated Vietnam veteran, and like the E. F. Hutton commercial, when Master Chief Watson talked, everyone listened.

"Like the boss said, for now it's a mount-out drill, but you better have it exactly right, 'cause you might have to use it. This one could well be for real. I don't care how many times you've checked your gear, you check it again. It might be some terrorist who jumps into your shit because you forgot something, instead of me.'' He flipped through his notebook, making individual assignments to various platoon petty officers.

"That's it, men. I want that gear on pallets and ready to go in twenty minutes. Let's move!''

Echo Platoon filed out of the briefing room and was escorted by four SEALs from the master-at-arms force to the platoon staging area. Isolation meant just that—once briefed into a mission, there was no contact with anyone outside the platoon until the mission was over. Two canvas-topped, olive-drab six-by-sixes throbbed at idle in the Team Three compound, waiting to take Echo Platoon and their gear across Coronado to North Island Naval Air Station.

Sunday, 12:07 P.M.—Andrews Air Force Base, Maryland

The sedan pulled up to the C-141 transport on the tarmac. The four big J-79 turbofan engines were silent, but the aircraft was alive. The navigational beacons were on and rotating, and a thick umbilical ran from the fuselage to a noisy portable generator that had been wheeled to the side of the plane. Three crewmen dressed in zippered overalls and blue fore-and-aft garrison caps stood talking quietly under the wing. An Air Force security guard, with a blue beret and a .45 strapped to his side, greeted Sclafani when he got out of the car.

"May I see your identification, sir?'' Sclafani removed the plastic ID badge clipped to his collar and handed it to the airman. He looked at the badge, front and back, to Sclafani's face, and again to the badge. The man saluted and handed it back to him. "Thank you, sir. You're cleared to board. Do you have any luggage or weapons?''

"I have some bags in the trunk and my service revolver, a .38 Special.''

"We'll see to your bags, sir. The aircraft commander has requested that all weapons be checked with the flight crew.''

Sclafani nodded, removed the holstered pistol from his brief-case, and handed it to the guard. Another security airman ap-peared to take charge of the weapon and to take his suitcase from the trunk. The first airman wished him a pleasant flight, and proceeded to direct the driver of the sedan across the tar-mac and away from the aircraft.

Sclafani walked over to the door of the plane, a rounded, rectangular cutout in the lower portion of the fuselage just for-ward of the wing. The belly of the C-141 was just a few feet off the ground, and the entry hatch was served by a short aluminum ladder. Sclafani waved casually to the men under the wing. All three came to attention and saluted. Sclafani smiled as he boarded. He'd served three years as an enlisted Marine be-tween high school and college. The Air Force had always seemed more like a support organization than an armed service, but then, the Marines were known to say that about the Army and Navy as well.

"Well, it looks like another gatherin' of the wild geese." Sclafani recognized the voice but could not yet see the speaker in the dark interior of the transport. A lanky form came up the aisle and extended his hand. "Howdy, Frank."

"Hello, Slim. I figured you might be on this lift. Have you been briefed on this?"

"The duty officer at the Quantico office gave me the general drift of things. This looks a little out of our line of work, doesn't it?"

William "Slim" Whitman was head of one of the HRT's SWAT elements, which included two sniper teams. He spoke with a soft West Texas drawl, and did in fact bear a resem-blance to the famous country-and-western singer. Slim would be in charge of the four "shooters"—two two-man teams that would operate in support of the SWAT element. Many gunmen and terrorists had sat in the cross hairs of the FBI snipers while men like Frank Sclafani reasoned with them. They were tightly controlled as the negotiations unfolded, but on occasion they were released to fire when they found a target or when there was imminent danger of harm to a hostage. The job called for a shooter's cool and the judgment of a good law-enforcement officer. Slim Whitman was one of the best on both counts.

"It's like I told the deputy director, we've never worked against an underway vessel. It's bound to be a Navy or Special Operations show, with the call being made by the White House through JCS. Our orders are to go out there and take charge until otherwise directed. As soon as that happens, we'll stand by to assist."

"You mean, provide assistance if requested—formally, in writing and notarized." Both men smiled. The FBI had a reputation of wanting to run the show or not wanting to play.

"Yeah, but we may have to be a little flexible this time. This could be pretty serious stuff."

Both men had been around long enough to know that most problems could be quickly resolved by the operators in the field. It was at the higher levels of the bureaucracy, both civilian and military, that the real battles were fought. The "turf wars," as they called them, could be intense. An air crewman served them coffee while Whitman introduced Sclafani to two of the snipers in his team. He knew the other two shooters from previous operations.

"Where's the rest of your group?"

"The SWAT guys'll be along directly—I caught the first bird out. Tell me, Frank, do you miss it now that you're doing the talking instead of the shooting?" Sclafani had done a tour as a sniper as a young agent. He was not a natural shooter, nor had he grown up with guns, like Slim Whitman. But he had a keen eye and was rock-steady, and had become one of the HRT's better marksmen.

"Sometimes, but honestly, Slim, I like the talking." Most of the snipers were like Whitman, avid hunters and outdoorsmen. Sclafani was a city boy. He'd tried hunting, but found he liked gun dogs more than guns, although he would occasionally drop a bird for Rachael.

A large helicopter landed nearby, and the ramp at the rear of the 141 opened up amid the screech of electric motors. A dozen men walked up the ramp, each carrying a parachute gear bag. They were dressed in casual outdoor clothes and had the look of a suburban gun club on an outing, which in some ways they were. They deposited the gear bags in a pile, and one of the crew members covered the bags with a cargo net and secured them to the floor of the plane. Half of them left and returned in a few minutes with three padlocked gun boxes, which were also tied to the floor.

"Got enough troops, Slim?"

"Well, they weren't too specific on what to expect, so I'd rather have too many than too few. Hell, I don't see how we're gonna be of any use out there, 'less they want us to hold off the press."

"In that case," offered Sclafani, "you're undermanned." The engines of the big transport began to spool up, and a crew member politely asked them to find their seats for takeoff.

Sunday, 12:45 P.M.—Pope Air Force Base, North Carolina

While the C-141 Starlifter with the FBI Hostage Rescue Contingent aboard climbed out over the Maryland countryside and turned west, another 141 sat on the tarmac at Pope Air Force Base, engines idling. Those who had just left Andrews rested comfortably in airline-type seating. The men in the transport at Pope were seated along each side of the fuselage on canvas benches with canvas-web backrests. They were hard young men who were as accustomed to discomfort as they were to waiting. They were dressed in camouflage utilities and polished jungle boots. Most wore green berets, but the flashes on the front varied, depending on their parent Special Forces unit. Some wore starched and blocked fatigue caps—they were from the Ranger Battalions. The only thing that detracted from their military appearance was their hair. A few had regulation military haircuts, but most wore their hair over their ears and a few of them had it over their collars.

These young men were a Delta Force platoon: three squad

elements of the best counterterrorist fighters in the world. Dressed in sneakers, blue jeans, and an old flannel jacket, as they often were on a mission, they could blend into the streets of almost any Western city. A number of them were olive-complected, dark-haired troopers whose Arabic or Farsi was good enough for them to freely roam the streets of Beirut or Tehran. They were a special group, and only a careful observer could tell that they were a little too clear-eyed and athletic, and a little too proud-looking, for your average Army soldier. Between the two lines of troopers, their equipment bags and weapons boxes were secured to the floor with straps and netting.

At the front of the aircraft, near the stairs to the flight deck, Captain Sherrard and Sergeant Blackwood waited. Sherrard stood passively with his arms folded, while Blackwood leaned against the padded forward bulkhead. After a while, Sherrard produced a tin of snuff and rolled the lid off in a practiced, one-handed motion, offering it to his sergeant. Both men slipped a pinch under their lip in an act of silent communion and continued their vigil.

"He just touched down, sir," called the crew chief, who was standing near the door of the aircraft. He wore a Mickey Mouse headset and lip mike, and was connected by a long cord that allowed him to speak with the flight deck while he roamed about the aircraft. Sherrard nodded and continued to wait. A few moments later, the crew chief approached Blackwood and handed him two foam cups.

"What's this?"

"It's for you and the cap'n," he shouted over the turbine whine. Blackwood gave him a puzzled look.

"It's for your snuce. My crew has to keep this plane clean, an' I don't want 'em having to wipe up your tobacco juice."

"It's all right," said Blackwood, handing the cups back to him, "we don't spit."

The crew chief looked at Blackwood and saw immediately that he was serious. He started to say something, but took the cups and moved away. While Delta platoon leader and his sergeant enjoyed their plug, a corporate jet with military markings taxied near the Starlifter and discharged a single passenger. A moment later an Army colonel stepped aboard the aircraft. He carried a kit bag in one hand and a map case in the other. He handed his bag to one of the crewmen, while the crew chief retrieved the stairs and closed the door behind him. The big transport had already started to roll.

"Good morning, Captain . . . First Sergeant. I'm Colonel Braxton from the Special Operations Command. I'll be your control for this operation." Braxton was a sparse, angular man with gray eyes. His Class B uniform trousers were bloused neatly into spit-shined Chocoran jump boots. Aside from the eagles on the shoulder flaps of his blouse, he wore only a Ranger Tab, Master Jump Wings, and a blue Combat Infantry Badge. His beret carried the yellow-and-red flash of the Fifth Special Forces Group. Braxton returned Sherrard's and Blackwood's salute and produced a copy of his orders. Sherrard read the paper carefully and handed it to Blackwood.

"I have some charts and the latest intelligence and message traffic," continued Blackwood. "We can commence an informal briefing as soon as we reach cruise altitude."

"Very well, sir," replied Sherrard. "Glad to have you along." He again produced the tin of snuff. "Would the colonel care for a dip?" Braxton's eyes widened as they went from Sherrard to the flat round can of black powder.

"Excuse me, gentlemen," interrupted the crew chief. "We're about to commence our takeoff roll. You'll have to take your seats immediately."

Sunday, 9:30 A.M.—Aboard the *Spokane*

"How soon will you be ready?" Jamil asked.

"The radios are in place and functional. The VHF has only line-of-sight range, but the UHF should be good for one hundred fifty kilometers or more." Ahmed had known the radios would not be a problem—and they were only a backup.

"And the television?"

"That will take us a little time. The system is operable, but proper adjustment has to be made for the antenna to acquire the satellite." Ahmed sat on the lid of an empty equipment crate, bent like a pretzel over the stack of electronic components. He connected wire leads and twisted dials while he spoke. "If we can hold a steady course for a period of time, it will greatly increase our chances for a good video transmission."

Jamil stepped over to the chart table. He wanted to stay in the middle of the channel as much as possible. They had just exited Admiralty Inlet and were midway between Partridge Bank Light to the north and the Quimper Peninsula to the south.

"Peck, turn left to a westerly heading and slow down to half speed." Peck added ten additional degrees to the left rudder he carried to compensate for the dead weight of the *Michigan* tied to the ferry's starboard side. Gradually the two vessels slowly began to come around to the west, and after a while, steadied on a course of 270.

Ahmed had become an expert with radios and tactical communication over the years. One of his tasks during the months of planning for the operation had been to design a plan that would turn the *Spokane* into a TV station. He found a video nut in Seattle who was a master at capturing TV satellite signals, and was also something of a pervert and had several large dish antennas so he could watch different X-rated channels at the same time. Won over by flattery and a little cash, he helped Ahmed to design a reasonably portable system that would co-opt a commercial TV satellite and use it to beam their signal back to earth, either from a videotape-player feed or from a Sony camcorder Ahmed had purchased for the system.

"How much more time?" Jamil had begun to pace between the bridge wings and to check the chart on every other lap through the pilothouse.

"We are almost ready. Let me check the antenna now that the boat is more steady."

Ahmed hurried down the stairs from the pilothouse to the promenade deck area behind the pilothouse. A 1.8-meter parabolic dish with a long, bulbous feed-horn projecting from its center rested on a heavy, complex-looking tripod. It looked like a death ray from an old Flash Gordon movie. There was an electrical box at the base of the tripod from which black electrical cords ran to the back of the antenna and to the equipment in the pilothouse. Ahmed adjusted the antenna manually, then began entering data on the small keyboard on top of the box. He toggled a switch on the back of the antenna, and the dish came alive. Electric motors in the gimballed base of the tripod began to whine and the dish first rotated around to a southerly heading and then rocked back to fifty-two degrees elevation. As Ahmed checked the meters on the control box, the antenna issued a periodic squeal as the stable element in the synchronous mount compensated for the motion of the ferry to hold its lock on a fixed point in the southern sky.

Telstar 307 sped along through space at over thirteen thousand miles per hour, but relative to a small patch of the Pacific Ocean 1,800 miles west of Isabela Island in the Galápagos and 2,340 miles south of Los Angeles, it was motionless. It was a communications satellite, placed in geosynchronous orbit to hover indefinitely, 22,500 miles over the equator at 118 degrees west longitude. Telstar 307 was a transponder—a spaceborne relay—which meant that it dutifully received ground signals on one frequency and transmitted them back to earth on another, much like an interpreter at the United Nations who listens to a speech in French and simultaneously translates it into English. The satellite would accept any KU band signal within range of its antenna, which included the western third of the United States, and retransmit the signal to the network news technical operations center, or TOC, in Burbank, California. The 307 had twenty-four transponders, or channels, so it could handle twenty-four receptions and rebroadcasts at the same time. It was not considered one of the brighter species of satellites, but Telstar 307 had performed its assigned task religiously and without any complaint from its creators for the last ten years. At least it did until that morning when it was interrogated by a maritime ground station on Puget Sound.

In the pilothouse of the *Spokane,* Ahmed interrogated each of 307's twenty-four transponders, noting that only five were in use. Sunday morning was a slow news time. *Well, we'll soon change that,* he thought.

Ahmed was an idealist and an intellectual, and by nature not an aggressive individual. But electronically he was vicious. His private and most secret passion was video games, at which he was not unskilled. Telstar 307 could tolerate a signal strength of three hundred watts. Ahmed once more verified that his antenna had a good lock, and boosted his transmission power up to five hundred watts. He then methodically punched out the five channels that were in use and two more for good measure, frying the transponders beyond repair. "That ought to get their attention," he murmured as he turned to Jamil.

"Channel eleven, your Islamic station, is on the air," he reported, and for the first time since they had boarded the *Spokane,* Ahmed smiled. Jamil threw an arm around his shoulders.

"My brother, it is time to tell the world why we have come here. Would you please do us the honor." Ahmed reduced the output to three hundred watts and found a good channel. Then he slid a videocassette into the VCR and punched the play button.

Tom Spears was the technician on duty at the TOC in Burbank. The suite of rooms connected to the large receiving dish on the roof of the building was a facility shared by all the major networks. Spears had perfected the technique of slouching on a stool, and periodically took a moment from his sci-fi novel to glance at the bank of twenty-four screens on his console. He and his girlfriend had sat up late the night before watching television and sharing a couple of joints, so it had been a struggle for him to stay awake. An audio alarm notified him of the first broken transmission, and he looked up in time to see the second screen turn to hash. Then more snow-filled screens and more alarms, like a symphony of smoke detectors. Spears stared openmouthed at the snowy screens until the phone buzzed. He switched the call to his headset and found the alarm-suppression buttons. Another two calls were soon waiting.

"What the hell's going on out there," screamed the caller

from New York. "I need that feed for our twelve-o'clock news!" Spears was a doper, but he was also pretty good at his job. He raked his eyes across the control panel and saw nothing wrong with his equipment. And it probably wasn't the ground-station transmission feeds—they couldn't have all failed at once.

"The hell if I know. My gear's up, so it must be the bird."

"Well, you get that goddamned thing fixed, or I'll have your butt."

"Hey, asshole," replied Spears, "I said it's the fuckin' bird. Whadda you think I am, a fuckin' shuttle astronaut?"

"I'm not kidding, you little prick, I'm gonna have your job for this. You just can't—"

Spears cut him off and looked at the blinking of the other four lines. *Maybe you will,* he thought, *but you'll have to get in line.* Spears felt a rush of panic. He'd always known that World War III would begin in space with each side knocking off the other's communications satellites, but the Russians were our friends now. Maybe the Visitors had finally come and had announced their arrival by taking out one of his birds. Then a sharp color picture appeared on one of the open channels. At first he thought one of the original users had shifted transponders and resumed transmitting, but this was certainly no news feed from an affiliate. Spears hesitated for a moment, then cut the signal in to the seven networks that shared the facility. *It's their satellite,* he reasoned, *and this looks a whole lot better than some of the human-interest crap that usually gets passed down during nonpeak hours.*

Jamil stood at a podium like a panelist on a quiz program, and looked straight into the camera.

"People of the United States of America, my name is Jamil. Your country is now under attack by the Islamic Brothers of Freedom. We have captured a Washington State ferry, and its passengers are our prisoners. We have also captured a U.S. Navy Trident submarine and its full complement of nuclear missiles.

"Our fight is not with you but with your government, which

provides arms and money to the Zionists who now occupy our lands in Palestine. On behalf of the displaced people of Palestine, we demand the return of the occupied territories, known as the West Bank and Gaza, to the Palestinian people and that the repatriation of these lands be immediate and without condition. We further demand that the United States and Israel recognize the sovereignty of these lands as the nation of Palestine by formal resolution in the United Nations. The time for talking is over.

"The United Nations ruled that Iraq had to abandon Kuwait, and the American Army was sent to enforce that ruling. Now we demand compliance with United Nations Ruling 242, which directs Israel to withdraw all forces from the occupied territories. Our demands also include the removal of all Jewish settlements from these lands.

"If these conditions are not publicly validated by a mutually binding agreement of both the United States and Israel, then the lives of the hostages will be forfeited and the submarine, with its lethal nuclear arsenal, will be destroyed. Your government has eight hours to provide public assurances that these demands have been met.

"We will broadcast again when your government has had sufficient time to consider the conditions we require for the release of those aboard the ferry and the return of your atomic-missile submarine."

Once the tape was in the offices of the major networks, there was a scramble to document its authenticity. Phone calls to local affiliates in Seattle strongly indicated there was some basis to the story, but no one aired it for fear it was a prank. The Washington State Police reluctantly admitted that there was a ferry overdue, but the Navy, following standard procedure, would "neither confirm nor deny" the in-port or deployed status of their Trident submarines.

The major networks sat on the story for an hour, trying to document a solid corroborating source. Finally, the chief of the news desk at CNN said, "Enough of this pussyfooting around—let's air it." The other major networks rapidly followed his lead. Shortly after the story was broken, the considerable resources and apparatus of the national media began to move on Seattle in a mass migration not seen since the San Francisco quake of '89.

"Well, Peck, your government has been put on notice." He had ceased to address him as captain, feeling that in many respects the title now belonged to him. "What do you think Mr. Bennett and your Congress will do now?"

"I have no idea. I do know that it's not the policy of the United States to negotiate with terrorists. Maybe they'll refuse to talk about it."

"It has been easy for America to endorse a policy of refusing to negotiate, especially if the terrorist—I prefer the term freedom fighter—has attacked the Rome airport or taken a British national hostage in Beirut. Would you not agree this situation is a little harder to ignore?"

"Sure it is, but the principle's the same."

"Principle!" spat Jamil. "What would you do, Peck, if you were President Bennett? Storm this vessel and risk everyone on board? Risk nuclear catastrophe? Do nothing and let me sail off with a nuclear submarine? Or do you contact the Israelis and talk in earnest about justice for the Palestinians?"

"Israel may not want us to get our submarine back bad enough to go along with this."

"Then I will destroy the submarine," Jamil said in an even voice.

"But what will that gain you?"

"Many things. Will America be so willing to send billions of dollars in military aid each year to a nation that would not surrender a captured desert land to save American lives and prevent contamination of this beautiful waterway? I think not. The relationship of America and Israel will be changed forever. And when my people see what just a few of us have done against you, they will take heart and renew their struggle against the Zionists who occupy our land. You see, Peck, I am not a terrorist—I am a *patriot*!"

He turned back to the chart table just as Michelle appeared

on the wing of the bridge. Her hair was pulled back behind her head and the shirt stuffed into her blue jeans was unbuttoned nearly to the waist. "Ah, *chérie*. I'm glad you have come." He put his arm around her waist and kissed her on the lips. "Stay here with the pilot and his assistant while I inspect the lower decks. Ahmed, call me if you hear anything on the radio."

Ahmed nodded and went back to his radio receivers, working carefully through the frequencies, but he had no indication their video transmission had been publicly aired. However, there was no activity on any of the Telstar 307's operable transponders, which meant the satellite was being held open to them for further traffic. Ahmed once again smiled. Someone had heard them.

Sunday, 9:35 A.M.—Sand Point Naval Station, Seattle, Washington

Rear Admiral John MacIntyre sat at his desk trying to prepare himself for the swift run of events that would accelerate throughout the day. He had set his staff on a crisis-action footing, and the naval reserve communicators had their part of it well in hand. In an effort to bolster his staff with needed expertise, he had asked Captain Bonelli at Bangor to send one of the in-port Trident skippers to his headquarters in Seattle to serve as a staff adviser. The commanding officer of the USS *Michigan* Gold Crew had been detached to him and should arrive within the hour. The media was still a problem, but his chief staff officer and PAO officer had been able to keep them pacified for the moment. Both had reported that their credibility was becoming thin, and MacIntyre knew some version of the truth would have to be told very soon. Information on the men killed at Bangor and those missing from the duty section of the *Michigan* could be managed for a short time, but there were too many casualties and witnesses at the Hood Canal bridge, and the *Spokane* was now six hours overdue.

The message traffic had kept him abreast of events at JCS and national command levels. A platoon of SEALs would be landing at McChord Air Force Base just south of Tacoma around noon, and an element of the Delta Force counterterrorist team would be arriving shortly behind them. A company of Rangers at nearby Fort Lewis had also been put on alert. These units would be held in readiness upon their arrival in an empty hangar at McChord. Six HH-60 Blackhawk helicopters had been assigned to MacIntyre for general use and as insertion platforms for these units should a heliborne assault of the two captured vessels be required. *God help us if it comes to that,* thought MacIntyre. He had asked that the team leaders of these units be flown to Sand Point as soon as they all had arrived. He wanted to meet some of the men whose lives he may have to put at risk.

The special agent in charge of the FBI Seattle field office had been fully briefed on PRESSURE POINT. Technically, the incident was still under FBI jurisdiction, but he was already starting to defer to MacIntyre.

The FBI man had just called and briefed MacIntyre on the interrogation of the captured terrorist. Apparently the man they had in custody had held nothing back, but he knew very little. After the *Spokane* and the *Michigan* cleared the Hood Canal bridge and the other three terrorists were killed, he had simply tied a white flag to the barrel of his AK-47 and begun waving it. The Jefferson County sheriff had taken him into custody and turned him over to the FBI. About all the man could tell them was that the attack had been planned for six months and that the leader's name was Jamil. He was able to provide the names of his three dead associates and the American whose boat they had chartered. He gave his name only as "Haj" and claimed to be a Palestinian. He also demanded to be treated as a prisoner of war.

The Kitsap County sheriff's deputies had found the boat where it had run aground near Port Gamble. A search of the vessel had revealed nothing but the dead American. MacIntyre had an on-line secure fax capability, and any additional information from or about the captured terrorist or his organization would come directly from FBI Headquarters in Washington.

The local FBI chief also relayed that the FBI Hostage Rescue Team was due to land at Boeing Field in Seattle just after 1:30 P.M. Terrorists and hostages were something MacIntyre admitted to knowing little about, and the advice and expertise of the HRT would be most welcome. The agent assured him that the senior member of the team was a highly experienced negotiator. *Maybe,* thought MacIntyre, *this guy can make everything else unnecessary. I'll sure need him—and probably soon, because we should be hearing from them anytime now.* He was rereading his incoming message file when one of his staff officers entered.

"Admiral, we have the photos developed that were taken from the P-3."

MacIntyre pushed the messages aside and stood up to take the stack of eight-by-ten glossy black-and-white prints. They were still damp and smelled of chemicals. He began to lay them out across his desk.

"They're not the best, are they, Norm?" Commander Norm Reasoner was the staff operations officer.

"No, sir. They were using a hand-held Minolta 35mm with a ten-power zoom. Normally, they get a lot closer for ship photography."

MacIntyre grimaced. *We can hunt submarines, but we can't even take a decent picture of a surface ship!*

"Well, we couldn't chance flying too close. What do you make of these?" MacIntyre pointed to the small structures on the deck behind the *Michigan*'s sail. "They look like a line of charcoal barbecue grills, but the enlargements are too grainy to really make them out."

"I can't tell either, Admiral, but I'll bet they aren't standard equipment. That captain from the *Michigan* should be able to help us when he gets here."

"Maybe so," replied MacIntyre, "but if those devices were put there by the terrorists, he may have no more idea than we do. I've got an idea—that photographer still here?"

"He's over at the photo lab working up another set of prints to send back to Washington."

"Good. When he finishes, get him back here." MacIntyre snatched the phone and put through a call to Admiral Tate at Coast Guard Headquarters.

"Jim, John MacIntyre here. Need a favor—any shipping traffic inbound on the Strait that will pass our problem in the next hour or so? . . . Right, I'll hold the line. Norm, we need some better pictures. . . . What's that, Jim . . . ? Okay . . . okay . . . about forty-five minutes, that's perfect . . . No, no word from them yet, but could you have one of your helos standing by— we may need it on short notice. . . . Right, thanks, Jim." MacIntyre walked over to the chart of the Strait of Juan de Fuca tacked to the wall.

"Okay, Norm, here's what I want you to do. Here's where the *Michigan* is and here's the location of the *Nissan Maru,* a Japanese car carrier inbound for Seattle. I want you and the photographer to get aboard that ship. Then you must convince the skipper to allow you to photograph the ferry and the submarine when they pass—the closer the better. You'll be able to get some good photos as you pass them."

"How much do I tell that Japanese master?"

"As much as you have to, but get the pictures!"

"Aye, aye, sir."

"And Norm, we need a shot from the starboard side of the *Spokane.* Ships normally pass port to port when meeting. You're going to have to get the Japanese master to pass starboard to starboard, understand?"

"Understood, sir."

MacIntyre walked over to his desk and again studied the pictures spread across the top of it. *Where the hell is that damn sub skipper, anyway, and when are those bastards going to break radio silence and tell us what they want?*

Sunday, 10:00 A.M.—Strait of Juan de Fuca

Gunnery Sergeant Jennings could easily see the *Spokane* and the dark shape of the *Michigan*'s sail against the white side of the ferry, but the low, black hull was almost invisible against the black waterline of the ferry. The rudder at the stern of the submarine rose six feet above the water and seemed to be trailing along behind both vessels. He put down the binoculars and keyed the radio.

"DeRosales, this is Gunny Jennings, are you there, over?" The answer came immediately.

"Roger, Gunny, this is DeRosales, over."

"Good to hear your voice, Jesús. How are you holding up, over?" Jennings had been unable to contact DeRosales at 7:00 A.M., but had talked with him on the hour at 8:00 and 9:00.

"Okay, I guess. I've been in every compartment of the boat, even the reactor room. They're all dead, Gunny—every one of them. This boat is a floating tomb. What's going to happen now?"

"Jesús, I don't know. I'm on a small craft, and we have you in sight right now. We're waiting for a Coast Guard cutter to join up with us. I'm sure we'll be hearing from the men who did this and there will be some negotiations to get you and the others on the ferry released, over."

"Gunny, I got an idea! I can probably slip over the side and they might never see me. Then you can pick me up—you said you're on a boat nearby, right?"

"That's affirmative. I'm on a boat close by, but, Jesús, we need you there—we need you to stay where you are for a while so you can call in reports. These guys killed your shipmates, and maybe you can help us nail them, okay?"

"I guess I don't have much choice, Gunny, but what can I do, over?"

"That's the ticket, sailor—where are you now, over?"

"I'm still in the sail. I don't want to be belowdecks unless I have to, over."

"Can you safely look back along the missile deck?"

"I think so."

"Give it a try, but be careful, and tell me exactly what you see, over."

After several minutes, DeRosales reported back with a fairly accurate description of the paint cans perched on tripods above the missile doors.

"That's super, Jesús. Now we want you to lay low, and if for some reason the terrorists come aboard the *Michigan,* I want you to go below and hide, okay?"

"Okay, Gunny, I'll do it, but why me? How come I'm the only one left alive?" Jennings had spoken with the *Michigan*'s chief engineer before he left Bangor. The man was nearly in shock about his dead shipmates and losing his boat, but he did tell Jennings why DeRosales might have been the only survivor.

"Jesús, we think they somehow pumped poisonous gas into the *Michigan.* The air-conditioning carried it throughout the boat. The torpedo room is at the end of the air-conditioning loop, so you were able to get your mask on before the gas got to you, over." There was a moment before DeRosales replied.

"I—I see. But still, why would God choose me and take all the others?" Jennings, who wasn't a particularly religious man, didn't really have an answer, but he knew DeRosales needed one.

"I guess the Lord wanted you to live. Maybe he left you there for a reason—to stay by the radio and help us. Now you gotta hang tough so we can try and save the others on the ferry. Can you do that, over?"

"I'll try, Gunny. Most of the time I'm all right, but sometimes I get so scared I can't think."

"You're doin' a good job, Jesús. Now you just keep your eyes and ears open, and I'll contact you again at eleven o'clock, over."

"Okay, Gunny, DeRosales out."

Jennings was on a sixty-five-foot torpedo retriever, a craft that looked like a patrol boat with a cut-out portion in the stern for recovering torpedoes that had been test-fired. It was a boxy-

looking craft, but powerful and seaworthy. They had left the
Bangor wharf at 7:30 A.M. in pursuit of the ferry and the stolen
submarine and taken station a mile and a half astern of them
shortly after 9:20.

"What do we do now, Gunny?" asked a rough-complected
man dressed in wash khakis who stood at the helm.

"Just lay back and shadow them, Chief. They'll tell us if
they want us to get any closer." Jennings reported back to Bangor by radio and passed along the information about the paint
cans on the tripods.

Jennings was concerned about DeRosales. The boy had put
his trust in him, just as Halasey had. His orders were to stand
clear of the two stricken vessels until the cutter arrived. That
might be hard to do if DeRosales got into trouble. *I don't know,*
he thought, *if I can stand by and allow those bastards to kill
another one of my men.* He stepped out of the deckhouse to the
railing and put the binoculars back on the *Spokane.*

Peck had managed to bring the two vessels back up to six knots,
but wind and a light chop on the water prevented them from
going faster. He had been on his feet at the helm almost nonstop
for nearly eight hours.

"Are all the ferryboat captains as handsome as you?" Peck
rubbed the stubble on his chin and eyed the woman who
lounged against the wall of the pilothouse. She draped her forearms across the barrel and stock of the AK-47 that hung from a
sling around her neck. Her breasts folded over the top of the
receiver. Ahmed looked up at her from the radio equipment,
shook his head imperceptibly, and went back to his work. Peck
hesitated. He didn't know what to make of this woman, but he
hoped he could learn something.

"What are you doing here?—you're not an Arab."

"No, I'm not, but you don't have to be from the Middle East
to want to fuck the United States."

"Is that what you want to do, fuck the United States?"

"Maybe. Or maybe we could get that fat little first mate of
yours to drive the boat, and we could go down to the crew's

lounge and fuck each other. What do you think about that, Monsieur Ferryboat Captain?''

Peck looked over at her, expecting to see that she was toying with him. Instead he saw a woman who wanted sex—lips apart, eyes wide, and breathing heavily. He could think of no reply, so he said nothing. Michelle got up and slowly walked behind him, placing her shoulder in the middle of his back and the muzzle of the assault rifle in his ribs. She ran her free hand along the inside of his thigh to his crotch, and then moved on past him.

''What do you think, First Mate—I'll bet the captain is hung like a bull?'' Janey stared at her coldly, then looked away. ''You don't agree, First Mate? Would you like to fuck the captain, or do you prefer women?'' Janey's head snapped around, and her eyes flashed. ''It's okay, *chérie*—sometimes I do too.'' Michelle laughed and walked back across the pilothouse and out onto the pilothouse wing.

''Is she a part of your Islamic Brothers or whatever you call yourselves?'' Peck asked, just loud enough for Ahmed to hear.

''She is a pig,'' spat Ahmed. ''She is here only for the terror and for the terrorist, not the Jihad. But she is dangerous, and you would do well to remember that.''

On the passenger deck, Jamil circled the passengers. They were dull-eyed, weary, and restless—like a herd of cattle in a holding pen. Food wrappers and cups littered the floor. Jamil had ordered the galley opened and seen to it that food was passed out. Affording prisoners a measure of care made them more manageable. Hassan and Yehya sat eating together at one of the nearby tables. Hassan offered him a cold sandwich, but he declined. Jamil was flush with power and pride and required nothing else.

''Salah?''

''He is on guard in the engine room,'' replied Yehya.

Then Fenton has lookout duty on the promenade deck, thought Jamil. He descended to the car deck and on down to the engineering spaces, where he found Salah near the propulsion control panel. The lithe brown man squatted on the deck with his buttocks resting on his heels, forearms draped on his knees. Had the rifle he held upright between his legs been a shepherd's staff, he could easily have been on a hill in Judea, tending goats like his grandfathers before him. *Will he go back to the life of a herdsman when this is over? The years of fighting and hiding have changed all of them, but if any of them can go back to the way it was before the Jews invaded—the way it used to be—it is this tough little man who now tends engineers instead of goats.* Jamil squatted beside him.

"*Al salam alaykom,*" he said in the traditional Islamic way of greeting. "How are they behaving?"

"They do their jobs, and occasionally look at the explosive you have placed on the pipe on the floor. I think you could leave them untended except for Gosnell. If he had the chance, I think he would make trouble—that one is a fighter."

"And the others?"

"They are sheep. All they want is to be safely off this boat—nothing else."

"Watch them, but watch our own people, too. You and I have been here before, waiting to negotiate after the demands have been made. The Americans could try to make us drop our guard and move against us, although it is too early for their special military units to have had time to respond. I know you are always vigilant, but the others will have to be made to stay alert."

"What if the Americans do try something—attack us in speedboats or helicopters?"

"I don't think they will—it would be too difficult. But if they do, we will set fire to their submarine, sink this ferry, and fight to the death."

Salah smiled at the thought. "It has been a long struggle, Sayeh. If we are not to be successful, it would be good death, would it not?"

"We are already successful. We have stolen their nuclear submarine and their nuclear missiles."

"I know, but we want our own nation, and we want to be free from domination by the Jews. If we are still to have no land, would it not be better to end it here? Promise me, Sayeh, that if we cannot do what we set out to do, then we die fighting.''

Jamil looked again at the man squatting beside him. *All he wants,* Jamil thought, *is his own land, and his only fear is that he will be denied an honorable death. And the Jews want to tell men like this to carry an ID card, to live where they tell him he has to live, and how much water he is to take from their wells.*

''You have my word, old friend. If the Israelis and the Americans do not guarantee what we ask, then it is to the death.''

Jamil walked along the car deck looking at the black monster tied to the side of the ferry, the nylon ropes stretched tight and hard as metal bands. Ahmed and Salah had placed additional lines between the two vessels, so the *Michigan* rode securely, if reluctantly, alongside. The black sail and low, flat deck gave only a hint of her huge underwater bulk. He checked the two transmitters attached to his belt, one for the explosives in the engine room and the other for the charges set on the submarine. Both showed an amber light, which indicated that the firing circuits were armed and on safe. Jamil completed a tour of the car deck and climbed the stairs to the passenger deck. *I should eat,* he told himself. *It will be a long day and I will have to negotiate with the Great Satan on behalf of my people.* He was walking forward on the port side when he heard a muffled weeping. Following the sound, he withdrew his pistol and crept toward the ship's office.

The weeping was now accompanied by grunting and muffled sounds of a struggle. Jamil peered carefully around the corner of the small crew's lounge, then stepped full into the doorway. Fenton was there with the teenage girl who had been tied to the rail during the attack on the *Michigan.* She still resisted, but her physical reserves were spent. The sweatshirt was up around her chest and her bra was torn away, as were her shorts and underpants. Fenton's own trousers were around his knees as he knelt between her thighs. He pinned her to the floor with one hand in the middle of her chest while he struggled with his undershorts, which were tangled on his erection.

''You PIG!''

Jamil's kick caught him in the rib cage and lifted him off the girl. Without thinking, Fenton reached for his rifle. Jamil pushed the weapon out of reach with his foot and whipped him across the face with the barrel of the silencer, carving a two-inch gash in his cheekbone. Fenton was dazed and started to say something, then, realizing his pants were down, reached to pull them up. Jamil hit him again across the mouth, splitting both lips and leaving him barely conscious and totally helpless. He then grasped him by the hair and dragged him from the room. Jamil deposited Fenton in the forward passenger cabin in full view of the shackled hostages.

"Hassan, get upstairs and stand lookout—where this miserable excuse for a soldier should have been—*now!*" Hassan spilled his tea as he scrambled to his feet and hurried out. Yehya, too, came to his feet, grasping his Uzi and assuming a vigilant pose.

Jamil stepped over and quickly cut free the woman who had stood at the rail with the girl. "She is in the crew's lounge—see to her." The woman left without a word.

"How did this happen?" he snapped. "Were you not supposed to be watching?" Yehya looked puzzled and apologetic. "Do none of you understand how important this is?" Jamil paced the floor between the group of passengers and the galley. All eyes were on him. The woman escorted the girl back into the passenger cabin, wrapped in a blanket. She gave him a malevolent look as they made their way to their seats.

"Hear this!" Jamil called to the hostages. "I will tolerate no disobedience from anyone on my vessel, including those in my prize crew. This wretched maggot is a traitor to your country and an embarrassment to our cause."

Fenton lay on his side on the linoleum in a semifetal position, still trying, with little success, to get his pants up. Jamil shot him twice in the crotch. Fenton grasped his genitals, mouth open in a noiseless scream. His eyes never left Jamil, silently pleading for mercy. Then he began to emit a low, primordial moan. At first it was almost inaudible, but it gathered strength and soon filled the cabin. Jamil waited until it reached a crescendo, fully documenting the man's pain, before he fired two more rounds into Fenton's heart.

"Retie the two hostages," Jamil said to Yehya as he placed a new magazine in the pistol, "then throw the carcass of this swine over the side." He grabbed two sandwiches and a carton of juice on his way back up to the pilothouse.

Sunday, 10:15 A.M.—Strait of Juan de Fuca, near Port Angeles

Kunio Kishida stood on the bridge wing of the *Nissan Maru* enjoying the peaceful transit down the Strait of Juan de Fuca. They had made radar landfall just after 3:00 that morning and had passed Cape Flattery Light abeam to starboard at dawn. The *Nissan Maru* was a clumsy-looking ship with a short, stubby bow; it resembled a large steel shoe box. She was a single-purpose vessel, designed to carry Japanese cars across the northern Pacific to the United States and return as quickly as possible for another load. And carry them she did—five thousand Nissan and Datsun cars and light trucks per crossing. Kishida always felt a surge of pride at the completion of a crossing. He was crisp and alert, having just showered and donned a fresh uniform.

The pilot, who had boarded the *Nissan Maru* at Neah Bay, stood nearby, occasionally giving course and speed instructions to Kishida, which he translated for the helmsman. He was a weathered-looking American with a large belly hanging over his belt and unruly mustaches that draped to either side of the meerschaum pipe that rested on his chin—a sharp contrast to the neat Japanese captain.

Kishida's family had been mariners for generations. His father had put to sea with the Imperial Navy during the war. He was a deck officer on the *Shokaku,* and young Kunio remembered him when he was home on shore leave after their victory at Pearl Harbor, resplendent in his dress uniform and samurai sword. He was lost at Midway when his ship was sunk with all hands by dive bombers from the *Hornet.* The *Shokaku* was also a strange-looking craft, a modified cruiser hull converted for duty as an aircraft carrier. She carried planes just as the *Nissan Maru* carried cars. Occasionally, Kishida thought of himself as a samurai, and those thoughts were never more apparent than when he brought a load of cars to America. *We lost the battle, honored Father,* he thought, *but we are winning the war.* Static from the portable transceiver carried by the pilot brought him out of his reverie. The American listened and said a few words into the microphone before turning to Kishida.

"From the Coast Guard at Port Angeles. We're supposed to slow to four knots and stand by to receive a helo."

Kishida wrinkled his brow and audibly sucked air through his teeth to show his concern. "So! This is unusual, is it not?"

"A little," said the pilot with a shrug. "Probably some customs agent following a drug tip. Nothin' I can do about it, though. You want to slow down?"

"*Hai.*"

Kishida issued instructions, and the *Nissan Maru* slowly began to lose way. While they waited, he swept the broad channel in front of him with his glasses—a superb pair of Nikon binoculars that had been a gift from the company for twenty years of service as a master. There was nothing on the water but the hazy outline of a ferry well to the east in the middle of the Strait.

Lieutenant Dan Mulvey was having a great time. He had just picked up a Navy commander and a third-class petty officer at the Sand Point Naval Station. His orders were to get them aboard a Japanese car carrier that was inbound on the Strait of Juan de Fuca near Port Angeles, and to get them there fast. He was also told to approach the Japanese vessel from the west so as to mask his flight path from any traffic on the eastern portion of the Strait. The orange and white Aerospatiale H-65 was racing across the Olympic Peninsula at 165 knots, hugging the foothills of the Olympic Mountains. Mulvey glanced back at his two passengers in the rear compartment. Both were white knuckled, and there was a noticeable layer of moisture on the commander's upper lip. Mulvey met the eye of his copilot, who smiled from behind his lip mike. They hadn't had this much fun since flying drug-interdiction missions off Key West.

Mulvey threw the helo into a sharp right-hand turn west of Crescent Bay and sped out over the Strait just thirty feet off the water. He immediately picked up the car carrier some ten miles to the east. When he was due west of her, he again banked into a hard ninety-degree turn to starboard and flew up the ship's stern. He now flew twenty feet off the water, keeping the bulk of the car carrier between his aircraft and the ferry that was farther east. Mulvey had been ordered not to break radio silence. *Maybe this is a narcotics bust,* he thought, *although the two white-faced Navymen in back don't look up to taking on any druggies.*

The *Nissan Maru* didn't really have a stern—it was a rectangular box welded onto a hull. Mulvey honked the machine back and covered the last hundred yards flying at a forty-five-degree angle, bleeding off airspeed and bringing the helo up to the aft lip of the huge superstructure. The H-65 rested on top of the ship for a few seconds while the two passengers scrambled off. Then the little helo jumped into the air and literally rolled off the back of the ship. Mulvey smoothly brought the craft to level flight a few feet off the water, and the helo screamed back to the west.

"If it's all the same to you, sir, I'll just ride this ship back to Seattle and get off at the pier."

Commander Norm Reasoner wiped his face with a handkerchief and took a deep breath. "Baker, I don't think there's enough Japanese guys on this tub to stuff me back aboard that helo. Let's see if we can find the captain."

They began walking forward across the top of the ship, dodging equipment-storage boxes and ventilators. They got halfway to the bow before two crewmen came running up to show them to the bridge. Reasoner carried in his briefcase a hastily drafted letter of authorization from Admiral MacIntyre, and Photographer's Mate Second Class Baker carried two anodized-aluminum camera cases. They were taken to the bridge, which was pasted to the forward end of the box-ship.

"Captain, I'm Commander Reasoner and this is Petty Officer Baker. We're sorry to drop in on you like this, but a situation of some urgency has come up, and we need your assistance. May I speak with you in private?" Kishida nodded curtly and led Reasoner to the port wing of the bridge, which extended out far enough to give the conning officer a view of the entire length of the ship. Kishida said a few terse words in Japanese, and a crewman who was sweeping the deck quickly disappeared.

"Commander, I am to be at my berth in Seattle at 4:00 P.M. If you delay me much longer, I will miss the proper tide for docking. Why have you boarded my ship in this manner?"

Reasoner handed him the letter from Admiral MacIntyre. "Captain, there has been an act of piracy aboard one of our commercial passenger ferries. The captured ferry has seized a nuclear submarine, and they are now just ahead of you in the Strait." Kishida looked out from the bridge to the east. Bow-on, the *Spokane,* with its large auto bay, looked like a flat, white O on the water.

"This does not concern my ship. What would you expect me to do?"

"Pass the ferry at two hundred yards on your starboard side."

"Pass to starboard? But that is against the rules of navigation."

"So is stealing a ferry and an American submarine."

"The submarine, is it armed?"

"Yes, sir. It is a nuclear ballistic-missile submarine, and it is armed."

"So!" replied the Japanese captain. His brow again wrinkled as he inhaled through clenched teeth. He took the glasses and studied the vessels ahead of him for a several moments. Then he spoke rapidly to his helmsman in Japanese while the pilot puffed contentedly on his pipe.

Sunday, 10:20 A.M.—Aboard the *Spokane*

Peck sensed there was something different about Jamil when he returned to the pilothouse. He abruptly dismissed Michelle, telling her to get below and keep an eye on the passengers. Then he checked the chart laid out on the table behind the helm and studied the shoreline to either side before marking their position on the chart. Ahmed, too, noticed the change.

"Jamil, what happened—is something wrong?"

"We are another man short," Jamil said casually. "I had to kill Fenton. No great loss, though—we are better off without the little swine. Any word yet?"

"None," replied Ahmed. He wondered about the dead American, but he knew Jamil would speak about it only when he was ready. "The standard VHF maritime frequency has been ordered clear by the authorities, but that could have been in response to our capture of the ferry."

"And the TV transmission?"

"The satellite through which we transmitted our video signal is still operable on the channels we did not destroy. So far, no ground stations have tried to use any of the functioning channels, which means they are restricting the use of the satellite. I can only assume that they are keeping the satellite clear for future communication." Jamil nodded his head in acknowledgment and again studied the chart. After a moment he turned to Peck, speaking in English.

"I have just executed the only American in my group. He was in the process of forcing himself on one of the female prisoners when I found him. The man was totally without honor. You see, Peck, even in war there is a need for honor."

"War?" said Peck. "You mean terrorism." A flash of anger flicked across Jamil's face. It passed quickly, and he regarded Peck critically as he sat down on the stool near the radar console. He placed one of the sandwiches within Peck's reach and began unwrapping the other for himself.

"War is a term that for you has dignity and honor. You have

your national holidays to celebrate your countrymen who fought and died in your wars. But don't forget, Peck, your country has billions to spend on the materials of war and you fight those wars thousands of miles from home. How was it your president labeled your actions in Kuwait—a 'just war'? You are a nation rich enough to define war and honor on your own terms.''

''Maybe, but I see nothing honorable in killing the crew of a submarine without warning, or holding innocent civilians hostage.''

''Of course you don't, Peck, but then, your homeland has never been occupied by a brutal, well-equipped mercenary force. You have never seen your parents forced to live in a refugee camp, stripped of everything they own and made to live in squalor. You have never had to watch your children grow up undernourished and with no hope for a better life because they are stateless persons. Peck, have you any children?''

''I have two sons.''

''Two sons—God has been good to you. Tell me, Peck, what would you do if your country were occupied by the Russians, and your wife and sons had to live in a dirt-floor shack with no water? What if you were allowed to work only at menial labor, even though you are a skilled ship captain? If terrorism were your only weapon, would you cast it aside and condemn your family to a life of wretched existence because you could not fight in a uniform in a proper war?'' Jamil stopped close beside him. Peck noticed that whenever he was close, the pistol was always in his hand. ''I don't think so, Peck,'' he continued quietly. ''You are not the kind of man who would passively accept that kind of oppression, just as you don't willingly accept my occupation of your ship. You are a warrior, Peck, and you would fight—with whatever means was at your disposal. You would even stoop to being what you call me, a terrorist.''

Jamil stepped away and thrust a piece of sandwich in his mouth. He carefully scanned the horizon around the *Spokane* before he spoke again ''But just remember, my friend, if you try anything here, you will die just as surely as if you were in a *real* war.''

For some reason, Peck thought, *it is important for him that he is thought of as a soldier—that there is nobility to his actions. Perhaps there is from his point of view, but that is of no concern to me—he's a zealot and he's taken my boat.*

"How were you able to do all this?" prompted Peck. "Knowing about the ferries and the bridge, and about the security at Bangor? It must have taken a lot of planning and some inside help."

"A democracy is a dangerously open society. People are always happy to talk about their work—or to complain about it. There is a surprising amount of detailed information published about your submarines and their bases. The library has books on this ferry with complete illustrations. The function of the Hood Canal bridge and its workings are not secrets. Your press is held in such esteem that anyone posing as a journalist gets answers to his questions—a spiral notebook and a pencil are all the identification that is required."

"You didn't get the information on a Trident submarine like that."

"No, I did not—I had to buy it, and one of your greedy businessmen was all too eager to furnish it. He lost the contract to provide repair services at Bangor to a rival company, and he was quite bitter about it. We hired him as a 'consultant' so he would feel better about being a traitor. His knowledge of the systems on the Trident and the base security was very specific. It was almost laughable, Peck. He treated us just like it was another business transaction."

"He'll pay for having given out that information," snapped Peck.

"He already has. I had to kill him for security reasons. But your government would only put him in jail—you don't kill murderers, let alone traitors. Take your countryman Walker, the spy who gave the Russians your most vital Navy secrets. He now enjoys life in one of your soft prisons, and he eats better than most of my people."

Peck squinted as he measured Jamil, who had once again settled on the stool by the radar. "You still won't get away with this. The hostages are one thing, but the submarine and those nuclear missiles are quite another matter. The President will have to stop you—you know that.''

''Your president can stop me at any time. He can send his commandos to storm this vessel. If that is what Mr. Bennett chooses to do, I accept it. But I will sink this ferry and destroy the submarine, and there will be much bloodshed. The nuclear contamination alone will be a major national disaster for you. But I also think your President Bennett will do everything in his power to get the Israelis to agree to our demands and to provide the guarantees we have asked for. I believe he will do this before he sends his commandos.''

Sunday, 12:45 P.M.—McChord Air Force Base, Tacoma, Washington

The C-130 had taxied right to the door of the hangar, and there was a squad of MPs there to provide security. Lieutenant Horner and his men quickly unloaded their gear and carefully staged it in one corner of the hangar. Master Chief Watson ordered the platoon diving supervisor to inspect and predive each Draeger scuba, and the platoon riggers to check the parachutes and fast-rope gear. The rest of the men busied themselves with their personal equipment. Cases of ammunition and grenades were waiting in the hangar when they arrived. Several of the SEALs were sitting cross-legged on the concrete floor, loading magazines. In the near corner of the hangar by the door was a field mess and steam tables, and there were cots in the far rear corner. The platoon was still in isolation, and would be confined to the hangar unless there was a mission or until the crisis was over. Horner stood at the hangar door with Chief Watson, watching the men prepare their equipment.

''Sir, we had a good load-out. Wildrick can't find his swim fins, and one of the Air Force guards went out to find a pair. Otherwise, the guys are in good shape.''

''Thanks, Chief. I just talked with the major in charge of the isolation, a G-2 type from Fort Lewis. He knows less than we do about what's going on, or he's not talking. You're from around here, aren't you, Chief?''

"Yes, sir. Grew up in Bellingham, up near the Canadian border.''

"Got any feelings about this one?''

"Not really, sir. If the terrorists are on a ferry and they make it out of the Hood Canal into Puget Sound with that submarine, it's going to be real hard to surprise them.''

"How cold is the water up here?''

"About fifty-four degrees. Let's hope they can negotiate this one. It could be a real sonofabitch.''

"Looks like we got company.''

Both men placed their hands over their ears as a C-141 taxied across the tarmac and parked next to the hangar. The engines wound down to an idle, and the ramp in the tail of the aircraft reluctantly ground open. The Delta Force troopers began to file out of the aircraft. All the soldiers had a weapon slung over one shoulder and a rucksack on the other. Most carried a parachute gear bag. The other SEALs had come to the door to watch, and the two groups looked at each other like rival high-school basketball teams at a holiday tournament.

"All right, you guys, let's give these men a hand with their gear.''

Watson spotted the first sergeant and took his kit bag from him. The rest of the Navymen hurried to help the others. The new arrivals were also prepared for multiple insertion, and had a great deal of additional equipment. The Starlifter was quickly unloaded and taxied away. The men had begun to mingle, and Horner found their platoon leader.

"Captain, I'm Brian Horner with SEAL Team Three.''

"Tom Sherrard with the Delta Operations Group. You guys based in San Diego, Brian?'' Sherrard was a lean man and spoke with what passed for a Texas drawl, though he was from Oklahoma. He had a patient, down-home way that made him appear almost indifferent, but when he spoke with someone, he looked directly at them and he listened carefully.

"That's right. Any idea what's going on?''

"Not really. I guess a group of ragheads hijacked a ferryboat an' stole a nuclear submarine. They must be pretty good to have pulled that off."

"I understand you brought a guy from SOCOM that's going to be our control?"

"Yeah, a bird colonel—flew in with us. Bit of a tight-ass. He jumped into a staff car and took off a few minutes ago. You never know about those REMFs."

"REMFs?"

"Rear-echelon motherfuckers."

"Oh, right. Well, I guess they'll tell us what's going on when they think we need to know. Say, do you know Richie Hulse?"

"Sure do. He's a member of our training cadre. How'd you know him?"

"We were in Ranger School together. He just beat me out for class honors."

"Ole Richie's a good trooper. Listen, Brian, I better check on my men and get my gear set up. We do a lot of waitin' on these things, so we'll probably have plenty of time to bullshit."

"Sounds good, Tom. See you later."

Across the hangar, the two senior enlisted men stepped away from the others. They had been around too long to waste time on trivia. Master Chief Watson accepted a dip from First Sergeant Blackwood and got down to business.

"What kind of a team you have, First Sergeant?"

"We're a Mideast, Delta response element," replied Blackwood. "A lot of my men speak Arabic, some Farsi. Our specialty is urban warfare and CQB. We're also a pretty fair conventional-assault unit. How about you?

"Standard direct-action SEAL platoon. The platoon's been together a while, so we're in a high state of readiness. We've been doing a lot of water work, so I feel pretty comfortable there."

"CQB?"

"It's part of our deployment workup and we're not all that

bad when it comes to working buildings, but basically, we're maritime raiders.''

''What about your officers, Master Chief?''

''They're okay, although my ensign's pretty green—just out of training. Neither has seen action. Yours?''

''The captain's as good as we get. We've been on two shows, and he's done a helluva job.''

Watson folded his arms as he shifted his plug to the other side of his mouth and traced a crack in the concrete floor with the side of his boot. Both men knew it would be a close-quarters battle with hostages at risk, and if there was any way to get the Delta team aboard, they were best trained for the job.

''First Sergeant, seems like even money that one or the other of us is gonna have to go in on this. I'd say if it's a helo assault, you guys are the best bet. If it's a waterborne assault and especially if it's wet work, it probably should go to us.''

''I agree. Think they'll ask us?''

''Oh, they'll ask us, but will they listen to what we have to say?'' Both smiled knowingly. ''Chances are the decision will be made pretty far up the line anyway.''

''Roger that, Master Chief. Let's us wander over to the field kitchen and see if these Air Force pukes know how to make coffee.''

Fifteen minutes later, Colonel Braxton walked back into the hangar and called Sherrard and Horner over to the hangar door. Accompanying Braxton was a blocky Army captain in camouflage battle dress and soft fatigue hat. He was black and very tough looking.

''Horner,'' said Braxton, extending his hand, ''pleased to meet you. Gentlemen, this is Captain Smith. He and his Rangers will be read into the problem.'' They shook hands around and Braxton continued. ''I will be the control for all special-operations elements. If this situation goes into extremis, it will be a Delta Force action, but we want the SEALs and the Rangers standing by with contingency plans and for possible follow-on actions. Naturally, a negotiated resolution to this situation is what we all hope for. However, if the President decides to use

force, or the lives of the hostages are in imminent danger, we
have to be ready.''

*He doesn't look like the kind who hopes for a "negotiated
resolution,"* thought Sherrard as he carefully studied the colonel, *but then, he doesn't have to make the assault.*

Braxton looked at his watch and continued. ''A Blackhawk
helicopter will be here shortly to take us to Seattle for a briefing
with an Admiral MacIntyre who has been placed in command
of the operation. He'll be looking for operational concepts for
an assault on this ferryboat.'' Braxton tamped a cigarette
against his thumbnail and lit it in practiced motion. ''Any questions?''

''Just one, Colonel,'' said Sherrard. ''I'd like to take my first
sergeant along for the briefing.''

''I'll want my chief there, too, sir.''

''Very well. Have them ready to go when that Blackhawk
arrives. That'll be all for now, gentlemen.''

Sunday, 2:10 P.M.—Andrews Air Force Base, Maryland

''Sir, we're parked at the gate and your helicopter is standing
by.'' The President waved his hand in dismissal of the uniformed crewman. Both he and Colonel Williams were glued to
one of the monitors in the President's cabin.

''Play it again.'' Williams hit the rewind button and the two
of them watched Jamil present his demands for the fourth time.
At the end of the tape, they both stared at a frozen frame of
Jamil.

''What do you think, Buck?''

''I don't recognize this guy or the name, and I've never heard
of the Islamic Brothers of Freedom. He's made no attempt to
conceal his identity. He either thinks we have nothing on him or
he doesn't care—probably the latter. We know he's got the

ferry and the *Michigan,* and we have to assume that he has the means to carry out his threat."

"Any ideas yet as to who may be behind this?"

"We'll probably be lucky to find out, even with something this big. There's usually a long trail of cutouts and cover organizations. And say we do track it to Abu Abbas or someone like him, it's still hard to prove who's backing him."

"So what do we do?" President Bennett now studied Williams with the same intensity that he had the terrorist.

"Play it by the book, sir. Establish communications, negotiate, buy time, and wait for him to make a mistake."

"It doesn't look like this guy has made any mistakes so far. What if he doesn't—what if he's prepared to go all the way with this?"

"Then if we want to try and stop him, we'll have to make an assault on that ferry." *And that,* thought Williams, *will be a decision made by the President, not a Marine colonel.*

"That's not going to be an easy call, Buck. I want you sitting in at the Security Council briefing Morton has scheduled. Sometimes it's not always just by the book, so if you have any gut feelings about this Jamil or what you think he might do, don't keep them to yourself."

"Aye, aye, sir."

Morton Keeney met them at the bottom of the boarding stairs and escorted them across the tarmac to the waiting helo. Once aboard, the modified presidential H-3 immediately lifted off and headed for the White House.

"Anything new, Mort?"

"No, sir. You've seen the tape and I assume you've had time to read the traffic?" *Air Force One* was a flying communications center. The President had been able to follow the situation reports from Seattle, and the meager flow of traffic from the FBI and the intelligence agencies.

"I have. Any word from the Israelis?"

"Not yet. I've just received confirmation that they have a tape of the terrorist demands."

"The briefing?"

"They're waiting for us at the White House. I've assembled the appropriate agencies and several experts whose opinions may be needed, and to be honest, that's a lot of people for a working session."

Morton Keeney liked to be in control, and if there was more time, he would have been. He preferred to make staffing assignments, request data, and to summarize and collate information. Then he and one or two key advisers would present a well-organized and, time permitting, well-rehearsed presidential briefing. Then, if Bennett had in-depth questions or required additional information, Keeney could go to the appropriate governmental agency or individual expert and get the required data. But there was no time now. The President had requested a special NSC meeting with specific governmental agency and military personnel. There would be no screening or manipulation of information, and Keeney would have no control of it.

"Would you like me to chair the meeting, Mr. President?"

"I'll do it myself, Mort. I have to get the facts and a clear understanding of what options are open to us, and I need to do it fast. Then you and I, along with General Scott, Grummell, and Baines, are going to have to come up with a plan of action."

As soon as the helicopter touched down, the President, Keeney, and Colonel Williams walked quickly across the lawn and into the White House. A Marine sentry preceded them as they hurried to the briefing room.

"The Commander in Chief!" announced another Marine sentry coming to attention just inside the conference-room door. There was a general rustling from those assembled around the long, polished wooden table as they fought the heavy chairs back through the thick carpet to get to their feet. Men seated along the walls of the conference room, many of them in uniform, also rose.

"Take your seats, please." The President strode purposefully to his place at the head of the table. Morton Keeney took the chair immediately to his right, while Williams found a seat along the wall. "I believe you all know as much as I do about this incident, but I'm going to have Morton Keeney provide us with a summary of events so we're all on the same sheet of music. Mort?''

"At approximately 5:50 A.M. eastern time, a group of armed terrorists took control of a Washington State ferryboat on Puget Sound and . . ." For the next five minutes, the National Security Adviser detailed the chain of events. "At 1:55 this afternoon, the following video transmission from the terrorists was first aired by CNN. It was then immediately released by the other networks." Jamil again made his speech from the large rear-projection screen at the end of the conference room. "And that's where we now stand," concluded Keeney.

"How were they able to tap into the news networks like that?" asked Bennett.

At the other end of the table, a portly man in his mid-fifties raised his hand as he spoke. He was the President's press secretary. "We believe they have a remote transmission capability, similar to the equipment carried by the roving news vans, and they were able to co-opt a commercial news satellite. We've been able to determine that this transmission was a prepared videotape done well in advance of the taking of the ferry and the submarine. We also have to assume that they have the ability to make live broadcasts using the same data-link.''

"Thanks, Brad," said the President. "And I assume that the whole world will be watching if they do?''

"Yes, sir, that is correct.''

"Damn! Who is this guy, anyway, Armand? Do we have anything on him?''

The President's comments were directed at a neatly dressed, scholarly-looking man sitting to his left. He was thoughtfully polishing his glasses, seemingly unaware that he had been addressed. He wrapped the wire frames first around one ear, then the other, and returned the linen handkerchief to his breast pocket. Armand Grummell had had time to study the video clip longer than anyone else at the table. A contact in the media had seen to it that the CIA got a copy of the tape thirty minutes before CNN broke the story. Until that time, no one at Langley had seen his face. But they did know of the man called "the

Shadow,'' and since the terrorist captured at the Hood Canal bridge had volunteered that his leader was a man called Jamil, Grummell was well prepared. The CIA director was also a former Beirut station chief and Mideast Division head, which had afforded him a long association with Arab terrorists.

"He is a Palestinian named Jamil Nusseibeh. However, he has operated under so many pseudonyms that it has been difficult to confirm if this is his true surname. We've had a 201 file on him since 1972, but this afternoon was the first time we've seen his face. He is approximately forty-two—quite old for an active terrorist, actually—but a highly capable one nonetheless. He goes by the name of Jamil, but he is most often referred to as the Sayeh, or simply, 'the Shadow.' His background is sketchy, but it seems his parents were intellectuals and were expelled from Palestine after the British Mandate. They were forced to live on the move as one Arab state after another made them unwelcome. They finally died in poverty in the Marka refugee camp in Jordan. Jamil attended the University of Beirut for a short time before leaving to join the PLO. His direct involvement with the Fatah was brief, and he has, for the most part, been an independent contractor. We feel the name of his current organization, the Islamic Brothers of Freedom, is a title of convenience, and taken only to lend legitimacy to this act. His reputation is that of a shrewd, ruthless, and accomplished terrorist, and unlike Ahmed Jibril or Abu Abbas, he has a phobia for publicity. This proclivity for anonymity has served him well, for we know very little about the man except that his skill and his experience make him a most formidable and dangerous enemy.'' Grummell paused to remove his glasses before continuing. "We haven't yet been able to confirm this, but based on the infirmation we received from the FBI, we believe one of the terrorists that was killed during the fighting on the Hood Canal bridge was his brother—and the only surviving member of his family.''

"If this Jamil is so publicity shy, then why did he so carefully arrange to have his face broadcast on national TV?"

Since the Iran-Contra affair, the administration had found that a spirited rivalry between the National Security Adviser and the Director of Central Intelligence to be in the national interest. Morton Keeney and Armand Grummell more than satisfied that requirement.

"It could be a number of things, Morton, but I believe one we shouldn't disregard is that this is his final act, and he wants us to know it—that he will succeed in forcing us to agree to his demands, or he is prepared to carry out his threat, even if it means his own death. I should think you would find that rather obvious."

"That'll do, gentlemen. Harry, what do you make of this?"

Harold Baines was the Director of the FBI. Domestic terrorism was under the jurisdiction of the Bureau, and this incident was by far the most serious attack on the United States the Bureau had encountered. Baines had none of the information on this Jamil character that they seemed to have at CIA. It was unreasonable to expect that he should, but it still made him uncomfortable. It was, however, very reasonable to expect that an operation of this magnitude mounted against a military base in the United States should have been detected.

"In all candor, Mr. President, we were taken totally by surprise on this one. As you know, we have previously uncovered numerous attacks planned against civilian and military targets. We have nothing on this Jamil, but then, our intelligence effort is primarily directed against domestic terrorist organizations. This guy must be good, though, because we had no hint it was coming." Harold Baines was a holdover from the previous administration. He was a prototype of the post-Hoover FBI directors—honest, straightforward, hardworking, and as apolitical as one could be in that position.

"Recommendations?" prompted the President.

"The Hostage Rescue Team is on the ground in Seattle, but I don't know how effective our SWAT and sniper teams will be against an underway maritime target. If it comes to an assault on those two vessels, it'll have to be done with military assets, and we have formally requested their help. Naturally, we'll lend any and all assistance. We do have our most senior negotiating team out there, and since the terrorist leader speaks good

English, I recommend that we retain our lead agency roll as the primary negotiator.''

"Who's in charge of your team?''

"The senior member and head negotiator is Frank Sclafani. If you may recall, sir, he's the one who handled the British Airways incident last year."

The President nodded and was silent for a few moments, then turned his attention to the tall black man in uniform sitting next to Baines. "General, I think it's time we heard from you."

"Mr. President, we have no military intelligence on this Jamil or his organization. The preliminary casualty figures and damage assessments are in front of you, and as you can see, they pretty well chewed up the wharf area at the Bangor Submarine Base. The loss of life to civilians and those aboard the *Michigan* has been appalling." There was rustling of paper at the other end of the table, but the attention of the President and his most senior advisers remained fixed on the Chairman of the Joint Chiefs of Staff.

"At the present time, we have three direct-action elements in place—a Delta Force element, a company of Rangers, and a Navy SEAL platoon. These military response teams are under the command of Colonel Stanton Braxton from the U.S. Special Operations Command. The Coast Guard cutter *Mellon* has taken station a few miles from the *Michigan*. The on-scene commander at this time is Admiral John MacIntyre, the senior naval officer in the Seattle area. He plans to remain in Seattle long enough to meet with Colonel Braxton and the response-team leaders. Then, subject to any direction to come out of this meeting, he will accompany the FBI negotiating team out to the cutter.

"It is our recommendation that this be a Delta Force action if there is to be a military operation to recover the two vessels. Our standard operating procedure for a maritime boarding calls for a nighttime assault by helicopter, with Delta Force men rappeling to the decks of the ferry and the *Michigan*. It would be a very risky insertion, but we have no other options."

The President sat with his elbows on the table, fingers interlaced and resting in front of his chin in a prayerful manner. *It's always like this,* he reflected. *We say that the military option is the last resort, but we always talk about it first. Is that why so many of these things come to a violent conclusion?*

"Any word from the Israelis?"

He directed his question to his secretary of state, Richard Noffsinger. Noffsinger was a tall, urbane man with a sophisticated veneer, but he was known in diplomatic circles as a street fighter.

"Not yet, sir, and I wouldn't look for any softening on their position regarding the occupied territories. Since the Gulf War and the defeat of Iraq, they have essentially treated the Palestinians as a conquered people. They sided with Saddam, and they are being made to pay for it. The Intifada is in remission, and the Israelis don't want that genie out of the bottle again. It's safe to say they'll make the most of this at the next round of peace talks, if there is a next round. As a practical matter, two hundred thousand Soviet Jews came to Israel last year, and they expect another four hundred thousand in the next eighteen months. Many of them will be settling in the occupied territories. Even a hint that the threat of force or a terrorist action could force them to change their position on the West Bank and Gaza is something they will avoid at all costs. They'll offer us the services of Mossad and some hard-line advice, but nothing else."

"How'd Mr. Mulroney take the news?" asked the President.

"He's concerned. He asked what he could do to help, and he wanted to know what might happen if the terrorists carry out their threat and explode the charges on the *Michigan.*"

The President glanced at the agenda items he had scribbled on the yellow legal pad in front of him. "I believe that's our next item. Aside from further risk to the hostages, what can we look for if Jamil sets off those charges?"

At the end of the table sat a stocky man whose florid face was in striking contrast to his thick shock of gray hair and white uniform. Four silver stars were woven into the gold braid on each of his shoulder boards. Admiral Truxton Matthews III, the chief of naval operations, was a submariner and felt the full weight of the tragic events at Bangor. He was a small man, but his vitality and presence made him appear much larger. The spark that had driven the admiral to the top of his service was noticeably dimmer this morning, but he did not flinch under the President's gaze.

"Mr. President, the *Michigan* was captured with a full complement of the new Trident II D-5 missiles. Since the maneuverable antimissile version of the D-5 has not yet been deployed to the fleet, all of the missiles were fitted with the standard twelve-MIRV warshot. There are two hundred twenty-eight nuclear devices aboard that submarine. As General Scott pointed out, our Bangor facility was badly shot up with small arms, and we believe thirty to thirty-three sailors died on the *Michigan.* One man, a second-class petty officer, is still alive and has maintained a radio watch aboard the *Michigan* since the incident.

"We received these photographs of the submarine ten minutes ago. They were taken by some of our people who managed to get aboard a passing Japanese merchantman, and they're remarkably clear." A Navy captain came forward and began passing out folders containing eight-by-ten glossy prints, beginning with the President and working around the table. "These photos show in some detail the tripodlike structures on the missile deck of the *Michigan.* Lieutenant Commander Bishop is here with us from the Navy's Explosive Ordnance Disposal School at Indian Head, Maryland. He is an expert on nonmilitary explosives and the best demolitions man in uniform, from what I'm told. I've asked him to tell us about these structures."

A tall and painfully thin man in his early thirties who was seated along the wall rose and approached the lectern at the foot of the table. He was dressed in a short-sleeved khaki uniform.

"Mr. President, members of the Security Council," he began as he shuffled through his notes. His prominent Adam's apple bobbed noticeably as he swallowed. "My apologies for being in working uniform—I was on leave when I got the call."

"Commander, I wouldn't care if you were in your underwear," replied the President, "just relax and tell us about the explosives on our submarine."

"Uh, thank you, sir. The position of these six one-gallon cans above the missile deck would indicate they are standard shaped charges. As you may know, a shaped charge is designed to project a jet of gas—a white-hot plasma that has exceptional armor-piercing capabilities. Judging from their height, I'd say each has seven to eight pounds of explosives—probably Semtex, C-4, or a similarly available commercial or military high explosive. Based on my calculations, and assuming a lower quality of explosive than is probably in the cans, those shaped charges can easily punch through the three and a half inches of steel in the missile doors, destroy the warhead, and continue into the solid fuel of the booster stages. I'm not that familiar with the configuration of the D-5 warhead, but from what I know of Trident I warshot, there's a reasonable chance for detonation of the conventional explosives that trigger the nuclear devices. And there is a very high probability, if not a certainty, that the jet from those shaped charges will start a fire in the third-stage booster." Bishop held up one of the photos. "Also, in the blowup of one of the charges, you will note there seem to be three or four wires coming from detonators in the top of the cans. An electrical firing circuit only requires two wires, so I would have to conclude there's some kind of antidisturbance device connected into the firing circuit—one designed to detonate if the firing circuit is tampered with." Bishop paused and quickly reviewed his notes. "It is my assessment that this is a simple, well-designed, and highly effective shaped-charge array, and that it will almost certainly set those six missile tubes on fire."

There was silence while the men around the table digested this information. Bishop shot a glance at Admiral Matthews, who nodded his approval.

"Commander, could you disarm those explosives?" asked the President.

Bishop bit his lower lip and again studied the photograph like a radiologist scrutinizing an X-ray. "There are no guarantees with improvised explosives or terrorist demolitions, sir, but I believe this firing circuit can be compromised." He looked up from the photos and directly at the President. "If those charges are capable of being disarmed, I can do it."

"Thank you, Commander." Then, turning to Admiral Matthews, "I hope his services will not be needed, but I want this man in Seattle as fast as you can get him there."

"Aye, aye, sir." Matthews summoned an aide, and after a few words, the aide and Bishop left the room.

"And now, Admiral, if the unspeakable happens and this madman does set off his explosives, what can we expect?"

"Again, and with your permission, sir, I'd like that to be addressed by an expert in the field. Captain Virgil Aspaugh has a doctorate in radiobiology from MIT and is in charge of our nuclear-weapons safety program."

The President nodded. A Navy captain rose from his place along the wall and walked to the lectern like a relief pitcher coming to the mound from the bullpen. He looked out of place—more like a Good Humor ice cream peddler than a naval officer in summer whites. His hair was too long and his uniform fit poorly. His ample buttocks made his sloping shoulders look all the more narrow, but a highly intelligent pair of eyes blinked behind the thick glasses. He addressed those around the table as though they were a group of undergraduates.

"Okay, each of the two hundred twenty-eight warheads aboard the *Michigan* has twenty-four and a half kilograms of fissionable material. Gentlemen, that's almost two tons of plutonium. If this material is not totally broken up by the initial penetration of the shaped charges or the possible detonation of the chemical explosives in the warheads, then it will surely be dispersed by the burning of the rocket fuel. Now, the fire will cause tremendous heat and pressure within the missile silo. Depending on the size of the hole in the missile hatch, the combustion products may initially vent through this hole, but ultimately, the wall of the silo will fail and the hot exhaust gases will be vented into the interior of the submarine. If just one of those missiles catches fire, the submarine is lost—and most, if not all, of the other missiles will eventually burn.

"In any case, a great deal of this plutonium will be vaporized and carried aloft as the hot gases escape. It's not the plutonium that's so much of a problem, but the alpha radiation that will be released. Alpha particles are helium nuclei or highly charged ions. When they come in contact with living tissue, they kill cells on contact and predispose other cells in the immediate vicinity to cancer. The extent of the contamination will depend on the wind and how much of the plutonium gets airborne before the *Michigan* sinks. Seawater is an excellent containment medium, but then we'll still have to deal with the lesser problem of waterborne and seabed pollution. Needless to say, the sooner the boat goes down, the better.''

Aspaugh was about to continue when the President interrupted. The color was starting to drain from his face.

''Captain, are you saying that we're looking at a Chernobyl-like event?''

''That's right, sir,'' replied Aspaugh evenly, ''with Washington State and British Columbia as the Ukraine and Byelorussia.''

''Godammit!'' said the President, slowly shaking his head. ''How in the hell did we let this happen!'' He slumped back in his chair in resignation. Looking at the faces around the table, he saw only concern and fear. Bennett took out a handkerchief and wiped his mouth. Nothing was said for a few moments, then the President sat erect and again focused his attention on Aspaugh.

''Is that the extent of the danger, this airborne contamination?''

''Yes, sir. However, I should mention the remote, but very real, problem that could arise should the containment vessel of the *Michigan*'s reactor be ruptured. The boat's uranium-fuel core is over five years old, which means it's about sixty percent expended. If the heat from the burning fuel breaches the containment vessel, the alpha radiation could be a secondary consideration.''

Bennett stared at him coldly. ''Thank you for your candor, Captain. As bad as all this appears, is there any chance for a nuclear explosion? Is that at least one possibility we can rule out?''

"Absolutely, sir. The process by which nuclear material in the warhead is imploded by conventional explosives to create the critical mass required for nuclear detonation is quite sophisticated and precise. We can safely rule out even low-order detonation. Our real problem is the alpha-radiation contamination."

"That's horseshit!" All eyes locked onto a sparse man in a brown suit who had been sitting in the corner behind the lectern. Aspaugh had to turn completely around to confront him.

"I'm sorry, Mr. President," the man continued as he stood up, "but the captain is dead wrong. There *is* a chance of nuclear detonation."

The President shot a puzzled look at Morton Keeney, who whispered, "Department of Energy—the secretary is out of town, and that's the DOE rep."

"Dammit, Al, we've been through this before," countered Aspaugh, "and you can't support that hypothesis." He addressed the man like a heckler at a political rally.

"And you're deliberately ignoring random theory and the nonuniform burn rate of the explosive chemical components."

"For Christ's sake, we're talking probabilities that are—"

"SILENCE!" The President was on his feet, glaring at both men. There was not a sound in the room.

"What's your name, young man?" he asked softly.

"Albert Patterson, sir—Assistant Secretary, Department of Energy."

"Very well," replied Bennett, taking his seat, "you have the floor. What's this about the possibility of a nuclear detonation?"

"Thank you, sir. At DOE, we do computer simulations and probability studies on the effects of fire and shock on all nuclear munitions in the inventory. Our studies suggest the W-88 warhead used with the Trident II missile could, under certain conditions of temperature and pressure, experience a low-order detonation. I admit," he continued, glaring at Aspaugh, "that this is a low probability, but given that the nuclear devices on the *Michigan* will be subject to extremes of temperature, pressure, *and* explosive shock, and that the probability of occurrence, however low, is multiplied by the number of missiles aboard, we simply can't just ignore it. Mr. President, if one of those warheads experiences low-order detonation, other warheads will low-order. The detonations may not be big, but they'll be very dirty. The State of Washington and British Columbia will be radioactive wastelands for centuries. Sure it's a long shot, but what if it happens?''

Patterson was physically and emotionally spent, and those seated close to him could see that he was trembling. He met the President's gaze, shrugged with his hands in a gesture of appeal, and crumpled back into his seat. Again, there was not a sound in the room.

''Captain?'' Unlike others in the room, Aspaugh had not been visibly affected by Patterson's speech. He was an academician—the matter was an intellectual and scientific question, not an emotional one.

''Patterson and I have had this discussion before, and I still maintain that the possibility of detonation, even low-order detonation, is so remote that it is not a factor for consideration. Our problem is alpha-particle contamination, and the farther the *Michigan* is moved from the population centers the better.'' Aspaugh retreated to his chair as the President rubbed his palms together looking around the table.

''Questions? . . . Comments?'' No one said a word. ''Thank you all for your time. I have to move this meeting into executive session and make some decisions. Needless to say, what has been spoken in this room is a matter of record, and it is absolutely top secret. I want all of you available by secure telephone until this crisis is resolved.'' While the President was talking, an aide delivered a piece of paper to Admiral Matthews. ''Something we should know about, Admiral?''

''Yes, sir. A Russian Akula Class fast-attack submarine has just been detected off the mouth of the Strait of Juan de Fuca in international waters. It has been running at periscope depth for a considerable period of time, presumably to receive coded-message traffic.''

''Just what we need!'' replied the President. ''General Scott, Morton, Armand, and Director Baines, I want you to remain. Admiral Matthews, you'd better join us too. The rest of you are excused.''

PART FOUR

DECISION

Sunday, June 21, 1992, 11:30 A.M.—Off the Coast of Washington State

Captain First Rank Viktor Molev was more than angry—he was livid. Occasionally, and without warning, he would crash his fist down on the communications console to punctuate his rage. Junior officers and petty officers around the control room did their best to busy themselves at their stations. They knew their captain to be a intense and volatile man, but they had never seen him quite like this. Their only consolation was that his fury was not directed at them or their boat. Only the executive officer dared approach the captain when he was like this.

"How much longer?" Molev said to the impassive officer standing nearby.

"I don't know, *Kapitan*. I can't imagine why they didn't take the time to encrypt this into burst-transmission format. It must be highly important for them to hold us on the surface to copy a standard coded message. It's almost as if they want us to be detected."

"As soon as they have finished, I want this boat at one hundred meters immediately!" replied Molev for the third time, although less forcefully than before. "It can't take that long to decode the message—see what's keeping them."

"Yes sir." The starpom hurried aft to the radio room.

Molev grasped the stopwatch hanging by a cord from the

225

overhead and looked at the elapsed time—six minutes! Again the hand crashed down. *It really doesn't matter now,* he thought. *We've already been at periscope depth too long to have possibly escaped detection by the Americans. Over two weeks of careful, tedious work down the drain!*

Sixteen days before, they had left Vladivostok on a fog-shrouded night and made their way through the Sea of Okhotsk and across the North Pacific. Carefully, they steamed and drifted south along the Canadian coast, blending with the Aleutian and Alaskan currents, which afforded them thermal and sonar protection. The objective of their clandestine transit nearly a third of a way around the world was to arrive off the coast of Washington undetected. It was not an easy task. There were the American RORSATs—radar ocean reconnaissance satellites—listening for their electronic transmissions, and the thermal-imaging satellites that tried to classify their temperature signature with IR sensors. Hydrophone arrays set around the approaches to the Strait of Juan de Fuca could detect all but a few Russian submarines, even at slow speed. And then there were the 680-Class attack boats, the Los Angeles series, with their sprint-and-drift tactics and their superb passive sonars. Often they lurked about the American Pacific coast, specifically looking for Russian attack boats that had come to stalk the Tridents.

Until a few minutes ago, Molev was confident they had been successful. Had they remained undetected, they would again wait for a Trident submarine to sortie from the Strait of Juan de Fuca on patrol, and again attempt to follow it. It was never an easy task, but this time Molev was convinced they might have had a chance.

His boat was the latest of the Akula Class, with a new and promising passive sonar array. The Akula was a follow-on generation to the very capable Victor III class. Western intelligence agencies called them Walker class, since many of the technical upgrades were from classified data passed by the Walker spy ring. After much trial and error, the yards at Komsomolsk and Severodvinsk were finally launching fleet submarines that were quiet and were equipped with sonar systems designed exclusively for passive operations. *They are,* reflected Molev, *becoming more like the American attack submarines.* And the newer boats were more than just hunter-killer submarines. The advanced tube-launched SS-N-21 cruise missile, with its 1,800-nautical-mile range and 200-kiloton warhead, made the Russian attack boats a formidable offensive threat.

"Message transmission received and acknowledged," reported the control-room phone talker.

"Flood negative!" shouted the young lieutenant at the diving station. "Down angle thirty degrees—all ahead standard. Make depth one hundred meters. Come to base course of one three five."

The control room burst into life as the duty section welcomed any activity that might break the sour mood of their captain. The Akula nosed over and headed for the sanctity of deeper water. Molev watched as the diving officer brought the boat smartly to depth.

"I'll be in my cabin, *Leytenant.* Have the communications officer and the executive officer report to me when they've decoded the message."

Once in his cabin, Molev lit a Camel and drew the smoke deeply into his lungs. His anger was partially shouldered aside by curiosity. *Something terribly important must be afoot to so blatantly compromise the position of a Russian attack boat off the North American coast. It is not something Admiral Zaitsev would do without reason, unless he is ordered to by one of the idiot politicians in Moscow—those same politicians who now grovel at the feet of the Western democracies. Now,* there *is something to be concerned about!* A sharp rap on the door brought him out of his reverie.

"Enter!" The starpom and the communicator, a junior lieutenant, shuffled into the captain's cramped stateroom. The younger officer laid a yellow sheet of paper on the captain's desk and stood against the locker with the executive officer. Both watched in silence as Molev read and reread the message.

"Get me the chart." The nautical chart that described the mouth of the Strait of Juan de Fuca out to the boundary of international waters was always referred to only as "the chart." The starpom handed the dog-eared nautical chart to the captain. Molev laid it out on the desk and grabbed the parallel ruler and dividers from the shelf. He drew several lines on the chart and checked distances along the latitude scale. Then he looked up and stared at the wall for a few moments, and a wisp of a smile began to work its way across his face.

"Our last satellite pass placed them here." He tapped the position on the chart with a pencil and looked at his watch. "They've made good progress since taking the Trident from its berth at Bangor." Molev drew a line from the *Michigan*'s position westerly to the mouth of the Strait and into the Pacific. "Say they can only maintain five knots. They'll be clear of the coast around 2:00 A.M. and be in international waters just after sunrise—unless the U.S. Navy intervenes." *There's no reason why they shouldn't*, he thought. But if there was one thing Molev had learned in his career of playing underwater games with the U.S. Navy, they often didn't do what they should. Molev drew down on the cigarette until it was a half-inch stub before parking it atop a pile of short, crushed butts in the ashtray on the desk. Then he turned back to the chart.

Sunday, 3:00 P.M.—The White House

"How much time do we have, Mort?" Following the meeting in the conference room, the President had led six of them up to the Oval Office. Now the small group was gathered around the coffee table, sitting in overstuffed chairs with cups and saucers balanced on their thighs.

"Their broadcast was sent from the *Spokane* about 12:45 our time and aired nationally by the networks just before 2:00 P.M. On his timetable, the deadline is 8:45 this evening, so we have just under six hours."

"Six hours—son of a fucking *bitch!* This bastard is in a position to devastate the whole state of Washington and the southwest portion of Canada, and he's able to broadcast it to the whole world on national TV. God *damn* him.''

President Bennett rose abruptly from his straight-back chair and walked over to the desk, where he could look out into the Rose Garden. Most of those in the room stared apprehensively at the back of the President, shocked at his outburst and wondering what would come next. Only Morton Keeney patiently sipped his coffee. He knew this president well, and this was a rare but not totally unexpected reaction. He had also known the President to be cool in a crisis, although this incident was potentially the most serious he had yet faced. The foul language was a carryover from his tour as a GI during the Korean War. *He'll quickly get it out of his system,* thought Keeney, *and settle down to the business of decision making and crisis management. He's been in war and he knows about life and death firsthand—that's why he's so upset. What'll we do when we have to elect presidents who haven't fought in our wars as young men? We'll certainly be the poorer for it.*

As if on cue, Bennett returned to his chair and sat with his forearms on his knees, offering no apology for the outburst or even acknowledging that it had taken place.

''Harry, you're our domestic-terrorism expert—what do you recommend?'' The FBI director pursed his lips and hesitated before he spoke.

''Mr. President, while this is by far the most dangerous incident we've ever encountered, I can only recommend that we follow those procedures that have worked before and have served us well in the past. Establish a dialogue, preferably a personal relationship between terrorist and negotiator, and encourage him to talk. Time is usually on our side in these matters. The terrorists become tired, they begin to identify with their hostages, and sometimes they will back away from unrealistic demands—especially if satisfying those demands is beyond our control. But the terrorist, especially a capable one like this Jamil seems to be, must be made to feel that we are negotiating honestly, not just stalling for time.''

''What do we have to negotiate with? We can't give him back his homeland—certainly not in the next six hours.''

"In a larger sense," continued Baines, "we have entered into a contract with him. He has the lives of the hostages and potential nuclear devastation with which to threaten us, although given what the experts have told us, I don't believe he realizes the scope of that devastation. In exchange, he has given us his life, and we can take it or give it back to him. No matter how committed the terrorist is, and I have no basis to suggest that Jamil is not prepared to carry out his threat, there are very few men who are really willing to die if a way out is left open to them. As a practical matter, we must appear to be *trying* to satisfy his demands—that we are willing to work with him, but we also have to make him understand there are factors beyond our control. At no time should he be made to feel that we are pushing him into a corner, or more importantly, that we are acting in bad faith. In this manner, we may effectively be able to play for time."

"So what do you recommend?"

"Sir, I recommend that we open negotiations with him as soon as possible, and that we convey to him that we take his demands and his threats very seriously—that we'll do what we can to work something out. We should also indicate that what he has asked for is very difficult, and whereas we sympathize with the plight of the Palestinians, what he has asked for will take time."

"You have a lot of confidence in your man out there, I take it?"

"Frank Sclafani is the best we have. He has a way of getting close to terrorists, and his insight on the mental stability and resolve of this man could be valuable. The more he can get Jamil to talk to us, the more we'll learn about him."

"Okay, for now we'll have to assume that this Jamil will wait until the time's up before he makes his next move. You buy that, Armand?"

"I do for the most part, but I agree only partially with the blanket assumption that time is on our side," replied the CIA director, again polishing his glasses. "Our experience with terrorists, especially Arab terrorists, is that they often become more volatile and unpredictable as time goes by. We must watch this very carefully. I'm having an in-depth psychological profile assembled on Jamil. It may give us a clue to his behavior, or something we can use against him. I also concur that a dialogue should be established as soon as possible with the man. We also have some highly capable negotiators should Harold's man not be up to the task.''

"Very well," said the President. *You'd think that the CIA and the FBI would close ranks a little in the face of an emergency,* he thought. *But then, the armed forces seldom do, even when there's a war—why should governmental agencies be any different?* "So we talk to the sonofabitch. The immediate decision I have to make is whether we should evacuate Seattle and the surrounding area. And how much do we tell the Canadians about this? So far, all I have to go on is the conflicting opinions of a midlevel civil servant and a Navy captain." Bennett looked full circle before his eyes came to stop on Morton Keeney.

"Mr. President, Secretary Davis is on his way to the capital and should arrive at DOE within the hour. I've asked him to get his top people at DOE cracking on this thing to see just what kind of probabilities we're dealing with regarding a possible nuclear detonation. And I've no reason to doubt Captain Aspaugh," he nodded politely to Admiral Matthews, "but we also need to corroborate his testimony about the nuclear contamination."

He took a deep breath and continued. "I believe it's inadvisable to order an evacuation at this time. I've consulted with FEMA, the Federal Emergency Management Administration, and they have no meaningful contingency plans for the evacuation of the Seattle area. As a matter of fact, Washington and Oregon have been among the least cooperative states in the nation on disaster preparedness. Mass evacuation is a nuclear-war contingency, and they just didn't believe something like this would happen. Since the terrorists went public with this thing, I'm sure there will be more than a few people leaving the area. Brad Holloway is working up a press release for your approval confirming that the submarine has been captured, and that any attempted sabotage on the part of the terrorists could possibly result in the release of some low-level contamination. Right now there are large numbers of weekend travelers on the Olympic Peninsula, a mountainous body of land that forms the southern border of the Strait of Juan de Fuca on the U.S. side and the west side of Puget Sound. Most of these travelers are on their way back to Seattle, and I'm told the ferries will be loaded to capacity with eastbound traffic. I know it's not totally honest, but FEMA feels that any stronger statement will result in panic and chaos. Sir, I recommend that for now we wait until we have better information.''

The President pinched his lower lip as he considered his NSA's advice. "Any comments on this?" Silence. If any of the men in the room had an opinion, they were keeping it to themselves. Nor did President Bennett really expect any serious discussion regarding the administration's public position—they were all politicians, even the men in uniform. Dissension and the passionate defense of one's beliefs was the province of younger, less important men like Captain Aspaugh and Patterson of DOE. *Besides,* he reflected, *deceiving the American people is a presidential prerogative—or at least it should be.*

"What about the Canadians, Dick?"

"We can tell them little more than we tell our own people," replied Secretary of State Noffsinger evenly. "If Mulroney knows the full story, he may feel compelled to take stronger civil action. If we get confirmation of a disaster scenario from DOE or DOD and the negotiations begin to deteriorate, we can advise the Canadians when we issue a more comprehensive public statement." Even though Noffsinger was a shrewd and experienced diplomat, a twisting of the truth was still not easy for him. For several moments, the President sat quietly erect with his hands folded on his lap. No one else moved. Finally, his eyes settled on Morton Keeney.

"Okay, we'll do it that way. Have Holloway get that press release ready as soon as possible. Now, what about the Israelis?" he continued, again looking to his secretary of state. "Is there any chance we can get them to give a little something on this?"

"As I mentioned earlier," Noffsinger continued, "they will

do nothing that would indicate the pressure of terrorism forced them to compromise.'' He was now on comfortable ground, and noticeably more at ease. ''But the cold facts are that we provide them over three billion dollars a year in military aid, plus that bonus they extracted from us for remaining neutral during the Gulf War. There's also the loan guarantees for the West Bank settlements. It's reasonable to expect that the Jewish lobby in Congress, which has so successfully protected that aid, will be unable to do so if the Israelis aren't willing to help us. I've taken the liberty of summoning their ambassador. He'll be waiting for an audience when we adjourn. We could try to force them to consent to a rehearing of UN Resolutions 338 and 242. Both deal with the 'land for peace' issue in the occupied territories, which have been the Palestinians' position since the talks began in Madrid. It would be a significant concession on the part of the Israelis, and consistent with our stand on the matter. It's a point of discussion, and it may buy us some time.'' Noffsinger looked at the CIA director, who nodded his assent. ''But don't look for them to go further than an agreement in principle. In reality, they're not about to abandon the West Bank—Gaza maybe, and only then with a lot of pressure and substantial guarantees and promises of additional aid on our part.''

''Thanks, Dick. I'll see the ambassador after we're finished here. General, if it comes down to military action, is there any way we can attack that submarine and surprise them before they have a chance to set off those explosives?''

''I don't believe so, Mr. President. We're still waiting for the mission concepts from the three response units in the field, but I'm doubtful. All Jamil has to do is push a button, so the surprise would have to be total. I'm relatively certain that we can make it a quick, surgical strike, and that we can gain control of both vessels in a matter of minutes, perhaps seconds, but I don't believe we can totally surprise them. Another thing, sir, I'd like permission to have the operational commanders and their units fully briefed on the ultimate disaster scenario. They need to know this. Normal antiterrorist doctrine allows the attacking-element commanders some latitude regarding lives at risk.

That is to say, they have the option of holding their positions
during an assault or aborting an attack altogether if lives, theirs
or the hostages', are placed at an unacceptable risk by pursuing
the attack. They'll not have that option in this case, and they'll
need to know why. The success of their mission may depend on
it, and they'll have to make their assault plans accordingly."
General Scott hesitated a moment, his words hanging heavy in
the room. "We owe this to them, sir," Scott continued.
"We're asking these boys to fight to the death and to possibly
die, even if they win the fight."

The President nodded his approval and was again silent for
a moment. When he spoke again, it was in a very quiet voice.
"What about one of those smart bombs, the laser-guided ones
like we used to stop the oil flow from Kuwait into the Gulf
during the war? Could one of them, dropped on the pilothouse
of the ferry, defeat those explosives?

"I'm afraid not, sir. We talked about that, and the munitions
experts tell us that the shock wave would probably cause the
initiator to function and set the charges off. The same with
gunfire from the cutter."

Bennett nodded and quickly moved on. "What do we know
about this MacIntyre who's in charge out there?"

"Admiral Matthews?" replied Scott. The admiral consulted
a file he held on his lap. "John MacIntyre is a fine officer with
a great deal of operational experience. He had three combat
deployments to Vietnam—shot down once and rescued at sea.
He was in command of VF-41 on the *Nimitz* during the Gulf of
Sidra incident back in 1981. MacIntyre himself was one of the
pilots who bagged the two Libyan SU-22s. He commanded the
Sacramento from October 1986 to October 1988. He then commanded the air group—we call them super-CAGs—aboard the
Kennedy from December '88 through the Gulf War. He led
several highly successful strikes and was awarded the Distinguished Flying Cross—he now has four of them. Promoted to
admiral just last year and assigned as Commander, Naval Base,
Seattle."

"Why Seattle?" asked the President. He knew the military
well enough to understand that shore duty in Seattle, while

perhaps not exactly a dead-end job, was not an assignment for a fast-track flag officer being groomed for bigger things.

"Well, sir," replied Matthews with a measure of contrition in his voice, "MacIntyre has a superb operational record, but in twenty-six years of service, he's somehow managed to avoid even a short tour of duty at the Pentagon. That's, well, not exactly a career pattern for senior flag rank."

"I can understand that, Admiral, and thank you for your candor." President Bennett looked carefully at each of the men seated in the room, then past them to the Marine standing at parade rest by the door. "Colonel," he commanded, "I'd like your opinion on this." Those with their backs to the door swiveled in their seats.

Colonel Williams came to attention and faced the group. "Sir, we have two things in our favor. We have a man on the submarine who is reporting in by radio, and may be in a position to be of some help. And the *Spokane* is moving west on the Strait of Juan de Fuca, away from the population centers. I agree with Mr. Baines that we must talk with Jamil until talking resolves the crisis or it appears that talking will no longer buy time. Then we'll have to assault the ferry and pray to God that the explosives aboard the *Michigan* are not set off." The President wanted to ask Williams about his decision to withhold information from the public—the information about the possibility of massive nuclear contamination or detonation—but Marine colonels weren't paid to comment on those decisions.

"Thanks, Buck. Gentlemen, is there anything else that needs to be said before we go to work?" Again, silence. "Very well, then. I want you in the situation room or in your office, where Morton can find you on very short notice. I've got a phone call to make and an ambassador to see."

Sunday, 12:20 P.M.—King County Airport, Seattle, Washington

"You sure this is gonna be okay?" asked Wilbur Snyder as they taxied down the service strip to the end of the runway.

"Hey look, we been over this before," replied his companion in the right seat of the Piper Seminole. "I'm not asking you to break any FAA regulations. You're allowed to fly at five hundred feet over water, and we're not going to fly directly over them—just circle 'em a few times. I'll snap some pictures and we'll be out of there. It's free airspace, right?"

Snyder nodded grimly and requested clearance from the tower. Running a one-man flying service wasn't the easiest game in town, but it was his game. For as far back as he could remember, he'd wanted to fly, and he couldn't imagine doing anything else. Nor had he had much luck working for someone else. It was just as well—there were a lot of pilots in Seattle, and good jobs in corporate aviation were scarce. Most of what he made went back into the aircraft. A few years back, his wife had told him it was either her or "that damned plane." For Snyder, it had been an easy choice.

They took off to the south and climbed out to nine hundred feet, turning sharply to the right to a heading of 310. They would stay at this altitude and well under the inbound traffic for Sea-Tac International until after they had crossed the Sound. Vashon Island crawled steadily under the port wing while the city of Seattle embraced the busy Elliott Bay waterfront off to the right. It was a superb day to be in the air.

Sunday, 12:30 P.M.—Strait of Juan de Fuca, near Dungeness Spit

The Coast Guard cutter *Mellon* had taken station fifteen hundred yards from the two captured vessels. She was almost due east of them, and steaming at a comfortable five knots to match their speed. They'd been on station for over half an hour, and Captain Libby thought it advisable to announce his position.

"This is the Coast Guard cutter *Mellon* calling the motor vessel *Spokane*. We are on your starboard quarter and will stand by should you require assistance." He repeated the call and added, "Cutter *Mellon,* out." Libby walked out onto the bridge wing and put his binoculars on the *Spokane*. He could see the white froth of prop wash as the ferry strained against the side of the submarine. *Just how in the hell could someone have hijacked a Trident submarine?* He thought of the line from the movie *Butch Cassidy and the Sundance Kid:* "Who *are* those guys?" Not far from Libby stood Gunnery Sergeant McGarther Jennings. The chief quartermaster had given him a pair of binoculars, and he, too, studied the *Spokane*. *I can't remember the last time I had a black enlisted Marine in camouflage fatigues standing on my bridge with a pair of ship's glasses around his neck,* mused Libby. *Every day in the Coast Guard's a little different.*

They had taken Jennings aboard just before noon and sent the torpedo retriever back to Bangor. The Marine had made his hourly call to the sailor on the *Michigan* from the bridge, and they had been able to get visual confirmation as DeRosales waved to them from the door in the base of the sail. In listening to their brief conversation, Libby sensed a strong bond between Jennings and the sailor—it was almost a parental thing. Jennings had the look of a man who could become nasty if rubbed the wrong way, and he was obviously concerned about DeRosales.

"How're you doing there, Gunnery Sergeant?" Jennings had just stepped out to the port wing of the bridge.

"Just fine, thank you, sir. Any word from Seattle as to what we're going to do about this? That kid's getting a little hungry over there. He's afraid to eat anything from the galley—it might be poison."

"We check in every fifteen minutes with our headquarters, but our orders remain the same—stand by and maintain station."

"Begging the Captain's pardon, sir, but are we just gonna let those assholes take that submarine all the way out to the Pacific Ocean?"

"I wish I could tell you, Sergeant. I know plans are being formulated at the highest level. Right now we have our orders, and they're very specific."

"Captain!" It was the lookout calling from the signal bridge on the level above the pilothouse. "We have a low flyer approaching from the south. Looks like he's heading right for the ferry." Libby picked him up immediately and brought his glasses to bear. It was a twin-engine, low-wing executive-type aircraft. *Let's hope he's just crossing the Strait for Canada.* The plane passed over the two captured vessels, dipped a wing, and began to circle.

"Get on the horn and raise that plane!" called Libby. "Order him to stand clear!" Inside the pilothouse, a petty officer grabbed a radio handset.

Stanley Lewis was a free-lance photojournalist, and he was capable of some very good work. His collection on the down-and-outers at Pioneer Square had received great reviews, but it didn't pay the bills. He'd been on his way to Green Lake in Seattle to take some action shots of the roller skaters who wheeled around the lake in outrageous attire, when he heard about the ferry hijacking on the news. He was driving north on I-5, and, on a hunch, he had turned off at the King County Airport exit.

"That's great," yelled Lewis. "Now make a pass from the front down the north side of the ferry, and tip the plane as we go past so I can shoot over the wing." Snyder nodded and banked steeply to bring the aircraft around for another run. He wasn't guarding 121.5 VHF-AM, the international distress frequency, but the Coast Guard operator found him on 122.8 Unicom.

"Unidentified aircraft circling the ferry *Spokane,* this is the United States Coast Guard cutter *Mellon.* You are flying in restricted and dangerous airspace. Stand clear and leave the area immediately. Please acknowledge, over."

"Hear that?" said Snyder. "We're outta here."

"I need just one more pass!"

"Sorry, man, they'll pull my ticket."

"One more pass and I'll double your fee." Lewis didn't have the money, but with these pictures, he could get it. "Just one more!" Snyder grimly brought the Seminole around for another pass. He needed the money, and he hoped this last run wouldn't cost him his license. *Grounded.* The thought of it sent a shudder through him. The Coast Guard called twice more before shifting to another frequency. Snyder shifted his radio to 121.5 and again monitored the call. *Great! I can acknowledge their call on this channel as I make this run, and be on my way. They can't get me for that!*

Salah "heard" the warbling from the conductance bar against his temple, which told him the sensor in the head of the missile had acquired the aircraft that now filled his sight ring. Just as many Americans refuse to buy foreign cars, he tried to avoid weapons made in the West. But the U.S. Stinger missile was just too available and too accurate. They only had three of them—they were terribly expensive, but he hoped they would need just this one. Knowing the missile needed five hundred meters of flight to arm itself and make target acquisition, Salah let the Seminole get well past the *Spokane* before he fired.

The Stinger, designed to look for the heat from a jet exhaust, was puzzled by the relatively mild thermal signatures from the two Lycoming piston engines. It couldn't make up its mind which one to go for, so it ripped through the fuselage just in front of the tail section, shredding the control cables and most of the tubular support members. The Seminole shuddered and crabbed to one side like an abused dog. The tail section, now being towed by the remaining control cables, began a circular oscillation and dragged the aircraft into a spin.

Lewis watched the deep blue of Puget Sound race madly from right to left as the plane spiraled for the water. That might have been the last thing he saw had not a crazed Wilbur Snyder grabbed him by the throat and screamed in this face, "You bastard, you wrecked my plane—you wrecked my plane!"

• • •

"Oh, my God!" Libby had never seen a surface-to-air missile before, but he instantly knew what it was. It took a full second for him to respond.

"Left standard rudder, all ahead flank! Make turns for twenty-four knots. Sound rescue stations and bring the lifeboat to the rail!" The bridge became a flurry of activity as Libby conned the ship toward the downed aircraft. Only the tail section remained visible, and it disappeared as soon as the *Mellon* steadied on her new course.

"Captain, our orders are to maintain station," said Libby's executive officer.

"Fuck the orders, XO. There may be survivors over there." Libby gave con back to the officer of the deck, or OOD, and took the radio handset. "Motor vessel *Spokane,* this is the Coast Guard cutter *Mellon.* We are closing on the site of the downed aircraft to look for survivors. I say again, we are closing to look for survivors, *Mellon* out."

Peck had seen the lithe Arab slip into the pilothouse and retrieve a long container that looked like a trombone case. He knelt behind the pilothouse wing combing to open it, and took out an olive-drab tube with a complex-looking trigger housing and boxlike appendage. He then ran down the steps to the promenade deck. When the twin-engined light plane made another low pass up the port side, it all became clear. Peck stretched to the limit of his cuffed wrist and yelled out the door.

"Don't fire! We can call them—we can call the cutter and warn them off. Dammit, you don't need to shoot at them!" Peck had a good view through the rear windows, and watched helplessly as the missileer tracked the aircraft down the starboard side of the boat. Peck involuntarily reached for the radio microphone, forgetting that Jamil had removed it. There was a sharp *whoosh* as the missile leapt from the man's shoulder. The aircraft wasn't more than one thousand meters from the ferry when the missile found it. The Seminole nosed over and fluttered down to the water. Jamil congratulated Salah on his kill and made his way back the pilothouse.

"You didn't have to do that! We could have warned them by radio."

"Possibly so, Peck, but there was—" Jamil was interrupted by the Coast Guard announcing their intention to rush to the scene of the crashed plane. "As I was saying, there was something to be gained here. You Americans are a curious people, and addicted to your television news. We have now effectively deterred any nosy cameramen or sightseers. More importantly, the fact that we have surface-to-air missiles will not be lost on your military planners. Helicopters and even small boats are most vulnerable to these missiles. Who knows, maybe there will be some survivors from the small plane and your Coast Guard can rescue them."

"You're still pretty sure of yourself, aren't you?" replied Peck quietly.

"I'm only sure of our cause, Peck, and that ultimately we must have our own nation or life means nothing. You call us terrorists, but this is a military operation. During the Second World War, if a group of your commandos had slipped into Germany and captured a Nazi submarine, they would have been hailed as heroes. It would have been the raid of the century."

"That was an unarmed civilian aircraft, and those were innocent people you killed."

"Don't talk to me about innocent people, Peck. What about the innocent civilians killed in your invasion of Panama or in the bombing of Baghdad? What about the civilians on the Iranian Airbus shot down over the Strait of Hormuz? This is now a warship, and those who approach, civilian or military, do so at their peril."

"The *Spokane* is not a warship, it's a passenger ferry."

"It was, but this vessel is no longer the *Spokane,* it is now the *Safinat al Horeya.* And it will be known as such in the many lands where my people wait in exile, as well as throughout the rest of the world." Jamil looked at his watch. "Perhaps it is time I again talked to your people, Peck. By now, I'm sure they are curious about what we are doing."

Jamil called Ahmed to the pilothouse, where he quickly

retuned the antenna and connected a hand-held camcorder to the transmitter. Jamil stepped out into the sunshine on the pilothouse wing, and Ahmed panned up on him from the promenade deck. It was like he was speaking from a balcony.

"Citizens of the United States. This is Jamil, and I am speaking to you from the deck of the *Safinat al Horeya,* the Ship of Freedom, formerly called the ferry *Spokane.* A few hours ago, you heard me demand that your government and the nation of Israel join together in a resolution that would restore the lands known as the occupied territories to the Palestinian people. We are no longer going to allow the Israelis to stall at the negotiating table while more Jews settle on our lands.

"The United States led the West in coming to the aid of Kuwait when that country was overrun by the legions of Saddam Hussein. The United Nations passed resolution after resolution condemning Iraq's invasion of Kuwait. But what of my people, the people of Palestine? After Israel annexed the West Bank and Gaza in 1967, the United Nations passed Resolutions 338 and 242, which required that Israel abandon those lands. These resolutions were passed almost twenty-five years ago. Yet the Jews still occupy those lands—our lands—and they continue to build settlements there. It seems the United States chooses which UN rules it will support and which rules it will ignore. We have no oil, or vast sums of money in Western banks, so we may seem very unimportant to you. But we are a people of much pride and spirit. Since your government supports the Jews in their aggression, the Intifada is now extended to America. In effect, we are at war with your government, and as your president proclaimed in your fight with Saddam, it is a just war. And while I fight the government of the United States here in America, I ask all my Palestinian brothers to rise up and strike the Zionists who occupy the land that is ours. Together, brothers, we will win our freedom and our homeland!

"An airplane that was spying on the *Safinat al Horeya* and our war prize, the missile submarine *Michigan,* has been destroyed. We will defend our ship against any aircraft or boat that approaches without permission. And our demands remain the same: The State of Israel must join the United States to guarantee that the West Bank and Gaza will become the nation of Palestine. Otherwise, we will destroy the *Michigan* and the lives of those Americans held aboard the *Safinat al Horeya* will be lost. Your government has less than five hours to respond. That is all.''

Peck again leaned toward the pilothouse door as far as his shackled hand would permit. *I don't believe it,* he thought. *The sonofabitch has just declared war on the United States.* That realization, and the downing of the civilian plane, changed something in Peck. Or was it that Jamil had changed the name of *his* boat? Peck knew his responsibilities to the *Spokane* and those aboard her were unchanged, but he felt he was no longer dealing with a criminal or a terrorist—he, too, was now at war. *Maybe the Navy or whoever isn't coming—or maybe they're waiting for an opening—for Jamil to make a mistake. Well, I can't wait—I've got to do something!* Peck was back behind the wheel when Jamil returned to the pilothouse.

''Bridge, this is the engine room, you there, Captain?'' Peck looked at Jamil, who was standing in the pilothouse door. He reached up and held the talk-listen switch.

''This is the captain. Go ahead, Andy.'' Andy Gosnell seldom addressed him as captain, nor did Peck often refer to himself by that title, but somehow it now seemed appropriate.

''The number-one and -two engines have been running hot for some time now, and I've asked this camel driver to let me shift to three and four, but he refuses. We're gonna burn 'em up if we keep going like this. You want to take this up with his boss?''

Peck studied Jamil, who had listened to Gosnell's request. Apparently the slur had gone unnoticed. ''The engineer's right. Those engines were not designed to push this much weight through the water. It would be prudent to give them a rest and to shift to the other two engines.''

''This doesn't mean that we must turn the ferry around and use the other propeller?'' he asked cautiously.

''No, we just start the other two engines and let them drive the electric-drive generator.''

Jamil thought for a moment and then waved his hand. "Very well, but do nothing that will impede our progress."

Peck nodded, and called Gosnell. "Engineer, this is the captain. Jamil says go ahead and shift power to three and four. And while you're at it, could you give us an accurate fuel reading and CASREP that lube-oil pump." The words came out before Peck even thought about them, and he was immediately challenged.

"What did you say—what was that about?" The pistol was suddenly in Jamil's hand.

"I asked him to check the status of our fuel—these gauges on the bridge are not that accurate, and I asked him to check the lube-oil pump. It's overdue for routine maintenance, and we've been keeping an eye on it." As if on cue, Gosnell called back.

"Captain, you're at about sixty-five-percent capacity on fuel, and we're using it pretty fast. If we're gonna shift power plants, then this monkey's gonna have to release me from the control panel."

Peck looked at Jamil, who reached for the lever on the speaker box. He exchanged several sentences in Arabic with the guard in the engine room and stepped back away from Peck. "Your engineer will be allowed free to change the engines and check his machinery, but he had better do nothing foolish."

Peck shrugged passively as he looked back out across the bow of the *Spokane,* but his heart was racing. They had come right slightly from their westerly base course, and he carefully added additional left rudder to correct it. He exchanged a glance with Janey and saw concern but nothing unusual—it had gone past her, too. CASREP is a Navy acronym for a "casualty report" on a piece of equipment that is broken. Peck had just told Gosnell to sabotage the lube-oil pump, and the old snipe seemed to have picked up on it. The pump served all four engines, and without it the Spokane could not move. A cold fear knifed through him as he reflected on the chance he had just taken. *It's a gamble,* he thought, *but I have to do something to stop them.* He casually glanced over his shoulder at Jamil, who was busy studying the chart.

Sunday, 1:15 P.M.—Sand Point Naval Station, Seattle, Washington

"Any ideas on what this boy might be able to do for us, Bob?" Admiral MacIntyre sat across from Captain Robert Hailey, commanding officer of the Gold Crew of the *Michigan*. It was his submarine that had been stolen, even if it wasn't under his command at the time of the theft.

"A Trident boomer is a pretty sophisticated piece of equipment. I doubt that there's anything DeRosales could do by himself other than what he's doing now—maintaining a radio watch."

"Could he scuttle her?"

"I beg your pardon?"

"You heard me, Captain, could he sink her?"

Hailey forced himself to think about it. "I don't believe so. There are scuttling charges aboard, but they're dual activated. I couldn't do it myself if I were aboard alone. There's air, but no emergency power to the ship, so he can't flood the ballast tanks. Every opening on a submarine is safeguarded, and designed to maintain the watertight integrity of the boat. There's really nothing he can do." Hailey almost seemed relieved at this conclusion.

"How about weapons aboard? Do you have a small landing-force locker that would have—"

"Excuse me, Admiral—you better look at the TV." MacIntyre grabbed the remote control on his desk, and a picture flickered across the TV screen on a console against the wall. The set, like those in offices of so many senior military officers and politicians around the world, was tuned to CNN. The picture cleared and Jamil's face came into focus. MacIntyre listened in silence, but came to his feet when the terrorist leader came to the part about destroying the "spy" aircraft. When the newscast began to repeat Jamil's message from the *Spokane*, MacIntyre yelled for his flag lieutenant. The young officer opened the door, but was quickly shouldered aside by the staff communications officer.

"Just in from the *Mellon*, sir. The terrorists shot down a light plane that looked like it was making a photo pass on the ferry. The *Mellon* didn't think there were any survivors, but she's searching the area."

MacIntyre frowned as he read the message. "Send a reply under my signature ordering them back on station. Get the chief of staff in here." MacIntyre, the aviator, felt the hair crawl on the back of his neck as he mentally pictured the panic in the cockpit of that plane during the last seconds. "And keep me posted on the status of any survivors."

"Aye, sir." The COS was there in less than fifteen seconds. Colin Gentry was a short, balding Navy captain with previous command tours aboard a destroyer and an Aegis cruiser. He was soft-spoken, often cynical, and highly competent. MacIntyre wasn't sure why so capable a seagoing officer had been sent to his staff, but he wasn't complaining. The Navy, like the other services, was shrinking and there was a surplus of good men.

"Looks like they've got a surface-to-air capability."

"I'll say. What's the story with the press, Colin—was that some reporter in the plane?"

"We're checking into it. The word was put out to the local press as well as the major wire services that the airspace and water within two miles of the *Spokane* was a military exclusion zone. They've been known to ignore warnings, but there're a lot of free-lancers out there. One thing, sir, we probably won't have any more problems with civilian low-flyers."

"How's the press behaving?"

"Not too bad. They're hungry, but they've learned to live with a certain amount of censorship in a crisis. I told them a DESERT STORM–type press pool will be organized to keep them informed."

"Is one being formed?"

"No"—Gentry laughed—"but it'll keep 'em guessing for a few hours."

"Have you told them anything?"

"Not really. I've been able to pacify them, saying that we're waiting to hear from CHINFO in Washington. They ask the same questions a dozen different ways, and we tell them the same thing—our orders are to stand by and take no action other than to keep everyone away from the *Spokane* and the *Michigan.* The statement from the White House press secretary and the broadcasts from the terrorists have given them plenty to work with.

"They are, however, starting to get pushy about the talk of low-level radiation in the White House press report. And Christ, there's a lot of them! There must be thirty out front and another thirty milling around the gate at Bangor. Mostly locals right now, but the national stringers are starting to arrive in waves. The clearing of wreckage on the Hood Canal bridge is also getting a lot of coverage."

"What about the families of those aboard the *Michigan?*" said MacIntyre, turning to Hailey.

"They've been told that the duty-section crew are hostages aboard the boat. Most of them have joined in a vigil at the Bangor chapel. My wife and most of the Gold Crew wives are there with the Blue Crew families. We can't keep this from them much longer, Admiral. It's not right, and they'll suspect the worst as time goes by."

"I know. And if Jamil carries out his threat, it won't matter one way or the other." A rush of pure hatred for Jamil surged through MacIntyre. *You can't help the families,* he told himself, *you've got to move ahead.* He turned back to Gentry.

"Colin, check again on those special FBI guys and this Colonel Braxton. I've got to get out to the *Mellon* as soon as possible." Gentry left, and MacIntyre turned his attention to Hailey.

"Okay, about the small-arms locker on the *Michigan . . .*" The flag lieutenant burst in without his customary knock, and MacIntyre turned irritably to meet him. "What *is* it, Dennis?"

"Telephone, sir—on the secure line!"

"I'll be just a moment longer with Captain Hailey, now—"

"But, Admiral, it's the President!"

• • •

President Bennett sat at his desk waiting for the call to go through. He had been looking at the file on MacIntyre left behind by Admiral Matthews. *This MacIntyre appears to be an excellent naval officer,* he thought, *with a great deal of operational and command experience. But could anything have prepared him for this crisis?*

"Good afternoon, Admiral. I assume that you were able to listen to the last broadcast from the terrorists on the ferry. Any other developments out there?"

"Yessir, I heard Jamil's last message. It seems they have a surface-to-air missile capability on the *Spokane.* We've confirmed that they shot down a light plane that was buzzing the ferry." The President didn't reply for a moment.

"I see. Admiral, what do you feel is their intent at this time—where are they going?"

"Sir, I don't know. The ferry service tells me they have fuel enough for about another twenty-four hours of operation. There's nothing along either side of the Strait of Juan de Fuca that would seem like a destination. The Washington State Police are checking out the communities and the few harbors along our side of the Strait. We have a good working relationship with the Canadians out here, and I've taken the liberty to ask the RCMP to do the same on their side."

The President listened carefully. He'd learned that a good politician uses his mouth, but a good Commander in Chief uses his ears. He had also learned that those closest to a crisis usually had a better feel for things than those in Washington.

"Very good. What are you doing now?"

"I'm waiting for the FBI negotiating team to get here. Then I plan to accompany them out to the *Mellon.* I also want to meet briefly with the senior special operations officer and his element commanders, who will be preparing military-response alternatives. Other than that, sir, we'll maintain communications through our chain of command, relay any new information, and await direction."

"What do you think our next move should be?"

MacIntyre was momentarily taken aback—he was prepared to take orders, not discuss strategy. But there was something in the tone of the President's voice that invited candor without surrendering any of its authority.

"Mr. President, I don't really know what this Jamil has in mind, and I'm concerned about the release of radioactive material if he does anything to the *Michigan*. There's also the hostages. Right now he's headed away from the major population centers, and that's a positive as I see it. I think we have to prepare military contingencies, while we try and talk to this guy. I think he's serious, and we know he's very capable. It seems to me that he'll do what he says unless we can somehow make a deal with him—or stop him."

The President was silent while he considered what MacIntyre had said. He knew that, ultimately, the major decisions and the responsibility were his. He also knew that a good on-scene commander, one given some flexibility to act on his own initiative, was sometimes the best chance for success. *God knows how many screwups have been caused by the White House trying to micromanage a crisis situation. Firsthand knowledge and common sense—those have often been lacking in decisions coming from this office. And it looks like I could probably do a lot worse than this MacIntyre fellow.*

"Are you still there, sir?" Thirty seconds had passed, and MacIntyre had wondered if the connection had been broken.

"I'm still here. Admiral, I want you to remain in charge of this operation, and you will report directly to me or to my National Security Adviser, Morton Keeney. Have Colonel Braxton and his special-operations people go ahead with their contingency plans, but our primary objective is to resolve this situation by negotiation. Get that FBI man on the cutter and get him talking as soon as possible. Director Baines has prepared a set of instructions for your negotiator." MacIntyre noticed that the President referred to the FBI man as *his* negotiator. "And now, Admiral, I'm going to tell you about the extent of the danger we face if Jamil carries out his threat."

The President omitted nothing about the potential catastrophe that awaited them, nor about their inability to effectively evacuate Seattle. Now it was MacIntyre's turn to be silent. *Massive contamination—possible nuclear detonation! So many lives at risk! And Sally—do I dare send her away?* It was hard for a combat veteran to comprehend so much danger and responsibility while seated at a desk.

"Are you with me, Admiral?"

"Yes, sir. This is far more serious than I imagined." He paused to think, struck momentarily with the incredulous circumstance of having the President of the United States on the telephone, patiently waiting for him to continue. "Mr. President, I'd like some idea of the latitude I have for direct action if negotiations break down. It's . . . well, sir, I'd like some rules of engagement."

"General Scott is preparing that now. You'll have them within the half hour. Obviously, I'll want your consultation on any course of action other than negotiation, time permitting. But understand this, Admiral, there's no book or set of rules that will cover everything that may come up over the next twenty-four hours. You're my on-scene commander, and I'll back you one hundred percent if you're forced to take any action you feel necessary. This is one of those situations where they don't pay us enough for the job we have to do." *Strange!* thought MacIntyre. *That's* exactly *what I've told my carrier pilots before a combat sortie.*

"Another thing. General Scott recommended that you brief Braxton and the special-operations people about the ultimate consequences if that sub blows up. I've agreed to this. Otherwise, this information is not to be shared with anyone unless you feel it's an absolute operational necessity. There's a special FBI security team being formed out there to ensure the compartmentation of all PRESSURE POINT–related information. I consider this vital, and you're to give them every cooperation." Again there was a pause on the line. "Admiral, I'm placing a great deal of trust in your judgment. Do you have reservations about what I'm asking you to do?"

You bet your sweet ass I do, flashed across MacIntyre's mind. "No, sir," he replied.

"Questions?"

"Not at this time. I'm sure there will be some as the situation develops.'' MacIntyre paused, then said, ''Mr. President, I'll do my best.''

''I'm counting on it, Admiral. Good luck to you.''

MacIntyre replaced the receiver and sat in silence. He had completely forgotten about Captain Hailey, who sat quietly by the side of the desk. The conversation and the terrible look on MacIntyre's face had frozen the submariner in his seat, and he neither moved nor spoke. The admiral's aide stuck his head inside the door.

''Sir, they're here.''

''What?''

''The FBI team—they're here.''

''Well, what are you waiting for—send them in.'' Captain Hailey moved to get up.

''Stay where you are, Bob. I'd like you to sit in on this.''

Admiral MacIntyre stood up to greet his visitors, trying to shake a vision of the snowcapped Olympic Mountains forming a backdrop for a mushroom-shaped cloud.

Sunday, 1:22 P.M.—Aboard the *Spokane*

Andy Gosnell alternately rubbed the red bands of flesh that circled each wrist where the handcuffs had been. The cocky Arab called Yehya handled him roughly as he released him, while the quiet chestnut-complected one called Salah covered him with his submachine gun. Gosnell looked impassively at his assistant, George Zanner, who remained cuffed to the propulsion control panel. Zanner had heard Gosnell's conversation with Peck, and he knew enough Navy slang to understand what was afoot. His hand was trembling as he was separated from Gosnell, and beads of sweat now appeared on his forehead. Gosnell saw this and tried to draw attention away from Zanner.

''Unless one of you monkeys knows something about diesels, I'm gonna need some help. I'll need my two helpers to shift the main drives.'' Yehya shoved him roughly away from the propulsion control panel and looked at Salah. He nodded, and the Egyptian walked across the room to release Burns and Gonzales. Both were tired and scared, and looked expectantly at Gosnell.

''Okay, girls, let's check out three and four, and get 'em warmed up. Georgie, cross-connect the panel and get ready to shift the load.'' Zanner stared vacantly at him for a moment and turned to the panel.

Gosnell and his two assistants, escorted by Salah, made their way back to the two silent Detroit diesels. They swarmed over one engine, then the other, checking fluid levels and throttle settings as they completed the prestart checklist. In the course of their ministrations to the two iron monsters, Gosnell found a chance to speak quietly to each of them. The two big diesels were soon purring at idle, and the three ferrymen returned to the control panel. Gosnell brought the two new engines up to full power and transferred the load from the electric drive to the two new diesels. They struggled as they accepted responsibility for driving the electric-drive generator and strained to maintain output rpm.

Gosnell shut down the two engines that had been relieved, and appeared to be concentrating on balancing the power output between the two new power plants, something he could almost do in his sleep. His mind was occupied on just how he could put the lube-oil pump out of action. *The captain chose well,* thought Gosnell. *It will take a while before the lack of oil causes the main engines to overheat and eventually seize up, perhaps long enough to avoid suspicion on his part for tampering with the pump. The big Detroits are tough engines, but they weren't designed to carry this kind of load for extended periods of time and most certainly not without proper lubrication. I got to be careful, though. The quiet one, the one they call Salah, is no fool. He doesn't shove people around or threaten them, but he's a very dangerous man.*

''Okay, Georgie,'' Gosnell said as he scanned the gauges on the panel. ''That's about as good as we can do given the load they're carryin'. Don't know how long we can run them diesels like this—they'd be real smart to slow down some.''

Zanner stared numbly at him from the other end of the panel, his eyes darting from Gosnell to Salah and back. He started to say something to Gosnell, but thought better of it. The engineer turned to Salah.

''I better make the rounds and check out the auxiliary equipment if you want this bucket of bolts to keep runnin'. An' you better let the oiler and wiper do the routine maintenance on their equipment. This gear don't run 'less you tend to it.''

Salah nodded, and motioned Gosnell away from the panel with the barrel of his Uzi. The engineer moved aft, wiping his hands with the rag he habitually carried in the back pocket of his coveralls. He paused to check the inspection tag on a motor-generator. *The lube-oil pump,* he thought. *I'll just close the main lube-oil circulation valve. The pump will appear to be doing its job but without actually pumping any oil. The main engines will eventually burn off the oil in their reservoirs and begin to starve.*

Sunday, 4:30 P.M.—The White House

The President knew he should make an appearance at the situation room, the crisis command center two levels below in the basement, but he liked to conduct business from his desk in the Oval Office, even at times like these. There was a rap at the door and his Director of Central Intelligence stuck his head through the opening.

''Come on in, Armand. What's up?'' In spite of Morton Keeney's disapproval, the President encouraged a policy of free access by his top advisers, especially in crisis situations. All presidents since Jimmy Carter had resisted a management style that would label them as having a ''siege mentality,'' or cause them to be accused of being sequestered by the White House staff.

"It's the Russian submarine, Mr. President. We were unaware of his presence until he began to run at shallow depth, presumably for communications purposes. He was undetected until that time, which, I might add, doesn't happen all that often. Since then, he's been evasive, but our hydrophone arrays have been able to hold his track. It's definitely an Akula Class attack boat, and a good one, from what the listeners tell us. His base course will take him to a position exactly where the *Michigan* is projected to enter international waters." The President pondered this, rubbing his hand over the side of his jaw. *I should have shaved while I was on the plane,* he thought.

"We don't need this shit now, Armand. Have State notify the Russian ambassador that I'd like a conference call with Mr. Stozahrov as soon as possible."

"Sir, may I ask what you have in mind?"

"Sure. I'm going to ask the fat little sonofabitch just what his goddamn sub is doing off our coast at a time like this!"

"Very well, sir."

Sunday, 1:35 P.M.—Sand Point Naval Station, Seattle, Washington

"Gentlemen, come in. I'm certainly glad you're here. This is Captain Hailey, the *Michigan*'s Gold Crew skipper. It was his submarine they took, but they took it from the other crew."

"Admiral . . . Captain. I'm Frank Sclafani and this is Special Agent Whitman." Both men presented MacIntyre with identification. They shook hands around, and MacIntyre motioned them to the seats in front of his desk.

"May I assume that you've been fully read into the scenario?"

"I was briefed at headquarters, and our local people filled us in on the ride over here, including his latest TV appearance. It looks like a difficult physical setup, and this Jamil seems to be a very determined character."

"So it would seem," replied MacIntyre. He rose abruptly from the desk and began to pace. "Have you been briefed as to what might happen if Jamil carries out his threat?" Sclafani and Whitman looked questioningly at each other.

"Just what was said in the White House press release," replied Sclafani.

"Apparently, it's a lot more extensive than that. My information is that the most probable scenario is a nuclear airborne contamination on a scale that could exceed that at Chernobyl. 'Massive alpha-particle contamination' was the term used." MacIntyre glanced at Hailey, who grimly nodded. "I'm also told there's a remote but very real chance of a nuclear detonation. So there's a lot more on the table here than hostages and an expensive piece of government property. If we fail, we risk national disaster on an unprecedented scale. I've been directed to prepare military contingencies, but the President was quite clear that our preferred option is a negotiated settlement. How about it, Mr. Sclafani—think you can talk this guy into throwing in the towel?"

Sclafani had been sitting forward in his chair with his forearms on his knees, listening intently. He leaned back and pursed his lips thoughtfully. He'd suspected there was a possibility of nuclear contamination, but not a potential disaster of this magnitude! *We've speculated about this very thing, but we always thought it would be a Third World nuclear device smuggled into a major city—not one of our own bombs!* He pushed the thought aside and studied MacIntyre.

"Please, call me Frank," he began. "I've studied the bio that the people at Langley put together on this guy, and very candidly, Admiral, he's going to be a tough nut to crack. This is not an *Achille Lauro*–type seizure that was done hastily and with minimal planning. This operation was no small undertaking, and has probably been in the planning stages for months, maybe years. Jamil, from what little is known about him, has a reputation for being smart, committed, and very secretive. Now, here he is on national TV, making no attempt to hide his identity. I think he wants us to believe this is a last, desperate operation for him." Sclafani paused and framed his words carefully. "I think we may be dealing with a man who is not bluffing and who may be prepared to die—one who may feel that blowing up the submarine or a heroic fight to the death are acceptable alternatives. I also sense from what he has said during the broadcasts that he has no idea just how deadly his threat is—*I* certainly didn't until a few minutes ago."

"What do you recommend?"

"I understand that you have a Coast Guard cutter shadowing the *Spokane* and the submarine?"

"That's right. The *Mellon* is about a mile from them now."

"How about communications?"

"We have UHF and VHF, but the terrorists have yet to respond to hourly calls from the cutter. There's also a secure SATCOM capability on the cutter, so we have a direct, real-time link with Washington. I thought you'd like to negotiate from the cutter, and they're prepared to receive you."

"Excellent. Right now I can only tell Jamil that our government is in high-level consultation with the Israelis, and restate our position on the UN land-for-peace resolutions being discussed at the Mideast peace talks. Basically, until we're given more to work with, I'll be playing for time. I'd also like to have a team of snipers set up on the cutter. It might be that we'll get an opportunity to take him out and deal with his second in command. It wouldn't be an easy shot, and we may not have the chance, but Slim and his shooters are the best there are."

"Anything else that you need?" asked MacIntyre.

"Just a ride out to the cutter. Once there, I'll need a communications station with some privacy. If possible, I'd like a radio link outside and up high on the ship. If I can see him as well as talk to him, it sometimes helps. Slim will find a concealed place on the ship to set up a shooting station." Sclafani again hesitated before continuing. "And just so we're clear on this, Admiral, I talk to Jamil and make my observations and recommendations to you. The decision to do anything but talk—any direct action—is your decision, is that correct?"

MacIntyre studied Sclafani carefully. *Is this guy trying to cover his ass, or is he just trying to verify the rules before he goes to work?* MacIntyre sensed it was the latter.

"Frank, I'm responsible for the tactical situation. The President wants recommendations and options. The decision to abandon negotiations and use force will be his, unless things start to move quickly—then I have the authority to respond. At this stage of the game, force is the last resort, and our best chance for a way out of this mess is with you. You're the expert. I'm counting on you to do the job, or to tell me when you can't and that we should begin to look at other options. If you can talk Jamil off that ferry, you get the credit; if the whole thing goes up in smoke, I'll take the blame."

Sclafani smiled and stood up, offering his hand. "You'd never make it at the FBI in Washington, Admiral, but I sincerely appreciate what you've said. We'll do what we can for you. Will you be joining us on the cutter?"

"Just as soon as I meet with the special-operations units. There's a Coast Guard helo waiting, and Captain Libby on the *Mellon* is expecting you."

Sunday, 4:45 P.M.—The White House

The President had just returned to the Oval Office from the situation room. He quickly put on his suit coat and straightened his tie before asking Secretary Noffsinger to show the ambassador in. Bennett met him at the door and shook his hand warmly before escorting him to a low cocktail table surrounded by two plush wing-back chairs and a settee. Noffsinger and the ambassador sat on the settee while the President took one of the chairs.

David Rosenblatt looked more like a graduate student on a job interview than the Israeli ambassador. He was in need of a haircut, and his gray pin-striped suit was just a shade too large. The Israelis joked that they never wore suits except when they came to Washington, and Bennett believed them. Rosenblatt was a tall, bony man with dark, shrewd eyes. He was American by birth, Harvard educated, and one hundred percent Israeli. He looked vulnerable and out of place, but the President knew better. Noffsinger was pinned against the arm of the settee, placing as much distance between himself and the Israeli as possible. He eyed Rosenblatt like a mongoose would a cobra. Bennett also measured the Israeli ambassador. He would have preferred to speak directly with Prime Minister Levin, but he was not available via a direct telephone line. Bennett strongly suspected this unavailability was intentional.

"Thank you for coming on such short notice, Mr. Ambassador. I'm sure you're aware of our problem out on the West Coast and of the demands made by the gunmen aboard our ferry for the release of the hostages and our nuclear submarine."

"Yes, Mr. President. Prime Minister Levin has asked me to convey his concern for the hostages and their families. He has also directed me to place my staff at your disposal on a consulting basis until the situation is resolved." *I'll bet he has,* thought Bennett. "Terrorists," Rosenblatt continued, holding his palms up in a gesture of appeal, "will we never be free of them?"

"That's most generous of you. As you are aware, we have pushed for a negotiated settlement of the Palestinian question for some time. Following the Persian Gulf War, we placed our support behind a negotiated peace process that would require Israel to end its occupation of the West Bank and Gaza in exchange for certain security guarantees. That was our basis for the Madrid talks. I realize this is a complex issue, and because of this, we have not pressed Israel regarding the occupation of their lands. How close is your government, at this time, to finalizing the conditions under which you will withdraw from the occupied territories?"

"You are correct in that it is a complex issue. And as you know, my government has refused to place a timetable on any withdrawal until the civil disobedience, and attacks on Israeli citizens and soldiers, has ended. We were most specific on this at Madrid and during subsequent negotiations. There is also the matter of the safety of Israeli citizens who will remain in these areas. And of course, there is the question of just who can speak for the Palestinians—there are so many factions who claim legitimacy, including that man in Tunis.'' Rosenblatt never referred to PLO chairman Yasser Arafat directly.

''Is your government in a position to issue a statement of intent regarding the occupied territories at this time?''

Rosenblatt stared at Bennett for a full ten seconds before he spoke. ''I will have to cable my foreign minister for instructions, but so there is no misunderstanding, are you asking for an immediate, general statement of intent on the part of my government to abandon the occupied territories?''

''I am.'' Again, a long silence.

Rosenblatt, for all his intelligence and experience, was totally unprepared for Bennett's request. Finally, he leaned forward, the fingers of his hands interlocked as if in prayer. ''Mr. President, may I remind you that it has been the policy of both our governments not to negotiate with terrorists. A statement like the one you are suggesting at this time would only serve to recognize the use of terror as a viable instrument of international arbitration. And if I may, sir, I can understand how difficult this recent attack may be for your administration. America has been relatively immune from terrorist acts until now, but the threat of terrorism is a way of life with us. If they succeed in forcing us to yield to their demands, and a declaration such as the one you have requested would be seen as just that, then all we have done over the last two decades to thwart terrorism will be lost.''

There was an uncharacteristic flush in Rosenblatt's cheeks. At first, Bennett listened impassively, but Rosenblatt's intimation that this request was motivated purely by political considerations was the wrong thing to say. The President bristled and was about to land on the young man when Noffsinger smoothly intervened.

''We appreciate the possible signal that could be sent to terrorist organizations, but we are facing a most difficult and potentially damaging situation out in Seattle. We feel that a statement such as the one President Bennett has suggested might assist us in disarming the situation, or at least allow us to draw out the negotiations until other alternatives can be found. Naturally, this statement by your government could be acknowledged as a special request by the government of the United States.''

Rosenblatt carefully phrased his reply. ''Of course, this is a matter that will be addressed well above the ambassadorial level, but let me suggest that such a statement at this time carries considerable risk for my country. While we will be seen as responding to your request, we are still being manipulated by terrorists—that if the threat is great enough, then demands will be met. And how will this be seen by the Palestinians who until now have been content to throw stones and stage an occasional riot? What will it do to the peace process now under way? Mr. President, they will come at us in a hundred different ways. There will be more bloodshed and more UN resolutions denouncing the brutality of Israel—UN initiatives that you have in the past supported.''

''Your point is well taken,'' replied the President, ''and I would not ask this if the situation we face were not so dangerous. Please remind Prime Minister Levin that the nation of Israel has enjoyed strong support from America in the past. That support has been based on friendship, strong cultural ties, and a commonality of regional interest. The situation we now face could conceivably result in substantial loss of life among our citizens. If we must suffer this, and it is later determined that you could have assisted us and refused, it could have a serious and lasting effect on our relationship.''

Rosenblatt stared coldly at Bennett for a moment and got to his feet. ''I will immediately convey your request to my government and inform you of their decision. Mr. President, Secretary Noffsinger.'' He left without shaking hands.

''Arrogant as a goddamn camel,'' said the President. ''Think they'll come through?''

''I think we knew the answer to that when Levin wouldn't take your call. At least they now know what's on the table. The Israelis depend on us, and you made it very clear that right now we need their help. They risk it all if they say no.'' Noffsinger watched as the President walked behind his large desk and looked down into the lawn.

''Y'know, Dick, sometimes I envy Levin and the Israelis.

Every decision is linked to national survival, so it's always black and white with them—no political shades of gray. Kind of like the fifties in this country when the Communists were everywhere.''

He took off his jacket and loosened his tie. ''Looks like this is going to be a long night—think I'll close my eyes for about fifteen minutes. Call me if there's any change.'' The President tipped his chair back and propped his feet on the desk while Noffsinger quietly let himself out.

Sunday, 1:50 P.M.—Aboard the *Spokane*

Did I do the right thing? Peck asked himself for the hundredth time. It had been almost an hour since he guardedly told his engineer to sabotage the lube-oil pump, which would eventually cause the main engines to shut down. The tachometers on his instrument panel told him that Gosnell had shifted power to number-three and -four engines. He could see they were straining under the load, just like their predecessors. *These diesels are tough, but they're not designed to carry this kind of load. And what about Gosnell? Maybe he wasn't able to get to the pump. They might not have even allowed him to leave his post at the propulsion control panel. Maybe he didn't understand the message or thought it was too dangerous to try. Maybe he tried and something happened to him!*

Peck closed his eyes for a moment and took a deep breath. He had been at the wheel for close to eighteen hours, and the strain of being on his feet for so long was beginning to show. There was a white dusting of stubble around his chin and upper lip. He took his cap off and laid it on the helm console. It was a beautiful cloudless day, and a mild westerly wind was causing a light, feathered chop on the ice-blue waters of the Strait. The temperature was in the mid-seventies.

If I were home, I'd just be waking up. Maybe a few chores around the house and a barbecue with Sarah and the boys.

Billy and Tom would be up to something—last week they were cutting the heads off kitchen matches, trying to make a rocket out of an old bicycle pump. Last week? It seems like last year.

He looked off the port beam to the plume of smoke rising from the pulp mill at Port Angeles. Ediz Hook was just barely visible through the light haze on the water, while the shoreline of Vancouver Island on the Canadian side was a solid purple-blue line. He noticed the absence of small-craft traffic, and he had yet to see the ferry that ran between Port Angeles and Victoria, British Columbia. The only other vessel was the white hull of the *Mellon,* keeping station off the starboard quarter. They had been a fixture there except when they broke to search for survivors from the plane that was shot down. *I wonder if they found any?* So far, there had been only the routine hourly radio calls from the cutter. Peck noticed that he was drifting off course and applied rudder to correct it. That seemed to be happening more often. *When will they begin to negotiate for our release?*

"You okay, Captain?"

"Yeah, Janey."

"You want me to try and steer for a while? As long as the wind is bow-on, I'm sure I can do it." Janey had been able to doze periodically on her stool, but was really no more rested than Peck.

"Thanks, maybe later."

He'll probably secure the circulation pump, thought Peck. *The engines will run for a while and then seize up, seemingly from the strain of having to pull the weight of the submarine. It's almost two o'clock. I'll bet that's what he did.*

Peck had just brought the *Spokane* slowly back to their base course of 285 when Andy Gosnell stepped into the pilothouse. Peck felt a stab of fear in his bowels as he tried to look surprised.

"Hello, Ross," Gosnell said.

Gosnell's hands were casually thrust into his overalls pockets, but there was a worried look on his face. Jamil stood behind him with the Sig Sauer .45 in his hand, the long silencer barrel running down along the outseam of his trousers.

''Well, Andy—they decide to let you out on deck for a little fresh air?'' Peck offered casually.

Gosnell forced a smile and turned to face Jamil. ''These rag-heads think I was tryin' to sabotage the main engines. They make me run 'em at full power all this time draggin' that hunk of iron tied alongside, an' then they say *I'm* tryin' to screw 'em up. Hell, we're lucky they haven't given out 'fore this with the load they been carryin'.''

''Let's stop the games, gentlemen. You closed the valve to the oil line that services the engines, knowing this would cause them to run out of oil. You did this deliberately as a means of trying to sabotage the engines.''

''What th' hell you even know about my eng—''

''SILENCE!'' The pistol came level, and both Gosnell and Peck froze. ''You think I am stupid—that I don't know what you were doing—that I was not prepared for something like this!'' Jamil lowered his voice, but the wild look in his eye remained. ''Did I not promise you that the punishment was death for such an offense?'' Jamil lowered the pistol and looked from Gosnell to Peck. ''Well, didn't I?''

Peck's knees were jelly, and his mouth was so dry he wasn't sure he could speak. He glanced at Gosnell, who stared fiercely back at Jamil. *I'm a dead man,* he thought! *Shit! Why did I try this? I don't owe the ferry system or this damned boat a thing. Oh God, Sarah, I'm so sorry!*

''I told him to do it,'' Peck managed in a steady voice.

Gosnell snapped a look at him and took his hand out of his pockets. ''Not really, Ross, I was the one that—''

''Never mind that, Andy,'' Peck said wearily. ''It was my order, and I think he knows it.''

''No, I did not, but I strongly suspected it.'' Jamil sighed and shot Gosnell twice in the chest. The impact of the bullets was louder than the explosions from the silenced automatic, like the slap of an open palm onto wet cement. Gosnell slumped back against the forward bulkhead and then to the floor.

''Fuckin' raghead . . .'' And then the fire went out of his eyes.

Peck stood frozen, watching Gosnell buck under the impact

of the .45 slugs and sink to the floor, almost in slow motion. Gosnell's right fist was tightly clenched except for the middle index finger, which was extended. Peck stared at his friend for a moment, then exploded. He flew at Jamil and almost got to him, but like a junkyard dog on a chain, he was jerked horizontally in the air and crashed heavily on the deck. The handcuff bit deeply into his wrist and the blood ran down his forearm to his elbow. Dazed, Peck stared up at Jamil, the hate plain in his eyes.

"God DAMN you! It wasn't his fault—I told him to do it!"

"Yes, yes, I know, Peck. You are the captain and he was just following orders. But this is war, and sometimes the officers are not offered the privilege—or the luxury—of dying for their mistakes. As is the usual case, it is those who carry out the orders who must die. But try me again, and I promise that I will oblige you. He was a brave man, Peck, and he does you honor by his death. But understand that it was *you* who killed him." Jamil looked at the chart and then back at Peck. "The engineer was right about the strain on the engines—slow to four knots. And we are drifting off course. Either get back to the wheel or have the woman do it. Hassan," he called to the Arab standing just outside the pilothouse, "give me a hand with the carcass of this dead *fares.*"

Peck watched numbly as they dragged his friend out and winced each time his head bounced on the steps that led down from the pilothouse.

Sunday, 2:00 P.M.—Sand Point Naval Station, Seattle, Washington

"Detail, atten-SHUN!"

The men around the table, all dressed in camouflage utility uniforms, scrambled to their feet. An Army colonel who stood by the door called them to attention. The admiral sensed something different about the colonel's attire, and then saw that only his uniform was freshly starched. He remained at attention with the tip of his right index finger touching his right eyebrow in a perfect salute. Navymen only saluted when covered, and MacIntyre had never become comfortable with the Army and Air Force custom of saluting bareheaded.

"Carry on, men." As those around the table took their seats, MacIntyre noticed the map case and notebook laid out at the head of the table, with an empty seat next to the end chair. He took the crisply starched fatigue cap from the chairman's seat and set it on the map case, which he slid off to his right. He stood to address the group from the end of the table. "I assume that you gentlemen have been fully briefed on the capture of the *Spokane* and the *Michigan?*"

"Yes, sir, we have," replied the colonel, who reluctantly took the seat to MacIntyre's right. "The staff G-2 at Fort Lewis provided us with an area briefing and a walk-through of the message traffic."

"Excellent. You must be Braxton, right?"

"Yes sir—we were just—"

"I'm Admiral John MacIntyre, and I'm the on-scene commander of this mess. Some wise guy in Washington codenamed it PRESSURE POINT, and he probably didn't know how right he was. Colonel, would you mind introducing me to your men?"

"Uh, not at all, sir." Braxton began introductions, and MacIntyre walked around the table and shook each man's hand.

"Thank you, Colonel. Gentlemen, it is our intention to resolve this crisis through negotiation. If that cannot be done and if so authorized by the President—or in extremis, authorized by me—you will be asked to storm the two vessels and recapture them. It has been made very clear to me by the President that this course of action will be taken only after all other avenues have been exhausted."

The door opened, and two naval officers entered. MacIntyre waved them to the seats at the far end of the table. "This is Captain Hailey, Commanding Officer of the *Michigan*'s Gold Crew, and Captain Gentry is my chief of staff. Captain Hailey and I will fly out to the Coast Guard cutter that is bird-dogging the captured vessels as soon as we've finished here. We need to be on our way as soon as possible, and I'm sure you men have plenty to do, so we'll keep this meeting brief. Captain Gentry will remain with Colonel Braxton and serve as your liaison to me. And now, Colonel, if the negotiations do fail, how do you propose to respond?''

Braxton stepped to the side of the table and turned the cover sheet on a tripod-mounted easel to reveal the beam-on profile of a Jumbo Class ferry.

''Taking down a moving ship is one the most difficult assignments we have. We have no viable underwater capability, so there is no way we can clandestinely approach these vessels. Our procedures call for a helicopter assault at night, with the pilots using night-vision goggles. A daylight action with their surface-to-air capability would be next to impossible. We hope to get aboard quickly and mount a coordinated attack before the terrorists have had time to react. It's a tall order, and risky, but we're trained for it.'' Braxton took what looked like a Cross pen from a slot pocket on his left sleeve and telescoped it into a pointer.

''This will be a Delta Force action, with Captain Sherrard leading the assault. Captain Smith and his Rangers will stand by in their rigid inflatable speedboats as a support element. The SEALs will be held in reserve. The main assault force will use three UH-60 Blackhawk helicopters from Fort Lewis. They will come in from the east and astern of the ferry in echelon formation at a forty-five-degree angle. This will allow the helos to be in autorotation on their final approach to suppress the noise from the rotor blades. The steep angle of descent will also eliminate the chance of being picked up on the ferry's surface-search radar. The predominant wind is from the west, which will also help to mask the noise of their approach. The first helo will flare fifty feet above the promenade deck here,'' he tapped the diagram with the pointer just behind the forward pilot-house, ''and the first squad will fast-rope to the deck. From here, they will assault the pilothouse. The second helo will hover over the stern, allowing the second squad to rope down to the observation platform on the passenger deck. From there, they can charge into the after cabin where the hostages are being held and engage the terrorists guarding them. After the hostages are liberated, they will post security and proceed to clear the car decks and engineering spaces.'' Braxton flipped the sheet over to a bird's-eye view of a ferry with the outline of a Trident submarine alongside. ''The third helo will put a light fire team on the missile deck of the *Michigan.* They will have ordnance specialists with them who will disarm or jettison the explosive charges on the deck of the submarine.''

He paused and turned away from the easel. ''There's a fifty-fifty chance the first helo will not be detected until it is directly overhead. It'll take about seven seconds for the members of the first squad to get to the deck and approximately fifteen seconds for them to form up and assault the pilothouse. They can have the pilothouse secured about thirty seconds from the time the first helo is over the deck, assuming we're not detected until our first bird is on top of the ferry. We can cut that a few seconds with some rehearsal time, but not a great deal.'' Braxton collapsed this pointer and addressed MacIntyre. ''Our chances for success rest entirely with getting the Delta Force on the deck of the ferry before the terrorists have time to react. The forty-five-degree, glide-slope approach is quiet, but the helos will be highly vulnerable to surface-to-air missiles at this time.''

''If you're able to get aboard, what do you estimate your chances for success?''

''One hundred percent. It won't be easy and we expect casualties, but intelligence indicates there are no more than ten terrorists aboard, probably less. We'll put sixteen men on the ferry and another six on the submarine. I don't believe any terrorist force, good as this one may be, can fight on equal terms with a platoon of Delta Force commandos.''

MacIntyre looked across the table to the Delta team leader. His face revealed nothing. ''Captain Sherrard, is there any chance of total surprise—a chance that if Jamil is in the pilot-house, you can get to him before he has time to explode those charges?''

"I'd say little or no chance, Admiral. Not unless we happen to catch him away from the firing device, and given the commercial availability of small, remote firing devices, I wouldn't put much faith in that. If he's any good at all, he'll carry it with him at all times."

"Is there any means at your disposal that would allow you to get aboard the *Spokane* undetected?" Braxton started to reply, and MacIntyre put his hand up. "Before you respond, I'd better tell all of you what's on the table besides the lives of the hostages and the embarrassment of losing a nuclear-capable ship—not to mention placing the lives of you and your men at risk. If the terrorists explode those charges, the most probable result will be a massive nuclear contamination of the greater Seattle area, the Olympic Peninsula, Vancouver Island, and southwestern British Columbia. Gentlemen, we are talking serious contamination to millions and potential fatalities in the thousands. That's the good news. The eggheads at the Naval Research Lab and DOE are working out the probabilities now, but it appears there may be a chance of a nuclear detonation. It appears to be only a slight chance, but as they say, close only counts in horseshoes and nuclear weapons." No one smiled, and there was not a sound in the room. "As you can see, the hostages and everything else are secondary to getting to Jamil and making sure those explosives don't go off. So I'll ask again, is there any way to get aboard undetected and disarm those explosives, or to kill Jamil before he can set them off?" Once again, the room was silent. Admiral MacIntyre looked around the room and turned to Braxton. "Now, you were saying, Colonel?"

"Captain Sherrard's right. If Jamil has a remote device and is determined to use it, there's little we can do to stop him. But there's a good chance that in the face of an assault, Jamil will try to defend himself rather than carry out his threat. Perhaps he'll surrender when it's clear that it's his only chance to live."

"Perhaps," replied MacIntyre, "but the behavioral science experts at the FBI think differently." He drummed his fingers on the table for a moment and looked at his watch—2:15. *I better get on out to the* Mellon *and let these men get on with their plans. God help us if we have to attack that ferry with a heliborne assault.* He was about to get up when the SEAL chief raised his hand.

"Admiral, I think there's a good chance we can get a SEAL squad aboard that ferry undetected." MacIntyre stared at him for a moment and settled back into his chair.

"Very well, Master Chief, let's hear about it." Chief Watson looked at Lieutenant Horner, who nodded for him to go ahead.

"We were just told the ferry has slowed to four knots—about twice as fast as a man with fins can swim for a short distance. A line of swimmers can be positioned at fifty-meter intervals in front of the ferry after dark. They can be cast by helo or by small craft. It's doubtful that anyone on board will be able to see men in the water at night. The first man in the line tosses a padded grappling iron over the rail of the car deck on the port side and hauls himself aboard. The lower car deck can't be more than six feet off the water, and the life rail a few feet higher. As the ferry works its way down the line of swimmers, the rest of the squad can be brought aboard. There's a chance that they'll have roving sentries on the car deck, but I doubt it. Most of them will be topside watching for an airborne attack. If there is a sentry, the first men over will have silenced weapons and can deal with it. Once aboard, we can try to get to the pilothouse undetected and try for Jamil, or we can go for the explosives. Given what you've just told us, I would recommend that we move across the ferry to the *Michigan* and try to disarm those charges. Then we can deal with the terrorists or call in the Delta teams."

MacIntyre studied the SEAL chief over steepled fingers. He was much smaller than his lieutenant, but he had a look of purpose about him. The camouflage blouse was rolled to just above his elbows, revealing knotted forearms and blunt, well-callused hands. He had a boyish face with a neatly trimmed mustache. A chestnut lock hung across his forehead, but his hair was running to gray, especially at the temples. *He's a master chief,* thought MacIntyre, *so he's got to be at least thirty-eight, probably older. He looks like a man who can do what he says, and God knows I don't need any bullshit at this stage of the game.* He glanced at Braxton, who stood by his easel, arms folded and glaring at the chief.

"What are your chances of getting aboard, Chief?"

"Right now I'd say they're better than half," replied Watson. "But if there's a ferry available for rehearsal, they'll go up a great deal. I'd like to be able to try it once in the daylight, and again as soon as it gets dark. If there's enough time for us to practice, sir, we'll get aboard all right. Then it's a matter of dodging the sentries and getting to the explosives on the submarine."

MacIntyre again studied him carefully. *The chief is a professional, but why is he pushing for the SEALs to be allowed to make the attack?* "Just why do you think this plan would have a better chance for success than the airborne assault outlined by Colonel Braxton?" pressed MacIntyre.

Chief Watson rubbed his hands together self-consciously and looked up at the admiral. "Sir, it seems to me this is the only way to get aboard that ferry undetected and to have a chance at disarming those explosives. I'm no terrorist expert, but I think this guy will do what he says—if he sees us coming, he's gonna crank those charges off." Watson looked at his lieutenant, at the others around the table, and back to MacIntyre. "Admiral, I grew up here. My folks still live up in Bellingham. We can't let him do this—not to all these people, not to this beautiful country."

"Lieutenant?" MacIntyre looked from Watson to Horner.

"If the master chief says we can get aboard, then we'll get aboard. My platoon has trained for maritime assaults at night. The ships weren't moving, but the sides were twenty feet of vertical metal. If we can practice it a few times, we can do it."

"It might help their chances," said Captain Sherrard, "if we could create a diversion when the SEALs are coming over the side."

"I may be able to help you there." It was Captain Hailey, seated at the far end of the table. "If that man on the *Michigan* is capable of taking some direction, we may be able to get their attention to starboard."

MacIntyre listened carefully. He glanced at Colonel Braxton and could tell this was not the option he had in mind. "Sounds promising so far," he said. "What about after you get aboard?"

"One of my petty officers is EOD qualified," continued Horner. "We'd move across to the starboard side and set up security while he disarmed the charges. Then, like Chief Watson said, we could call in the Delta teams, or begin our own search-and-clear operations on the ferry."

"Admiral," said Chief Watson, "we're probably not as good as Captain Sherrard and Sergeant Blackwood's men, but we can hold our own in close-quarter battle. And really, sir, I think we all know that taking down the terrorists is a secondary objective." MacIntyre was silent for a moment, then got to his feet, motioning the others to remain seated.

"Very well, I want both of these plans rehearsed and available as soon as possible, as well as Captain Smith's Rangers in the small assault craft. If force is to be used, we may elect one or more of these options. Captain Gentry will get you a ferry for your rehearsals and see to any other support requirements you may have. Colonel Braxton, report to me when your men are staged and ready to go. Once they're in place, I'd like you to be on the *Mellon* with me. You can direct the operation from there."

MacIntyre paused and swept the group seated around the table, holding each man's gaze for a moment. "Gentlemen, I sincerely hope that this is a false alarm for you—just another training exercise. But if you are called on to do your job, please understand that a great number of lives will depend on our success. Good luck to each of you." MacIntyre again shook each man's hand, then stepped out into the hall followed by Gentry and Hailey.

"Captain Hailey and I are heading out to the cutter right now," he said to Gentry. "I want you to stay with these men, and I want you to observe the rehearsals. Give them whatever they need to get the job done. Let it be known I'll have any bureaucrat's ass that doesn't cooperate and do so smartly. I'll want your opinion as well as Braxton's as to just how good those SEALs are at getting aboard a moving ferry. Take your cellular phone and stay in constant communication.''

''Aye, sir.''

MacIntyre looked back over Gentry's shoulder into the room. The two enlisted men and the three young officers were crowded around the easel in animated conversation, pointing to different parts of the ferry. Braxton observed them from the side, arms still folded. *The operators seem to be working together,* thought MacIntyre. *That's good, because I don't need any of this interservice-rivalry crap right now.*

He shook Gentry's hand and motioned Hailey to follow as he walked out the door to where the bright-red Coast Guard helo was turning on the pad.

Sunday, 2:20 P.M.—Aboard the Coast Guard Cutter *Mellon* (WHEC-717)

Frank Sclafani rested his elbows on the rail of the cutter's bridge wing to steady the binoculars. He could clearly see one of the terrorists walking back and forth on the promenade deck, an AK-47 rifle slung on a strap around his neck. The weapon was suspended horizontally and seemed to bisect him at the waist. At Sclafani's request the cutter had crept forward to just abaft the *Spokane*'s starboard beam. From this position, he could just see through the stair railing into the pilothouse door. There were several people inside, and he assumed that the large man in the dark trousers and white shirt standing at the helm must be the captain. Periodically a tall Arab wearing a dark sweater would step out onto the pilothouse wing for a moment and then go back inside. Once, a man wearing glasses came down the pilothouse steps and made some adjustments to the tripod-mounted dish antenna on the promenade deck just behind the pilothouse. One deck below, he could see the silhouettes of the hostages seated in the forward passenger cabin.

There was some movement, but he was unable to distinguish between prisoner and guard.

"What do you think?" Up on the signal bridge, one level above the *Mellon*'s pilothouse, Slim Whitman was settled in behind the "big eyes," a large pair of swivel-mounted binoculars. Each ocular was six inches in diameter. He wore a headset and lip mike identical to Sclafani's. It was critical that the negotiator and the shooters have real-time communications, especially toward the end of the negotiations.

"Looks like the horses are in the pilothouse, which is what we figured from the last video transmission. I'm sure the guy in the black sweater who just stepped back into the pilothouse is our boy—he's dressed the same as the guy on TV. I can see Captain Peck and what looks like a female crewman inside the pilothouse. The stoop-shouldered guy with glasses must be the technician running the video uplink."

"Do you have a shot?"

"Maybe later, but I doubt it. The relative wind is about fifteen miles per hour, and it's gustin'. I'd say its fifty-fifty for a body shot from here with no wind—maybe not that good. An' I wouldn't even try a head shot." The FBI sniper teams had learned from experience that only a head shot would keep a terrorist from pulling the trigger—or in this case pushing a button. "We're set up as best we can, but it'll be a low-percentage shot unless we can get closer and the wind dies down." Whitman had placed a two-man shooting team amidships, well hidden behind one of the cutter's lifeboats. This position, three levels below the flag bridge, sacrificed height as a shooting platform but minimized the effects of the ship's roll and pitch.

Captain Libby had found Sclafani a space in the ship's radio room located just behind the bridge. He would do most of his work from there, but he thought he would begin from out here on the bridge. He had a maritime VHF circuit patched to the bridge wing with enough power output to easily reach the *Spokane*, but, he hoped, not enough to be monitored on either shore. He took a deep breath as he ran his finger down the checklist to the first item: *Establish communication and bona fides.*

"This is Assistant Secretary of State Frank Jefferson on the cutter *Mellon* calling Mr. Jamil Nusseibeh on the M/V *Spokane.*" Using his surname would indicate that Sclafani knew something of Jamil and, in fact, had been briefed by U.S. intelligence. Unless he was dealing with domestic criminals, he almost always used the name Jefferson and a State Department title—both made him sound more official. "Mr. Nusseibeh, I represent the government of the United States, and have been authorized by the secretary of state to negotiate with you regarding the conditions that you have made for the release of the hostages and the return of the USS *Michigan.*" He repeated the call and waited, studying the *Spokane* through the glasses. He smiled as he saw increased activity in the pilothouse. The speaker at his elbow hissed a few times as someone keyed a microphone.

"This is Jamil of the Islamic Brothers of Freedom aboard the *Safinat al Horeya.* How do I know that you represent the government of the United States?"

Item two on the checklist: *Be formal and polite.*

"Sir, if you will ask Captain Peck for a pair of his binoculars, please train them on the bridge of the cutter, for that is where I am now standing." When Jamil did, he saw a man in a dark suit and tie on the bridge wing of the cutter. The man in the suit took a pair of glasses from his eyes and waved.

"Very well," replied Jamil, "is your government prepared to meet my demands?"

Item three: *Be sympathetic, show good faith, and work for time.*

"Mr. Nusseibeh, Jamil if I may, my government takes your requests very seriously. As you know, we have always supported a return of the occupied territories to the Palestinian people in return for peace. We are in consultation at this time with the government of Israel, but as you are well aware, they can be difficult. I have been directed to tell you that we are doing everything we can to support a repatriation of the West Bank and Gaza, but I also must remind you that the nation of Israel is a sovereign state and that they may feel no urgency to comply with what you ask."

"That is your problem, Jefferson. The Israelis may be arrogant Zionists who pursue only their own interests, but they are also your hirelings and your money controls them. The decision is yours, and you will have to bring them to heel."

Four: *Establish your willingness to work with him, but emphasize your limited authority.*

"Again, Jamil, we take your position very seriously, and I personally respect the risk you have taken for your people. I will convey your position to my government, but I must emphasize that the time frame you have specified and the anticipated reluctance of the Israelis make this a most difficult situation."

"Listen carefully, Jefferson. By now you have had a chance to study the explosives on the submarine, and the destruction that will result if I am forced to detonate those explosives. I am a soldier, and this is my duty. If you know who I am, then you must surely know that I will not shrink from that duty. The Israelis may be difficult, but they are your problem, not mine. You have less than four hours to meet my demands, or I will do exactly what I told you I would do. Your country has supported the Jews for decades, Jefferson. It is now time that you ask them to support you. Call me when you and your Jewish allies are prepared to meet my demands. This conversation is over."

On the cutter, Sclafani put the microphone down and replaced the headset. "Did you get a good look at him, Slim?"

"He's the one on TV, all right. He's carryin' something on his belt, possibly an electronic device. It'd be my guess that it's a remote triggering device for the explosives."

"Do you have a shot?"

"Not yet. The quartermaster up here says the wind usually dies down by late evenin', but then we may not have enough light. And I'd still like to get closer. We'd be lucky to take him out, and one of the others could still push the button."

"Thanks, Slim."

Sclafani pulled the headset off and thought about the initial interview. There had been no softening of the terrorist's position—he hadn't expected there would be—but he judged it a successful exchange. Jamil had been willing to talk, and he had at least acknowledged the difficult U.S. position in dealing with the Israelis. Sclafani felt there may possibly be some room for the give-and-take that must be part of a successful negotiation. But in his past experience, he had always dealt from a position of strength—no deals unless the hostages were set free, and ultimately, the fate of the hostages had been subordinated to the principle of not giving in to the hard demands of a terrorist. This was different—the hostages could number in the thousands, maybe the tens of thousands, and the advantage was clearly with the terrorist.

Sclafani rubbed his eyes wearily and looked across the water at the *Spokane* and the black shape alongside. He perceived a toughness and resolution on the part of Jamil he rarely experienced. Unless he was given something meaningful to bargain with, something that was in line with what Jamil was asking, Sclafani judged this was a man who would not hesitate to carry out his threat. He looked at his watch and made his way back to the radio room to listen to a tape of their conversation.

Sunday, 5:23 P.M.—The White House

President Bennett drummed his fingers on the desk while he waited for the security connections, many of them done manually, to be made along the line. *If I were calling a Western capital,* he thought, *everything would be automated and would take a fraction of the time. The Russian phone system is like their economy—slow and twenty years behind the times.* Bennett had not used the NSA emergency communication channels, which were far more efficient, because he didn't want to give undue urgency to the call.

"The President of the Russian Republic conveys his good wishes to you, and asks how he may be of service."

"Please deliver to President Stozharov my greetings, and ask his pardon for disturbing him at this late hour." The American translator spoke in Russian directly to the president of the

Russian Republic and his translator on the other end of the connection. Speaking through interpreters was like watching a foreign film with subtitles—it was awkward at first, and you had to pay attention. Communication was possible, but subtle inferences were often lost, at least until the recorded text could be analyzed by the experts at State and Langley.

"As you are aware, President Stozharov, one of our ballistic submarines on our Pacific coast has been captured by terrorists, and they are threatening to sink it with explosives."

"Yes, Mr. Bennett, we are aware that the Trident submarine *Michigan* is now in the hands of terrorists. Can I be of service?"

"Not at this time, thank you. However, I would like to ask that your Akula Class nuclear attack submarine currently operating off the coast of Washington State move out to sea. It has positioned itself in the path of the captured ferry, and we consider that an unnecessary complication at this time."

"Our submarine is in international waters, is it not? All our naval vessels have been carefully instructed not to violate the territorial waters of any nation."

He's screwing with me, thought Bennett as he concentrated on the translation. *That or he doesn't know what's going on. And now is not the time to remind him of his Whiskey Class submarine that grounded itself well inside Swedish territorial waters some years back.* "The Russian submarine has not penetrated American territorial waters, but under the circumstances, we feel the presence of one of your submarines in the close proximity of this unfortunate situation could be viewed as a provocation." *Provocation,* he mused. *Khrushchev would have hung up on Jack Kennedy if he'd talked to him like that.*

"I understand your position. Our submarines regularly patrol in international waters near your ballistic-missile-submarine bases, just as your submarines cruise near some of our naval ports. I will contact the commander of the Red Banner Pacific Fleet immediately, and confirm the mission and location of this particular submarine. Are you sure there is no way we can be of assistance in this unfortunate incident?"

"That is most kind of you, President Stozharov, but no,

thank you. The movement of your submarine away from our coast is all that is required.''

"I understand. I will take this up immediately with my fleet commander. Good luck with the recapture of your submarine."

Bennett hung up the phone and looked questioningly at Noffsinger, who sat across the desk. He also put down a receiver.

"My guess is that he doesn't know, and there's no reason he should. Langley can probably tell us from an analysis of their ELENT intercepts. The submarine is in a routine patrol station in international waters, although it's rare that one of them comes right up to the twelve-mile limit. I think he'll get that boat out of there, but it could take a while. Their command-and-control procedures are not as efficient as ours. There will be a communications delay between Moscow and Pacific Fleet headquarters in Vladivostok, and a further delay in their communications with the sub. As you know, our Trident D-5 missiles have been a central issue at the arms-reduction talks. I'm sure this is giving them a great deal of satisfaction, but I doubt that he'll deny your request to move that Akula out to sea."

President Stozharov sat at his desk in the office adjacent to his Moscow apartment, wrapped in his bathrobe and a pleasant smile. He was a plump man, which the political cartoonists in the Western press exaggerated unmercifully. He moved gingerly from behind the desk and began to pace. *It is true! A ragtag group of Arab terrorists has actually stolen one of their Trident submarines. What a stroke of luck—or is it luck? Could this be one of the KGB's elaborate plots, initiated by a more aggressive KGB chief during the pre-glasnost/pre-coup era and carried forward by some reactionary cell buried within the First Directorate? Reform came slowly to the chekists. Many of Kryuchkov's men were still in place, and there were even pockets of Andropov's people still lurking within the huge bureaucracy.*

A mild stab of fear shot through Stozharov. The old Soviet Union had been forced to court the West, for without Western capital and technology, the Russian Republic and the Confederation, or what was left of it, was doomed. In pursuit of those precious commodities, they had virtually abandoned their global superpower status. Now, for some reason, if this was a KGB-sponsored terrorist action and his government was held responsible, the damage would be incalculable—far worse than the KGB's aborted plot to assassinate the Polish Pope or their support of the coup against the central government. Stozharov was lost in thought for a moment, formulating contingencies and damage assessment. *God help those idiots at Dzerzhinsky Square if they are behind this, and it's laid at my doorstep. This may not be the old days, but heads will roll— literally.*

"Mikhail," he said to the aide sitting at the desk just inside the door, "please notify the Director of the KGB that I request the honor of his person in my office at his convenience within the hour, and get Admiral Zaitsev on the phone as soon as possible." Then Stozharov, attired in his bathrobe and slippers, and looking more like Nero on his way to a pool party than the President of the Russian Republic, padded back to his apartment to change into one of his many plain, dark suits.

Sunday, 3:00 P.M.—Ollala, Washington

Harlan Boesh was sitting on his deck enjoying the afternoon sun and a wedge of his wife's apple pie. He was a retired pipe fitter from the Puget Sound Naval Shipyard, and his time was equally divided between fishing, gardening, and taking trips to California in their motor home to visit the grandkids. Harlan had built the house himself, and he was especially proud of the large cedar deck with its expansive view across Clovos Passage to Vashon Island. Maritime traffic bound for Tacoma and lower Puget Sound usually took East Passage around the other side of Vashon, but West Passage always held a few pleasure boats, some Indian gill-netters, and an occasional tugboat dragging a log boom down to the mill in Shelton. He was just about to slip back into the kitchen for seconds when he happened to look across the water to the north.

"Hey, Clara, you wanna come out here and take a look at this?"

"What's the problem, Granddad, the Indians stealing your salmon again?"

"No, look at this. Ever see one of those out here?" A large Washington State ferry was slowly making its way through the Passage.

"Why, no, I can't say that I have."

Harlan and Clara Boesh always welcomed something interesting to watch on the water, so they both settled down in their deck chairs to watch the big white ferry make its way past their home. Being natives of Puget Sound, they'd seen plenty of ferries, but they were not prepared for what came next. A helicopter swooped noiselessly in behind the ferry and came to an abrupt hover over the forward part of the top deck. As it halted in midair, the *whap-whap-whap* of the rotors echoed across the water. A thick rope appeared, followed immediately by a half-dozen or more men who dropped swiftly down the line to the deck. They were like drops of oil sliding down a thread. It happened so quickly it didn't seem real, but a few moments later, another helicopter did exactly the same thing.

"Harlan, what in the world are they doing?"

"Maybe it's some a them Rangers from Fort Lewis practicing, although I can't figure why they'd be using a ferry. Maybe it's got something to do with that terrorist business up at Bangor we been hearin' on the news."

On the deck of the M/V *Walla Walla,* Captain Sherrard and his men swarmed around the pilothouse. The door burst open and two men darted in, crouched behind submachine guns. The captain and his first mate knew it was coming, but it was still terrifying. The two men slid to either side of the door, swinging their weapons in broad arcs to cover the room. Behind them Sherrard and another man popped through the door, the latter dropping to one knee.

"CLEAR!" shouted Sherrard as an Arab-looking sergeant

and another trooper then piled thorough the opposite pilot-house door, gun barrels pointed up but at the ready.

"Not bad," said Sherrard, who stepped back out onto the pilothouse wing. One soldier was strategically positioned just below on the promenade deck, with his weapon covering the door. Sherrard turned and nodded to a man on the roof of the pilothouse. "All right, that one's a take. But let's go through it again just to be sure."

"I can't believe how fast they get in here," said the mate after Sherrard and his men filed down the steps.

"I know," replied the *Walla Walla*'s captain, "but that doesn't mean there's not going to be a lot of bullets flying. Y'know, Fred, they could just as easily have taken our boat. God, I hope Ross Peck and his people get through this okay."

On the passenger deck, a team of Delta Force troopers under Sergeant Blackwood were conducting assault practice. They leapfrogged through the main cabin, moving silently on rubber-soled boots while flash-bang grenades with their pins safely taped in place periodically rolled across the deck. The Delta Force men moved with the practiced grace of a ballet troop.

Behind them in the wake, four small craft stalked the *Walla Walla*. They were the Rangers in their RIBs, or rigid inflatable boats—light, fast craft with rubber spray tubes mounted on fiberglass V-hulls and powered by large twin Mercury outboards. They now moved on the ferry, porpoising out of the water as they met a swell. One man in each boat braced himself against a postmounted M-60 machine gun in the bow. The first pair rushed up to the stern on either quarter. The coxswain held the boat against the ferry while a squad of men scrambled aboard. The first two boats veered off and were replaced by the second pair. They formed into squad elements and swarmed over the ferry.

The Rangers didn't move with the grace of the Delta Force men, but they were no less professional and more heavily armed. They wore flak jackets and helmets, and had a look of permanence about them.

"Rehearsal briefing in five minutes, guys. We'll meet over

on the port side of the boat.'' While the men busied themselves with their equipment, Lieutenant Horner walked around the cavernous empty car deck trying to get the feel of it. When Master Chief Watson had approached him with the idea of boarding the slow-moving ferry, he immediately agreed, for he was certain they could do it. It wouldn't be easy, but Brian Horner was a competitor and everything was a contest.

Around SEAL Team Three, Horner was known as a ''hacker,'' and much was put in store by those who could hack it. He had been an all-American swimmer at Santa Clara, and had qualified for the NCAA championships three times, although he'd never won a medal. For him, the rigorous UDT/SEAL training had just been a continuation of sports—another athletic season. At Team Three, he was always first in the timed swims and placed in the top three on the five-mile beach runs. Each morning, he pushed his platoon through a rigorous hour of PT—one hundred push-ups, one hundred sit-ups, twenty-five pull-ups, and countless repetitions of other conditioning exercises. Echo Platoon was physically ready, and so was Horner—they had been years in the preparation. Now he had just a few hours to mentally prepare himself for the real thing.

After the briefing in Seattle with Admiral MacIntyre and the flurry of activity that followed their load-out from the hangar at Fort Lewis, there had been little time to think about the reality of taking his platoon into action. He had been totally absorbed by the mechanics of preparation, even though that was largely arranged by Chief Watson. Now he had to face the prospect of a fight—this was not going to be just another athletic event. Nor would it be a training exercise with blank ammunition, safety observers, or other SEALs posing as the aggressor force. *Please God, make them give up so we don't have to do this. I'm scared,* thought Horner as he stood by rail of the slow-moving ferry. *Maybe I shouldn't have let the master chief speak up.* There was a sick churning in his stomach, and for a moment he thought he was going to throw up. His hand was shaking as he wiped the moisture from around his mouth. *I've got to get a hold of myself—even my legs feel rubbery.*

''You're not thinking of feeding the fish, are you, sir?''

"No way, Master Chief," replied Horner. His tan seemed to have faded for the moment, leaving only a bloom of color across his cheekbones. "It's just—well, I guess I'm a little nervous about this one."

"Bullshit, sir, you're scared as hell." Horner looked at Watson as though he had slapped him. "An' I'll tell you something else. I'd think there was something wrong with you if you weren't. Tell me, sir, have I ever steered you wrong—ever given you bad advice?"

"Well, no—not that I can think of."

"Now, you listen to me. Every time you have a free moment to do nothing but think about what's happening, like now, you run the risk of pissing in your pants. That's normal. But when we're in the water and doing our thing, whether it's for practice or for real, it'll seem like just another training evolution. Don't ask me why, but it will. You'll have to keep reminding yourself that this is not training—*it's for real!*" Horner gave his platoon chief a look of disbelief.

"That somehow doesn't seem right, Chief."

"Trust me, sir," said Watson as he put his hand on the taller man's shoulder and guided him away from the rail and forward along the port side. "I've been through this before—and really, so have you. Our training and conditioning take over. This operation has a different twist to it, but most of what we'll have to do is part of our standard procedures. It's another game of catch-me, fuck-me, sir. Yeah, it's for real, but it'll seem like a game."

During basic SEAL training, there were night tactical problems in which the student attackers would have to take an objective defended by the instructor staff. If the students could sneak in and hit the objective and slip away, they could sleep off the rest of the night. If they were discovered by the instructors, they spent the rest of the night doing push-ups in the surf—catch-me, fuck-me. Horner smiled. He was beginning to feel better, and he looked it.

"You wouldn't shit me about a thing like this, would you, Master Chief?"

"Not on your life, sir." Watson laughed. They turned to

walk back to the port quarter of the ferry, where the men were gathering for the rehearsal briefing. ''This is a pretty good platoon we got here, Mr. Horner. You lead 'em and they'll do a job for you. But remember one thing, sir, *you* have to lead them.'' Horner looked at Watson again. The humor was gone, and the chief was deadly serious.

''Thanks, Master Chief. I'll be okay.''

''Damn straight you will, sir,'' he said with a wink. Then he walked on ahead and began barking at a few of the stragglers who had not yet assembled with the rest of the platoon for the briefing.

They used two of the Rangers' RIBs to cast them in front of the *Walla Walla* at fifty-meter intervals. Horner was third in line with two of his strongest swimmers ahead of him, both equipped with three-pronged grappling hooks trailing fifteen feet of knotted nylon line. The flukes of the grapnels had been wrapped with neoprene rubber.

The lead swimmer was a rangy first-class petty officer named Bob Garniss. Garniss wasn't quite the swimmer Horner was, but he had wide shoulders and long, lean muscles. As the *Walla Walla* bore down on him, he moved left a little, then right as he positioned himself in front of the ferry.

The stem of the *Walla Walla* passed no more than eighteen feet from Garniss. The bow wave gently pushed him away, but at four knots it was not a problem. A kick of his fins and he was back alongside. Per his instructions, he waited until he was nearly amidships to make his move. A series of strong kicks brought his chest out of the water. It was an eight-foot toss, and all he had to do was get it over the inch-and-a-half metal pipe that served as the rail above the car-deck combing. The grappling iron sailed gracefully over the rail as the black nylon line paid out of his open palm. Garniss felt the momentum of the ferry engage the grapnel and the line go taut. Three rapid overhand pulls on the line jerked him free on the water, and he was perched on the side of the *Walla Walla,* crouched on the lip that was formed by a six-inch extension of the deck outboard of the deck combing. He quickly dropped the line back into the water as the second SEAL drifted past Garniss and hooked the ferry thirty feet aft with his grapnel. He skipped on the water once as he pulled himself up, but had no trouble getting aboard.

Horner elected to use the first line. There was a small white marker-float tied about a foot off the water to guide him to the line—this would be important at night. Like Garniss, he was brought halfway out of the water by his fins, and his arms did the rest. Garniss grabbed him by the back cross-strap of his harness and dragged him onto the deck lip. Horner quickly slipped under the rail to the deck inside the combing, while Garniss looked for the next SEAL. The procedure was made awkward only by the fins. On the real thing, they would jettison their fins at the rail. Garniss retrieved his line so the last four SEALs would have to be brought aboard by the number-two swimmer. Horner watched each of the remaining SEALs scramble aboard. The entire platoon would participate in the rehearsals, but only half of the fifteen-man platoon would attempt the real boarding, if it came to that. *It'll be a tough choice,* thought Horner. *They're all getting aboard well, and none of them will want to be left out.*

"Lookin' good."

"Thanks, Tom," said Horner. He had been intently watching the other SEALs climb aboard, and hadn't noticed Captain Sherrard at the rail beside him. "We'll get better with practice, and I don't think we'll have any problems at night."

"Those things keep you dry?" Horner, like the rest of the SEALs, was dressed in a rubberized vinyl dry suit with watertight neoprene rubber wrists and neck dams. A long waterproof zipper ran across his back and shoulders.

"Just like wearing a jogging outfit—warm and dry." Underneath the exposure suit, Horner wore black coveralls fitted with pockets and Velcro straps. They were almost identical to the ones worn by Sherrard.

"I've got some water wings in my kit bag. You sure you don't want me on your team?"

"Hey, thanks, but if we go in first, we may need you guys coming in right behind us in the helos." As if on cue, one of the Blackhawks came whistling quietly down on the *Walla Walla* on another practice run. The bird flared over the promenade deck, and the pounding of the rotor blades became deafening.

"As you can see, we won't get aboard unannounced. If those charges are going to be neutralized," Sherrard said seriously, "you guys might have the best shot. You get that raghead's demolitions away from him, and we'll make him wish he was back in the desert herding camels."

"Fair enough, Army."

Sherrard clapped him on the shoulder and headed for the stairs to the passenger deck. Horner rejoined the group of SEALs who were standing around dripping on the deck, talking about the boarding. "Okay, guys, that wasn't bad. Now let's strap on the ammunition, grenades, and weapons and see how well we can get up that line. Some of you who've been cheating on your pull-ups may find it a little more difficult."

The chief's right, thought Horner as he unzipped his dry suit and strapped on his ammunition vest. *I haven't thought about this being for real since we started the rehearsals. Maybe it is just a big game.*

Sunday 6:45 P.M.—The White House

President Bennett sat at his desk wearing a haggard look. His elbows were on the desk blotter, and his left hand was curled around a foam cup. He held his chin and a cigarette in his right hand. He looked more like a labor negotiator than a United States president. Across from him sat his secretary of state and the Director of Central Intelligence. A plate of BLT wedges and several empty juice glasses cluttered the desk.

"So you feel that there's no way that the Israelis will come our way."

"I seriously doubt it," replied Richard Noffsinger, wondering how the American public would react if they could see their President with the cigarette that was now dangling from the corner of his mouth. "Even the liberal factions who have advocated a 'land for peace' solution in the occupied territories will not support it under these conditions. Jamil's last broadcast, especially the 'rise up, brothers, and fight' portion, has not been particularly well received by members of the Knesset, conservative or liberal.''

''Any more on who might be behind this, Armand?''

''Nothing. We have good sources close to Abu Abbas and the Ahmed Jibril organizations. They're the primary groups we thought capable of something like this or had the most to gain, and my information is that they are as surprised as we are. Our liaison with Mossad also confirms this.'' Grummell wiped his hands with his napkin and continued. ''This may sound a little farfetched, but I think Jamil is acting alone.'' Both the President and Noffsinger moved forward in their chairs to speak, but Grummell raised his hand, asking for patience. ''Now, I know we've come to think that major acts of terrorism like this are always state sponsored, and I'm not saying our friend didn't possibly get some funds put on deposit in a numbered Swiss account. But I don't think this particular action has direct state backing.''

''That doesn't seem likely, Armand. What makes you think so?''

''Well, sir, this thing came right out of the blue. Security on it had to be tight—so tight that only one or two people could have known about the ultimate objective. Usually, when something big is afoot, the Brits or the Israelis or FBI counterintelligence or somebody gets a tip that something is happening. They may not know exactly where, when, or who, but we get information that a terrorist event is in the making. This time, nobody heard a peep. My experience in these matters tells me that this is all Jamil's doing—his own personal coup. The whole operation could have been financed with less than two million dollars, an amount that could have been made available to him by any number of sources, including our friends in Moscow.''

''So what are you saying, Armand?—what does this have to do with where we are now?''

''It means that Jamil has his reputation, his ego, and his personal honor all on the line. No one is pulling his strings on this one. These people have honor, you know, and an honorable death can be most important to a true believer—or a fanatic. If this is the case and Jamil is on his own, it could mean that he may freely elect martyrdom, even welcome it, if he cannot achieve his goal.''

''Christ, is there any good news to all of this?'' the President replied as he viciously stabbed the ashtray with his cigarette butt.

''Possibly,'' said Grummell. ''This is his hour—his day in the sun, if you will. An appeal on our part to extend the deadline he has set may well serve to allow him to bask in the limelight a bit longer.''

''Recommendation?''

''Let's offer him the commitment to back a new and stronger resolution in the UN for an Israeli withdrawal from the occupied territories,'' replied Grummell, ''and follow that with a request for more time, at least another twenty-four hours. It's reasonable that we would need a full day to try to wring something out of the Israelis—not that I think there's much chance of it.''

''Dick?''

''I concur.''

''Okay, have Baines give those instructions to his man in Seattle—Staloni, is it?''

''It's Sclafani, sir.''

''Whatever, let's get moving on it.''

The two secretaries stood up as Morton Keeney stepped through the door. He had just come up from the situation room. ''Mr. President—Dick, Armand—I just got off the secure line with Admiral MacIntyre in Seattle. He's now aboard a Coast Guard cutter that's shadowing the *Spokane* and the *Michigan.* He provided me with some mission concepts being worked out by the special-operations units, and it looks like there may be a way to sneak some men aboard the *Spokane* undetected.''

''Well, good Lord, man, let's hear it!'' Noffsinger and Grummell sat back down while Keeney remained standing. He quickly reviewed the assault plans of Rangers, SEALs, and

Delta Force, dwelling primarily on the covert boarding techniques of the SEALs.

"They're conducting rehearsals on a sister ship of the *Spokane* right now. They want to try it after dark in open water with combat equipment before estimating chances for success. However, the daylight trials look promising."

"Hot damn!" replied the President. "Maybe there's a chance to pull this thing out, even if we can't work a deal with Jamil."

"Or," cautioned Armand Grummell, again buffing his lenses, "bring about the result we fear most."

Sunday 4:15 P.M.—Aboard the *Mellon*

Frank Sclafani sat at a small desk in the radio room of the cutter trying to collect his thoughts. The noise of the air-conditioning was almost deafening. There comes a time in all negotiations when the negotiator has to challenge his opponent. He must tell him something he doesn't want to hear—that something he wants, he can't have. Normally, Sclafani chose that moment very carefully. It usually came well into the negotiation process, after he had established rapport and credibility with the terrorists—or clients, as he liked to call them. It also helped if they were in the second or third day of a hostage situation. The terrorists' reasoning became addled from lack of sleep, and a bond between hostage and terrorist sometimes became a factor that supported a peaceful solution. Now he hadn't the time, and the hostages were not his only consideration, nor were they the terrorists' only bargaining chip. With these clients it was different, and Sclafani sensed that Jamil probably knew it.

"Calling the M/V *Spokane,* this is Under Secretary Jefferson on the cutter *Mellon.* I would like to speak with Jamil, please."

"What is it, Jefferson? Have your government and the Jews agreed to allow us to go home?" Sclafani concentrated on a still color photo taken from the videotape and mounted on a piece of cardboard. It sat on the desk leaning against the metal bulkhead. He talked to the photo as would a civilian attorney to an important client in a private law office.

''We have strongly urged the government of Israel to seriously discuss your request. Our communication with that government at this time has been inconclusive. It is still early morning in Tel Aviv, and while we have as yet only been able to make contact on the ministerial level, we are still waiting for their reply. Naturally, President Bennett has asked for discussions at the head-of-state level. Jamil, I will not lie to you, for that would serve no purpose for either of us. I don't believe that the government of Israel can be pressured on such short notice into such a course of action.'' Sclafani paused a moment before he continued. As he stared at the picture, he thought he could feel Jamil weighing his words.

''I have been authorized by the President of the United States to tell you that he will publicly offer to unilaterally support a new and stronger initiative in the General Assembly *and* the Security Council of the United Nations for the establishment of the State of Palestine in the occupied territories. We will also support this position at the peace talks. In return, he asks for another twenty-four hours to try to work out an agreement with Israel. Since you feel we have influence with the Israelis, we must have the time to use that influence if we are to bring about an acceptable solution. Surely that is a reasonable request.'' There was a long silence, and Sclafani knew that the first one to speak was usually the loser. He studied his watch and measured the tension by the sweep of the second hand. After forty-five seconds, Jamil's voice came through the speaker.

''I sense that you are just buying time, Jefferson, but I will consider what you have said. And in case you are planning an assault on the *Safinat al Horeya* by your special forces, I have only to press a button and the explosives we have placed on the ferry and the submarine will be detonated. I will not hesitate to do this at the first sign of trouble, do you understand?''

''Yes, Jamil, that is quite clear.''

''You still have two hours on the original time period. I will consider your request and advise you later. For now, my demands and the deadline stand, and do not forget that I will tolerate no hostile or threatening act toward my ship.''

''I understand, Jamil. I am also authorized to ask if there is anything that you or the hostages require in the way of food or medical care. We can put a small boat in the water or send an unarmed helicopter.'' The response was immediate.

''We require nothing but our freedom and our homeland, Jefferson. And your countrymen aboard the *Safinat al Horeya* are not hostages; they are prisoners of war and will be treated accordingly. If you wish to send a Red Cross representative to verify their welfare, that can be arranged. I will let you know of my decision for more time. This discussion is ended.''

Sclafani sat and gazed at the picture on the desk as he absent-mindedly patted his bald spot. ''You're not bad, my friend, not bad at all.'' There was a trace of a smile at one corner of his mouth, but it faded quickly as he remembered the destructive potential at his client's fingertips. ''And, my Arab friend, it's sure to get more interesting.''

''You say something, sir?'' It was the *Mellon*'s chief radio-man.

''Just talking to myself, Chief. Did you get a good tape of the transmission?''

''Yes, sir. It's already been encrypted and is on its way to Washington. I'll have a copy ready for you in a— Attention on deck!''

''Carry on, please—as you were.'' Admiral MacIntyre stepped across the cramped space to where Sclafani was seated. He had listened to the exchange from a speaker on the bridge. ''Think he'll give us more time?''

''I think he will. Time is not really against him, at least not yet. I think he just put us off now to retain a measure of control. You heard him say they had explosives on the *Spokane* as well?''

''I did. That's a complication, but it's still a secondary issue. What's this about a Red Cross representative?''

''It's my guess he wants to be treated as a combatant under

the terms of the Geneva Convention—terrorists are not afforded Red Cross visits. I don't advise it at this time, but it's something we may want to consider later. I think he brought it up hoping we will treat him as someone with national status rather than a stateless person.''

''Any weaknesses we can get a handle on?''

''He's an arrogant bastard. Other than that, he's not giving us much time or much of an opportunity to find something to work with. It's still his move.''

In the pilothouse of the *Spokane,* Jamil clipped the microphone back to the side of the VHF transceiver and smiled confidently. ''You see, Peck, your President Bennett is talking with his Jewish allies. Now that we hold something of value—something he wants back very badly—he is forced to support our claim to the occupied territories.'' Jamil's eyes flashed with excitement and triumph—he felt invulnerable. He turned and embraced Ahmed, who smiled softly. ''You still doubt that we will be successful, old friend? That is good, for with each victory that brings us closer to our goal, I need to be reminded that our journey is far from complete.''

''That is correct, Jamil—we are getting closer, but there is still a great deal to be done. The Americans say they will work with us, but it is the Israelis who occupy our homeland.'' He hesitated before he continued. ''So far, we have been unable to get the Jews at the peace talks to discuss the surrender of land, and we have been unable to dislodge them with the Intifada. Do not forget, the Israelis have nothing to gain from this arrangement. Perhaps the American President, who controls their money, will have some success. Presently, we must still be very careful—the Americans have a taste for military action and their special forces can be very dangerous.''

''Yes, yes—perhaps you are right,'' Jamil conceded, ''but our defiance of the Americans will rally our brothers in the occupied lands, and put additional pressure on the Zionists. We have already started something here that cannot be stopped. The victory will be ours!''

''What will you tell Jefferson about the time?'' Ahmed

asked. Jamil walked out to the pilothouse wing and looked at the cutter, which now seemed a part of the seascape.

"I will give them until eight o'clock tomorrow morning to meet our terms. The whole world is following our journey to freedom, and a few more hours will only serve to focus more attention on our cause. Keep watch on our captain and the mate while I inspect the lower decks. Call me if there is any further radio communication." Jamil walked down the steps and headed aft.

On the port side of the pilothouse, Janey McClure sat on the stool where she had been for most of the time since the terrorists took the *Spokane*. Occasionally Janey relieved Peck at the wheel, and for short periods of time, she kept the ferry and the *Michigan* on a straight course. It was a very tricky helm, but after a short while she found that she could keep the two vessels on a steady heading. However, she sensed it was important for her not to be *too* good at steering the boat, for she felt that Peck's life could depend on his being the only competent helmsman. She also thought Peck understood this. That afternoon, she had intentionally allowed the *Spokane* to wander off course. He had given her a questioning look but said nothing. Jamil and the other Arabs readily accepted her incompetence—after all, she was a woman.

Janey had been scared from the beginning, but now she was terrified. She had always thought of herself as a woman who could take it as well as any man—and a lot better than most—but after watching Jamil kill Andy Gosnell, she wasn't so sure. Maybe it was the absence of violence at the exact moment of his death—one instant he was there, and the next he was gone. You could almost see his spirit leave him. In life, Gosnell had been a cocky little rooster, but highly likable, even if he did make it clear that he thought women had no place on the crew of a ship. It was as if Jamil had casually snatched the life out of him, like plucking a ripe fruit from a tree. She stood there dazed, hoping Gosnell would just get up. A dark stain around his crotch and the smell told her that death also brought loss of bowel and bladder control. The realization that it could have been her lying on the pilothouse floor in her own excrement, while others watched, kindled a fear in her as strong as death itself. Then the captain flew across the pilothouse and crashed to the deck. For a moment, she had thought he, too, was dead.

The dark red blood dripping from Peck's left wrist had finally stopped, but not before the wooden deck grating around the helm had become slick with it. When he went for Jamil, it was like an explosion—one instant he was standing by the helm looking at Gosnell, and the next he was at the end of his chained wrist, almost close enough to grasp him. She saw the surprise register on Jamil's face at the swiftness of the assault. After the captain had regained his feet and they had dragged Gosnell out, he seemed to be a different man. She wasn't sure what it was, but Ross Peck was not the same. He moved slowly and carefully as he went about the business of piloting the ferry. Each movement was measured and very deliberate. He seemed compliant, and there was a calm about him that was unnatural and anything but reassuring.

"Captain, can I . . . is there anything I can get you—water or coffee?" The one called Ahmed who tended the radios as well as the two of them hadn't objected to their talking.

"No, thanks, Janey."

"What do you think will happen—do you think the government will be able to get these people what they want?"

"Perhaps—I don't know. There's very little we can do in any case except what we're told."

"Captain, I'm scared." She choked back a sob, but was unable to keep her voice from cracking. He looked at her, his blue eyes both sad and calm.

"I know, Janey, but this can't go on much longer. One way or another it will resolve itself. We just have to be patient and hope for the best." There was no reassurance in the tone of his voice or the detached, tranquil expression on his face. He smiled grimly and turned his attention back to the ferry, which was exactly on course.

Aboard the *Michigan,* Petty Officer DeRosales huddled inside the base of the sail. He occasionally looked out the metal door to reassure himself that the white-hulled Coast Guard cutter was still there, hovering a mile away like a guardian angel. The hull of the submarine thumped and banged as it worked against the side of the ferry. DeRosales had yet to become comfortable with these sounds, and periodically he scrambled below, fearing it was the sound of the terrorists boarding the submarine. He lived for the hourly radio transmissions, so he was startled when the radio crackled at 4:45 P.M.

"Jesús, this is Gunny Jennings, are you there, over?"

"Yeah, sure, Gunny, right here—is anything wrong?"

"Not a thing, buddy. I got someone here who wants to talk with you. I think you may be glad to hear from him—hold on."

"Petty Officer DeRosales, this is Captain Hailey. I'm the captain of the Gold Crew, and I'm working along with Sergeant Jennings and many others to try to get you and the *Michigan* back. How are you getting along, over?"

"Okay, sir, although I could sure use some food and something to drink. I guess you know they killed everyone in my duty section—they're all dead."

"I know, son, and I'm sorry, but we can't help them now. Now listen closely. I talked with the medical officer, and they're sure it was some kind of cyanide gas that was released aboard the boat. This gas will not affect food or water that it has not yet come into contact with. Now, you're still inside the sail, am I right, over?"

"Yes, sir. I've been belowdecks several times, but I try to stay up here as much as possible, over."

"DeRosales, you can go below through the mess deck to the galley. There in the cooler you'll probably find some milk or juice and some canned food. It may not be a regular meal, but it'll get you by. When this is over, you can have steak and eggs on me, okay?"

"Sounds good, sir. You sure it's all right to eat the food that's aboard, over?"

"I'm positive. Just take things that are wrapped or are covered and bring them back up to the sail, where you can take your mask off. You're not having any trouble getting around the boat with your EBA mask, are you, over?"

"No, sir. It's just like the drills."

"Excellent, DeRosales. Now, do you think you'd have any trouble getting back down to the torpedo room, over?"

"No, sir, but why would I want to go back there?"

"You may be able to help us when it comes time to free you and the others on the ferry. Now lay below and get yourself something to eat, and when you go below, take the radio with you. We want to get a radio check to see if you can transmit and receive while belowdecks. I'll be talking with you later when it comes time for you to help us, okay?"

"Aye, sir."

Captain Hailey handed the microphone back to Jennings in the *Mellon*'s pilothouse and joined Admiral MacIntyre and Sclafani on the port wing of the cutter.

"What do you think?" asked MacIntyre.

"He seems fine, and Sergeant Jennings thinks he'll be all right. He's a torpedoman, and that's a big plus."

MacIntyre looked at his watch as he turned to Sclafani. "And what do you think, Frank—what can I tell the White House Jamil's going to do?" Sclafani's white shirt was rumpled, and the sleeves were rolled to the elbow. His wrinkled tie was draped around his open collar in a loose knot. A dense stubble that made the lower half of his face a shade darker served as a backdrop for the cigarette jammed in the corner of this mouth. He looked like a futures trader at the closing bell.

"At this stage of the game, anything can happen. I think we'll get some more time out of him, or he'll let the eight-o'clock deadline pass without doing anything. But I don't see a lot of flexibility in him. He may negotiate, but I doubt that anything falling short of his demands will be acceptable." Sclafani passed a hand across his stubbled jowl and looked at MacIntyre. "Candidly, Admiral, I think there's a good chance he'll fight to the finish if we push him. Or he could set off the explosives on the submarine and cast it adrift, holding the ferry and the hostages for further negotiations—maybe to bargain for his freedom. He's tough and he's smart, and I don't think he'll give us the time to wear him down in a protracted negotiation."

"You're saying he won't back down?" asked MacIntyre.

The FBI man thrust his hands deep into his trouser pockets and shrugged. "I'm saying anything can happen, and he's one rugged customer. My guess is that he'll do what he says if we can't give him what he's asking for."

MacIntyre nodded curtly and headed for the radio room and the dedicated secure comm-link to Morton Keeney at the White House situation room.

Jamil walked the length of the passenger deck, digesting his last dialogue with Jefferson. He was elated that the Americans were seemingly willing to support his demands, but as Ahmed had pointed out, they must be vigilant—especially after dark. He had known the Israelis would be difficult to deal with, even with the Americans pushing them. And even the Americans could say one thing and do yet another. Their military-response teams were quite proficient, but he was confident that his position on a moving vessel with hostages and the charges on the submarine were sufficient to keep them in check. They would at least want to do more talking before they acted, and the world, specifically the Arab world, would be watching while he bargained for Palestinian freedom.

"They are quiet," he said as he surveyed the Americans scattered around the cabin. Some slept, while others stared slack-eyed at him. The lack of sleep and tension had exhausted them.

"There is very little spirit left to them," replied Salah. "Nothing in their soft Western life has prepared them for this." He squatted comfortably on the floor in the dining area while Yehya sat at a table. According to the duty rotation, it was Salah's time to be resting. The others napped when their turn came, but Salah was a man who needed very little sleep.

"How are they performing in the engine room?"

"Like their life depended on it," he replied with a smile. "Hassan watches them now, and I believe we'll have no more problems."

"Excellent." He tossed Salah a vial of pills. "These will help you and your two men to remain alert, for none of us dare sleep after the sun goes down."

"As you wish, Sayeh. I will send Hassan to you when it gets dark—Yehya and I can manage the prisoners and the engines."

Six of them! thought Jamil as he made his way back up to the promenade deck. *With God's help, six of us will be enough. If only I had a few more like Salah.*

Sunday, 5:50 P.M.—Aboard the *S-570*

Captain Molev sat at his station in the control room and lit another cigarette. They had gone to periscope depth several times for communications, and now they were at a hundred meters making five knots, steaming in circles some fifteen miles off the Washington State coast. *The Arab terrorists have held the Trident submarine for nearly fourteen hours now,* mused Molev. *Why haven't the Americans made an attempt to take it back?*

Terrorism was something the Russians could deal with. Molev remembered a story told him by a GRU colonel over a bottle of vodka one night when he attended the Voroshilov General Staff Academy in Moscow. It seems that in the early days of the Beirut debacle, when the Soviets had a large delegation there, one of the radical Arab factions had taken two Russian nationals hostage along with several Westerners. The KGB had quietly gone about identifying the men involved, then begun to systematically kill their family members. The Russians who were abducted were quickly returned to the embassy compound, and the legation never bothered again. *That is the way to deal with terrorists.* The Western hostages taken were never seen again.

Molev looked at his watch—*time for another fucking communications drill.* He nodded to the diving officer and the boat began to make its way up to shallow water where they could deploy the long floating-wire antenna.

"Comrade Captain, fleet headquarters is once again asking for our position. How should I reply?"

"Tell them we are on patrol in our assigned sector," growled Molev, "then take us back down." Molev assumed the bootlicking politicos in Moscow were now being interrogated by their American friends as to what his boat was doing there. *And those spineless bastards at fleet headquarters don't have the balls to tell them to shut up and let the Navy do its job. Now they will probably order me away from the area. This could be an unprecedented opportunity—surely Zaitsev must know this. We have a chance to learn something about the Trident or at the very least, to embarrass the American Navy.* He had to smile—the American submariners were so proud of it. While Molev admired their technology and freely admitted that the Trident system was the most sophisticated and deadly weapon in any navy, he had a professional disdain for his American counterparts. Now a handful of terrorists had managed to swipe their marvelous toy from their most closely guarded base. *Incredible! Such an opportunity, and at this very minute, I'll bet those soft old men in Moscow are trying to figure a way to squander it. It wouldn't surprise me if we were directed to offer assistance—to help the Americans get their property back.*

"Help them. . . . Help them!" He slammed his fist on the top of an electrical panel, causing his ashtray and its contents to take flight. "By God—why not!"

"Sir?" said the rating standing nearby.

"I said we'll help them! Summon the communications officer and have him meet me in my quarters."

"At once, Captain!"

Five minutes later, Captain Molev strode back into the control room, trailing his communications and executive officers.

"Stand by to surface."

"I—I beg you pardon, Captain! Surely you don't mean to surface—I mean, *here* . . . ?" The watch officer stared openmouthed at Molev, just as a junior officer on an American submarine would if his skipper had ordered him to surface off the coast of Petropavlovsk.

"*Leytenant*, you are relieved—go to your quarters! Starpom, take charge of the watch section and bring the boat up.

Raise all communications masts as soon as we are on the surface.''

Sunday, 6:56 P.M.—Aboard the *Spokane*

Janey had taken the wheel from Peck, who now sat on a stool in the forward corner of the pilothouse to the left of the helm. When Janey relieved the helm, Peck was given the key to the handcuffs and allowed to unlock himself while Jamil or Ahmed trained a gun on Janey. Then he was directed to cuff himself to a metal ring on the bulkhead and to return the key. After the rest period, the process was reversed. Peck rested with his eyes closed, but they flew open at the slightest disturbance.

Jamil had just stepped from the small toilet that adjoined rear of the pilothouse. He radiated pride and confidence. Peck watched as Jamil took the microphone from the side of the radio and quickly glanced around the pilothouse.

"This is the *Safinat al Horeya* calling the Coast Guard ship—are you there, Jefferson?" After a moment's delay, he was answered.

"Yes, Jamil, I am here. How can I be of service?"

"Have the Jews agreed to give us back our land?" Again, a pause.

"Jamil, my government has placed your request and our support of that request before the government of Israel. I can assure you that President Bennett has made a personal appeal for them to join us in positive steps to guarantee the immediate repatriation of the West Bank and Gaza. Unfortunately, the political climate in Israel has not allowed for Prime Minister Levin to give us those assurances. I must report that while we are doing our best, Israel has not yet agreed to your request."

"It was not a request, Jefferson, it was a demand."

"I understand the urgency on your part, but surely you must understand that a matter so complex as this issue will take more than eight hours to resolve. And certainly a person like yourself can appreciate the difficulties involved. My government is acting in good faith, Jamil, but we simply must have more time."

"Very well, Jefferson. I will allow you until eight o'clock tomorrow morning. As spokesmen for the new government of Palestine, it is our intention to be reasonable, but my patience has limits. And remember, if there is any attempt to attack us or I find that you are lying to me, the people of Palestine will then rally to the martyrs who died on the *Safinat al Horeya* when it was blown up with your Trident submarine. Do you understand me, Jefferson?"

"I understand, Jamil. My government appreciates your patience as we try to work this out. However, while I assure you we will do everything possible, I cannot make any promises concerning the Israelis. They can be very difficult concerning the occupied territories."

"It will not do, Jefferson. Your president will have to talk directly with Levin in terms he will understand—money and arms. He depends on American aid, and Israel is as much your prisoner as the Trident submarine *Michigan* and the Americans aboard the *Safinat al Horeya* are my prisoners. You will meet my terms by eight o'clock tomorrow or my prisoners will die, is that understood?"

"Yes, Jamil, that is quite clear, and I will convey that to my government. Is there anything you require for the safety and comfort of those aboard your vessel?" Sclafani repeated the offer of assistance, but again there was no response.

Jamil had abandoned the radio and was now pacing the pilothouse, pausing momentarily during each circuit to glare at the white hull of the cutter.

"The Americans are trying to play with us. Well, I will not be fooled! If they think we are afraid to die—that I will allow them to be passive in this matter—they will be sadly disappointed." He continued to pace, occasionally pounding the fist of one hand into the palm of the other. Then the radio speaker again came to life.

"This is the *S-570* calling the Palestinian vessel *Safinat al Horeya*—this is the *S-570* calling the *Safinat al Horeya,* come in please, over.'' Jamil stared at the radio for a moment, then snatched the handset.

''This is the *Safinat al Horeya,* please identify yourself.''

''This is the Russian submarine *S-570,* Captain First Rank Viktor Molev commanding. I am off the American coast in international waters. Do you require any assistance, over?'' *A Russian submarine off the coast offering assistance!* Jamil's mind raced. *Could this be a trick? They have recognized my ship as a Palestinian vessel. The Russians have been an ally— opponent of the West really—in the past. Can this be a genuine offer of assistance, and how can I use it? What could they want in return? The* Michigan! *A Russian submarine captain would go to considerable trouble and risk to get aboard an American Trident submarine.*

''This is the United States Coast Guard cutter *Mellon* calling the Russian submarine *S-570.*'' A voice that was not Jefferson's blared into the pilothouse of the *Spokane* as the cutter transmitted at a power level boosted to reach the Russian submarine off the coast. ''This is a restricted frequency! You are directed to cease all transmissions, I repeat, you are to cease all transmissions—please acknowledge, over!'' Jamil stared at the radio speaker, still lost in thought, then grabbed the microphone.

''This is Jamil of the Islamic Brothers of Freedom on the Palestinian ship *Safinat al Horeya,* calling the *S-570.* What is it that you propose?''

''Captain Jamil, this is the *S-570.* We are a Russian warship steaming independently in international waters. My boat has trained medical personnel aboard. If you require any medical or mechanical assistance, we are prepared to provide it, over.''

''That is most generous of you, Captain Molev. We will be in international waters early tomorrow morning. At that time we will see if your services are required. However, a boarding by you and some of your officers on a courtesy visit would be most welcome, over.''

''Thank you, Captain Jamil. We will certainly look forward to that. We will also guard this frequency during your transit along the Strait of Juan de Fuca. Please keep us updated on your progress, over.''

''I will do that, and thank you for your kind offer of assistance.''

On the *S-570,* Molev returned the handset to the cradle and held on to a railing to steady himself as the Akula wallowed in the shallow North Pacific swells. Nuclear submarines were not designed for surface operations, but the seas were relatively calm and should allow them to comfortably remain surfaced. *A chance to board a Trident submarine! But would the Americans allow it?* He had not been able to copy the transmission from the American ship to the terrorists, but Jamil's side of the conversation made it clear that he had taken a very aggressive posture in the negotiations.

''That was a very brave move, Comrade Captain.''

''Perhaps, but then, you know what a humanitarian I am. The mission of this submarine is to find enemy submarines, is it not? Perhaps we have found one.'' Molev was speaking to Captain Third Rank Mikhail Gurtovoi, the boat's *zampolit,* or political officer. Since the fall of the Communist party, he remained a political officer in name only. In the old days, the political officer's authority rivaled that of the commanding officer. On modern Russian combatants, while he still reported to a different chain of command than did the captain, he usually had seagoing experience and served as a personnel officer and security officer. Molev had also found this *zampolit* to be a loyal confidant as well as politically shrewd, and he valued his counsel.

''Captain, I sense this is not what Moscow would have you do in this situation.''

''Perhaps not, but what would the Americans do if one of our newer surface combatants in the Black Sea defected into Turkish waters?''

''Do you intend to board the ferry and the Trident?'' parried Gurtovoi.

''The chance to see a Trident missile submarine up close is

worth any risk. And I do not believe I have violated my orders.''

Your orders did not anticipate the piracy of an American Trident submarine, thought Gurtovoi. He studied his captain carefully. Molev was among their most capable submariners, and his record was spotless. *He is bold and aggressive,* Gurtovoi admitted, *and very arrogant, but is that not what makes a good submarine commander? The Navy will defend such a man against the political forces in Moscow, but only so far.*

"The mood in Moscow is not to confront the West, especially the Americans. You also know that I must make a report of this through my channels.''

"Of course, and perhaps you can tell me which way the wind blows at the seat of power—wherever that is these days.''

"Betray my political responsibilities, Captain,'' Gurtovoi said mockingly. "Well, perhaps just this one time, but you know that what you are doing is very dangerous. Our Navy still answers to the Russian government, and the Kremlin is very sensitive these days to any military action that could be construed as, shall we say, independent.''

"Thank you, Mikhail. I understand the risks, but this opportunity is unique—we must not squander it.''

"That sonofabitch! He's trying to sneak aboard the *Michigan* and have a look around. She still has her full complement of crypto gear and codebooks, doesn't she?'' Admiral MacIntyre stood at the rail on the *Mellon*'s bridge wing and glared at the *Spokane.*

"Yes, sir. She's fully outfitted for patrol,'' replied Captain Hailey.

"Do you think the Russians might be on our side on this one? Maybe they're trying to help us,'' said Don Libby, the *Mellon*'s skipper. MacIntyre raised an eyebrow as he considered the possibility.

"I doubt it,'' said Hailey. "Moscow and Washington may have abandoned the cold war, but out at sea, the boomers and the attack boats still play the game, and we play it with deadly seriousness. *Perestroika* has not brought an end to nuclear de-

terrence. I can easily understand that Russian skipper's thinking. I'd give my eyeteeth to get aboard one of their Typhoon
Class missile boats.''

''Well, there's nothing we can do about it right now,'' concluded MacIntyre. ''We taping that circuit?''

''Yes, sir,'' replied Captain Libby.

''Good. Let's get it on the wire as soon as possible, while I
get on the horn to the White House. They're not going to be real
happy with this turn of events.''

''Americans, citizens of the world community, and people of
the new nation of Palestine. We have a new ally in our struggle
for freedom!''

Jamil stood on the promenade deck of the ferry just forward
of the pilothouse. Above him, the wooden placard with ''Spokane'' in gold lettering had been covered by a crude white
board with black stenciling that proclaimed the vessel as the
Safinat al Horeya. Ahmed stood out on the starboard wing of
the promenade deck with the video camera shooting back toward the pilothouse. The western sun was well on its way to the
horizon as the ferry strained under its burden to follow it to the
Pacific. The fading rays played across Jamil's face and bur-
nished his animated features.

''A Russian submarine has been sent to serve as our escort
and is waiting off the coast of America in the Pacific Ocean.
They have offered to help us and are no doubt interested in our
war prize, the American Trident missile submarine. We appreciate this gesture of goodwill and the recognition of our status
as an equal among the family of nations. If America and Israel
have not recognized the West Bank and Gaza as the new and
independent nation of Palestine by 8:00 A.M. tomorrow, I will
allow our Russian friends to inspect the Trident submarine
before it is destroyed.

''My brother Palestinians, this is our hour. The Americans
have said they will honor our request for nationhood and the
expulsion of the Jews from our new homeland. But the Zionists, who have supported illegal settlements in the occupied
territories, have yet to join the Americans in recognition of our

nation. While I fight in America for our freedom, will you not arise and defend our land against the Jews? The Israelis respond only to force—you must take to the streets and expel them. The Intifada must be reawakened, and it must conclude with a victory for the people of Palestine. If we are to be free from our chains, we must fight, and we must fight now! Rise up, brothers, for your children and your children's children—rise up and strike!"

He repeated the message in Arabic, again with the measured confidence of a natural leader. Above him, Ross Peck watched as he grimly applied himself to the task of piloting the ferry. Michelle stood on the pilothouse wing where she could listen to Jamil and still keep an eye on Peck and Janey. *He seems more docile than before, even complacent,* she thought. *Perhaps he is not the lion I thought he was.* She took the AK-47 from her shoulder and walked into the pilothouse. She stood close to Janey and cycled the action of the weapon, knowing it made her cringe.

Sunday, 10:54 P.M.—The White House

President Bennett, Secretary Noffsinger, DCI Grummell, Director Baines, and General Scott sat around the coffee table in the Oval Office and watched the most recent video from the *Spokane.* After Jamil signed off, there was depressing silence. Finally, the President of the United States spoke.

"Son of a fucking *bitch.* As if we don't have enough to worry about, this goddamn Russian submarine off the coast is giving them encouragement. Dick, just what the hell is Stozharov trying to pull? I thought we had an understanding with those people."

"We're trying to sort that out now. There's no reason for the Russians to be doing this. But if there's one thing we've learned in dealing with the Russians, it is to expect the unexpected. The decentralization of the economy has unfortunately carried over to the military. I've no reason to believe Stozharov didn't give the order for that sub to clear the area, but either due to the bureaucracy, communications problems, or who knows what, the boat is not only still there—it's in contact with terrorists on the *Spokane.*''

''Just exactly what did the foreign minister say when you talked to him?

''Basically, it was a lot of tap-dancing. He cited communications problems and asked for time to verify the recording of the transmission we gave them between Jamil and the captain of the submarine.''

''So you feel they aren't sandbagging us?'' pressed Bennett.

''No, sir. I've been able to read egg in their face before, and I believe they are having a problem calling that sub off. Diplomatically, the theft of the *Michigan* will be a real blow to our START negotiating team and a big plus for them. This move on the part of the Russian attack submarine risks squandering that advantage. Since the coup attempt last year, we've made a big deal about the Republic's control of strategic nuclear weapons by the Russian government. Right now, they can charge us with, excuse the expression, carelessness with the security of our nuclear arsenal.'' Bennett looked at Armand Grummell, who nodded solemnly.

''Okay, Dick. Get back to the Russian foreign minister, and convey in appropriate language our shock and dismay at their actions and our insistence on an immediate recall of that attack boat. What else?''

''Well, sir,'' continued Noffsinger, ''there are serious problems developing in the occupied territories. Every kid over the age of six is out throwing rocks, and there have also been a number of shootings. Several Israeli soldiers and a dozen Palestinians have been killed. Prime Minister Levin has ordered a twenty-four-hour curfew until this situation is resolved. A number of Palestinian organizations have come out in support of Jamil and the Islamic Brothers of Freedom—the PLO and George Habash's Islamic Freedom Movement, to name two. It's much the same as when Saddam invaded Kuwait— Christ, you'd think they'd learn. Basically, sir, the Intifada has exploded, and the Israelis are moving infantry and armored units to the West Bank and Gaza to deal with it. If the Palestinians keep it up, there'll be a great deal more bloodshed.''

"Can the Palestinians succeed?''

"Not a chance. The Israelis won't force it—not after the Temple Mount affair, but if those poor people come at them with rocks and small arms, it'll be a massacre.''

"General,'' said Bennett, addressing his Chairman of the Joint Chiefs, "how are we coming with the special-operations teams out in Seattle?'' Bennett called his other top advisers by their first name, but his tour in the Army as an enlisted man somehow prevented him from addressing Scott as anything but "General.''

"The Delta Force and the Rangers are ready, and the rehearsals on the sister-ship ferry have made them familiar with the layout of the *Spokane*. The SEALs have been surprisingly effective in coming over the side of the moving ferry, and there's every reason to expect they have a chance of getting aboard the ferry at night undetected. Since the deadline has been moved up, giving us more time, Admiral MacIntyre wants as much rehearsal time as possible. Commander Bishop, the EOD specialist, has arrived out there, and is now working with the SEALs.''

The President pondered this a while before shrugging his shoulders and turning to his CIA director. "Armand, you have something for us.''

"Yes, sir. Our technical staff has been going over the last tape, and we found something that may be of help. Go ahead, Gary.''

One of Grummell's technicians from CIA headquarters began flipping switches on several electrical modules stacked on a video cart beneath a large high-definition monitor. As Jamil finished his speech and before the tape ended, the camera operator swung the camera to the left, providing a brief shot down the starboard side of the ship.

"Right there,'' said Grummell, and the picture was frozen. The technician with his sophisticated video equipment was able to zoom in and magnify a small section of the picture at the lower left of the screen. "See that line looping down from the top deck of the ferry to the submarine? My people at Langley tell me it's a firing cable from the ferry to the charges on the *Michigan.* This would indicate that the remote firing device is on the *Spokane,* not on the submarine."

"So?" replied Bennett.

"What this means," said Grummell patiently, "is that if we can get a man aboard the ferry, he has only to cut the firing lead in this cable and Jamil cannot detonate the charges."

"That's great, Armand, but it sounds too easy. Why wouldn't he put the remote device on the submarine?"

"As I understand it from some of our folks who train sappers, remote devices are sometimes unreliable or are subject to electronic jamming. By keeping the receiver of the remote firing device on the ferry, it would be much more reliable. Also, if it fails, he probably has a backup friction-blasting machine tied into the circuit—a variation of the old plunger box you see in the movies."

"So we can just cut the cord and that's it?"

"Possibly," said Grummell, "unless there's an antidisturbance circuit associated with this cord. Based on the aerial photographs taken earlier, Commander Bishop thinks there is, and my people concur. We know Jamil isn't stupid, and from what we've been able to learn so far, this is a highly professional setup. That's why we need to get Bishop aboard the *Spokane* to deal with it."

"Well, we face certain catastrophe if Jamil decides to press the button—or push the plunger." The President sighed and looked around at his advisers.

"Okay, gentlemen, the military option is looking more and more likely. Dammit, I didn't want it to come to this. General, get your special-operations people ready. I'll want to speak personally with MacIntyre when they've completed their rehearsals." They all rose as the President got up. "And, Harry, brief your man Sclafoni out there about the potential bloodbath that's brewing in the occupied territories. Maybe it's something he can use in negotiating with Jamil."

"Yes, sir, and it's Sclafani."

"Whatever."

Sunday, 9:55 P.M.—Aboard the *Spokane*

Peck squinted into a sun that was about five degrees off the western horizon. It was one of those beautiful Northwest summer evenings that seemed to go on forever—evenings that made him think of his front-porch swing and quiet times with Sarah. The *Spokane* was still making a good four knots, and the reduced speed seemed to tax the engines less. Peck was less familiar with this part of the Strait, but he knew they were somewhere off Clallam Bay and the small community of Sekiu. He and the boys used to come to Sekiu to fish for salmon.

Jamil stood on one pilothouse wing and Michelle stood on the other. Together they had a 360-degree vantage of the water around them.

"I'd like to see my boat."

"You would like to what?" said Jamil, walking back inside.

"I haven't been out of the pilothouse in almost twenty hours," said Peck. "I need to walk around a bit, and I'd like to see my boat." Jamil looked at him carefully, then shrugged.

"Very well, Peck. It is now my boat, but I will allow you to look at it. Have the girl take the helm." Peck stepped back as Janey moved over to take the wheel. Jamil tossed him the key to the handcuffs, and Peck freed himself. He motioned to Ahmed, who left his radios and walked behind Peck. He drew Peck's hands behind him and passed one of the manacles under his leather belt and clipped it around his free wrist. Peck now effectively had his hands tied and secured behind his back. Jamil raised Salah on the Motorola and asked him to send Hassan to the promenade deck to stand lookout while he and Peck toured the ferry. Then he turned to Ahmed.

"Call me the instant there is any communication from Jefferson on the cutter or from our Russian friends."

Peck winced from the stiffness in his legs as he descended the pilothouse stairs to the promenade deck. The two remaining Stinger missile launchers rested on a row of seats amidships. He cast a long look at the cutter and started down the stairs to the passenger deck. They walked aft past the galley area to where the hostages were scattered in groups around the after passenger cabin. A few held their nylon collars to allow the wire cable to pass without chafing. He recognized several of the hostages. The shock and petition in their faces told the story. Peck looked coldly at Jamil as he paused before the girl who had been assaulted by Fenton.

"So this is how you fight a war?" he said evenly.

"In my country," Jamil replied, "young women her age have been prisoners of the Zionists their entire lives and suffered years of indignities. What is a few days in captivity?" The girl clung to the older woman who had shared her trial on the promenade deck. The woman held the girl protectively and glowered like a she-bear at Jamil as they continued on.

"How're you feeling?"

"I'll be okay, Captain," said Brad Johnson. The side of his face around his eye was blue-black where Jamil had struck him. The eye was a slit, but he could still see with it. "I'm sorry about the engineer. I . . . just hope it's over soon. If there's anything I can do, let me know. I'm still dizzy, but I'm feeling a lot better."

"Thanks, Brad. Janey and I'll do fine." Peck saw the compassion in Brad's face and the faces of several others. *I must be a real inspiration to them—trussed up like a Christmas turkey. God protect them, because I certainly can't!*

"Can we go to the engine room?"

"After you, *Captain.*"

Peck had learned that Jamil did nothing without a reason. He knew he was being allowed to tour the boat for the effect on the passengers of seeing their captain manacled like a common criminal. While Jamil was behind him, he managed to wink at Johnson, and he could see that it helped. They made their way through the engine room and to the propulsion control panel.

George Zanner was cuffed to the panel, and gave Peck as sad a look as he'd ever seen.

"I'm so sorry about Andy, Captain—I just don't know what to say."

"Try not to think about it, George—you're the engineer now. Just do what they tell you and don't make any trouble." Peck could tell from the terrified look on Zanner's face that he would be no threat to the terrorists.

"Don't let 'em set off that dynamite, please. I don't want to die like this!" His voice cracked, and Peck knew he was at the end of his rope. He looked down the passageway to the block of explosives on the main sea suction and made a mental note of it. *If it's detonated, the* Spokane *is lost. The seawater will gush in much faster than the pumps can handle it.* Burns and Gonzales sat against the wall. Both had the look of young men who had lost hope.

"The government is negotiating with these people for our release. Just do what they say, and it'll all be over soon, okay?" Gonzales stared at him and blinked rapidly, while Burns acted as if he hadn't heard a word.

"Look after them, George, and let me know if there's any problems with the engines." Zanner nodded and gave him another sad look. Peck turned to Jamil. "All right, I've seen enough. I'm ready to go back to work."

Sunday, 11:30 P.M.—Aboard the *Mellon*

Frank Sclafani walked aft down the port side of the *Mellon*'s boat deck. He said a few words to the two FBI men who were standing amidships by the rail. Just behind them on the deck under the motor whaleboat was a mattress and a 30.06 sniper rifle. It was a composite weapon with a Remington action, a Douglas barrel, and a McMillan stock, and it was one of the most accurate sniper rifles in the world. He continued on back past the hangar to the helo deck. There was a serenity about a ship under way on a quiet night that was almost religious. Only the muted hum of the ship's ventilation system and the gentle slap of the water against the vessel's side marked her passing. He had become accustomed to the acrid smell of stack gas and the reassuring, baritone throb of the two Fairbanks-Morse diesels idling deep within *Mellon*'s bowels. Sclafani lit a cigarette, conscious of the noise made by his old flip-top Zippo. The Milky Way stretched cleanly across the heavens, dimmed only in the east by the quarter moon that had risen over the stern, and now followed them westward on the Strait. He leaned his forearms on the life rail and stared at the well-lighted ferry, which looked much closer than it had in the daytime. *What can you say to this man?* thought Sclafani. *He believes what he is doing is right, and he's said that he's prepared to die. If I could isolate him—get him alone—he might not choose death so readily, but as long as his followers are watching, I think he'll not hesitate to take the final step. And then there's the hatred. I can feel it over the radio—it drips from the speaker as a form of personal contempt because I represent the government he despises. How can I overcome a lifetime of hatred and injustice in a few hours? How can I get past the obsession and the despair that must stalk this man? All I can really do, I suppose, is to listen to him and keep him talking.* Sclafani shrugged and flipped the cigarette butt over the side as he walked forward.

Admiral MacIntyre stood quietly on the bridge wing looking at the *Spokane*. The night steaming watch moved softly around the pilothouse like altar boys about their duties. The inside of the pilothouse was bathed in red light like a cheap strip-bar to protect the night vision of those on watch.

"This is the hardest part, the waiting," said Sclafani. He liked the admiral. The negotiator worked best under a strong on-scene commander who took care of all details and communication up the line but didn't interfere in his dialogue with his client. Sclafani also sensed MacIntyre had that seasoned, unflappable quality of a man who is experienced in matters of crisis and danger. "If it's any consolation, he's waiting too, and there's tremendous pressure on him."

"What's he thinking about over there, Frank? What's going

on in that bastard's mind?'' Sclafani lit another cigarette. The OOD didn't allow smoking on his bridge, but he'd make an exception for the admiral's friend.

"I expect he's running on pure adrenaline by now. He's probably becoming moody and arbitrary in dealing with the hostages as well as his own people. He's got it pretty well thought out, but he's now likely starting to review his options in response to any number of moves we might make. As long as it's dark, he'll have to be on the alert for the possibility of an attack. In the end, Jamil will act on instinct. He's smart and he's committed, and I suspect there's a rage burning inside the man that's about to consume him.'' Sclafani drew heavily on his cigarette. "And I would think he's preparing himself for his own death—something we Westerners don't do on the eve of battle.''

"Anything we can do?''

Sclafani shook his head. "We can give him what he wants or we can't. An offer to set him free if he surrenders would only insult him. I think there's maybe a seventy-five-percent chance of his blowing up that submarine if the Israelis don't come through.''

"So we chance an assault on the ferry?''

"Possibly. If we do, we squander that twenty-five-percent chance he's bluffing or will settle for something less than he's asking.'' Sclafani stared at the admiral a moment, the pressure of his responsibilities clearly written on his face.

"Hang in there with him, Frank,'' MacIntyre finally replied. "We may not have much longer to talk.''

Sclafani made his way back to the cutter's radio room and sat at the desk. Jamil looked back at him from the picture, proud and defiant. "What can I say to you, my friend, that will turn you away from this madness?'' Sclafani had called every hour on one pretext or another to keep Jamil awake and to look for some break in his resolve. He stared at the picture a moment longer and picked up the microphone.

"This is Jefferson on the cutter *Mellon* calling Jamil, over.'' It was the first time Sclafani had abandoned the State Department title when calling Jamil.

"Yes, Jefferson, what do you want?" It was there, the arrogance and the impatience.

"Jamil, have you been following the news from the occupied territories? Do you know what's happening there?"

"Yes, of course. The radio news says that the Palestinians are rising in mass protest against the Jews. We are united in our common goals."

"I can understand that, Jamil, but your people in Palestine are women and children armed with rocks and sticks, and only a few of the men even have rifles. The Israelis have moved in tanks and soldiers to deal with the disturbance. If you continue to call for this mass uprising, large numbers of your people will die."

"The price of freedom is never cheap, Jefferson. Your ancestors had to fight the British for your independence."

My ancestors had to fight with the Mafia, thought Sclafani, *unless, of course, they were in the Mafia.* "Jamil, please listen to me. I am not speaking for the United States, but as a man concerned with needless killing. The people you are asking to take to the streets and fight are not soldiers like yourself. They don't have a submarine and prisoners and automatic weapons. They are poor and they have no experience in these matters. The Israelis have tanks and mechanized infantry. If the riots there become a full-scale attack on the Jews, it will be a massacre. Your people have suffered too long to die like this. I've promised that we will help, and I'm asking you to seek a negotiated resolution to this matter—give the peace talks more time. You're about to kill the people you're trying to save!" Sclafani's emotions had begun to play in his voice, and that seldom happened to him. There was no immediate reply, and for the first time, Sclafani felt some hesitation in Jamil.

"I believe you, Jefferson." His voice was softer, less combative, but still full of conviction. "And it gives me no pleasure to order children into the streets to do what should be done by men, but there is no other way. The Israelis will talk, but they will never abandon captured land and their settlements—it is not their way. We *will* win this battle, you will see. But if this battle should go against us, then we must surely win the war, for the world will condemn the men in the tanks, and expatriate Palestinians in Jordan and Lebanon and East Jerusalem and Golan will take up the Intifada with a vengeance. Those in Gaza and the West Bank who survive will fight again, because if we don't fight, we will become like your red men, relegated to second-rate reservation land under strict regulations and control—and we will be forgotten. It is better to struggle and die. American children can't understand this, but Palestinian children do. I'm sorry, Jefferson. Their blood will be on my hands, but there will be enough blood to splash on all of us. The Jews in Israel now live in occupied Palestine—we have allowed them that. Is the West Bank and Gaza too much to ask? Talk to me when you have convinced them to allow us to have at least a portion of what is ours.''

Sclafani sat for a while staring at the microphone. Then he got up and quietly walked back out on deck.

Commander William Bishop bicycled on the large duckfins as he watched the lighted monster bear down on him. He had been able to hear the rumble of the approaching ferry for some time, and now he could feel the vibrations. In the darkness, Bishop was just able to catch a glimpse of the man in front of him in the line of swimmers as he jockeyed to line up properly. Bishop was an EOD diver, so he was not uncomfortable in the water. But he was not a SEAL combat swimmer, nor was he in anything like the condition of the young men with whom he must board the captured ferry. He was shivering, both from the cold water and from the prospect of the boarding. Even so, he was beginning to sweat, which caused the black face paint to run into his eyes and burn. There was a harness strapped over his dry suit with one end of a thirty-meter line tied to a D ring on his chest and the other tied to the SEAL in front of him. There wasn't time for him to practice scaling the side of the moving ferry, so he would be lifted aboard by the SEALs. Bishop was a little embarrassed at being handled like so much baggage, but there was no other way in the time allowed to ensure that he got aboard.

''Get ready, sir,'' whispered the SEAL ahead of him, a mus-

cular second-class petty officer named Rhorbach—his pla-
toonmates called him "the Kraut." Bishop waved, immediately pulling his hand back into the water. He had been briefed
to stay low in the water and create a minimum silhouette. As the
bow of the ferry passed, he kicked toward the side of the boat
as he had been instructed in the briefing. *God help me—here we
go!* The glare of light from the windows on the passenger deck
partially blinded him, but he finally picked out two dark lumps
clamped to the side of the auto-deck railing. From water level
looking up, the sheer size of the ferry was imposing—nothing
like he'd imagined it. The line went taught and the harness
constricted his chest as he was jerked from the water. He found
himself kneeling between the two dark forms on the rim of the
car deck for an instant, then strong hands grabbed the fabric of
his dry suit and flipped him over the rail. He crouched inside
the railing and watched two other men scuffle over the side and
move quietly about the deck.

"Okay, hold it there." Bishop blinked as neon lights washed
the car deck. The SEALs were scattered along the side and
interior walls of the car deck, crouching over their weapons.
Rhorbach was at his side, his white, even teeth cutting a slit-
smile in his blackened face. "Well done, sir. Just like I told
you—it's a piece of cake." Lieutenant Horner called them together for a critique of the boarding evolution before they again
took their positions and continued the rehearsal. Off to one
side, two men watched.

"Well, it looks like they can do it at night."

"Apparently," replied Colonel Braxton, "but it could be
different under actual conditions out in less-protected water.
And if there's a sentry on the car deck, he's sure to hear them
come over the side."

Colin Gentry had thought they had slipped aboard rather
quietly, but then, he was a shipboard officer, not a commando.
He didn't particularly like Braxton, and he sensed the Army
man felt much the same about him. He had watched while
Braxton directed the rehearsals for the three assault groups.
The man knew his business, but Gentry could tell that Braxton
favored the Delta Force and that he resented Gentry's presence

as MacIntyre's deputy. He also seemed to object to the emphasis that was being placed on a covert boarding of the *Spokane* by the SEALs.

"Look, Braxton, I think it's time we put the bullshit aside. Your job is to prepare military options for use at the discretion of Admiral MacIntyre—he's the on-scene commander. My job is to observe these preparations and report my observations to the admiral, okay? Now, you seem determined that this be a Delta Force action. You want to tell me why, or is that some big military secret?"

Braxton regarded Gentry coldly. "Captain, I've been at the business of special operations all my life, and our country's track record in this area has been less than spectacular. Most of our problems have been the result of meddling politicians and conventional military thinking. How the hell'd you like me telling you how to fight an engagement at sea? Somewhere along the line, the special operators have to be assigned a target and allowed to do it their way, without interference by bureaucrats and the regular military. That's why the British SAS and the Israeli commandos are so effective. The politicians assign them a target, but they don't tell them how to do it."

"So you think the Army men have a better chance than the SEALs?"

"Look, Captain," Braxton said with an exaggerated show of patience, "this SEAL platoon is a direct-action platoon. These men are generalists, and their training has been primarily in over-the-beach reconnaissance and demolition raids. They're a superb maritime tactical unit, but they are *not* counterterrorist specialists or close-quarter battle specialists. These SEALs have never trained in CQB as a primary mission requirement. Even their boarding, while it looks good during rehearsal, is an improvised tactic. Once aboard, it's going to take them a while to capture the *Spokane,* and if they meet stiff resistance, they'll take a lot of casualties doing it. On the other hand, the Delta Force has spent *years* of training for this exact scenario—many of these men are combat veterans with tactical experience in CQB. The terrorists won't have a chance against them. If Captain Sherrard and his men are sent in, they'll swarm across that ferry like Genghis Khan through a gay bar—they'll own that ferry in two minutes tops!''

Gentry heard him out, arms folded on top of his generous stomach, pawing the deck with one shoe. ''I have no argument with you, Colonel. The Delta men are probably far more capable of defeating the terrorists than the SEALs, but that is *not* our primary mission.'' Braxton gave him a cautious look. ''Our number-one priority is to defeat the explosives on the *Michigan,* and the SEALs give us a chance to do that before the maniac on the ferry pushes the button. It's our *only* covert option.''

The Army man glared at him for a moment. ''I understand that. But there are a dozen things that can compromise them— they can be seen in the water, they can meet a sentry coming over the side, they can be detected moving across the ferry to the submarine, to name just a few. I'm convinced that the shock of a coordinated heliborne assault is the better option. This Jamil will be too busy fighting for his life to reach for a detonator. It's our best chance!'' Braxton was almost shouting, and several of the SEALs couldn't help but turn from their positions along the deck to stare.

''Very well, Colonel,'' said Gentry quietly. ''You'll need to point that out to the admiral. He's the one calling the shots, and I'm sure he'll want your opinion.''

Monday, June 22, 3:30 A.M.—The White House

President Bennett, Morton Keeney, and Richard Noffsinger sat staring at the speakerphone on the President's desk. Bennett drummed his fingers irritably on the desk, suspecting that he was being made to wait intentionally. Finally, a heavily accented voice spoke to them.

''My dear Mr. President, gentlemen, I offer my apologies for having you wait, but *ach,* the political factions within my own government that I must indulge! It's a difficult road we must follow sometimes, is it not?'' It was an excellent connection, and the forced good humor on the part of the Israeli prime minister came across clearly.

"If you mean that sometimes we must take positions we do not like, then I am in agreement with you, Prime Minister.''

"I see,'' said Levin guardedly. ''My foreign minister has advised me of your situation. How goes it with the terrorists who have taken your submarine and the hostages on the ferry-boat?''

"It's not going well at all. The terrorists have a highly secure position, and they are capable of creating a nuclear incident with the explosive charges they have placed aboard the submarine. I fully understand the rationale for not dealing with terrorists and the implications of setting a precedent by making an exception, but in this case, I am forced to try to accommodate them.''

"Forgive my bluntness, Mr. President, but I see this not as an accommodation, but a capitulation. If we allow these people to use terror successfully, then we are all in serious trouble.''

The President knew the communications security on the SATCOM link to Tel Aviv was airtight, but still he hesitated. ''I may already have serious trouble. There is a possibility that our problem could be more than an incident. What I'm saying, Mr. Levin, is that there is the possibility of a nuclear catastrophe.''

"*Elohim Adirim!* Are you suggesting a nuclear explosion?''

"That is a possibility.''

There was a long pause at the other end of the line, and for a moment Bennett thought the connection was broken.

"Mr. President, this . . . this is terrible.'' Levin paused again. When he continued, the anguish was evident in his voice. ''We had suspected something like this because of your insistence to meet the demands of the terrorists, but it is most distressing to have it confirmed. And it is all the more painful to me, sir, for I must tell you that we simply cannot comply with what you ask.'' Bennett started to speak, but Levin continued. ''Please, Mr. President, let me speak. What you face is a catastrophe, but what is at stake for us is national survival. The occupied territories, too, are poised for a large and dangerous explosion. If we allow this terrorist to force us from these lands at gunpoint, other madmen like him will not stop there. The dissident factions will flood into the West Bank from Jordan and into Gaza from Lebanon. Then it will only be a matter of time before they become a conventional threat on our very borders. Can you imagine the Russians on your Canadian border in the old days? This is how it will be with us. This Jamil cannot be allowed to succeed. I pray to God that you can deal with the situation— that he is bluffing or that you can seize the vessels, but I cannot and I will not allow the occupied territories to be captured by terror. I am very sorry.''

Bennett started to protest but thought better of it. Levin had made his position clear—neither he nor his government was susceptible to threats, bribes, or any external pressure at this point. And the President of the United States was not going to beg.

''Prime Minister Levin, so there is no misunderstanding, I will ask again—plainly and directly—will you help us?''

''No, Mr. President, I cannot help you.''

''I see. Thank you for your time.''

Bennett casually reached over and pressed the disconnect button before the prime minister could reply. There was silence in the room as all three men stared at the speaker. The President was buffeted by an emotional medley of anger, frustration, and despair. He was also very tired, and he was cornered. He issued a short, weary sigh and looked at his three advisers as he pressed the intercom button on his desk.

''Ask General Scott to please come up here.''

The President had just finished lighting another cigarette when there was a sharp rap on the door and the JCS Chairman stepped inside.

''Please join us,'' Bennett said, gesturing to a chair between Keeney and Noffsinger.

''Thank you, sir.''

''General, the military option seems to be a little stronger than it was a few minutes ago. Could you give us an update on the preparations of your special-operations teams?''

Monday, 12:50 A.M.—Off the Coast of
Washington State

The *S-570* was making just enough turns for steerageway. She displayed a grimes light that properly identified her as a submarine running on the surface at night, something Russian submarines almost never did. Molev sat on a metal stool in the cockpit on top of the sail while two lookouts with binoculars swept the horizon. The only noticeable movement was from the small Snoop Pair radar that rotated atop one of the extended periscope masts. Russian submarines rarely surfaced outside of their own territorial waters and almost never in such a temperate climate. The gentle swells and fresh, sweet night air were a pleasant respite from the submerged transit. Only the constant drone of a low-flying U.S. Navy P-3 Orion disturbed the soft breaking of waves as they crawled over the massive rounded hull of the sub. The executive officer made his way up the ladder into the cockpit.

"Captain, another message from Pacific Banner Fleet Headquarters. It is most insistent that we leave the area immediately and open the American coastline." The *starpom* would have added that it was the third such message, but he knew his captain resented being crowded. "How shall I respond?"

"Get the engineering officer up here."

"The engineer?" Molev looked sharply at his second-in-command, who immediately pressed the lever on the communications box and asked the diving officer in the control room to summon the engineer. Three minutes later, another form crowded onto the sail. He had a sparse beard, and was dressed in blue coveralls and dirty white combination cap.

"You sent for me, Captain?"

"I did, Yuri. It's about your engineering casualty—that rupture in one of the secondary high-pressure steam lines that has forced us to the surface. I believe it is time that we sent a message to Fleet Headquarters and notified them of our problem. You can report that the boat and all personnel aboard are in no danger, and that we estimate the repairs will take about eight hours.'' There are no secrets on a submarine, and the engineer knew full well why the *S-570* was on the surface. Nonetheless, he was surprised by such a request. He had seen a few Russian commanders refuse to report equipment breakdowns, as such failures looked bad on their performance ratings, but never had he known one to invent an engineering casualty and falsely report it.

''Prepare the message for transmission,'' said Molev, ''and, *Starpom*, I want it entered in the ship's log under your signature that this engineering casualty and its reporting were made at the direction of the commanding officer.''

The engineer looked at his captain impassively and breathed a quiet sigh of relief. ''That was not necessary, Captain, but thank you.''

Molev inclined his head. ''It may not seem necessary now, my friend, but you may think differently if there is a squad of GRU security men waiting at the pier on our return home.'' The engineer saluted and climbed back down the scuttle leading to the control room. Molev shifted on his stool and called down the hatch to his *starpom*, who had followed the engineer below. ''Make that transmission in the clear, without encryption. There is no reason to make our situation a secret.''

Molev then made himself comfortable by propping his feet on the top of the sail combing and mentally noting the twenty-second intervals of the Tatoosh light off Cape Flattery just visible on the eastern horizon. A short time later, another officer joined Molev on the sail. The captain didn't have to look around to know who it was.

''Good evening, Mikhail Gurtovoi, or if we go by the Americans' time, good morning. I've been expecting you.''

''Good morning to you, Comrade Captain,'' replied the political officer. ''I am given to understand that we have an engineering emergency that will keep us in the area and on the surface for the next several hours.''

''It is true, but I believe we can correct the problems and be on our way before midday. Your concern, however, is duly noted.''

"Captain," replied the *zampolit*, moving closer and out of earshot of the lookouts, "your decision to contact the terrorists who captured the American submarine was foolhardy, but admirable. At best, you would have been publicly censured and perhaps privately praised. More likely, you would have been relieved for cause. These new orders from Fleet Headquarters to leave the American coast come directly from President Stozharov's office. These are orders you cannot ignore. Before, you were risking your career—now you are risking your life!"

"Comrade," said Molev, turning to look him in the eye, "my father, whom I never knew, died at Leningrad during the Great Patriotic War, as did three of my uncles. My father's younger brother raised me, and until the day of his death, he carried with him a kind of self-imposed humiliation of having lived while so many others died. He never forgave himself, Mikhail, for having been twelve years old and made to stay at home to look after me. Imagine that—he was ashamed to be alive because he felt that he could have fought and died for the Rodina at the age of twelve!"

Molev was silent for a moment, then he continued in a quiet voice. "The West is winning, at least for the time being. We are on the defensive economically and militarily, but we must still fight a holding action—we must retreat in good order. These Palestinians have offered us a rare opportunity to win a battle in our retreat. The politicians in Moscow have adopted a policy of total appeasement and are incapable of taking the initiative. Our senior military commanders are interested only in safeguarding their privileges and their pensions, and have overlooked their duty—they, too, are impotent." Again he paused and continued in a hushed voice. "You see, Mikhail, I am not twelve years old, and unlike my uncle, I *do* have the chance to serve my country—more than that, I have a duty. No orders from Moscow can absolve me of that duty."

"Captain," replied Gurtovoi carefully, *"my* orders are to relieve you if you do not comply with the fleet directives. Would that make it easier for you?"

Molev eyed him critically. "Perhaps. May I please see the

communication granting you that authority?'' Gurtovoi hesitated, then nodded before he retreated down the ladder. As soon as he had left the sail, Molev toggled the lever on the intercom.

''*Starpom!*''

''Yes, Captain.''

''See that some sandwiches and tea are sent up for me and my two lookouts. Then place Comrade Gurtovoi under arrest, and confine him to his quarters under guard. He is to communicate with no one, and he is to be treated with the utmost courtesy and respect.''

''Understood, Captain,'' replied the executive officer calmly. Again, there are no secrets on a submarine.

Monday, 1:15 A.M.—U.S. Coast Guard Station, Port Angeles, Washington

The SEALs sat in a tight circle in the corner of the brightly lit hangar. A shining red H-65 squatted nearby. The men were dressed in black overalls and their faces and hands were stained black with camouflage paint. The only color variant was the hair of those who didn't wear a black watch cap. Petty Officer Rhorbach, who had been charged with the responsibility of Commander Bishop, sat close to him in the circle. Behind them, dressed in black coveralls but without the paint, were the Echo Platoon SEALs who were not scheduled for the operation. They shuffled about restlessly, like bench-warmers around the team huddle.

''Okay, guys, it looks like this operation may just be going down. This will be our last mission briefing before the final go–no go decision. We've rehearsed it—now it's just a matter of going out and doing it.'' Lieutenant Horner flipped a page of his pocket notebook and looked around—nothing but eyes and teeth. ''We'll board the chopper in reverse order of exit: Chief Watson, Wildrick, Commander Bishop, Rhorbach, Mantalas, myself, Peppard, and Garniss. Everyone but Garniss and the commander will be carrying silenced MP-5s with sixty rounds, a pair of flash-bangs and side arms. Your gear and ammo loading should already be set up. Wildrick and Mantalas will carry the extra gear bags—Garniss and Peppard will toss the hooks. When we're done here, we'll gear up for inspection and a radio check. Then it's on the helo, and we stand by to stand by.

"Our mission is unchanged from the rehearsal briefing and the practice sessions: get Commander Bishop aboard the ferry without detection and get him to the explosives so he can disarm them. Everything else is secondary. We'll board to port and move to the starboard side of the ferry, just like we rehearsed. Initially, we're just a security element, and we protect the commander at all costs until he gets his job done. When that's finished, Rhorbach stays with him and the remaining six of us will attempt to free the hostages and retake the ferry. For now, I want you to forget about the explosives, the terrorists, the missiles, the radiation, everything. This is a maritime boarding drill. Get lined up—maintain your interval—stay low in the water. Bob and Charlie will get the lines over; the rest of us just have to kick to the ropes and pull ourselves aboard. Once the commander is aboard, it's a sneak-and-peek drill across the ferry. You guys know your jobs, and you're good at it. We've busted our asses for the last year in predeployment training, and now it's money time. There's *nobody* who can do this job better than we can. Concentrate on the small things—stick to procedure and you'll do just fine. Any questions?"

Horner looked at his watch and then at his chief. "Master Chief?"

Watson stood up and surveyed the group. All eyes were on him. "We've been well briefed, and we've rehearsed it. Everybody knows exactly what they're supposed to do. Now, I know we've all got the jitters, and that's normal—this is our first real operation and our first opportunity for combat. But trust me on this one, men, and it's important—you've all been there before. It may seem hard to believe, but there's no difference between the real thing and a paint-gun fight."

The SEALs trained extensively with pistols and rifles that fired paint pellets. Close-quarter battle training usually consisted of SEALs armed with paint guns and eye goggles moving from room to room, attacking other SEALs with paint guns and eye goggles dressed up like terrorists. The paint pellets clearly marked a hit, and a good-sized welt let a SEAL know he'd been shot.

"You'll get the same rush, and you'll get the same tunnel vision. After the first few rounds, you won't hear or see much of what's going on around you—just like a paint-gun fight. So, just like you've been trained, you must concentrate on your shooting mechanics and constantly be aware of where the other guys are. Remember, if we're engaged before Commander Bishop can disarm the explosives, it'll be a squad action. Once he's disarmed the demolitions, it'll be a standard room-clearing drill—tap 'em twice and keep moving. We've done this all before, and like Lieutenant Horner said, concentrate on the little things—move quietly, follow the SOPs, keep your eyes moving—and you'll do just fine."

Watson looked around the circle and met each man's eyes. They looked calm and ready, but deep inside, each of them knew it would be more than a paint-gun fight. *They're scared, all right, and that's as it should be,* thought Watson. *SEALs are no braver than anyone else, but they've been trained to bury their fear deep within themselves so they can do their job.*

"Okay, let's gear up. Inspection in ten minutes!"

The SEALs stood and moved to the neat piles of equipment that were lined up in squad-file order. One end of the hangar doubled as a basketball court, and the equipment was arranged along the baseline. Some of the men stretched or bent to touch their toes, like athletes prior to the game. The nonpainted SEALs moved among them, quietly kidding them, offering advice, and helping them with their gear.

"Okay, Chief?" said Horner as they walked off to the side.

"They're ready, sir—how about you?"

"I think so, and you were right—every time I get a free moment and start to think, I get the willies."

"You're doing everything right, sir, including being scared. Once we get started, the training takes over—you'll see."

"What was it like, Master Chief, your first combat action?"

Watson flashed quickly back to a steamy mangrove swamp in the Mekong Delta and the unsuspecting Vietcong squad walking casually past his ambush site. Seaman Watson and his SEAL squad had shredded the five VC like a scene from a Sam Peckinpah movie. Looking back, it was really nothing more than premeditated murder.

"Sir, Vietnam was a long time ago, and it was so different from this, it isn't worth talking about."

"Any last-minute advice, then?"

"Just this—let the men do the work. Your job is to know what everybody's doing and to think ahead. These things don't often go as planned, so you need to keep a fix on the big picture and give new orders as things change."

"Just like we trained, huh, Chief?" Horner smiled.

"Just like we trained." Watson put his hand on the taller officer's shoulder. "You're gonna do just fine, sir. Now, we better gear up." A short while later Horner and Watson started down the line of men.

"All set, Bob?"

"You bet, sir," replied Garniss, "let's do it!"

Garniss was a fixture at SEAL Team Three, a fifteen-year veteran. He should have made chief petty officer several years before, but he didn't seem to care about advancement. He did only the minimum amount of physical training, but on the weekly five-mile team race, he always finished near the front. He was impervious to cold weather, and when walking point, he moved like a cat.

Garniss, like the others, was dressed in loose-fitting black canvas coveralls, tightly Velcroed at the wrists and ankles. He wore black sneakers and vinyl gloves with leather pads on the palms and fingers. Strapped to his torso was a custom-made vest called a SOMAVS—Special Operations Modular Assault Vest System. It was constructed of nylon and cordura, and held his grenades, extra magazines, penlight, and a small first-aid kit. On one side hung a holstered Glock Model 17 9mm Parabellum pistol and on the other, a standard Navy K-bar knife. Centered between Garniss's shoulder blades was a vest pouch that held his Motorola MX300 squad radio. A cord led up from the transceiver to the voice-actuated throat microphone that was held against his larynx by a Velcro strap. Another cord went to the small piece that fitted snugly in his ear. The radio was designed for an on/off button to be attached to the front of the vest, but the SEALs had modified the unit to locate the button on the pistol grip of their weapons. Horner walked around him, checking his equipment and tugging on straps. On the floor beside Garniss were his fins, the grapnel hook, a tight coil of black nylon line, and a Steyr 5.56mm Bullpup automatic rifle. The Steyr was a very compact weapon made mostly of high-density plastic and was complete with silencer and single-point night sight.

"Looking good, Bob—go ahead and get dressed." Garniss didn't move until Master Chief Watson, who was following Horner, gave him an imperceptible nod.

"Hoo-yah!" yelled Garniss as he dropped to the deck and began to pull on the pants of his dry suit. Horner and Watson worked their way down the line, checking equipment and weapons. Everyone worked at casual conversation.

"All set, Commander?" Horner asked Bishop.

"As far as I can tell." His SOMAVS carried only his squad radio, a pistol, and a first-aid kit. "Lieutenant, rather than over-load some of your men, I'm sure I could carry some of my equipment."

"Better let the guys do that, sir," replied Horner. "They'd get real embarrassed if you showed them an EOD man could pack as much gear in the water as they can. Dry suit fit okay?"

"It's a little loose, but it does the job." One of the platoon SEALs remaining behind had been as tall as Bishop, but heavier.

"Stay close to the Kraut, sir, and we'll get you there to do your job." Rhorbach already had his dry suit on and was standing by to help Bishop with his. Horner and Watson moved on to the last SEAL in the line. He was a big man and had two waterproof containers clipped to his vest.

"You missed a spot on your neck with the camouflage, Willie."

"I'll get right to it, sir," he replied with a grin. Wildrick was just an average swimmer for a SEAL, but he had tremendous upper-body strength. In addition to his own gear, he'd carry most of Bishop's EOD equipment aboard the ferry. The camouflage face paint didn't do much to change Wildrick's color, since he was already black, but it gave a flat cast to his skin and reduced reflected light.

"You comfortable with the extra gear?"

"No problem, sir."

"Good show. Go ahead and suit up."

Watson and Horner then inspected each other. Both carried a Motorola hand radio for communication with Braxton on the cutter. Watson's radio was attached to his vest. Horner's was encased in a special waterproof housing, and fitted to a pocket of his dry suit so he'd be able to talk to Colonel Braxton while he was in the water. Satisfied, they both pulled on their dry suits, carefully working their sneakers down into the suit booties. They joined the other SEALs, who were still adjusting their neoprene wrists and neck dams to ensure a proper seal. The watertight zipper that ran across the back and shoulders would be left open for ventilation until just before they entered the water.

"Radio check, radio check. How do you hear me, Bob?"

"Loud and clear, boss."

"Charlie?"

"Hear you five by, sir."

"Manny?"

"Okay, boss."

"Kraut?"

"Loud an' clear."

"Commander Bishop?"

"I hear you fine, over."

"Willie?"

"Gotcha, skipper."

"Master Chief?"

"Loud and clear, sir."

"Okay, all radios check," said Horner aloud to the group as he signaled for the men to gather around him.

He looked at his watch—1:45 A.M. Outside the hangar door,

a Navy H-3 had begun to whine. On Watson's recommendation, Horner had insisted on a Navy helo with an experienced Navy ASW pilot. The Army pilots were excellent and the HH-60 was a superior bird for special operations, but only Navy helo pilots with antisubmarine warfare experience had multiple hours of flying low over water at night.

"Men, that's our limousine spooling up out there. As soon as we get aboard, we'll be in full standby. Any last-minute questions?" After a long pause, he continued. "Then hoo-yah, let's do it! Load 'em up and lock 'em."

There was a ripple of metallic clattering as magazines clicked into place and cartridges were chambered. The SEALs held their weapons up for inspection as Master Chief Watson passed down the line carefully looking at each man's piece, including Horner's.

"Locked and on safe, sir." He held out his own silenced MP-5 for Horner's inspection.

"Very well, Master Chief," he replied, checking the weapon, "let's board 'em."

Watson lead the file of warriors out of the hangar to the waiting helicopter amid words of encouragement from the other SEALs.

"Good hunting, guys!"

"Kick ass!"

"Knock their dicks in the dirt!"

Once aboard, Lieutenant Horner was handed an aircraft headset by one of the crew members.

"This is Sundance 27 calling the cutter *Mellon,* over."

"Roger, Sundance 27, this is the *Mellon.* I read you loud and clear, over."

"This is 27, my element is in ground standby. I say again, my element in ground standby, over."

"Uh, roger, Sundance 27, we copy you in ground standby, *Mellon* out."

Monday, 1:50 A.M.—U.S. Coast Guard Station, Pier 36, Seattle, Washington

"Okay, now this is the coast of Vancouver Island, this is the U.S. coast, this blip here is the Swiftsure Light marking the entrance to the Strait, and this large blip is the *Spokane* and the *Michigan,* right?"

"Yessir, you've got it," said Carol Peschel. *You've also got,* she thought, *the dreamiest brown eyes I've ever seen.* "And this one here is the *Mellon.* We're looking at them from the Cape Flattery antenna, and they're almost due east of the Cape right now. The ferry and the submarine are making about four knots, so they'll be at the mouth of the Strait in a little over two hours."

"Tell me about the helos circling the *Spokane.*" Ensign Dave Santee stood looking over Carol's shoulder at the radarscope. The glow of the rotational cursor brushed their faces with a pale-lime tint.

"Since that light plane was shot down, we've kept a helicopter circling them at a mile and a half or so to warn off any low flyers or small craft that might stray into the area. All merchant traffic has been ordered to stand clear. One of the helos had to herd a few fishing boats away near Pillar Point earlier this evening, but everyone else seems to have gotten the word to stay off the Strait."

"Can you paint the helos on radar?"

"Sometimes, if they're low enough. Let me try and bring one down." Peschel keyed the mike on her headset. "Coast Guard Barrier Patrol, this is Seattle VTS, over."

"Roger, this is Barrier Patrol, go ahead, VTS."

"Barrier Patrol—VTS. I need to track you for a while on my surface search. Request you bring it down to deck for a few minutes, over."

"This is Barrier Patrol, wilco, out."

Peschel toyed with several knobs on the radar console and soon the cursor began to paint a dim, rapidly moving blip of light circling the large spot that was the *Spokane* and the slightly smaller one that marked the *Mellon*. Santee studied the scope with a puzzled expression.

"It's right here, sir."

"Oh, right." Santee gave her a boyish grin. *He's awful cute,* she thought, *but he couldn't cut it as a radarman. The chief has always said that guys in the Navy weren't too smart, especially the officers.* He watched as the helo made a complete circle. "I understand that in fog or low visibility, you can give directions to a ship to help them steer?"

"Sure, we do that a lot in the winter in really bad weather, and sometimes at night when a merchantman's lost his radar."

"Think you can do that with a helo?"

Peschel thought about it for a moment. "I don't see why not, so long as he stays low enough for me to paint him on the scope." Santee dropped to one knee beside her with his arm on the back of her chair and his eyes level with hers. Suddenly the grin was gone.

"Carol, here's what I need you to do. Ask the helicopters to stay low, and every ten or fifteen minutes send them out on a bearing away from the *Spokane* like they were checking out a contact. They need to fly out on a steady bearing for about five minutes, then you can bring them back to the patrol circle. Can you do that?"

"That's not normal procedure, but yessir, I can do it. But why?" *He's still cute, but his face is deadly serious.*

"In a while, a helicopter with SEALs from my platoon is going to relieve the helo that's now on patrol, and they will continue to circle, just like the others. If orders are given for us to attack, I need you to direct the helo out away from the ferry, and this is very important, they need to fly out *exactly* along the course of the ferry, do you understand?"

"I think so, sir. You want me to vector the patrol helo out from the patrol circle exactly on the ferry's projected track."

"That's right—can you do it?"

"No sweat, sir." Santee put his hand lightly on her shoulder, and in the dim light from the scope, she swore he winked at her. He got to his feet and turned to Chief Dearing.

"Chief, you have that secure line to my helo up yet?"

"Right here, sir." Dearing handed him a headset while a Coast Guard lieutenant commander looked on.

"Thanks, Chief." Santee put on the headset, adjusted the lip microphone, and found the button on the cord. "Sundance 27, this is Sundance Junior, how do you hear me, over?" After a moment and burst of static, Horner came through on the circuit.

"Junior, this is 27. I hear you fine, Dave, how about me, over?"

"Loud and clear. Brian, we're all set here, and we are capable of directing you on your spotting run, over."

"Roger, Dave, understand you can control us to spot our swimmers. I'll pass that along to my pilot. We're on airborne standby now. All we need is the green light, you copy that, *Mellon*?"

"Roger, this is the *Mellon,* we copy. Green light and the execution code word will be given on mission authorization. Continue airborne standby, *Mellon* out."

Monday, 5:15 A.M.—The White House

Dawn was filtering through the curtains of the Oval Office and a weary President Bennett sat looking across his desk at Morton Keeney. Bennett had been able to grab a few fifteen-minute catnaps. Keeney had not slept a wink, yet he looked as urbane and unruffled as he had twenty hours ago when he was so abruptly called away from his church service.

"I don't think we can put this off much longer, Mort. Why don't you get them in here."

"Yes, sir." Keeney got up and returned several minutes later with Harold Baines, Armand Grummell, Richard Noffsinger, and General Scott. The President didn't invite them to the more casual environment of the coffee table and settee. He sat upright behind his huge desk while his advisers took straight-back chairs in front of him. Colonel Buck Williams stood quietly by the door.

"Gentlemen, it's just about crunch time. It'll be dawn on the West Coast in a few hours, and I'm told we'll have very limited military options once the sun comes up. First of all, does DOE have any better numbers for us on the possibility of a nuclear explosion?"

"I just spoke with Secretary Rogers and Patterson's immediate supervisor. It seems that there's a controversy even within DOE about the chance of nuclear detonation. The consensus is that it's a very remote possibility, but there's a few well-respected people there who seem to think it's much higher. The Navy still maintains that the chance of the *Michigan* going nuclear, even low-order nuclear, is so unlikely as to be negligible."

"Christ almighty! What kind of an answer is that? Those people are supposed to be the experts—they supervised the building of the goddamn bombs." Bennett frowned as he drew his hand across his face. He hadn't time for this, and he knew it. "Okay, so a nuclear blast is still a possibility. Dick, how about that Russian sub?"

"Since they declared an emergency, there's been an exceptionally high volume of coded traffic on their fleet broadcast bands. Officially, they haven't acknowledged that they have a submarine in trouble, and they claim they're making every attempt to recall the boat. It's either a very convincing and plausible cover, or that sub skipper is acting on his own."

"If I may," said General Scott, "our military attaché in Moscow reported through DIA channels that one of his contacts in the Russian Army said it's a rogue submarine captain, and that President Stozharov is furious. The Army has been smarting for years over what they feel has been a disproportionate share of military funding going to the Navy, especially their submarine service. And since the Army didn't come away as clean during the coup attempt as the Navy, they don't mind seeing their rival service get a little soiled. The Russian generals are openly gloating over the Navy's predicament."

"Thank you, General. Armand?"

"It fits, and our sources would seem to confirm that the Akula boat's actions are totally without authorization. If it's a ploy, it's a very well-conceived one. Five years ago, I would have been skeptical, but not today—the Russians have too much to lose by toying with us."

"All right," said the President, spreading his fingers, palms down, on the desk, "neither the Israelis nor the Russians can or will help us to solve our problem. The question for us—for me, really—is, do I take the military option? General, are your forces in place?"

"Yes, sir. The Delta Force contingent is standing by aboard three HH-60 Blackhawks at Fort Lewis. They are ready to lift off and can hit the *Spokane* on thirty-five minutes' notice. The SEALs have just become airborne and are circling the target in place of the Coast Guard Barrier Patrol. They can be in the water in less than ten minutes. Once in the water, it will take the ferry approximately thirty minutes to get to their location so they can attempt a boarding. The Rangers are in place and hiding behind the breakwater in Neah Bay. They have a fully equipped thirty-two-man assault platoon in four high-speed RIB-type boats. The *Spokane* is near Neah Bay right now, but the Rangers would have to traverse four miles of open water. They can be there in six to eight minutes, but they'll be highly visible the whole way."

After Scott had given his report, the President sat lost in his own thoughts, giving no acknowledgment or indication that he had even heard him. The JCS Chairman glanced at the others, and Morton Keeney gave him a reassuring nod. Finally, Bennett reached across the desk and pressed the button on the front of his speakerphone.

"Yes, Mr. President?"

"Connect me with Admiral MacIntyre."

"Right away, sir." The group sat in silence for a moment while the connection was made.

"This is Rear Admiral MacIntyre, sir."

"Admiral, this is the President. I'm here with several of my advisers. Time is getting short and I need to make a decision. Are you by yourself?"

"No, sir. I have Frank Sclafani here, who's been negotiating with Jamil, and Colonel Braxton of the Special Operations Command. We are in a secure space and they are able to hear you. I'd like them to remain as a part of this meeting if you approve."

"I do. Can you bring us up to date on your situation there?"

"Yes, sir. Special Agent Sclafani has been in contact with Jamil on an hourly basis, and it's his opinion that Jamil will carry out his threat unless we can in some way guarantee his demands. He feels that Jamil may permit the Russians to board the *Michigan* first, but that he'll then destroy her. By our plot, the *Spokane* and the *Michigan* will reach international waters and the Russian boat between 6:30 and 7:00 A.M. Pacific time."

"Mr. Sclafani?"

"Yes, Mr. President."

"What makes you so sure that Jamil isn't bluffing?"

"Sir, I'm convinced he's a very committed and dedicated man. He has a single-minded passion about his cause—the freedom of his people—and a very deep-seated hatred for Israel and the United States. It's . . . well, sir, he's known a lifetime of bitterness and frustration, and now it's all on the line—everything he believes in.

"But how can he save himself if he blows up the *Michigan*?"

"If he cared about living, I could perhaps deal with him. I don't think he does, and that's a problem. Sir, he's a very dangerous and unpredictable man. He knows the world is watching, and I don't think he will be the first one to blink." Bennett watched FBI Director Baines while Sclafani was speaking. Baines nodded his head in grim acknowledgment.

"Thank you, Mr. Sclafani. Admiral, if I'm to attack this man, how do you recommend we do it?"

"Mr. President, it's between the Delta Force and the SEALs for an assault on the *Spokane*. The Rangers should be held back as a follow-on capability. Colonel Braxton favors the Delta Force for their experience and proven effectiveness in these situations. And there's a chance that the shock and surprise of their attack may overwhelm Jamil before he has a chance to detonate the explosives. As you know, the SEALs have come up with an improvised plan to covertly board the *Spokane* with Commander Bishop, the EOD specialist. The plan has merit, and they were successful in rehearsals, but as Colonel Braxton has pointed out, if they are discovered in the water or while they are boarding the ferry, Jamil would surely detonate the explosives.''

''Colonel, I take it you would send the Delta Force?''

''Most definitely, Mr. President. The shock and firepower of a Delta Force attack may be able to overpower Jamil and take him out before he can blow up the sub. These men have been highly trained for this kind of an action, and I believe it's our best chance for success.''

''Thank you, Colonel.'' President Bennett looked to each of his advisers in turn. There was no help there, nor did he expect any. ''Admiral . . . what do you recommend?''

''Mr. President, I recommend the SEALs.''

President Bennett stared at the speaker a moment, then replied, ''Admiral, send your SEALs to board the *Spokane.* Place the Delta Force on standby in case the SEALs fail to get aboard or they need assistance. Keep me continually informed on the progress of the assault.''

''Aye, aye, sir.''

''Do you have any questions?''

''No, sir.''

''Convey my personal regards to your assault-team leaders, and God bless all of you.''

''Thank you, sir.''

Bennett again hit the speaker button to sever the connection, and surveyed the somber men seated across the desk. ''Gentlemen, I think we better wait this one out in the situation room. I'll join you there in a few minutes.'' As the men filed out, he caught the eye of his military aide. ''Buck, why don't you stay for a minute.'' After the others had departed, the President called Colonel Williams over and motioned him to a chair. ''Take a load off, Buck.''

''Thank you, sir.'' The colonel sat down, but still at attention.

"Keeney and the others, with the exception of General Scott, think we should wait Jamil out—press for further negotiations—and Scott's worried that if this goes badly, he and his Special Operations Command will be blamed. But you approve of my decision. You want to tell me why?"

"I approve, sir?"

"Buck, I've gone from private in the Army to President of the United States. Along the way I got pretty good at reading people. Now, you think this is the proper course of action, and I'd like to know why. This was a tough decision, and quite frankly, I can use all the support I can get, even from a lowly Marine colonel."

Both men smiled, and Williams relaxed just a bit. "Very well, sir, I do approve. I don't think you can make deals with terrorists, and especially not with this one. He's too much of a leader, and he's committed. I also feel strongly that unless we have better information, you have to back the people that are there—trust their judgment, like we did the military commanders during the Gulf War. Sclafani is convinced that Jamil isn't bluffing, and Admiral MacIntyre seems to be doing a pretty good job out there. After all, if this thing turns bad, they could be the first to die."

The President sat motionless for a moment, then slowly nodded his head. "That's exactly the way I see it. God knows I'd like to talk our way out of this, but it just doesn't seem possible." He again paused before he continued. "Why don't you go ahead on down—I'll be there in a few minutes."

"Yes, sir." Williams got to his feet and quietly let himself out.

Monday, 2:10 A.M.—Torpedo Room, USS *Michigan*

DeRosales labored at the manual hydraulic pump, moving the lever back and forth with one arm, then the other. It was very

cool in the submarine, but the exertion had caused him to fog
the faceplate of his EBA mask and made the battle lantern appear as a dull light in the mist. He didn't bother to clear it, since
he didn't really need to see anything to work the pump. Finally,
there was a distinct metallic clunk. He took off the mask and
held his breath while he swabbed the inside of it with his handkerchief. Once the mask was back in place, he reached for the
radio.

"Okay, sir, the outer doors are open."

"Good job, Jesús." It was the patient voice of Captain Hailey. "Now I want you to go through the prelaunch checks carefully, but do not, I repeat do not, release the tube-weapon locks,
do you understand, over?"

"Understood, sir, do not release the weapon locks."

As a torpedoman, DeRosales knew the weapon-launch sequence by heart, but under the glare of the lantern, he went
down the checklist item by item as he prepared the tube for
firing. As a Trident skipper, Hailey also knew the launch sequence, just as he knew every other system aboard his submarine. The *Michigan* had no electrical or hydraulic power, but
she still had an abundance of compressed air. That was all that
was physically required to fire torpedoes or, in the case of this
tube, launch a false target canister. Normally the canister,
which was nothing more than a large sophisticated Alka-Selt-
zer tablet, would be ejected clear of the sub to create a cloud of
air bubbles in its wake. It was specifically designed to decoy an
enemy torpedo away from the *Michigan*.

"Prelaunch checklist complete, sir—weapon locks in place,
over."

"Very well, DeRosales. Stand by your tube and wait for my
command to fire the canister, over."

"Roger, sir, standing by."

Monday, 2:15 A.M.—Aboard the *Spokane*

"Ahmed, what's this contact out here? Why wasn't I notified about this?" Ahmed's station was the radios and the radar.

"They have a helicopter circling about a mile and a half or so from us. The Coast Guard called earlier and said they were on patrol to warn off boats and small craft. Occasionally they fly farther out to check on a contact and then return to their circle route. I do not think they want another plane shot down."

Jamil thought about it. "It's good that they keep everything away from us. That makes it easier to see any attacking boats or aircraft." He studied the scope for a moment, then looked out the window to the west.

"It should be dawn in another hour and a half, right, Peck?"

Ross Peck stood at the wheel of the *Spokane* and stared straight ahead. He ached with fatigue and his mind was starting to drift off to warm, comfortable places like his living-room couch, the hammock in the front yard—his own *bed!* When Jamil spoke, he was quickly jerked back to reality and the plight of his vessel. *I've got to stay sharp and hold on until dawn. If the Navy or whoever is going to attempt a rescue, they'll probably try it before sunup. Maybe this offer of help by the Russian submarine was a trick, and the Russians will try to rescue them.*

"I said daylight in an hour and a half, Peck. Is that about right?" Peck made a show of looking at his watch.

"That's about right," he said evenly.

"Then we'll see if your President Bennett has struck a deal with the Jews. If not, perhaps we can strike a deal with the Russians. They seem quite eager to get aboard my Trident submarine."

"What makes you think the Russians will help you? They supported my country during the Gulf War." *When was the last time I called it "my country"?* thought Peck.

"The Russians are most predictable, because they always act in their own interest. I would imagine that it's in their interest to get aboard the Trident and into her code room. And if they do start to feel noble, I will blow them up along with the submarine. You just steer us out into the Pacific Ocean, Peck, and I will tend to the rest.''

Monday, 2:19 A.M.—Aboard Navy 317 near Neah Bay

Lieutenant Horner sat in the crowded bay of the helicopter and looked around at the dark lumps jammed into the compartment. All equipment and weapons were tied securely to their vests inside the dry suits. Only the fins were carried wet, strapped around their waists on a nylon belt with a quick-release catch. Like his men, Horner was hot, uncomfortable, and anxious. They had been airborne for almost twenty minutes and were flying very close to the water. It was a clear night, and Horner could easily see the *Spokane* in the center of their racetrack pattern. On one circuit he was able to recognize the Coast Guard cutter as they passed over her stern. *When will they give us the word? There's still a chance we'll be recalled. If we do go, will they see us coming over the side and pick us off? Closequarter battle—what will it be like with* real *bullets? I just hope I don't let the men down.* Horner jumped as Chief Watson tapped him and extended his hand with a stick of gum.

"A little jumpy there, sir?" Watson shouted with a grin over the roar of the helo's rotor blades.

"You could say that, Master Chief," replied Horner, pulling one earphone off as he accepted the gum.

"Piece of cake," replied Watson. "Easy day."

Horner had just stuffed the gum into this mouth when he jumped again and quickly pulled the earpiece back in place. "Sundance 27, this is the *Mellon,* over."

Horner fumbled for the transmit button on the headset cord. "Roger, *Mellon,* this is Sundance 27."

"Sundance 27, you have a green light, I say again, you have

a green light. Execution code word LABRADOR, I repeat LABRADOR. How copy, over?''

''This is 27, understand green light and code word LABRA-DOR.''

''That is affirmative, Sundance. Good hunting. *Mellon* out.'' Horner hesitated for a second, then pulled the headset down around his neck and shouted at the rest of the SEALs.

''Okay, guys—it's a green light! Stand by for the cast!'' He replaced the headset and quickly adjusted the lip mike. ''Sundance Junior, this is Sundance 27, you there, Dave?''

''Roger 27, this is Sundance Junior. We copy your green light—you all set to go there, over?''

''That's affirmative. Where are we on the pattern, over?''

''27 . . . Junior, we hold you four o'clock from the ferry's heading moving counterclockwise, over.''

''Okay, Dave, take us around once and then send us out on a bearing from the ferry when we get back to twelve o'clock, over.''

''Understand, 27, once more around the circle and then we'll control you for the spotting run. Good luck, Brian.''

''Break, Sundance 27, this is Cobra. Understand you have the ball. Go get 'em, Navy, and save a few of 'em for us. Cobra out.'' Horner instantly recognized Captain Sherrard's voice. He had no authorization to come up on the circuit, but Horner deeply appreciated his encouragement.

''Roger, Cobra, thanks for the kind words, break—Sundance Junior, tell your controller to give us a good spot. This is Sundance 27, out.'' Horner took the headphones off and passed them to Chief Watson. Since Watson would be the last man out of the helo, he would serve as jumpmaster and control the swimmer cast. He pulled the waterproof zipper across Watson's shoulders to seal him in his suit and turned around for the chief to close his zipper.

At Coast Guard headquarters in Seattle on Pier 36, Radarman Third Class Carol Peschel leaned over her scope and made a final adjustment. The large eighteen-inch scope painted the mouth of the Strait of Juan de Fuca from the Cape Flattery antenna.

"Navy 317, this is Coast Guard VTS Control. I'll be spotting your cargo delivery. Continue around the pattern and stand by to come right to a heading of 290 on my mark, over."

"This is Navy 317. Uh, roger, I copy—continuing around patrol pattern and will turn to 290 on your mark, over."

"That's affirmative, 317. When you have executed your turn, stand by to deliver your cargo on my mark, over."

"Understand deliver my cargo on your mark after my turn to 290—317 out."

Peschel glanced up at Ensign Santee, who stood behind her also wearing a headset. He gave her a quick smile and a squeeze on the shoulder. They both watched in silence as the faint, fast-moving blip on the screen circled the large dot that was the *Spokane*. The helo was flying at a leisurely sixty knots and made the circuit in eight minutes.

"Navy 317 . . . VTS. Stand by to come right to new course 290, over." The moving blip was now west-northwest of the *Spokane*.

"317, standing by."

"Roger 317. Five, four, three, two, one . . . Mark! Execute turn 290, over."

"This is 317. On new heading 290 and coming to delivery speed and altitude, over." The helo and the blip were now moving away from the ferry almost due west and slowing down.

"Sundance 27, this is Sundance Junior, prepare to cast your swimmers, over."

"Roger, Sundance Junior. Wait, out." Through the secure-voice scrambler, Ensign Santee recognized the steady, unhurried voice of Master Chief Watson.

Aboard Navy 317, Garniss was seated on the floor in the starboard door with his legs hanging out. A bar had been bolted to the side of the helo; it extended four feet straight out from the door. Garniss was twisted as he sat in the opening, leaning forward with his right hand on the bar and the other on the leading edge of the aircraft door. Chief Watson, wearing the headset, knelt beside him with a restraining hand on his shoulder. Both men braced themselves as the helo rolled sharply into the turn. The bird then rocked back as they slowed to twenty knots and descended to twenty feet. It was here that the pilot's skill became critical. The crew chief gave Watson a thumbs-up.

"Junior, this is 27. We are at cast speed and altitude, over."

"Roger 27, stand by . . . stand by . . ." There was a grease-pencil line on the scope marking the *Spokane*'s projected course. Carol Peschel brought Navy 317 to the line and gave a last course correction to vector the helo directly in the ferry's path. The helo was moving more slowly, so it took a moment to ensure the helo was tracking on the proper heading. She looked at Santee and nodded.

". . . Go, Sundance, Go!"

"Sundance, Roger out."

Master Chief Watson slapped Garniss on the shoulder. There was no hesitation as he popped out of the helo and swung forward on the bar to launch his body forward in a forty-five-degree angle toward the water. The angle was required to offset the forward motion of the helo, and if done properly, allowed the cast SEAL to cleanly enter the water. Petty Officer Charlie Peppard immediately took Garniss's place in the door. Watson had a hand on his shoulder and his lips by Peppard's hooded ear.

"One thou-sand, two thou-sand, three thou-sand, four thou-sand—Go!"

Horner dropped to the seat in the door and was tapped out. Down the file they went until Wildrick took the ready position. When he left, Watson stripped off the headset and sat in the door. He carefully counted to one thousand four and piked out into the dark.

Monday, 2:32 A.M.—Aboard the *Mellon*

"Sir, the SEALs are in the water. Navy 317 reports a good cast. Coast Guard VTS plot has them at about three thousand yards in front of the *Spokane*. Boarding estimated at 0255—about twenty-three minutes from now."

"Very well," replied Admiral MacIntyre to the *Mellon*'s communications officer, who was serving as bridge communicator. He turned to Captain Hailey, who stood to his left on the port wing of the bridge. "Everything ready on the *Michigan?*" Hailey looked at Gunnery Sergeant Jennings, who nodded.

"All set, Admiral. We'll start the bubbles in fifteen minutes."

"Think they'll notice it?"

"Unless they're deaf, blind, and asleep, they'll notice it!"

"Excellent. Frank, you ready?"

"Yessir," replied Sclafani. "I'm not due to talk to Jamil until 3:00 A.M. If he calls, I'll play dumb and keep him talking as long as I can."

MacIntyre nodded and turned to look at the brightly lit ferry. He rested his forearms on the metal rail of the bridge combing, wondering about those men out there the in cold, black water, waiting for the ferry to run them down. *If they're not successful, then what? A fiery eruption from the missile deck of the* Michigan, *a blinding white flash, then oblivion?* His attention was captured by the crackling of a bridge speaker.

"That's the SEALs circuit, Admiral," said Colonel Braxton.

"Victoria Harbor Control, this is the *Brian Foss*. Request permission to take my barge alongside Pier 47, over." Horner's radio was not secure, so his transmission, which told them that the SEALs were in the water and in position for their boarding attempt, sounded like the tugboat chatter that was common on Puget Sound waters.

"This is Victoria Harbor Control to the *Brian Foss,*" replied Braxton. "Permission granted—proceed to Pier 47, Harbor

Control, out.'' Two bursts of static told them that Horner had copied their transmission.

MacIntyre looked once again at the *Spokane* before turning to the comm officer. ''The line to Washington, Lieutenant?''

''Right here, sir,'' he replied, pointing to the handset on the side of the padded captain's chair. The chair, identical to the one on the starboard bridge wing, was reserved for the commanding officer—unless there was a visiting flag officer aboard. MacIntyre had yet to take advantage of this privilege, preferring to interfere as little as possible with Captain Libby's normal shipboard routine. Now he heaved himself up into the comfortable seat and took the handset from the keeper.

''This is Admiral MacIntyre. Put me through to the President.'' He sat gazing across the water for a few moments while the connection was made. As the scrambler circuits finally clicked into place, MacIntyre sat a little straighter in the chair.

''Admiral, this is the President. I have you on the speakerphone in the situation room. What is the status out there?'' President Bennett sounded as if he were talking from the bottom of a garbage can.

''Sir, the SEALs have been successfully cast into the water in front of the ferry.'' He looked at his watch and back to the *Spokane*. ''They should be starting to board in about fourteen minutes.''

''Understood, Admiral. So long as it doesn't interfere with your duties there, I want you to stay on the line and keep us informed as events happen.''

''Aye, aye, sir.''

Monday, 2:43 A.M.—Aboard the *Michigan*

''Jesús, this is Gunny Jennings. You still there, buddy?''

DeRosales, shivering in the cold of the torpedo room, grabbed the handset. ''Yeah, Gunny, this is Jesús, over.''

''Time to go to work, pal—here's the captain.''

"DeRosales, this is Captain Hailey. Are you ready to fire that tube, over?"

"Yessir, uh . . . over."

"Very well, proceed with your firing sequence, and again, be sure *not* to disengage the weapon locks."

"Aye, sir."

Aboard the *Spokane,* Hassan was walking up the starboard side of the promenade deck. His weapon was slung, and he was very sleepy. The Dexedrine tablet he had taken had caused his heart to beat more rapidly than normal, but his eyes had continued to droop. He wanted desperately to sit down and rest—just for a moment—but he feared Jamil's wrath if he were caught. Then the noise came. At first, it sounded like thunder. He scanned the sky over Vancouver Island, but there were no clouds. It grew louder—*oh, no, helicopters!* He quickly unslung his weapon and searched the sky, but there was nothing. Then he saw the frothing waterspout on the side of the submarine, illuminated by the lights from the passenger-deck windows. It came in spurts and was now leaving a trail of foam in the water. He sprinted toward the forward pilothouse, meeting Jamil as he came charging out onto the pilothouse wing.

"What is it!" Jamil called. His pistol was drawn and he was looking skyward.

"The submarine," yelled Hassan, pointing over the rail. "It's sinking!"

"What can this be!" Jamil said to Ahmed, who had just joined him and was looking over the side. The starboard side of the submarine continued to boil.

"I—I don't know," Ahmed replied.

"Is it really sinking?"

"It shouldn't be. All the open hatches are well above the water. From what I know of submarines, perhaps a valve has failed and the air tanks are venting."

"If this is the doing of the Americans, I'll end it here and now!" Jamil moved his hand to the remote control on his belt.

"I think we should wait," said Ahmed. "We will know if the submarine is sinking if it begins to settle lower in the water.

It seems like a lot of air, but that is a very big submarine.'' They watched for several more minutes, and finally the bubbles began to subside. Jamil was relieved, but wary. He carefully searched the empty sky and water around the *Spokane*.

''Perhaps you were right—it was only a faulty valve. The submarine seems no lower in the water. But we must watch it carefully. If it happens again, I will not hesitate to set off the charges.''

He looked to the promenade deck where Michelle and Salah had joined Hassan to watch the submarine. ''Back to your places. It will be light in another hour and we will be safe. Hassan, keep watch off the back of the boat—I will keep an eye on our submarine.'' Hassan slung his rifle and walked aft. Michelle walked around in front of the pilothouse and mounted the stairs to the port wing, while Salah went below to check on his prisoners.

''Never a dull moment, eh, my friend?'' said Jamil. Ahmed gave his leader a tired smile and went back to the radar. The Coast Guard cutter was where it should be, and the protective helo continued to circle them.

Aboard the *Mellon*, Admiral MacIntyre watched the bubbling on the side of the *Michigan*.

''Is the diversion working, Admiral?''

MacIntyre took the glasses from his eyes. ''It seems to be, Mr. President,'' he replied, looking at his wristwatch. ''Five of them are standing on the upper deck with their heads over the starboard rail. The SEALs should be boarding on the port side.''

On the *Spokane*, Garniss hesitated outboard of the car deck combing for a moment while he pulled the Steyr Bullpup off his back and kicked off his fins. Only a few of the overhead fluorescent lights were on—few enough, he allowed, to provide for covering shadows. He held the rail with one hand while he shook the rifle, barrel down, to drain out the water. The 5.56mm rounds of the Bullpup had little tolerance for foreign matter in the chamber or barrel. Peppard drifted past him, preparing to toss the second grapnel. Garniss slithered over the side and quickly swept the port side of the car deck with his weapon—nothing. He checked the grapnel hook to make sure it had a good bite on the rail. The line went taught, and seconds later Horner popped over the side, making more noise than he should have.

"Yer fins, sir."

"Oh, right!" whispered Horner as he kicked off his flippers.

Garniss moved off to his security position while Horner waited for Mantalas, who was next up the line. Within five minutes, all the SEALs and Commander Bishop were aboard. They were paired off and scattered along the port side of the *Spokane,* squatting in pools of water. The K-bars came out, and the men cut themselves from their dry suits. All looked to Horner, who was kneeling on the port car-deck island with Garniss. He pulled the Motorola from his vest.

"Victoria Harbor Control, this is the *Brian Foss.* We have just passed channel-buoy number one, over."

"*Brian Foss,* this is Victoria Harbor Control. We hold you at channel buoy one, VHC out."

Horner signaled for them to move out, and Garniss began to work his way across to the starboard side, using the cars parked close to the bow in the main auto bay for cover. Once on the starboard island, he motioned Horner to follow. The officer was halfway across the bay when Yehya stepped from the starboard door that led down to the engine room. His AK-47 slung across his chest, he was searching his pockets for a match. He saw Horner and reached for his weapon as the cigarette dropped from his mouth. Garniss tapped him twice, catching him full in the chest with two two-round bursts. The Bullpup was well silenced, but there was a clattering from the gas-operated action and a sharp whine as one of the rounds passed through Yehya and ricocheted down the stairwell. The Egyptian fell back across the threshold mortally wounded, and tried to get up. Garniss was on him like an attack dog. He slid into Yehya, pinning him to the deck with his knees while he brought the butt of his rifle down sharply to unhinge his jaw. His prey still moved, so Garniss applied two more butt strokes to his head.

When Horner arrived, Garniss was looking over the top of his rifle down the stair access to the engine room. Horner prayed that the noise of the engines running at full power would cover the sound of the encounter.

"Should we check out the engine room sir?"

"Negative. Stash him and let's get the commander to the explosives."

Garniss nodded, grabbing the fallen man by the front of his jacket. He carried him like a suitcase, legs dragging, and put him in the cleaning-gear locker that faced the engine-room stairway door. Horner was peering down the starboard side of the car deck when Peppard and Mantalas arrived.

"Charlie, you and Manny set up a security position here. Shoot anyone who comes up that stairwell." Both nodded and crouched by the door.

When Garniss returned, Horner signaled him to move aft down the starboard side, checking to be sure that Rhorbach and Commander Bishop were following. His heart beat wildly, and he felt a wave of giddiness. *SEALs one, ragheads zero,* he thought. *These guys aren't so tough!* Then he saw the sail of the *Michigan* riding some twenty feet off the starboard side. The large black fin was well lighted by the lights on the passenger deck, and very sinister looking. Horner felt a stab of fear as he realized he was possibly just a few feet from ground zero. Garniss was kneeling amidships by the starboard island when Horner caught up with him.

"That what we're lookin' for?" Horner followed his gaze to a black line that looped down from the promenade deck to the submarine. It, too, was clearly illuminated by the passenger deck just above them.

"Right on the money, Bob. Move on back to the stern and set up—I'll get the commander cracking."

Garniss faded quietly aft as Rhorbach and Bishop arrived. Bishop had already spotted the wire. Wildrick and Master Chief Watson set up security on the port side of the starboard car-deck island after Wildrick had dropped off the pouches that contained Bishop's gear. The EOD man checked the equipment, quickly arranging his tools and several pieces of metered test equipment in the light nylon bag he'd carried in his vest.

Horner tapped the button on the side of his MP-5 to turn on his squad-radio mike.

"Garniss, report."

"All clear, boss."

"Chief?"

"Main auto bay clear."

"Manny?"

"Bow area clear and nobody's come up from the engine room."

"Commander Bishop's going to work now—sing out if you see anything."

Horner nodded to Rhorbach, who escorted Bishop across the two car lanes that separated the starboard island from the starboard rail. Rhorbach was also an EOD technician; most SEAL platoons had at least one. But Rhorbach hadn't the experience and special training of Bishop. Bishop watched while Rhorbach tossed a small, weighted grapnel tagged with a monofilament line over the firing lead. Then, slowly and carefully, he began to take up slack in the bow of the line to bring it into the car deck.

While Rhorbach was doing this, Bishop laid out his tools and tried to catch his breath. He was in good shape for a thirty-seven-year old, but he hadn't done a helo cast in well over five years. He'd tried to climb the rope by himself during the boarding, but it was Rhorbach and Horner who had hauled him aboard. And then there was the killing of the terrorist. The point man had pounced on the dying man like a tiger on a gazelle, and destroyed the man's face with his rifle butt. He'd never seen anything so brutal. Now he was about to attempt to disarm a firing circuit that could possibly trigger a nuclear explosion.

As Rhorbach reached for the wire, he remembered that he'd promised to coach his son's Little League game this evening. He flashed on a picture of Tommy and a group of boys in ill-fitting uniforms as they waited at the field for him to show up. Tommy was telling them to hold their horses and that his dad would be there in a few minutes. *Now, why is* that *on my mind at a time like this!*

"Sir . . . sir, you with me?"

"Yeah, sure."

He took the rubber-coated wire from Rhorbach and carefully rolled it between his thumb and forefinger. *Just as I thought—there's more there than a firing lead in there.* He took out a scalpel-like knife and began to cut the rubber outer coating. A strange tranquillity settled on him as he carefully circumscribed the wire, blocking out everything else. It was always the same when he worked on a particularly dangerous piece of ordnance or on a terrorist device. In the trade, they called it the Bomb Calm. Bishop took a long, thin penlight and put it in his mouth, directing the highly focused beam on the wire. He took a probe and lifted back the rubber sheathing. It was just what he had expected and hoped for—four wires. Carefully he cut lengthwise along the rubber coating and laid back a flap to see better. He then looked up at Rhorbach and smiled, the penlight now in the side of his mouth like a cheroot.

"Good news?" whispered the SEAL.

Bishop nodded, then extended his cut twelve inches along the wire and stripped back the coating to fully expose the four internal wires. Then he began to check each lead with a clamp-on DC ammeter. There were two with no reading, while the other two indicated two amps of current, one with current going toward the sub and the other bringing it back to complete the loop. It was the antitampering circuit. If the flow of current was disturbed, it would trip a capacitor, dumping a charge into the firing circuit and detonating the charges. The antitampering circuit could also be used as a backup firing circuit. He took a wire-stripping tool and bared an inch-long section of the current-carrying wires. Bishop took a breath and held it while he twisted the two bare wires together. He again checked to ensure that the two-amp current of the antitampering circuit was still there, but that the current in the loop went no farther than the splice. Now for the big cut—the firing circuit.

"You wanna do it?"

"Not on your life, sir. That's why you draw 0-5 pay."

"Here goes." They both winced as Bishop cut cleanly through the one lead, then the other. Both exhaled audibly into the silence.

"You officers are so clever," said Rhorbach. He was grinning, but his voice wavered slightly.

Bishop cut one leg of the antitampering circuit running down to the *Michigan,* and Rhorbach helped him tape the rubber coating back into place. The SEAL then slowly paid out the monofilament, and the firing line took its original slack position. Bishop crept back to where Horner waited.

"The firing lead's cut, and I've shunted the antitampering circuit. Unless there's something pretty exotic on those charges, it's safe."

"You sure?"

"If I'm wrong, Lieutenant, I'll be just as dead as you."

"Sorry, sir—just checking." The Motorola was already in Horner's hand. "Uh, Victoria Harbor Control, this is the *Brian Foss.* My barge is safely in the channel, and we are proceeding to the pier, over."

"Roger, *Brian Foss.* Understand your tow is safely in the channel, over."

"That is correct. We'll keep you advised on our approach to the pier. This is the *Brian Foss,* out."

Horner stowed the Motorola and recovered his weapon. Phase one was complete and one terrorist had been wasted—*so far, so good.* He waved his hand over his head with this index finger and pinky extended, like an infielder signaling two down in the bottom of the ninth. Six of them rallied at the after starboard stairwell. Commander Bishop and Rhorbach would wait there for an opportunity to board the *Michigan* to further inspect the explosives. Horner nodded, and Chief Watson led Wildrick and Mantalas across the auto bay to the port after stairway.

"Ready, Chief."

"Ready."

"Go!"

Garniss preceded Horner and Peppard up the starboard stairwell, while Mantalas was on point for Watson and Wildrick on the port side. Both stairwells canted forward, delivering the SEALs just aft of amidships on opposite sides of the passenger deck. The point men stepped into the passenger deck and dropped to a shooting crouch, carefully checking the area forward. Horner and Watson were behind their points, sweeping the side passageway areas aft.

"Starboard clear," said Horner.

"Port clear," replied Watson, "now checking aft." Watson sent Mantalas and Wildrick into the after passenger cabin. They expected everyone to be forward, but it had to be verified.

"After cabin clear," reported Mantalas as the two SEALs rejoined Watson.

"Okay, gang, let's take down the forward cabin—just like the rehearsal. Ready?"

"Ready."

"Go!"

The three-man SEAL elements began to leapfrog from booth to booth toward the forward passenger area and cafeteria. The plan was for both elements to advance until contact was made. The group that was not engaged would move forward to provide support and establish a blocking position. They wanted to avoid having the terrorists between them in a cross fire and ending up shooting at each other.

Salah was pacing restlessly between the hostages and the cafeteria area—port to starboard and back to port. Experience told him that the Americans would try something. *They didn't hesitate to use force in the Arabian Gulf—why would they not take action on their own soil?* He also knew just how stubborn the Israelis could be. He was thinking about the Jews and the young heavy-handed Israeli soldiers who so arrogantly patrolled the streets of his home village. Suddenly, he saw in the window the reflection of a crouched man moving quickly along the port side of the cafeteria. His AK-47 had just come level when Mantalas wheeled around the corner looking over the top of his submachine gun. Both men fired. Mantalas's MP-5 was set for a three-round automatic burst, and he instinctively went for the center of mass. Two of the rounds went into Salah's midsection, while the third slammed into the AK. The rifle was knocked from his hands, but not before he had fired a five-round burst, two of which struck Mantalas in the head, killing him instantly.

Master Chief Watson was around the corner a fraction of a second later. He quickly stepped over the fallen SEAL, pointing his submachine gun down at the little Arab who sat on the deck holding his stomach, his rifle flat on the linoleum by his side.

"Freeze," ordered Watson as he advanced to within five feet of the downed man. Salah smiled warmly at him.

"Allahu Akhbar," he said through the pain, and very deliberately he reached for his rifle. There was an instant of mutual understanding, almost respect; then Watson's silenced MP-5 coughed rapidly as it buried two 9mm rounds in Salah's face. The veteran SEAL looked quickly around the cabin—only frightened, cowering hostages. "Clear!"

Garniss and Peppard quickly moved to the hostages, looking for terrorists hiding among them. Peppard took his side cutters and began to cut them loose, quietly ordering them to lie quietly on the deck. Horner rushed across the cabin to Watson. The chief quickly checked Mantalas and stood up.

"Manny, is he . . ."

"He's dead. Sir, we gotta keep moving." Horner stared at Mantalas a second, then started to bend down to him. Watson caught him hard by the shoulder. "It's over for him, sir. We have to get topside—now!"

"Uh, right—Peppard, stay here with the hostages. Chief, you take Wildrick up the starboard side—Garniss an' I'll go port side."

"Aye, sir. Willie, let's go." Watson and Wildrick headed for the starboard stairwell to the promenade deck. Horner signaled Garniss to follow him and ran for the port stairs.

Jamil had just walked into the pilothouse to look at the chart when Salah's rounds went off. The *Spokane* was a well-built and well-insulated vessel, and there was a breeze over the bow that carried the sound aft. The AK-47's report sounded like a metallic woodpecker. He wasn't sure what it was, but he knew it wasn't right.

"What was that?"

Ahmed, seated at the radar, cocked his head for a moment and shrugged.

"Peck?"

"It could be an air-compressor safety. They sound like that." Peck tried to sound unconcerned, but he had spent too much time aboard boats in Vietnam not to recognize that sound—it was automatic-weapon fire.

"I don't like it." Jamil brought the Motorola to his mouth. "Salah, are you there?" Silence. "Salah, answer me!" He paused a moment, perplexed. "Hassan, where are you?"

"Here, on the back of the boat."

"Is everything all right?"

"All quiet here, but I heard a noise. Could it have been shooting?"

"Get back here . . . quickly!" *Perhaps some of the hostages could have tricked Salah and taken his weapon, although that is unlikely. If someone had sneaked aboard, we would have seen a boat.*

"Ahmed, go below with Hassan and see what's become of Salah. If some of the hostages are to blame, shoot them."

Ahmed blanched, but took up his Uzi and made his way out the starboard pilothouse door and started down the stairs.

"Michelle, keep a sharp eye out for helicopters and small craft." Michelle nodded from her place on the port pilothouse wing.

Jamil again raised the transceiver. "Yehya—come in, engine room. Are you there, Yehya!?"

Master Chief Watson stepped through the passageway from the stairs and dropped to one knee. The promenade deck from amidships to the forward pilothouse was clear. Then a quick motion behind him—*thuk . . . thuk.* Watson whirled around to see a man some ten feet behind him slump to the deck. The sound of his rifle hitting the deck was deafening. He groaned, and Wildrick put two more rounds into him.

"Nice shootin', Willie," Watson whispered. "Let's move."

A tall man stumbled down the pilothouse steps and walked aft. He was preoccupied with his weapon, turning it from one side, then the other. He mumbled something and finally found the slide pull knob on top of the receiver, cycling the action to cock the Uzi. Watson and Wildrick were now crouched among a group of chairs just aft of the forward solarium. Unsuspecting, the man walked not more than six feet from them. *Thuk . . . thuk.* There was enough moon for Watson to try a head shot, and Ahmed was dead before he hit the steel deck. Again they listened for an alarm, but there was none. Wildrick collected the Uzi and pulled the dead Arab back among the seats.

"Chief?"

"Watson here."

"Whatta you got?" Horner and Garniss had worked their way to the seats just behind the stairs of the pilothouse.

"Two more bandits down. We're at the solarium."

"Move up and hold. Garniss and I will try the port stair to the pilothouse."

"Watson, aye—good luck, sir."

Jamil knew something was very wrong. He stepped out to the starboard pilothouse wing and looked aft—all clear. When he looked over the rail at his submarine, he saw two men, one with a weapon slung across his back, taking the charges from the tripods and throwing them into the water. His hand shot to the remote detonator on his belt and pressed the button—nothing.

"No!" The anguished cry echoed across the water. The Sig Sauer was suddenly in his hand, and he quickly emptied the magazine down onto the missile deck.

Commander Bishop had the last charge cradled against him when the .45 slug sank into the middle of his back, severing his spinal chord. He waltzed with the can in a drunken circle before he toppled from the missile deck into the dark water.

Rhorbach was hit in the thigh by a ricochet and knocked off his feet. "Pull your life vest!" he yelled from the deck.

Bishop surfaced once, spitting water. "The game!" he cried. "I've got to get to Tommy's game!" Then the can of Semtex he still clutched to his chest took him down for good.

Jamil ejected the empty magazine from the butt of the pistol and was ready to insert a fresh one when two wrists slammed heavily on his shoulders and a chain jerked viciously across his throat. Then he was lifted nearly off his feet as his assailant levered his forearms between his shoulder blades. Jamil couldn't breath, and only his turtleneck kept the chain from cutting into his flesh. Each time he got the magazine close to the butt of the pistol, the chain ratcheted tighter and lifted him higher. The struggle had brought them through a grunting, shuffling half-circle, until Jamil was looking back into the pilothouse. The helm was vacant, and one of the spokes from the wheel was broken and bent out. Then he became aware of the grizzled chin that raked his ear.

"Peck!" he rasped.

"That's right, motherfucker," Peck replied between clenched teeth, "and you can give Allah my regards!"

Horner and Garniss had worked their way up the port side near the pilothouse. When the rapid single-fire of Jamil's pistol erupted from the other side, Horner assumed that Watson and Wildrick had been engaged. As he mounted the stairs to the pilothouse, a figure appeared at the top. He automatically dropped to a shooting crouch. The dim light from the pilothouse illuminated the shape of a woman, her ample breasts swelling in the light. *Good-looking,* flashed in Horner's mind, and as he hesitated, Michelle ripped him across the chest with her AK-47. He bolted straight upright, blocking Garniss's line of fire. She shot him again, sending him sprawling back to the deck as she jumped for the protection of the pilothouse door. She was almost inside when a hand gripped the muzzle of her rifle and a shoulder under her rib cage began to shove her back outside.

"Let go of me, you fucking dyke," shrieked Michelle as she tried to force her way back in. The hot barrel and gas tube of the

AK seared Janey's hand, and Michelle began to dig at her face with her nails. But the smaller, stockier woman, with her deck shoes and low center of gravity, was winning the battle.

"Shoot, dammit—Shoot her!" cried Janey as she steadily pushed her back through the door.

"No . . . no, please. I didn't mean to . . ."

Janey looked up at Michelle and watched as she shook four times in succession, as though she was taken with a rapid set of hiccups. Then she stumbled backward, coughing blood from her nose and mouth, and dropped to her knees.

"Die, bitch!" spat Janey as she tore the rifle from her feeble grasp and slammed the barrel across the side of her head, knocking her to the deck. She stood glaring over her until a tall, very quick man in black coveralls jumped to the top of the stairs. In one quick movement, he jerked her down flat on the deck beside Michelle and trained his weapon back across the pilothouse.

Watson climbed the stairs with the two struggling men in his sights. He recognized Peck's uniform as the same as those worn by officers on the *Walla Walla*. He placed Jamil from a film clip shown during one of their briefings, but it was not easy, as his face was swollen and almost black.

"Let him go—I've got him covered." Jamil was barely conscious, but Peck still jerked spasmodically on the handcuffs.

"I said let him go!" Watson advanced to the top of the stairs as Peck shook Jamil and held him between the SEAL and himself.

"Fuck you. He's a dead man—me, too, if you want to shoot us both." Watson moved up onto the pilothouse wing, quickly glancing inside.

"Clear, Chief!" Garniss stood by the helm with the Bullpup trained on Peck and Jamil.

With his carotid arteries blocked and his brain starved for blood, Jamil fought the red curtain that pressed in on him. *Death I can accept, but not failure. How did they get aboard? If only I could . . .* Then an idea burned through the scarlet fog that was choking him. His hand fumbled for his waist and found a button. *No, that one didn't work—it was* that *one . . .* WANG! Jamil was past hearing, but he felt the vibration. Then he allowed the crimson blanket to smother him.

"What was that?" said Watson.

"Damn!" shouted Peck. He savagely slammed Jamil's body to the deck. As he stood, blood dripped from his cuffed wrist and from the fingers of the other hand, which had pulled the manacle across Jamil's throat. "There was a bomb in the engine room—I've got to get down there!"

"Hold on—there may be more of them."

"There were only six of them—how many did you get?" asked Peck, bending down to check Jamil. He grunted with satisfaction as he noted the dilation in his eyes.

"Four—five, counting him," said Watson.

"I killed a broad on the other side," said Garniss, "but not before she shot Mr. Horner. He's dead, Master Chief."

"And Rhorbach's down on the missile deck of the sub," added Wildrick. He was crouched at the bottom of the stairs, covering the midships portion of the promenade deck.

"Goddammit!" whispered Watson as he took out his Motorola. *"Mellon,* this is Master Chief Watson on the *Spokane.* Vessels secure, I repeat, both vessels secure. I've got dead and wounded, and there may have been a bomb exploded in the engine room of the ferry. Request you bring that cutter alongside and get some medical assistance here ASAP, over."

"We copy you secure, Master Chief." Watson recognized the admiral's voice. "Bravo Zulu—we're on the way, over." Watson provided the admiral a few quick details before turning to Garniss.

"Stay here with the lieutenant, and secure the upper deck till help gets here. Willie, get Peppard and see what you can do for Rhorbach. Captain, let's check out your engine room."

"I'll mind the helm, Cap'n," Janey called from the pilothouse. "I signaled for all-stop, but there's no response." Peck nodded. He stepped over Jamil and bounded stiffly down the stairs after Watson.

Monday, 6:23 A.M.—The White House

"MacIntyre, what's going on out there!" President Bennett sat in an elevated leather captain's chair reserved for him in the situation room. The room was a mini–command center, staffed with an appropriate balance of civilian and military personnel. There were two rows of padded seats reserved for VIPs. Morton Keeney, Secretary Noffsinger, Director Baines, and Armand Grummell sat in the first row, while General Scott, Energy Secretary Rogers, and Press Secretary Brad Holloway lined up behind them. Colonel Williams stood by the door with Admiral Matthews. It was like a group of serious fans listening to the Super Bowl on the radio.

"Admiral, I need to know what's—"

"Dammit, sir, I can't talk now—please wait!"

There was absolute silence in the room. None of the civilians nor most of those in uniform could imagine someone talking to the President of the United States like that. Those few who had given orders in battle understood and mentally nodded their approval. Bennett drummed his fingers on the arm of his chair, shrugged, and looked around. He, too, understood, but he didn't like it.

"I guess the man's a little busy." He replied casually, but it was forced. Three thousand miles away, Admiral MacIntyre was barking orders to those around him, calling for support from the Delta Force, the waterborne Rangers, and prepositioned medevac units. The *Mellon* heeled to starboard and came to flank speed. But the admiral didn't make the President wait long.

"Mr. President, MacIntyre here. The SEALs aboard the *Spokane* report the ferry secure, and the charges aboard the *Michigan* have been pushed over the side. All the terrorists have been killed, but the SEALs have dead and wounded. Assistance teams and the *Mellon* are now en route to the ferry and the *Michigan*. A bomb may have been exploded aboard the

Spokane, but we have no further information. Sorry to be so short with you, sir, but I've been pretty busy."

"No apologies required, Admiral. You did the job I asked you to do, and we all owe you and your people out there a debt of gratitude. Is the submarine in danger?"

"Not that we can see from here. I'll have Captain Hailey aboard in a few minutes and he can tell us more about that later."

"Excellent. Tell that SEAL leader I want to personally shake his hand."

"I wish I could, Mr. President. He was killed in the assault. I have to tend to my duties, sir—may I call you in a few minutes?"

"Yes, yes, of course. Again, well done." Bennett nodded to the technician to break the connection.

For a moment, Bennett felt euphoric, but that was quickly replaced by feelings of relief and fatigue. He straightened wearily in his chair, looking every bit like a man who had been up for twenty-six hours. He was dead tired, and he knew he would have to have a few hours of sleep before tackling the complex political questions that were sure to follow this near-disaster.

"Gentlemen, we just dodged a bullet. It was the Navy this time, but we need to review our nuclear-weapons security across the board." General Scott met his eye and nodded.

"Morton, this afternoon I'd like to brief a small, nonhostile group of congressional leaders on the events as they happened, and present them a preliminary agenda of what we are doing to repair the damage and prevent future occurrences. See to it. Brad, schedule a press conference following that briefing." *Jesus, I'm not looking forward to facing those reporters,* thought Bennett, *or the congressmen.*

"Dick," he said, turning to Secretary Noffsinger, "brief Mr. Mulroney on these latest developments immediately. Then I want to see two stinging communiqués for my signature—one to President Stozharov and the other to Premier Levin. Now, I need a few hours to myself. We'll meet in the Oval Office at ten o'clock." He paused, deep in thought, and looked at Morton Keeney. "We may have to wait a few months for this to blow over," he said softly, "maybe a few years. But this Palestinian issue *has* to be settled once and for all."

Everyone stood as Bennett stiffly slipped down from the chair and walked out.

Monday, 3:28 A.M.—Aboard the *Spokane*

When they reached the passenger deck, Peck stopped at a fire-control station and removed two fire axes, handing one to Watson.

"What's this for?"

"C'mon," he replied, and headed down the stairs to the car deck. When he stepped from the stairwell near the stern, he found himself looking into the muzzle of an automatic weapon. He froze, afraid to move until Watson caught up with him.

"Stand easy, Rhorbach," said Watson, "it's all over. Who's this guy?" Rhorbach sagged back against the bulkhead of the car-deck island. "It's the sailor who was aboard the sub. Name's DeRosales—Oh, shit!" The submachine gun clattered to the deck as the SEAL slumped to a sitting position.

"Where're you hit?"

"It's my legs, Chief. The fucker shot me in the legs. An' they got the commander. He went over the side." Watson cut away the trouser leg with his K-bar. There were two bullet wounds. One round had grazed his calf; the other had entered his thigh and was still there. Watson made him lie down and took a morphine serrate from a pouch on his vest. He plunged it through the coverall fabric into the wounded man's good thigh.

"Keep him quiet—there'll be a medical team here in minutes. Know how to use these?" He handed DeRosales two field dressings.

"I can bandage him," replied the sailor.

"Good." Watson stood up and plucked the transceiver from his vest. "This is Watson on the *Spokane* calling the *Mellon*, over."

"Go ahead, Master Chief."

"We lost a man over the side during the fighting. He was shot, but maybe he's still alive. Request you initiate a SAR effort along our route."

"On the *Spokane,* understand you have a man overboard, maybe wounded. Our search-and-rescue helo is airborne, over."

"Roger, Watson out."

Wildrick and Peppard arrived and began to help DeRosales tend Rhorbach. Watson had been aware that Captain Peck was wielding his ax along the starboard side. Now he was amidships, limping forward.

"What are you doing?" he yelled, catching up with him.

"We gotta cut that sub loose and get her away from us."

"You sure we should be—"

"Look, Chief, my boat's sinking. If I'm gonna save her, I got to get clear of the sub. Now cut that spring line and I'll get the one on the bow." A moment later, both men were chopping the remaining lines that bound the ferry to the *Michigan.*

On the promenade deck, Garniss was facing an air-traffic-control problem. Military, medical, and Coast Guard helicopters were lined up for an approach. The *Spokane* wasn't designed to receive helos, so the choppers had to hover six feet off the deck while the boarders jumped. The first man aboard was Captain Sherrard. Behind him, his men fanned out across the deck to provide additional security. Sherrard made his way straight for Garniss. The SEAL nodded to him as Sherrard lifted the corner of a jacket that shrouded a form on the deck near Garniss's feet.

"Shit," he said softly. "Anybody else?"

"One more dead, another wounded. The EOD commander went over the side after they shot him. I think he's gone too."

"The terrorists?"

"Six of 'em—all dead, sir."

"You guys did a helluva job, Navy," said Sherrard. "I'm sorry about your lieutenant." The howl of an approaching helo made further talking impossible. He tossed Garniss a casual salute, stepped over Horner's body, and moved off.

• • •

The nitrous smell of exploded C-4 was still thick in the engine room. A fountain of seawater boiled up through the severed pipe where the explosives had ripped a two-foot seam in it. Seawater was just starting to come over the deck gratings. Zanner sat on the floor in front of the propulsion control panel, his wrist still cuffed to the panel bar. He was semiconscious and bleeding from one ear. Steve Burns and Gonzales were around the corner, tied to a piece of auxiliary machinery and shielded from the blast. They were tied loosely with rope and had almost freed themselves. Peck took a set of bolt cutters from the repair locker and cut the cuff chain, while Watson helped Burns and Gonzales to their feet.

"Bridge, this is the engine room—you there, Janey?"

"Yessir. We're free of the submarine."

"I know. Come left and steer for the nearest point of land."

"Come left and head for the shore. Aye, aye, Cap'n."

Brad Johnson arrived, sloshing across the deck plates. He and Burns got on either side of Zanner and began to assist him up the ladder.

"You going to put her in the beach?" asked Watson.

Peck nodded. "If she'll stay afloat that long." He looked around at the water that was now to their ankles. They turned to follow the others up the stairs when Peck pulled out Jamil's pistol.

"What's going on?" demanded Watson.

"Suppose you tell him, Gonzales."

"Captain?"

"These people knew too much about the *Spokane* to get it all from the tech manuals. And how did they find out about Gosnell and the lube-oil pump so quickly?"

"I don't know what you're talking about!" Gonzales's eyes widened as Watson now gave him a questioning look. "Honest!" He ran his tongue across his lips, looking from one grim face to the other.

Peck raised the pistol to Gonzales's head. "You bastard, it was you who killed Andy Gosnell."

Gonzales hesitated a moment, backing away until he was flat

against a bulkhead. Then a sneer came to his lips. "You can't prove that I had anything to do with it. Anyway, I demand to be treated as a political prisoner." He now spoke with just a trace of an accent. "I am not a terrorist—I am a freedom fighter and I have rights. And I want a lawyer—a good American lawyer!"

Peck whipped the .45 across his face, cutting a gash in his cheek and knocking him to the deck. Watson started to intervene, and Peck swung the pistol toward him.

"You stay out of this."

"Don't do this, Peck—it's murder."

"Is it? Is it, really?" Peck stomped his foot in the middle of Gonzales's back. He lay on his stomach, head back, straining—just barely able to keep his nose above the rising water. "I guess maybe I'm something of a terrorist too, Gonzales. You're going to drown, just like you'd have let George Zanner and Steve Burns drown."

"No! You can't do this! You . . . ," he pleaded, gasping between words as the rising water washed over his nose and mouth. He looked to Watson. "Stop him, please—I can't . . . !"

"Peck, let the feds have him. Maybe he can tell them something. The law'll punish him."

"Bullshit. Some lawyer'll get him off or he'll plea-bargain his way to a short sentence. Nobody wants that, certainly not you." Peck looked down at the man pinned under his foot. "You're a dead man, Gonzales, or whatever your name is." He shoved down, pushing the man's head down to eye level. He began to thrash the water with his arms and legs, but he couldn't get his nose above the surface. Watson again moved to intervene, but the pistol and the look on Peck's face held him in check—it was the same malevolent expression he'd seen earlier on the pilothouse wing. Gonzales quit struggling in about thirty seconds, and the two men stood quietly looking at each other for another full minute.

"Here," Peck finally said, handing the pistol to Watson as he walked past. "I've got to get topside and try to save my boat."

Watson stepped past Gonzales, who was beginning to float facedown, and followed Peck up the stairs.

Monday, 4:50 A.M.—Strait of Juan de Fuca, off Cape Flattery

The *Spokane* sat with a slight starboard list, hard aground on Duncan Rock. Peck had thought about trying to ground her in Neah Bay where the bottom was a little softer, but that was another three miles up the coast. The way she was taking water, he might have lost her. He had put her on the rocks as gently as he could, but there was sure to be some additional damage to the hull and the forward propeller. The old gal was a sad sight with her bow on the rocks and her stern low in the water, but she was safe. The *Evelynn Foss* had just tied up to the stern quarter, and a salvage team had gone below with pumps and shoring.

Out on the Strait, the *Mellon* and another tug bracketed the *Michigan.* The sun had risen above the Cascade Mountains to the east and clearly marked the dark outline of her sail against the white hull of the cutter. The tug was made up to the sub's stern like a remora to a great black shark. They'd have her under way for Bangor before long.

Peck stood on the port pilothouse wing on the grounded end of the ferry and watched the activity. Helicopters came and went, and a trawler out of Neah Bay was taking the passengers off by the stern. The small craft used by the Rangers were nested off the port side. Just aft of the forward solarium, the soldiers had brought up the last of the dead. The two SEALs and Andy Gosnell had been carefully placed in body bags, while the terrorists were lined up and covered with a tarp. The decks were crawling with FBI men.

A husky black Marine continued to circle the deck with the sailor who had been on the *Michigan.* They walked slowly, the larger man periodically placing his hand on the younger man's shoulder. They looked like a pair at a father-and-son outing. Peck was weary almost beyond sleep.

"Captain, I request permission to come onto your bridge."

"Uh, yessir, please do." The man in khakis coming up the stairs had a star on each collar point. He, too, looked exhausted.

"I'm John MacIntyre." He extended his hand, but withdrew it when he saw that Peck had both hands bandaged. "How're you feeling?"

"I'm tired, sir—tired and relieved. I lost a good friend in my engineer, Andy Gosnell."

"My condolences, Captain. And, Master Chief," he continued, returning Watson's salute, "I'm sorry for the loss of the lieutenant and your petty officer. You men did an outstanding job."

"Thank you, sir."

"Captain, I understand that you found a terrorist mole in your crew."

"Yessir. He was part of the engine-room gang. I confronted him just after the explosion when we were evacuating the engineering spaces. He tried to run back down the stairs and he fell."

"He fell?"

"That's right, sir," said Watson. "He banged his head when he tumbled into the water and drowned."

MacIntyre carefully scrutinized the two men. They wore an expression he'd seen before, on the faces of young carrier pilots in the Tonkin Gulf when they tried to explain how their bombs had strayed onto restricted targets—targets that needed to be bombed but were placed off-limits for political reasons. *Hell,* mused MacIntyre, *I was one of those pilots.*

"I see," he replied.

There was an awkward silence while the three of them watched a disheveled man with a bald spot on top of his head as he circled the dead terrorists on the promenade deck. His short-sleeved white shirt was soiled and his tie was askew. He talked with the Ranger posted by the corpses, who looked at his credentials and pulled back a corner of the tarp. They were laid out in a row, shoulder to shoulder. The man squatted for several minutes by the body of an Arab wearing a black turtleneck sweater and a Seattle Seahawks jacket. Finally, he nodded his thanks to the guard and walked back along the deck.

An Army colonel in tailored camouflage utilities approached the bottom of the ladder and saluted. "Admiral, excuse me. Chief Watson, could I see you for a moment." MacIntyre smiled and shook Watson's hand.

"Good luck, Master Chief. I intend to see that you receive a commendation for your work here."

"That's not necessary, sir."

"Oh, yes it is. Carry on." He returned Watson's salute and turned to Peck. "Anything I can do for you, Captain?"

"Can you get word to my wife that I'm okay?"

"Why don't you call her yourself." He handed Peck the red cellular phone he cradled in his left hand.

"Uh, Admiral, can you do that? I thought this was a dedicated line to the President."

"It is, but it worked when I called my wife. Just give the operator your number."

458

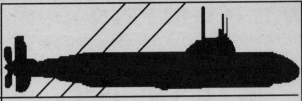